"NO ONE ELSE in America tells so well as Edna Ferber the story of the American people in their various backgrounds. . . . She is the legitimate daughter of the Dickens dynasty," writes William Allen White.

Miss Ferber's career as a novelist began with a work she did not like and threw away. Her mother rescued it and sent it to a publisher, and in 1911 *Dawn O'Hara* was published.

Her tremendous popularity began in 1924, with the success of *So Big*. Each masterpiece that followed—*Showboat, Saratoga Trunk, Ice Palace, Giant*—increased her reputation as one of the bestselling woman novelists of this century.

EDNA FERBER

Cimarron

A FAWCETT CREST BOOK

Fawcett Publications, Inc., Greenwich, Conn.

TO MY MOTHER
JULIA FERBER

ACKNOWLEDGMENT: For certain descriptive passages in the portion of this book concerned with the Opening of Oklahoma in 1889 acknowledgment is made to HANDS UP, by Fred E. Sutton and A. B. MacDonald, published and copyright MCMXXVII by the Bobbs-Merrill Company.

CIMARRON

THIS BOOK CONTAINS THE COMPLETE TEXT OF THE ORIGINAL HARDCOVER EDITION.

A Fawcett Crest Book reprinted by arrangement with Doubleday and Company, Inc.

Selection of Doubleday's Dollar Book Club, June 1962

Printed in the United States of America
August 1971

Foreword

ONLY the more fantastic and improbable events contained in this book are true. There is no attempt to set down a literal history of Oklahoma. All the characters, the towns, and many of the happenings contained herein are imaginary. But through reading the scant available records, documents, and histories (including the Oklahoma State Historical Library collection) and through many talks with men and women who have lived in Oklahoma since the day of the Opening, something of the spirit, the color, the movement, the life of that incredible commonwealth has, I hope, been caught. Certainly the Run, the Sunday service in the gambling tent, the death of Isaiah and of Arita Red Feather, the catching of the can of nitro-glycerin, many of the shooting affrays, most descriptive passages, all of the oil phase, and the Osage Indian material complete—these are based on actual happenings. In many cases material entirely true was discarded as unfit for use because it was so melodramatic, so absurd as to be too strange for the realm of fiction.

There is no city of Osage, Oklahoma. It is a composite of, perhaps, five existent Oklahoma cities. The Kid is not meant to be the notorious Billy the Kid of an earlier day. There was no Yancey Cravat—he is a blending of a number of dashing Oklahoma figures of a past and present day. There is no Sabra Cravat, but she exists in a score of bright-eyed, white-haired, intensely interesting women of sixty-five or thereabouts who told me many strange things as we talked and rocked on an Oklahoma front porch (tree-shaded now).

Anything can have happened in Oklahoma. Practically everything has.

EDNA FERBER.

One

ALL the Venables sat at Sunday dinner. All those handsome inbred Venable faces were turned, enthralled, toward
Yancey Cravat, who was talking. The combined effect was
almost blinding, as of incandescence; but Yancey Cravat was
not bedazzled. A sun surrounded by lesser planets, he gave
out a radiance so powerful as to dim the luminous circle
about him.

Yancey had a disconcerting habit of abruptly concluding
a meal—for himself, at least—by throwing down his napkin
at the side of his plate, rising, and striding about the room,
or even leaving it. It was not deliberate rudeness. He ate
little. His appetite satisfied, he instinctively ceased to eat;
ceased to wish to contemplate food. But the Venables sat
hours at table, leisurely shelling almonds, sipping sherry;
Cousin Dabney Venable peeling an orange for Cousin Bella
French Vian with the absorbed concentration of a sculptor
molding his clay.

The Venables, dining, strangely resembled one of those
fertile and dramatic family groups portrayed lolling uncon-
ventionally at meat in the less spiritual of those Biblical
canvases that glow richly down at one from the great gallery
walls of Europe. Though their garb was sober enough, being
characteristic of the time—1889—and the place—Kansas—
it yet conveyed an impression as of purple and scarlet robes
enveloping these gracile shoulders. You would not have been
surprised to see, moving silently about this board, Nubian
blacks in loincloths, bearing aloft golden vessels piled with
exotic fruits or steaming with strange pasties in which night-
ingales' tongues figured prominently. Blacks, as a matter of
fact, did move about the Venable table, but these, too,
wore the conventional garb of the servitor.

This branch of the Venable family tree had been transplanted from Mississippi to Kansas more than two decades
before, but the mid-west had failed to set her bourgeois
stamp upon them. Straitened though it was, there still obtained in that household, by some genealogical miracle, many
of those charming ways, remotely Oriental, that were of the
South whence they had sprung. The midday meal was, more

often than not, a sort of tribal feast at which sprawled hosts of impecunious kin, mysteriously sprung up at the sound of the dinner bell and the scent of baking meats. Unwilling émigrés, war ruined, Lewis Venable and his wife Felice had brought their dear customs with them into exile, as well as the superb mahogany oval at which they now sat, and the war-salvaged silver which gave elegance to the Wichita, Kansas, board. Certainly the mahogany had suffered in transit; and many of their Southern ways, transplanted to Kansas, seemed slightly silly—or would have, had they not been tinged with pathos. The hot breads of the South, heaped high at every meal, still wrought alimentary havoc. The frying pan and the deep-fat kettle (both, perhaps, as much as anything responsible for the tragedy of '64) still spattered their deadly fusillade in this household. Indeed, the creamy pallor of the Venable women, so like that of a magnolia petal in their girlhood, and tending so surely toward the ocherous in middle age, was less a matter of pigment than of liver. Impecunious though the family now was, three or four Negro servants went about the house, soft-footed, slack, charming. "Rest yo' wrap?" they suggested, velvet voiced and hospitable, as you entered the wide hallway that was at once so bare and so cluttered. And, "Beat biscuit, Miss Adeline?" as they proffered a fragrant plate.

Even that Kansas garden was of another latitude. Lean hounds drowsed in the sun-drenched untidiness of the doorway, and that untidiness was hidden and transformed by a miracle of color and scent and bloom. Here were passion flower and wisteria and even Bougainvillea in season. Honeysuckle gave out its swooning sweetness. In the early spring lilies of the valley thrust the phantom green of their spears up through the dead brown banking the lilac bushes. That coarse vulgarian, the Kansas sunflower, was a thing despised of the Venables. If one so much as showed its broad face among the scented élégantes of that garden it suffered instant decapitation. On one occasion Felice Venable had been known to ruin a pair of very fine-tempered embroidery scissors while impetuously acting as headsman. She had even been heard to bewail the absence of Spanish moss in this northerly climate. A neighboring mid-west matron, miffed, resented this.

"But that's a parasite! And real creepy, almost. I was in South Carolina and saw it. Kind of floating, like ghosts. And no earthly good."

"Do even the flowers have to be useful in Kansas?"

drawled Felice Venable. She was not very popular with the bustling wives of Wichita. They resented her ruffled and trailing white wrappers of cross-barred dimity; her pointed slippers, her arched instep, her indifference to all that went on outside the hedge that surrounded the Venable yard; they resented the hedge itself, symbol of exclusiveness in that open-faced Kansas town. Sheathed in the velvet of Felice Venable's languor was a sharp-edged poniard of wit inherited from her French forbears, the old Marcys of St. Louis; Missouri fur traders of almost a century earlier. You saw the Marcy mark in the black of her still bountiful hair, in the curve of the brows above the dark eyes—in the dark eyes themselves, so alive in the otherwise immobile face.

As the family now sat at its noonday meal it was plain that while two decades of living in the Middle West had done little to quicken the speech or hasten the movements of Lewis Venable and his wife Felice (they still "you-alled"; they declared to goodness; the eighteenth letter of the alphabet would forever be ah to them) it had made a noticeable difference in the younger generation. Up and down the long table they ranged, sons and daughters, sons-in-law and daughters-in-law; grandchildren; remoter kin such as visiting nieces and nephews and cousins, offshoots of this far-flung family. As the more northern-bred members of the company exclaimed at the tale they now were hearing you noted that their vowels were shorter, their diction more clipped, the turn of the head, the lift of the hand less leisurely. In all those faces there was a resemblance, one to the other. Perhaps the listening look which all of them now wore served to accentuate this.

It was late May, and unseasonably hot for the altitude. Then, too, there had been an early pest of moths and June flies this spring. High above the table, and directly over it, on a narrow board suspended by rods from the lofty ceiling sat perched Isaiah, the little black boy. With one hand he clung to the side rods of his precarious roost; with the other he wielded a shoo-fly of feathery asparagus ferns cut from the early garden. Its soft susurrus as he swished it back and forth was an obbligato to the music of Yancey Cravat's golden voice. Clinging thus aloft the black boy looked a simian version of one of Raphael's ceilinged angels. His round head, fuzzed with little tight tufts, as of woolly astrachan through which the black of his poll gleamed richly, was cocked at an impish angle the better to catch the words that flowed from the lips of the speaker. His eyes, popping

9

with excitement, were fixed in an entrancement on the great lounging figure of Yancey Cravat. So bewitched was the boy that frequently his hand fell limp and he forgot altogether his task of bestirring with his verdant fan the hot moist air above the food-laden table. An impatient upward glance from Felice Venable's darting black eyes, together with a sharply admonitory "*Ah*-saiah!" would set him to swishing vigorously until the enchantment again stayed his arm.

The Venables saw nothing untoward in this remnant of Mississippi feudalism. Dozens of Isaiah's forbears had sat perched thus, bestirring the air so that generations of Mississippi Venables might the more agreeably sup and eat and talk. Wichita had first beheld this phenomenon aghast; and even now, after twenty years, it was a subject for local tongue waggings.

Yancey Cravat was talking. He had been talking for the better part of an hour. This very morning he had returned from the Oklahoma country—the newly opened Indian Territory where he had made the Run that marked the settling of this vast tract of virgin land known colloquially as the Nation. Now, as he talked, the faces of the others had the rapt look of those who listen to a saga. It was the look that Jason's listeners must have had, and Ulysses'; and the eager crowd that gathered about Francisco Vasquez de Coronado before they learned that his search for the Seven Cities of Cibolo had been in vain.

The men at table leaned forward, their hands clasped rather loosely between their knees or on the cloth before them, their plates pushed away, their chairs shoved back. Now and then the sudden white ridge of a hard-set muscle showed along the line of a masculine jaw. Their eyes were those of men who follow a game in which they would fain take part. The women listened, a little frightened, their lips parted. They shushed their children when they moved or whimpered, or, that failing, sent them, with a half-tender, half-admonitory slap behind, to play in the sunny dooryard. Sometimes a woman's hand reached out possessively, remindingly, and was laid on the arm or the hand of the man seated beside her. "I am here," the hand's pressure said. "Your place is with me. Don't listen to him like that. Don't believe him. I am your wife. I am safety. I am security. I am comfort. I am habit. I am convention. Don't listen like that. Don't look like that."

But the man would shake off the hand, not roughly, but with absent-minded resentment.

10

Of all that circlet of faces, linked by the enchantment of the tale now being unfolded before them, there stood out lambent as a flame the face of Sabra Cravat as she sat there at table, her child Cim in her lap. Though she, like her mother Felice Venable, was definitely of the olive-skinned type, her face seemed luminously white as she listened to the amazing, incredible, and slightly ridiculous story now being unfolded by her husband. It was plain, too, that in her, as in her mother, the strain of the pioneering French Marcys was strong. Her abundant hair was as black, and her eyes; and the strong brows arched with a swooping curve like the twin scimitars that hung above the fireplace in the company room. Sabra was secretly ashamed of her heavy brows and given to surveying them disapprovingly in her mirror while running a forefinger (slightly moistened by her tongue) along their sable curves. For the rest, there was something more New England than Southern in the directness of her glance, the quick turn of her head, the briskness of her speech and manner. Twenty-one now, married at sixteen, mother of a four-year-old boy, and still in love with her picturesque giant of a husband, there was about Sabra Cravat a bloom, a glow, sometimes seen at that exquisite and transitory time in a woman's life when her chemical, emotional, and physical make-up attains its highest point and fuses.

It was easy to trace the resemblance, both in face and spirit, between this glowing girl and the sallow woman at the foot of the table. But to turn from her to old Lewis Venable was to find one's self baffled by the mysteries of paternity. Old Lewis Venable was not old, but aged; a futile, fumbling, gentle man, somewhat hag-ridden and rendered the more unvital by malaria. Face and hands had a yellow ivory quality born of generations subjected to hot breads, low-lands, bad liver, port wine. To say nothing of a resident unexplored bullet somewhere between the third and fifth ribs, got at Murfreesboro as a member of Stanford's Battery, Heavy Artillery, long long before Roentgen had conceived an eye like God's.

Lewis Venable, in his armchair at the head of the table, was as spellbound as black Isaiah in his high perch above it. Curiously enough, even the boy Cim had listened, or seemed to listen, as he sat in his mother's lap. Sabra had eaten her dinner over the child's head in absent-minded bites, her eyes always on her husband's face. She rarely had had to say, "Hush, Cim, hush!" or to wrest a knife or fork or forbidden tidbit from his clutching fingers. Perhaps it was the curiously

11

musical quality of the story-teller's voice that lulled him. Sabra Venable's disgruntled suitors had said when she married Yancey Cravat, a stranger, mysterious, out of Texas and the Cimarron, that it was his voice that had bewitched her. They were in a measure right, for though Yancey Cravat was verbose, frequently even windy, and though much that he said was dry enough in actual content, he had those priceless gifts of the born orator, a vibrant and flexible voice, great sweetness and charm of manner, an hypnotic eye, and the power of making each listener feel that what was being said was intended for his ear alone. Something of the charlatan was in him, much of the actor, a dash of the fanatic.

Any tale told by Yancey Cravat was likely to contain enchantment, incredibility (though this last was not present while he was telling it), and a tinge of the absurd. Yancey himself, even at this early time, was a bizarre, glamorous, and slightly mythical figure. No room seemed big enough for his gigantic frame; no chair but dwindled beneath the breadth of his shoulders. He seemed actually to loom more than his six feet two. His black locks he wore overlong, so that they curled a little about his neck in the manner of Booth. His cheeks and forehead were, in places, deeply pitted, as with the pox. Women, perversely enough, found this attractive.

But first of all you noted his head, his huge head, like a buffalo's, so heavy that it seemed to loll of its own weight. It was with a shock of astonishment that you remarked about him certain things totally at variance with his bulk, his virility, his appearance of enormous power. His mouth, full and sensual, had still an expression of great sweetness. His eyelashes were long and curling, like a beautiful girl's, and when he raised his heavy head to look at you, beneath the long black locks and the dark lashes you saw with something of bewilderment that his eyes were a deep and unfathomable ocean gray.

Now, in the course of his story, and under the excitement of it, he left the table and sprang to his feet, striding about and talking as he strode. His step was amazingly light and graceful for a man of his powerful frame. Fascinated, you saw that his feet were small and arched like a woman's, and he wore, even in this year of 1889, Texas star boots of fine soft flexible calf, very high heeled, thin soled, and ornamented with cunningly wrought gold stars around the tops. His hands, too, were disproportionate to a man of his stature; slim, pliant, white. He used them as he talked, and the eye followed their movements, bewitched. For the rest, his costume was a Prince Albert of fine black broadcloth whose skirts swooped and spread with the vigor of his movements; a pleated white shirt, soft and of exquisite material; a black string tie; trousers tucked into the gay boot-tops; and, always, a white felt hat, broad-brimmed and rolling. On occasion he simply blubbered Shakespeare, the Old Testament, the Odyssey, the Iliad. His speech was spattered with bits of Latin, and with occasional Spanish phrases, relic of his Texas days. He flattered you with his fine eyes; he bewitched you with his voice; he mesmerized you with his hands. He drank a quart of whisky a day; was almost never drunk, but on rare occasions when the liquor fumes bested him he would invariably select a hapless victim and, whipping out the pair of mother-o'-pearl-handled six-shooters he always wore at his belt, would force him to dance by shooting at his feet—a pleasing fancy brought with him from Texas and the Cimarron. Afterward, sobered, he was always filled with shame. Wine, he quoted sadly, is a mocker, strong drink is raging. Yancey Cravat could have been (in fact was, though most of America never knew it) the greatest criminal lawyer of his day. It was said that he hypnotized a jury with his eyes and his hands and his voice. His law practice yielded him nothing, or less than that, for being sentimental and melodramatic he usually found himself out of pocket following his brilliant and successful defense of some Dodge City dancehall girl or roistering cowboy whose six-shooter had been pointed the wrong way.

His past, before his coming to Wichita, was clouded with myths and surmises. Gossip said this; slander whispered that. Rumor, romantic, unsavory, fantastic, shifting and changing like clouds on a mountain peak, floated about the head of Yancey Cravat. They say he has Indian blood in him. They say he has an Indian wife somewhere, and a lot of papooses. Cherokee. They say he used to be known as "Cimarron" Cravat, hence his son's name, corrupted to Cim. They say his real name is Cimarron Seven, of the Choctaw Indian family of Sevens; he was raised in a tepee; a wickiup had been his bedroom, a blanket his robe. It was known he had been one of the early Boomers who followed the banner of the picturesque and splendidly mad David Payne in the first wild dash of that adventurer into Indian Territory. He had dwelt, others whispered, in that sinister strip, thirty-four miles wide and almost two hundred miles long, called No-Man's-Land as early as 1854, and, later, known as the

Cimarron, a Spanish word meaning wild or unruly. Here, in this strange unowned empire without laws and without a government, a paradise for horse thieves, murderers, desperadoes, it was rumored he had spent at least a year (and for good reason). They said the evidences of his Indian blood were plain; look at his skin, his hair, his manner of walking. And why did he protest in his newspaper against the government's treatment of those dirty, thieving, lazy, good-for-nothing wards of a beneficent country! As for his newspaper—its very name was a scandal: The Wichita *Wigwam*. And just below this: All the News. Any Scandal Not Libelous. Published Once a Week if Convenient. For that matter, who ever heard of a practising lawyer who ran a newspaper at the same time? Its columns were echoes of his own thundering oratory in the courtroom or on the platform. He had started his paper in opposition to the old established Wichita *Eagle*. Wichita, roaring, said he should have called his sheet the *Rooster*. The combination law and newspaper office itself was a jumble and welter of pied type, unopened exchanges, boiler plate, legal volumes, paste pots, loose tobacco, old coats, and racing posters, Wichita, professing scorn of the *Wigwam*, read it. Wichita perused his maiden editorial entitled Shall the Blue Blood of the Decayed South Poison the Red Blood of the Great Middle West? and saw him, two months later, carry off in triumph as his bride Sabra Venable, daughter of that same Decay; Sabra Venable, whose cerulean stream might have mingled with the more vulgarly sanguine life fluid of any youth in Wichita. In spite of the garden hedge, the parental pride, the arched insteps, the colored servants, and the general air of what-would-you-varlet that pervaded the Venable household at the entrance of a local male a-wooing, Sabra Venable, at sixteen, might have had her pick of the red-blooded lads of Kansas, all the way from Salina to Winfield. Not to mention more legitimate suitors of blue-blooded stock up from the South, such as Dabney Venable himself, Sabra's cousin, who resembled at once Lafayette and old Lewis, even to the premature silver of his hair, the length of the fine, dolichocephalic, slightly decadent head, and the black stock at sight of which Wichita gasped. When, from among all these eligibles, Sabra had chosen the romantic but mysterious Cravat, Wichita mothers of marriageable daughters felt themselves revenged of the Venable airs. Strangely enough, the marriageable daughters seemed more resentful than ever, and there was a noticeable falling off in the number of young ladies who had been wont to drop round at the *Wigwam* office with notices of this or that meeting or social event to be inserted in the columns of the paper.

During the course of the bountiful meal with which the Venable table was spread Yancey Cravat had eaten almost nothing. Here was an audience to his liking. Here was a tale to his taste. His story, wild, unbelievable, yet true, was of the opening of the Oklahoma country; of a wilderness made populous in an hour; of cities numbering thousands literally sprung up overnight, where the day before had been only prairie, coyotes, rattlesnakes, red clay, scrub oak, and an occasional nester hidden in the security of a weedy draw.

He had been a month absent. Like thousands of others he had gone in search of free land, and a fortune. Here was an empire to be had for the taking. He talked, as always, in the highfalutin terms of the speaker who is ever conscious of his audience. Yet, fantastic as it was, all that he said was woven of the warp and woof of truth. Whole scenes, as he talked, seemed to be happening before his listeners' eyes.

Two

COAT tails swishing, eyes flashing, arms waving, voice soaring.

"Folks, there's never been anything like it since Creation. Creation! Hell! That took six days. This was done in one. It was History made in an hour—and I helped make it. Thousands and thousands of people from all over this vast commonwealth of ours" (he talked like that) "traveled hundreds of miles to get a bare piece of land for nothing. But what land! Virgin, except when the Indians had roamed it. 'Lands of lost gods, and godlike men!' They came like a procession—a crazy procession—all the way to the Border, covering the ground as fast as they could, by any means at hand—scrambling over the ground, pushing and shoving each other into the ditches to get there first. God knows why— for they all knew that once arrived there they'd have to wait like penned cattle for the firing of the signal shot that opened the promised land. As I got nearer the line it was like ants swarming on sugar. Over the little hills they came, and out of the scrub-oak woods and across the prairie. They came from Texas, and Arkansas and Colorado and Missouri. They

15

came on foot, by God, all the way from Iowa and Nebraska! They came in buggies and wagons and on horseback and muleback. In prairie schooners and ox carts and carriages. I saw a surrey, honey colored, with a fringe around the top, and two elegant bays drawing it, still stepping high along those rutted clay roads as if out for a drive in the Presidio. There was a black boy driving it, brass buttons and all, and in the back seat was a dude in a light tan coat and a cigar in his mouth and a diamond in his shirtfront; and a woman beside him in a big hat and a pink dress laughing and urging the horses along the red dust that was halfway up to the wheel spokes and fit to choke you. They had driven like that from Denver, damned if they hadn't. I met up with one old homesteader by the roadside—a face dried and wrinkled as a nutmeg—who told me he had started weeks and weeks before, and had made the long trip as best he could, on foot or by rail and boat and wagon, just as kind-hearted people along the way would pick him up. I wonder if he ever got his piece of land in that savage rush—poor old devil."

He paused a moment, perhaps in retrospect, perhaps cunningly to whet the appetites of his listeners. He wrung a breathless, "Oh, Yancey, go on! Go on!" from Sabra.

"Well, the Border at last, and it was like a Fourth of July celebration on Judgment Day. The militia was lined up at the boundary. No one was allowed to set foot on the new land until noon next day, at the firing of the guns. Two million acres of land were to be given away for the grabbing. Noon was the time. They all knew it by heart. April twenty-second, at noon. It takes generations of people hundreds of years to settle a new land. This was going to be made livable territory over night—was made—like a miracle out of the Old Testament. Compared to this, the Loaves and the Fishes and the parting of the Red Sea were nothing—mere tricks."

"Don't be blasphemous, Yancey!" spoke up Aunt Cassandra Venable.

Cousin Dabney Venable tittered into his stock.

"A wilderness one day—except for an occasional wandering band of Indians—an empire the next. If that isn't a modern miracle——"

"Indians, h'm?" sneered Cousin Dabney, meaningly.

"Oh, Dabney!" exclaimed Sabra, sharply. "Why do you interrupt? Why don't you just listen!"

Yancey Cravat raised a pacifying hand, but the great buffalo head was lowered toward cousin Dabney, as

16

though charging. The sweeetest of smiles wreathed his lips. "It's all right, Sabra. Let Cousin Dabney speak. And why not? *Un cabello haze sombra.*"

Cousin Dabney's ivory face flushed a delicate pink. "What's that, Cravat? Cherokee talk?"

"Spanish, my lad. Spanish."

A little moment of silent expectation. Yancey did not explain. A plump and pretty daughter-in-law (not a Venable born) put the question.

"Spanish, Cousin Yancey! I declare! Whatever in the world does it mean? Something romantic, I do hope."

"Not exactly. A Spanish proverb. It means, literally, 'Even a hair casts a shadow.'"

Another second's silence. The pretty daughter-in-law's face became quite vacuous. "Oh. A hair—but I don't see what that's got to do with . . ."

The time had come for Felice Venable to take charge. Her drawling, querulous voice dripped its slow sweetness upon the bitter feud that lay, a poisonous pool, between the two men.

"Well, I must say I call it downright bad manners, I do indeed. Here we all are with our ears just a-flapping to hear the first sound of the militia guns at high noon on the Border, and here's Cousin Jouett Goforth all the way up from Louisiana the first time in fifteen years, and just a-quivering with curiosity, and what do we hear but chit-chat about Spanish proverbs and shadows." She broke off abruptly, cast a lightning glance aloft, and in a tone that would have been called a shout had it issued from the throat of any but a Venable, said, *"Ah*-saiah!"

The black boy's shoo-fly, hanging limp from his inert hand, took up its frantic swishing. The air was cleared. The figures around the table relaxed. Their faces again turned toward Yancey Cravat. Yancey glanced at Sabra. Sabra's lips puckered into a phantom kiss. They formed two words, unseen, unheard by the rest of the company. "Please, darling."

"Cede Deo," said Yancey, with a little bow to her. Then, with a still slighter bow, he turned to Cousin Dabney. "'Let there be no strife, I pray thee, between thee and me.' You may not recognize that either, Dabney. It's from the Old Testament."

Cousin Dabney Venable ran a finger along the top of his black silk stock, as though to ease his throat.

With a switch of his coat tails Yancey was off again,

pausing only a moment at the sideboard to toss off three fingers of Spanish brandy, like burning liquid amber. He patted his lips with his fine linen handkerchief. "I've tasted nothing like that in a month, I can tell you. Raw corn whisky fit to tear your throat out. And as for the water! Red mud. There wasn't a drink of water to be had in the town after the first twenty-four hours. There we were, thousands and thousands of us, milling around the Border like cattle, with the burning sun baking us all day, nowhere to go for shade, and the thick red dust clogging eyes and nose and mouth. No place to wash, no place to sleep, nothing to eat. Queer enough, they didn't seem to mind. Didn't seem to notice. They were feeding on a kind of crazy excitement, and there was a wild light in their eyes. They laughed and joked and just milled around, all day and all night and until near noon next day. If you had a bit of food you divided it with someone. I finally got a cup of water for a dollar, after standing in line for three hours, and then a woman just behind me——"

"A woman!" Cousin Arminta Greenwood (of the Georgia Greenwoods). And Sabra Cravat echoed the words in a shocked whisper.

"You wouldn't believe, would you, that women would go it alone in a fracas like that. But they did. They were there with their husbands, some of them, but there were women who made the Run alone."

"What kind of women?" Felice Venable's tone was not one of inquiry but of condemnation.

"Women with iron in 'em. Women who wanted land and a home. Pioneer women."

From Aunt Cassandra Venable's end of the table there came a word that sounded like, "Hussies!"

Yancey Cravat caught the word beneath his teeth and spat it back. "Hussies, heh! The one behind me in the line was a woman of forty—or looked it—in a calico dress and a sunbonnet. She had driven across the prairies all the way from the north of Arkansas in a springless wagon. She was like the women who crossed the continent to California in '49. A gaunt woman, with a weather-beaten face; the terribly neglected skin"—he glanced at Sabra with her creamy coloring—"that means alkali water and sun and dust and wine. Rough hair, and unlovely hands, and boots with the mud caked on them. It's women like her who've made this country what it is. You can't read the history of the United States, my friends" (all this he later used in an Oklahoma

18

Fourth of July speech when they tried to make him Governor) "without learning the great story of those thousands of unnamed women—women like this one I've described—women in mud-caked boots and calico dresses and sunbonnets, crossing the prairie and the desert and the mountains enduring hardship and privation. Good women, with a terrible and rigid goodness that comes of work and self-denial. Nothing picturesque or romantic about them, I suppose—though occasionally one of them flashes—Belle Starr the outlaw—Rose of the Cimarron—Jeanette Daisy who jumped from a moving Santa Fé train to stake her claim—but the others—no, their story's never really been told. But it's there, just the same. And if it's ever told straight you'll know it's the sunbonnet and not the sombrero that has settled this country."

"Talking nonsense," drawled Felice Venable.

Yancey whirled on his high heels to face her, his fine eyes blazing. "You're one of them. You came up from the South with your husband to make a new home in this Kansas——"

"I am not!" retorted Felice Venable, with enormous dignity. "And I'll thank you not to say any such thing. Sunbonnet indeed! I've never worn a sunbonnet in my life. And as for my skin and hair and hands, they were the toast of the South, as I can prove by anyone here, all the way from Louisiana to Tennessee. And feet so small my slippers had to be made to order. Calico and muddy boots indeed!"

"Oh, Mamma, Yancey, didn't mean—he meant courage to leave your home in the South and come up—he wasn't thinking of——Yancey, do get on with your story of the Run. You got a drink of water for a dollar—dear me!—and shared it with the woman in the calico and the sunbonnet . . ."

He looked a little sheepish. "Well, matter of fact, it turned out she didn't have a dollar to spare, or anywhere near it, but even if she had it wouldn't have done her any good. The fellow selling it was a rat-faced hombre with one eye and Mexican pants. The trigger finger of his right hand had been shot away in some fracas or other, so he ladled out water with that hand and toted his gun in his left. Bunged up he was, plenty. A scar on his nose, healed up, but showing the marks of where human teeth had bit him in a fight, as neat and clear as a dentist's signboard. By the time I got to him there was one cup of water left in the bucket. He tipped it while I held the dipper, and it trickled out, just an

19

even dipperful. The last cup of water on the Border. The crowd waiting in line behind me gave a kind of sound between a groan and a moan. The sound you hear a herd of cow animals give, out on the prairie, when their tongues are hanging out for water in the dry spell. I tipped up the dipper and had downed a big mouthful—filthy tasting stuff it was, too. Gyp water. You could feel the alkali cake on your tongue. Well, my head went back as I drank, and I got one look at that woman's face. Her eyes were on me—on my throat, where the Adam's apple had just given that one big gulp after the first swallow. All bloodshot the whites of her eyes, and a look in them like a dying man looks at a light. Her mouth was open, and her lips were all split with the heat and the dust and the sun, and dry and flaky as ashes. And then she shut her lips a little and tried to swallow nothing, and couldn't. There wasn't any spit in her mouth. I couldn't down another mouthful, parching as I was. I'd have seen her terrible face to the last day of my life. So I righted it, and held it out to her and said, 'Here, sister, take the rest of it. I'm through.' "

Cousin Jouett Goforth essayed his little joke. "Are you right sure she was forty, Yancey, and weather-beaten? And that about her hair and boots and hands?"

Cravat, standing behind his wife's chair, looked down at her; at the fine white line that marked the parting of her thick black hair. With one forefinger he touched her cheek, gently. He allowed the finger to slip down the creamy surface of her skin, from cheek bone to chin. "Dead sure, Jouett. I left out one thing, though." Cousin Jouett made a sound signifying, ah, I thought so. "Her teeth," Yancey Cravat went on thoughtfully. "Broken and discolored like those of a woman of seventy. And most of them gone at the side."

Here Yancey could not resist charging up and down, flirting his coat tails and generally ruining the fine flavor of his victory over the Venable mind. The Venable mind (or the prospect of escaping it) had been one of the reasons for his dash into the wild mêlée of the Run in the first place. Now he stood surveying these handsome futile faces, and a great impatience shook him, and a flame of rage shot through him, and a tongue of malice flicked him. With these to goad him, and the knowledge of how he had failed, he plunged again into his story to the end.

"I had planned to try and get a place on the Santa Fé train that was standing, steam up, ready to run into the

20

Nation. But you couldn't get on. There wasn't room for a flea. They were hanging on the cow-catcher and swarming all over the engine, and sitting on top of the cars. It was keyed down to make no more speed than a horse. It turned out they didn't even do that. They went twenty miles in ninety minutes. I decided I'd use my Indian pony. I knew I'd get endurance, anyway, if not speed. And that's what counted in the end.

"There we stood, by the thousands, all night. Morning, and we began to line up at the Border, as near as they'd let us go. Militia all along to keep us back. They had burned the prairie ahead for miles into the Nation, so as to keep the grass down and make the way clearer. To smoke out the Sooners, too, who had sneaked in and were hiding in the scrub oaks, in the draws, wherever they could. Most of the killing was due to them. They had crawled in and staked the land and stood ready to shoot those of us who came in, fair and square, in the Run. I knew the piece I wanted. An old freighters' trail, out of use, but still marked with deep ruts, led almost straight to it, once you found the trail, all overgrown as it was. A little creek ran through the land, and the prairie rolled a little there, too. Nothing but blackjacks for miles around it, but on that section, because of the water, I suppose, there were elms and persimmons and cottonwoods and even a grove of pecans. I had noticed it many a time, riding the range."

(H'm! Riding the range! All the Venables made a quick mental note of that. It was thus, by stray bits and snatches, that they managed to piece together something of Yancey Cravat's past.)

"Ten o'clock, and the crowd was nervous and restless. Hundreds of us had been followers of Payne and had gone as Boomers in the old Payne colonies, and had been driven out, and had come back again. Thousands from all parts of the country had waited ten years for this day when the land-hungry would be fed. They were like people starving. I've seen the same look exactly on the faces of men who were ravenous for food.

"Well, eleven o'clock, and they were crowding and cursing and fighting for places near the Line. They shouted and sang and yelled and argued, and the sound they made wasn't human at all, but like thousands of wild animals penned up. The sun blazed down. It was cruel. The dust hung over everything in a thick cloud, blinding you and choking you. The black dust of the burned prairie was over everything.

We were like a horde of fiends with our red eyes and our cracked lips and our blackened faces. Eleven-thirty. It was a picture straight out of hell. The roar grew louder. People fought for an inch of gain on the Border. Just next to me was a girl who looked about eighteen—she turned out to be twenty-five—and a beauty she was, too—on a coal-black thoroughbred."

"Aha!" said Cousin Jouett Goforth. He was the kind of man who says, "Aha."

"On the other side was an old fellow with a long gray beard—a plainsman, he was—a six-shooter in his belt, one wooden leg, and a flask of whisky. He took a pull out of that every minute or two. He was mounted on an Indian pony like mine. Every now and then he'd throw back his head and let out a yell that would curdle your blood, even in that chorus of fiends. As we waited we fell to talking, the three of us, though you couldn't hear much in that uproar. The girl said she had trained her thoroughbred for the race. He was from Kentucky, and so was she. She was bound to get her hundred and sixty acres, she said. She had to have it. She didn't say why, and I didn't ask her. We were all too keyed up, anyway, to make sense. Oh, I forgot. She had on a get-up that took the attention of anyone that saw her, even in that crazy mob. The better to cut the wind, she had shortened sail and wore a short skirt, black tights, and a skullcap."

Here there was quite a bombardment of sound as silver spoons and knives and forks were dropped from shocked and nerveless feminine Venable fingers.

"It turned out that the three of us, there in the front line, were headed down the old freighters' trail toward the creek land. I said, 'I'll be the first in the Run to reach Little Bear.' That was the name of the creek on the section. The girl pulled her cap down tight over her ears. 'Follow me,' she laughed. 'I'll show you the way.' Then the old fellow with the wooden leg and the whiskers yelled out, 'Whoop-ee! I'll tell 'em along the Little Bear you're both a-comin'.'

"There we were, the girl on my left, the old plainsman on my right. Eleven forty-five. Along the Border were the soldiers, their guns in one hand, their watches in the other. Those last five minutes seemed years long; and funny, they'd quieted till there wasn't a sound. Listening. The last minute was an eternity. Twelve o'clock. There went up a roar that drowned the crack of the soldiers' musketry as they fired in the air as the signal of noon and the start of the Run.

You could see the puffs of smoke from their guns, but you couldn't hear a sound. The thousands surged over the Line. It was like water going over a broken dam. The rush had started, and it was devil take the hindmost. We swept across the prairie in a cloud of black and red dust that covered our faces and hands in a minute, so that we looked like black demons from hell. Off we went, down the old freight trail that was two wheel ruts, a foot wide each, worn into the prairie soil. The old man on his pony kept in one rut, the girl on her thoroughbred in the other, and I on my Whitefoot on the raised place in the middle. That first half mile was almost a neck-and-neck race. The old fellow was yelling and waving one arm and hanging on somehow. He was beating his pony with the flask on his flanks. Then he began to drop behind. Next thing I heard a terrible scream and a great shouting behind me. I threw a quick glance over my shoulder. The old plainsman's pony had stumbled and fallen. His bottle smashed into bits, his six-shooter flew in another direction, and he lay sprawling full length in the rut of the trail. The next instant he was hidden in a welter of pounding hoofs and flying dirt and cinders and wagon wheels."

A dramatic pause. Black Isaiah was hanging from his perch like a monkey on a branch. His asparagus shoo-fly was limp. The faces around the table were balloons pulled by a single string. They swung this way and that with Yancey Cravat's pace as he strode the room, his Prince Albert coat tails billowing. This way—the faces turned toward the sideboard. That way—they turned toward the windows. Yancey held the little moment of silence like a jewel in the circlet of faces. Sabra Cravat's voice, high and sharp with suspense, cut the stillness.

"What happened? What happened to the old man?"

Yancey's pliant hands flew up in a gesture of inevitability. "Oh, he was trampled to death in the mad mob that charged over him. Crazy. They couldn't stop for a one-legged old whiskers with a quart flask."

Out of the well-bred murmur of horror that now arose about the Venable board there emerged the voice of Felice Venable, sharp-edged with disapproval. "And the girl. The girl with the black——" Unable to say it. Southern.

"The girl and I—funny, I never did learn her name—were in the lead because we had stuck to the old trail, rutted though it was, rather than strike out across the prairie that by this time was beyond the burned area and was

23

covered with a heavy growth of blue stem grass almost six feet high in places. A horse could only be forced through that at a slow pace. That jungle of grass kept many a racer from winning his section that day.

"The girl followed close behind me. That thoroughbred she rode was built for speed, not distance. A race horse, blooded. I could hear him blowing. He was trained to short bursts. My Indian pony was just getting his second wind as her horse slackened into a trot. We had come nearly sixteen miles. I was well in the lead by that time, with the girl following. She was crouched low over his neck, like a jockey, and I could hear her talking to him, low and sweet and eager, as if he were a human being. We were far in the lead now. We had left the others behind, hundreds going this way, hundreds that, scattering for miles over the prairie. Then I saw that the prairie ahead was afire. The tall grass was blazing. Only the narrow trail down which we were galloping was open. On either side of it was a wall of flame. Some skunk of a Sooner, sneaking in ahead of the Run, had set the blaze to keep the Boomers off, saving the land for himself. The dry grass burned like oiled paper. I turned around. The girl was there, her racer stumbling, breaking and going on, his head lolling now. I saw her motion with her hand. She was coming. I whipped off my hat and clapped it over Whitefoot's eyes, gave him the spurs, crouched down low and tight, shut my own eyes, and down the trail we went into the furnace. Hot! It was hell! The crackling and snapping on either side was like a fusillade. I could smell the singed hair on the flanks of the mustang. My own hair was singeing. I could feel the flames licking my legs and back. Another hundred yards and neither the horse nor I could have come through it. But we broke out into the open choking and blinded and half suffocated. I looked down the lane of flame. The girl hung on her horse's neck. Her skullcap was pulled down over her eyes. She was coming through, game. I knew that my land—the piece that I had come through hell for—was not more than a mile ahead. I knew that hanging around here would probably get me a shot through the head, for the Sooner that started that fire must be lurking somewhere in the high grass ready to kill anybody that tried to lay claim to his land. I began to wonder, too, if that girl wasn't headed for the same section that I was bound for. I made up my mind that, woman or no woman, this was a race, and devil take the hindmost. My poor little pony was coughing and sneezing and trembling.

Her racer must have been ready to drop. I wheeled and went on. I kept thinking how, when I came to Little Bear Creek, I'd bathe my little mustang's nose and face and his poor heaving flanks, and how I mustn't let him drink too much, once he got his muzzle in the water.

"Just before I reached the land I was riding for I had to leave the trail and cut across the prairie. I could see a clump of elms ahead. I knew the creek was near by. But just before I got to it I came to one of those deep gullies you find in the plains country. Drought does it—a crack in the dry earth to begin with, widening with every rain until it becomes a small cañon. Almost ten feet across this one was, and deep. No way around it that I could see, and no time to look for one. I put Whitefoot to the leap and, by God, he took it, landing on the other side with hardly an inch to spare. I heard a wild scream behind me. I turned. The girl on her spent racer had tried to make the gulch. He had actually taken it—a thoroughbred and a gentleman, that animal—but he came down on his knees just on the farther edge, rolled, and slid down the gully side into the ditch. The girl had flung herself free. My claim was fifty yards away. So was the girl, with her dying horse. She lay there on the prairie. As I raced toward her—my own poor little mount was nearly gone by this time—she scrambled to her knees. I can see her face now, black with cinders and soot and dirt, her hair all over her shoulders, her cheek bleeding where she had struck a stone in her fall, her black tights torn, her little short skirt sagging. She sort of sat up and looked around her. Then she staggered to her feet before I reached her and stood there swaying, and pushing her hair out of her eyes like someone who'd been asleep. She pointed down the gully. The black of her face was streaked with tears.

"Shoot him!' she said. 'I can't. His two forelegs are broken. I heard them crack. Shoot him! For God's sake!'

"So I off my horse and down to the gully's edge. There the animal lay, his eyes all whites, his poor legs doubled under him, his flanks black and sticky with sweat and dirt. He was done for, all right. I took out my six-shooter and aimed right between his eyes. He kicked once, sort of leaped—or tried to, and then lay still. I stood there a minute, to see if he had to have another. He was so game that, some way, I didn't want to give him more than he needed.

"Then something made me turn around. The girl had mounted my mustang. She was off toward the creek section.

Before I had moved ten paces she had reached the very piece I had marked in my mind for my own. She leaped from the horse, ripped off her skirt, tied it to her riding whip that she still held tight in her hand, dug the whip butt into the soil of the prairie—planted her flag—and the land was hers by right of claim."

Yancey Cravat stopped talking. There was a moment of stricken silence. Sabra Cravat staring, staring at her husband with great round eyes. Lewis Venable, limp, yellow, tremulous. Felice Venable, upright and quivering. It was she who spoke first. And when she did she was every inch the thrifty descendant of French forbears; nothing of the Southern belle about her.

"Yancey Cravat, do you mean that you let her have your quarter section on the creek that you had gone to the Indian Territory for! That you had been gone a month for! That you had left your wife and child for! That——"

"Now, Mamma!" You saw that all the Venable in Sabra was summoned to keep the tears from her eyes, and that thus denied they had crowded themselves into her trembling voice. "Now, Mamma!"

"Don't you 'now Mamma' me! What of the land that you were to have had! It was bad enough to think of your going to that wilderness, but to——" She paused. Her voice took on a new and more sinister note. "I don't believe a word of it." She whirled on Yancey, her black eyes blazing. "Why did you let that trollop in the black tights have that land?"

Yancey regarded this question with considerable judicial calm, but Felice, knowing him, might have been warned by the way his great head was lowered like that of a charging bull buffalo.

"If it had been a man I could have shot him. A good many had to, to keep the land they'd run fairly for. But you can't shoot a woman."

"Why not?" demanded the erstwhile Southern belle, sharply.

The Venables, as one man, gave a little jump. A nervous sound, that was half gasp and half shocked titter, went round the Venable board. A startled "Felice!" was wrung from Lewis Venable. "Why, Mamma!" said Sabra.

Yancey Cravat, enormously vital, felt rising within him the tide of irritability which this vitiated family always stirred in him. Something now about their shocked and staring faces, their lolling and graceful forms, roused in him an unreasoning rebellion. He suddenly hated them. He wanted to be free of them. He wanted to be free of them—of Wichita—of convention—of smooth custom—of—no, not of her. He now smiled his brilliant sweet smile which alone should have warned Felice Venable. But that intrepid matriarch was not one to let a tale go unpointed.

"I'm mighty pleased, for one, that it turned out as it did. Do you suppose I'd have allowed a daughter of mine—a Venable—to go traipsing down into the wilderness to live among drunken one-legged plainsmen, and toothless scrags in calico, and trollops in tights! Never! It's over now, and a mighty good thing, too. Perhaps now, Yancey, you'll stop this ramping up and down and be content to run that newspaper of yours and conduct your law practice—such as it is—with no more talk of this Indian Territory. A daughter of mine in boots and calico and sunbonnet, if you please, a-pioneering among savages. Reared as she was! No, indeed."

Yancey was strangely silent. He was surveying his fine white hands critically, interestedly, as though seeing them in admiration for the first time—another sign that should have warned the brash Felice. When he spoke it was with utter gentleness.

"I'm no farmer. I'm no rancher. I didn't want a section of farm land, anyway. The town's where I belong, and I should have made for the town sites. There were towns of ten thousand and over sprung up in a night during the Run. Wagallala—Sperry—Wawhuska—Osage. It's the last frontier in America, that new country. There isn't a newspaper in one of those towns—or wasn't, when I left. I want to go back there and help build a state out of prairie and Indians and scrub oaks and red clay. For it'll be a state some day—mark my words."

"That wilderness a state!" sneered Cousin Dabney Venable. "With an Osage buck or a Cherokee chief for governor, I suppose."

"Why not? What a revenge on a government that has cheated them and driven them like cattle from place to place and broken its treaties with them and robbed them of their land. Look at Georgia! Look at Mississippi! Remember the Trail of Tears!"

"Ho hum," yawned Cousin Jouett Goforth, and rose, fumblingly. "This has all been very interesting—odd, but interesting. But if you will excuse me now I shall have my little siesta. I am accustomed after dinner . . ."

Lewis Venable, so long silent, now too reached for his cane and prepared to rise. He was not quick enough. Felice

Venable's hand, thin, febrile, darted out and clutched his coat sleeve—pressed him back so that he became at once prisoner and judge in his chair at the head of the table.

"Lewis Venable, you heard him! Are you going to sit there? He says he's going back. How about your daughter?" She turned blazing black eyes on her son-in-law. "Do you mean you're going back to that Indian country? Do you?"

"I'll be back there in two weeks. And remember, it's white man's country now.".

Sabra stood up, the boy Cim grasped about his middle in her arms, so that he began to whimper, dangling there. Her eyes were startled, enormous. "Yancey! Yancey, you're not leaving me again!"

"Leaving you, my beauty!" He strode over to her. "Not by a long shot. This time you're going with me."

"And I say she's not!" Felice Venable rapped it out. "And neither are you, my fine fellow. You were tricked out of your land by a trollop in tights, and that ends it. You'll stay here with your wife and child."

He shook his great head gently. His voice was dulcet.

"I'm going back to the Oklahoma country; and Sabra and Cim with me."

Felice whirled on her husband. "Lewis! You can sit there and see your daughter dragged off to be scalped among savages!"

The sick man raised his fine white head. The faded blue eyes were turned on the girl. The child, sensing conflict, had buried his head in her shoulder. "You came with me, Felice, more than twenty years ago, and your mother thought you were going to the wilderness, too. You remember? She cried and made mourning for weeks."

"Sabra's different. Sabra's different."

The reedy voice of the sick man had the ghostly carrying quality of an echo. You heard it above the women's shrill clamor. "No, she isn't, Felice. She's more like you this minute than you are yourself. She favors those pioneer women Yancey was telling about in the old days. Look at her."

The Venable eye, from one end of the table to the other, turned like a single orb in its socket toward the young woman facing them with defiance in her bearing. Not defiance, perhaps, so much as resolve. Seeing her, head up, standing there beside her husband, one arm about the child, you saw that what her father said was indeed true. She was her mother, the Felice Venable of two decades ago; she was the woman in sunbonnet and calico to whom Yancey had given his cup of water; she was the women jolting endless miles in covered wagons, spinning in log cabins, cooking over crude fires; she was all women who have traveled American prairie and desert and mountain and plain. Here was that inner rectitude, that chastity of lip, that clearness of eye, that refinement of feature, that absence of allure that comes with cold white fire. The pioneer type, as Yancey had said. Potentially a more formidable woman than her mother.

Seeing something of this, Felice Venable said again, more loudly, as though to convince herself, "She's not to go."

Looking more than ever like her mother, Sabra met this stubbornly. "But I want to go, Mamma."

"I forbid it. You don't know what you want. You don't know what you're talking about. I say you'll stay here with your mother and father in decent civilization. I've heard enough. I hope this will serve a lesson to you, Yancey."

"I'm going back to the Nation," said Yancey, quite pleasantly.

Sabra stiffened. "I'm going with him." In her new resolve she must have squeezed the hand of the child Cim, for he gave a little yelp. The combined Venables, nerves on edge, leaped in their chairs and then looked at each other with some hostility.

"And I say you're not."

"But I want to go."

"You don't."

Perhaps Sabra had not realized until now how terribly she had counted on her husband's return as marking the time when she would be free to leave the Venable board, to break away from the Venable clan; no more to be handled, talked over, peered at by the Venable eye—and most of all by the maternal Venable eye. Twenty-one, and the yoke of her mother's dominance was beginning to gall her. Now, at her own inner rage and sickening disappointment, all the iron in her fused and hardened. It had gone less often to the fire than the older woman's had. For the first time this quality in her met that of her mother, and the metal of the older woman bent.

"I *will* go," said Sabra Cravat.

If anyone had been looking at Lewis Venable at that moment (which no one ever thought of doing) he could have seen a ghostly smile momentarily irradiating the transparent ivory face. But now it was Yancey Cravat who held their fascinated eye. With a cowboy yip he swung the defiant Sabra and the boy Cim high in the air in his great arms—

29

tossed them up, so that Sabra screamed, and Cim squealed in mingled terror and delight. It was the kind of horseplay (her word) at which Felice Venable always shuddered. Altogether the three seemed suddenly an outrage in that seemly room with its mahogany and its decanters and its circle of staring high-bred faces.

"Week from to-morrow," announced Yancey, in something like a shout, so exulting it seemed. "We'll start on a Monday, fresh and fair. Two wagons. One with the printing outfit—you'll drive that, Sabra—and one with the household goods and bedding and camp stuff and the rest. We ought to make it in nine days. . . . Wichita!" His glance went round the room, and in that glance you saw not only Wichita! but Venables! "I've had enough of it. Sabra, my girl, we'll leave all the goddamned middle-class respectability of Wichita, Kansas, behind us. We're going out, by God, to a brand-new two-fisted, rip-snorting country, full of Injuns and rattlesnakes and two-gun toters and gyp water and desper-*ah*-dos! Whoop-*ee*!"

It was too much for black Isaiah in his perilous perch high above the table. He had long ago ceased to wield his asparagus fan. He had been leaning farther and farther forward, the better to hear and see all of the scene that was spread beneath him. Now, at Yancey's cowboy whoop, he started violently, his slight hold was loosed, and he fell like a great black grape from the vine directly into the midst of one of Felice Venable's white and virgin frosted silver cakes.

Shouts, screams, upleapings. Isaiah plucked, white-bottomed, out of the center of the vast pastry. The sudden grayish pallor of his face matched the silver tone of his pants' seat. Felice Venable, nerves strained to breaking, lifted her hand to cuff him smartly. But the black boy was too quick for her. With the swiftness of a wild thing he scuttled across the table to where Yancey Cravat stood with his wife and child, leaped nimbly to the floor, crept between the man's legs like a whimpering little dog, and lay there, locked in the safety of Yancey's great knees.

Three

INDIANS were no novelty to the townspeople of Wichita. Sabra had seen them all her life. At the age of three Cim was held up in his father's arms to watch a great band of them go by on one of their annual pilgrimages. He played Indian, of course, patting his lips to simulate the Indian yodeling yell. He had a war bonnet made of chicken feathers sewed to the edge of a long strip of red calico.

Twice a year, chaperoned by old General "Bull" Plummer, the Indians swept through the streets of Wichita in their visiting regalia—feathers, beads, blankets, chains—a brilliant sight. Ahead of them and behind them was the reassuring blue of United States army uniforms worn by the Kansas regiment from Fort Riley. All Wichita, accustomed to them though it was, rushed out to gaze at them from store doorways and offices and kitchens. Bucks, braves, chiefs, squaws, papooses, tepees, poles, pots, dogs, ponies, the cavalcade swept through the quiet sunny streets of the midwestern town, a vivid frieze of color against the drab monotony of the prairies.

In late spring it was likely to be the Cheyennes going north from their reservation in the Indian Territory to visit their cousins the Sioux in Dakota. In the late autumn it was the Sioux riding south to return the visit of the Cheyennes. Both of these were horse Indians, and of the Plains tribes, great visitors among themselves, and as gossipy and highly gregarious as old women on a hotel veranda. Usually they called a halt in their journey to make camp for the night outside the town. Though watched over by martial eye, they usually managed to pilfer, in a friendly sort of way, anything they could lay hands on—chickens, wash unwisely left on the line, the very clothes off the scarecrows in the field.

Throughout the year there were always little groups of Indians to be seen on the streets of the town—Kaws, Osages, and Poncas. They came on ponies or in wagons from their reservations; bought bacon, calico, whisky if they could get it. You saw them squatting on their haunches in the dust of the sunny street, silent, sloe eyed, aloof. They seemed to be studying the townspeople passing to and fro. Only their eyes moved. Their dress was a mixture of savagery and civilization. The Osages, especially, clung to the blanket. Trousers, coat, and even hat might be in the conventional pattern of the whites. But over this the Osage wore his striped blanket of vivid orange and purple and red. It was as though he defied the whites to take from him that last insignia of race.

A cowed enough people they seemed by now; dirty, degraded. Since the Custer Massacre of '76 they had been pretty thoroughly beaten into submission. Only occasionally there seemed to emanate from a band of them a sullen, enduring hate. It had no definite expression. It was not in their bearing; it could not be said to look out from the dead black Indian eye, nor was it anywhere about the immobile parchment face. Yet somewhere black implacable resentment smoldered in the heart of this dying race.

In one way or another, at school, in books and newspapers of the time, in her father's talk with the men and women of his own generation, Sabra had picked up odds and ends of information about these silent, slothful, yet sinister figures. She had been surprised—even incredulous—at her husband's partisanship of the redskins. It was one of his absurdities. He seemed actually to consider them as human beings.

Tears came to his own eyes when he spoke of that blot on southern civilization, the Trail of Tears, in which the Cherokees, a peaceful and home-loving Indian tribe, were torn from the land which a government had given them by sworn treaty, to be sent far away on a march which, from cold, hunger, exposure, and heartbreak, was marked by bleaching bones from Georgia to Oklahoma. Yancey and old Lewis Venable had a long-standing feud on the subject of Mississippi's treatment of the Choctaws and Georgia's cruelty to the Cherokees.

"Oh, treaties!" sneered Yancey's father-in-law, outraged at some blistering editorial with which Yancey had enlivened the pages of the Wichita *Wigwam*. "One doesn't make treaties with savages—and expect to keep them."

"You call the Choctaws, the Creeks, the Chickasaws, the Cherokees and the Seminoles savages! They are the Five Civilized Tribes! They had their laws, they had their religion, they cultivated the land, they were peaceful, home-loving, wise. Would you call Chief Apushmataha a savage?"

"Certainly, sir! Most assuredly."

"How about Sequoyah? John Ross? Stand Waitie? Quanah Parker? They were wise men. Great men."

"Savages, with enough white blood in them to make them leaders of their dull-witted, full-blood brothers. The Creeks, sir" (he pronounced it "suh") "intermarried with niggers. And so did the Choctaws; and the Seminoles down in Florida."

Yancey smiled his winning smile. "I understand that while you Southerners didn't exactly marry——"

32

"Marriage, sir, is one thing. Nature, sir, is another. Far from signing treaties with these creatures and giving them valuable American land to call their own——"

"Which was their own before we took it away from them."

"—I would be in favor of extermination by some humane but effective process. They are a sore on the benign bosom of an otherwise healthy government."

"It is now being done as effectively as even you could wish, though perhaps lacking a little something on the humane side."

From her father and mother, too, Sabra had heard much of this sort of talk before Yancey had come into her life. She had heard of them at school, as well. Their savagery and trickiness had been emphasized; their tragedy had been glossed over or scarcely touched upon. Sabra, if she considered them at all, thought of them as dirty and useless two-footed animals. In her girlhood she had gone to a school conducted by the Sisters of Loretto, under the jurisdiction of the Jesuit Fathers. Early in the history of Kansas, long before Sabra's day, it had started as a Mission school, and the indefatigable Jesuit priests had traveled the country on horseback, riding the weary and dangerous miles over the prairies to convert the Indians. Mother Bridget, a powerful, heavy woman of past sixty now, shrewd, dominating, yet strangely childlike, had come to the Mission when a girl just past her novitiate, in the wild and woolly days of Kansas. She had seen the oxen haul the native yellow limestone of which the building was made; she had known the fear of the scalping knife; with her own big, capable, curiously masculine hands she had planted the first young fruit trees, the vegetable and flower garden that now flourished in the encircling Osage hedge; she had superintended the building of the great hedge itself, made of the tough yet supple wood that the exploring pioneer French had called *bois d'arc*, because in the early days the Indians had fashioned their bows of it. The Kansans had corrupted the word until now the wood was known as "bodark." The Mission had been an Indian school then, with a constantly fluctuating attendance. One day there would be forty pairs of curiously dead black Indian eyes intent on a primer of reading, writing, or arithmetic; the next there would be none. The tribe had gone on a visit to a neighboring friendly tribe. Bucks and squaws, ponies and dogs and children, they were off on society bent, the Osages visiting the Kaws, or the Kaws the Quapaws. At other times their

33

absence might mean something more sinister—an uprising in the brewing, or an attack on an enemy tribe. Mother Bridget had terrible tales to tell. She could even make grim jokes about those early days. "Hair-raising times they were," she would tell you (it was her pet pun), "in more ways than one, as many a poor white settler could prove to you who'd had the scalp lifted off him by the knife." She had taught the Indian girls to sew, to exchange wigwams for cabins, and to wear sunbonnets and to speak about their souls and their earthly troubles as well to a Great Father named God who was much more powerful than the Sun and the Rain and the Wind to whom they attributed such potency. These things they did with gratifying docility for weeks at a time, or even months, after which it was discovered that they buried their dead under the cabins, removing enough of the puncheon floor to enable them to dig a grave, laying the timbers back neatly, and then deserting the cabins to live outdoors again, going back to the blanket at the same time and holding elaborate placating ceremonies to various gods of the elements. Mother Bridget (Sister Bridget then, red cheeked in her wimple, her beads clicking a stubborn race against the treachery of the savages) and the other Sisters of Loretto had it all to do over again from the start.

All this was past now. The Indians were herded on reservations in the Indian Territory. Mother Bridget and her helpers taught embroidery and music and kindred ladylike accomplishments to the bonneted and gloved young ladies of Wichita's gentry. The Osage hedge now shielded prim and docile misses where once it had tried to confine the wild things of the prairie. The wild things seemed tame enough now, herded together on their reservations, spirit broken, pride destroyed.

Sabra had her calico pony hitched to the phaëton (a matron now, it was no longer seemly to ride him as she used to, up and down the rutted prairie roads, her black hair in a long thick braid switching to the speed of the hard-bitten hoofs). Mother Bridget was in the Mission vegetable garden, superintending the cutting of great rosy stalks of late pie plant. The skirt of her habit was hitched up informally above her list shoes, muddied by the soft loam of the garden.

"Indian Territory! What does your ma say?"

"She's wild."

"Do you want to go?"

"Oh, yes, yes!" Then added hastily: "Of course, I hate

34

to leave Mamma and Papa. But the Bible says, 'Whither thou——' "

"I know what the Bible says," interrupted the old nun shrewdly. "Why does he want to go—Cravat?"

Sabra glowed with pride. "Yancey says it's a chance to build an empire out of the last frontier in America. He says its lawmakers can profit by the mistakes of the other states, so that when the Indian Territory becomes a state some day it will know wherein the other states have failed, and knowing—uh—avoid the pitfalls——"

"Stuff!" interrupted Mother Bridget. "He's going for the adventure of it. They always have, no matter what excuse they've given, from the Holy Grail to the California gold fields. The difference in America is that the women have always gone along. When you read the history of France you're peeking through a bedroom keyhole. The history of England is a joust. The womenfolks were always Elaineish and anemic, seems. When Lady Guinevere had pinned a bow of ribbon to her knight's sleeve, why, her job was done for the day. He could ride off to be killed while she stayed home and stitched at a tapestry. But here in this land, Sabra, my girl, the women, they've been the real hewers of wood and drawers of water. You'll want to remember that."

"But that's what Yancey said. Exactly."

"Did he now!" She stood up and released the full folds of her skirt from the waist cord that had served to loop it away from the moist earth. She lifted her voice in an order to the figure that stooped over the pie-plant bed. "Enough, Sister Norah, enough. Tell Sister Agnes plenty of sugar and not like the last pie, fit to pucker your mouth." She turned back to Sabra. "When do you start? How do you go?"

"Next Monday. Two wagons. One with the printing outfit, the other with the household goods and bedding. Yancey will have it that we've got to take along bedsprings for me, right out of our bed here and laid flat in the wagon."

Mother Bridget seemed not to hear. She looked out across the garden to where prairie met sky. Her eyes, behind the steel-rimmed spectacles, saw a pageant that Sabra had never known. "So. It's come to that. They've opened it to the whites after all—the land that was to belong to the Indians forever. 'As long as grass grows and the rivers flow.' That's what the treaty said. H'm. Well, what next!"

"Oh, Indians . . ." said Sabra. Her tone was that of one who speaks of prairie dogs, seven-year locusts, or any like Western nuisance.

35

"I know," said Mother Bridget. "You can't change them. Nobody knows better than I. I've had Indian girls here in the school for two years at a stretch. We'd teach them to wash themselves every day; they'd learn to sew, and embroider, and cook and read and write. They were taught worsted and coral work and drawing and even painting and vocal music. They learned the Gospel of the Son of God. They'd leave here as neat and pretty and well behaved as any girl you'd care to see. In two weeks I'd hear they'd gone back to the blanket. Say what you like, the full-blood Indian to-day is just about where he was before Joshua. Well——"

Sabra was a little bored by all this. She had not come out to the old Mission to hear about Indians. She had come to say farewell to Mother Bridget, and have a fuss made over her, and to be exclaimed over. Wasn't she going to be a pioneer woman such as you read about in the books?

"I must be going, dear Mother Bridget. I just came out—there's so much to do." She was vaguely disappointed in the dramatics of this visit.

"I've something for you. Come along." She led the way through the garden, across the sandstone flagging of the porch, into the dim cool mustiness of the Mission hall. She left Sabra there and went swiftly down the corridor. Sabra waited, grateful for this shady haven after the heat of the Kansas sun. She had known this hall, and the bare bright rooms that opened off it, all through her girlhood. The fragrance of pie crust, baking crisply, came to her nostrils: the shell, of course, that was to hold the succulent rhubarb. There was the sound of a heavy door opening, shutting, click, thud, somewhere down a turn in the corridor. She had never seen Mother Bridget's room. No one had. Sabra wondered about it. The Sisters of Loretto owned nothing. It was a rule of the Order. The possessive pronoun, first person, was never used by them. Sabra recalled how Sister Innocenta had come running in one morning in great distress. "Our rosary!" she had cried. "I have lost our rosary!" The string of devotional beads she always wore at her waist had somehow slipped or broken and was missing. They kept nothing for themselves. Strange and sometimes beautiful things came into their hands and were immediately disposed of. Sabra had seen Mother Bridget part with queer objects. Once it had been a scalping knife with brown stains on it that looked like rust and were not; another time an Osage papoose board with its gay and intricately beaded pocket in which some Indian woman had carried her babies strapped to her

36

tireless back. There had been a crewelwork motto done in bright-colored wool threads by the fingers of some hopeful New England émigrée of years ago. Its curlycue letters announced: Music Hath Charms to Soothe the Savage Breast. It had been found hanging on the wall just above the prim little parlor organ in the cabin of a settler whose young wife and children had been killed during a sudden uprising of Indians in his absence.

Suddenly, as she waited there in the peace of the old building, there swept over Sabra a great wave of nostalgia for the very scenes she was leaving. It was as though she already had put behind her these familiar things of her girlhood: the calico pony and the little yellow phaëton; the oblong of Kansas sunshine and sky and garden seen through the Mission doorway; the scents and sounds and security of the solid stone building itself. She was shaken by terror. Indian Territory! Indian—why, she couldn't go there to live. To live forever, the rest of her life. Yancey Cravat, her husband, became suddenly remote, a stranger, terrible. She was Sabra Venable, Sabra Venable, here, safe from harm, in the Mission school. She wouldn't go. Her mother was right.

A door at the end of the corridor opened. The huge figure of Mother Bridget appeared, filling the oblong, blotting out the sunlight. In her arms was a thick roll of cloth. "Here," she said, and turned to let the light fall on it. It was a blanket or coverlet woven in a block pattern of white and a deep, brilliant blue. "It's to keep you and little Cim warm, in the wagon, on the way to the Indian Territory. I wove it myself, on a hand loom. There's no wear-out to it. The blue is Indian dye, and nothing can fade it. It's a wild country you'll be going to. But there's something in the blue of this makes any room fit to live in, no matter how bare and ugly. If they ask you out there what it is, tell 'em a Kansas tapestry."

She walked with Sabra to the phaëton and produced from a capacious pocket hidden in the folds of her habit a little scarlet June apple for the pony. Sabra kissed her on both plump cheeks quickly and stepped into the buggy, placing the blue and white blanket on the seat beside her. Her face was screwed up comically—the face of a little girl who is pretending not to be crying. "Good-bye," she said, and was surprised to find that her voice was no more than a whisper. And at that, feeling very sorry for herself, she began to cry, openly, even as she matter-of-factly gathered up the reins in her strong young fingers.

Mother Bridget stepped close to the wheel. "It'll be all right. There's no such thing as a new country for the people who come to it. They bring along their own ways and their own bits of things and make it like the old as fast as they can."

"I'm taking along my china dishes," breathed Sabra through her tears, "and my lovely linen and the mantel set that Cousin Dabney gave me for a wedding present, and my own rocker to sit in, and my wine-color silk-warp henrietta, and some slips from the garden, because Yancey says there isn't much growing."

Behind her spectacles the eyes of the wise old nun were soft with pity. "That'll be lovely." She watched the calico pony and the phaëton drive off up the dusty Kansas road. She turned toward the Mission house. The beads clicked. Hail, Mary, full of grace . . .

Four

THE child Cim had got it into his head that this was to be a picnic. He had smelled pies and cakes baking; had seen hampers packed. Certainly, except for the bizarre load that both wagons contained, this might have been one of those informal excursions into a nearby wood which Cim so loved, where they lunched in the open, camped near a stream, and he was allowed to run barefoot in the shadow of his aristocratic grandmother's cool disapproval. Felice Venable loathed all forms of bucolic diversion and could, with a glance, cause more discomfort at an al fresco luncheon than a whole battalion of red ants.

There was a lunatic week preceding their departure from Wichita. Felice fought their going to the last, and finally took to her bed with threats of impending dissolution which failed to achieve the desired effect owing to the preoccupation of the persons supposed to be stricken by her plight. From time to time, intrigued by the thumpings, scurryings, shouts, laughter, quarrels, and general upheaval attendant on the Cravats' departure, Felice rose from her bed and trailed wanly about the house, looking, in her white dimity wrapper, like a bilious and distracted ghost. She issued orders. Take this. Don't take that. It can't be that you're leaving those behind! Your own Aunt Sarah Moncrief du Tisne embroidered every inch of them with her own—

"But, Mamma, you don't understand. Yancey says there's very little society, and it's all quite rough and unsettled—wild, almost."

"That needn't prevent you from remembering you're a lady, I hope. Unless you are planning to be one of those hags in a sunbonnet and no teeth that Yancey seems to have taken such a fancy to."

So Sabra Cravat took along to the frontier wilderness such oddments and elegancies as her training, lack of experience, and Southern family tradition dictated. A dozen silver knives, forks, and spoons in the DeGrasse pattern; actually, too, a dozen silver after-dinner coffee spoons; a silver cake dish, very handsome, upheld by three solid silver cupids in carefree attitudes; linen that had been spun by hand and that bore vine-wreathed monograms; many ruffled and embroidered and starched white muslin petticoats to be sullied in the red clay of the Western muck; her heavy black grosgrain silk with the three box pleats on each side, and trimmed with black passementerie; her black hat with the five black plumes; her beautiful green nun's veiling; her tulle bonnet with the little pink flowers; forty jars of preserves; her own rocker, a lady's chair whose seat and back were upholstered fashionably with bright colored Brussels carpeting. There were two wagons, canvas covered and lumbering. Dishes, trunks, bedding, boxes were snugly stowed away in the capacious belly of one; the printing outfit, securely roped and lashed, went in the other. This wagon held the little hand press; two six-column forms; the case rack containing the type (cardboard was tacked snugly over this to keep the type from escaping); the rollers; a stock of paper; a can of printer's ink, tubes of job ink, a box of wooden quoins used in locking the forms.

There was, to the Wichita eye, nothing unusual in the sight of these huge covered freighters that would soon go lumbering off toward the horizon. Their like had worn many a track in the Kansas prairie. The wagon train had wound its perilous way westward since the day of the old Spanish trail, deeply rutted by the heavy wheels of Mexican carts. The very Indians who trafficked in pelts and furs and human beings had used the white man's trails for their trading. Yet in this small expedition faring forth there was something that held the poignancy of the tragic and the ridiculous. The man, huge, bizarre, impractical; the woman, tight lipped, terribly

39

determined, her eyes staring with the fixed, unseeing gaze of one who knows that to blink but once is to be awash with tears; the child, out of hand with excitement and impatience to be gone. From the day of Yancey's recital of the Run, black Isaiah had begged to be taken along. Denied this, he had sulked for a week and now was nowhere to be found.

The wagons, packed, stood waiting before the Venable house. Perhaps never in the history of the settling of the West did a woman go a-pioneering in such a costume. Sabra had driven horses all her life; so now she stepped agilely from ground to hub, from hub to wheel top, perched herself on the high wagon seat and gathered up the reins with deftness and outward composure. Her eyes were enormous, her pale face paler. She wore last year's second best gray cheviot, lined, boned, basqued, and (though plain for its day) braided all the way down the front with an elaborate pattern of curlycues. Her gray straw bonnet was trimmed only with a puff of velvet and a bird. Her feet, in high buttoned shoes, were found to touch the wagon floor with difficulty, so at the last minute a footstool was snatched from the house and placed so that she might brace herself properly during the long and racking drive. This article of furniture was no more at variance with its surroundings than the driver herself. A plump round mahogany foot rest it was, covered with a gay tapestry that had been stitched by Sabra's grandmother on the distaff side. Its pattern of faded scarlet and yellow and blue represented what seemed to be a pair of cockatoos sparring in a rose bush. Yancey had swung Cim up to the calico-cushioned seat beside Sabra. His short legs, in their copper-toed boots, stuck straight out in front of him. His dark eyes were huge with excitement. "Why don't we go?" he demanded, over and over, in something like a scream. He shouted to the horses as he had heard teamsters do. "Giddap in 'ere! Gee-op! G'larng!" His grandmother and grandfather, gazing up with sudden agony in their faces at sight of this little expedition actually faring forth so absurdly into the unknown, had ceased to exist for Cim. As Sabra drove one wagon and Yancey the other, the boy pivoted between them through the long drive, spending the morning in the seat beside his mother, the afternoon beside his father, with intervals of napping curled up on the bedding at the back of the wagon. All through the first day they could do nothing with him. He yelled, "Giddap! Whoa! Gee-op!" until he was hoarse, pausing only to shoot imaginary bears, panthers, wildcats and Indians, and altogether working himself up into such a state of excitement and exhaustion that he became glittering eyed and feverish and subsequently had to be inconveniently dosed with castor oil.

Now, with a lurch and a rattle and a great clatter of hoofs the two wagons were off. Sabra had scarcely time for one final frantic look at her father and mother, at minor massed Venables, at the servants' black faces that seemed all rolling eyeballs. She was so busy with the horses, with Cim, so filled with a dizzy mixture of fright and exhilaration and a kind of terror-stricken happiness that she forgot to turn and look back, as she had meant to, like the heroine in a melodrama, at the big white house, at the hedge, at the lovely untidy garden, at the three great elms. Later she reproached herself for this. And she would say to the boy, in the bare treeless ugliness of the town that became their home, "Cim, do you remember the yellow and purple flags that used to come up first thing in the spring, in the yard?"

"What yard?"

"Granny's yard, back home."

"Nope."

"Oh, Cim!"

It was as though the boy's life had begun with this trip. The four previous years of his existence seemed to be sponged from his mind like yesterday's exercise from a slate. Perched beside his father on the high wagon seat his thirsty little mind drank in tales that became forever part of his consciousness and influenced his whole life.

They had made an early start. By ten the boy's eyes were heavy with sleep. He refused stubbornly to lie on the mattress inside the larger wagon; denied that he was sleepy. Sabra coaxed him to curl up on the wagon seat, his head in her lap. She held the reins in one hand; one arm was about the child. It was hot and still and drowsy. Noon came with surprising swiftness. They had brought along a precious keg of water and a food supply sufficient, they thought, to last through most of the trip—salt pork, mince and apple pies, bread, doughnuts—but their appetites were enormous. At midday they stopped and ate in the shade. Sabra prepared the meal while Yancey tended the horses. Cim, wide awake now and refreshed, ate largely with them of the fried salt pork and potatoes, the hard-boiled eggs, the mince pie. He was even given one of the precious oranges with which the journey had been provided by his grandparents. It was all very gay and comfortable and relaxed. Short as the morning had been, the afternoon stretched out, somehow, endless.

Sabra began to be horribly tired, cramped. The boy whimpered. It was mid-afternoon and hot; it was late afternoon; then the brilliant Western sunset began to paint the sky. Yancey, in the wagon ahead, drew up, gazed about, got out, tied his team to one of a clump of cottonwoods.

"We'll camp here," he called to Sabra and came toward her wagon, prepared to lift her down, and the boy. She was stiff, utterly weary. She stared down at him, dully, then around the landscape.

"Camp?"

"Yes. For the night. Come, Cim." He lifted the boy down with a great swoop.

"You mean for the night? Sleep here?"

He was quite matter-of-fact. "Yes. It's a good place. Water and trees. I'll have a fire before you can say Jack Robinson. Where'd you think you were going to sleep? Back home?"

Somehow she had not thought. She had not believed it. To sleep out of doors like this, in the open, with only a wagon top as roof! All her neat conventional life she had slept in a four-poster bed with a dotted Swiss canopy and net curtains and linen sheets that smelled sweetly of the sun and the air.

Yancey began to make camp. Already the duties of this new manner of living had become familiar. There was wood to gather, a fire to start, water to be boiled. Cim, very wide awake now, trotted after his father, after his mother. Meat began to sizzle appetizingly in the pan. The exquisite scent of coffee revived them with its promise of stimulation.

"That roll of carpet," called Sabra, busy at the fire, to Yancey at the wagon. "Under the seat. I want Cim to sit on it . . . ground may be damp. . . ."

A sudden shout from Yancey. A squeal of terror from the bundle of carpeting in his arms—a bundle that suddenly was alive and wriggling. Yancey dropped it with an oath. The bundle lay on the ground a moment, heaving, then it began to unroll itself while the three regarded it with starting eyes. A black paw, a woolly head, a face all open mouth and whites of eyes. Black Isaiah. He had found a way to come with them to the Indian Territory.

Five

BY NOON next day they were wondering how they had got on at all without him. He gathered wood. He started fires. He tended Cim like a nurse, played with him, sang to him, helped put him to bed, slept anywhere, like a little dog. He even helped Sabra to drive her team, change and change about, for after all there was little to it but the holding of the reins slackly in one's fingers while the horses plodded across the prairie, mile on mile, mile on mile.

Yancey pointed out the definiteness with which the land changed when they left Kansas and came into the Oklahoma country. "Okla-homa," he explained to Cim. "That's Choctaw. Okla—people. Humma—red. Red People. That's what they called it when the Indians came here to live."

Suddenly the land, too, had become red: red clay as far as the eye could see. The rivers and little creeks were sanguine with it, and at sunset the sky seemed to reflect it, so that sometimes Sabra's eyes burned with all this scarlet. When the trail led through a cleft in a hill the blood red of the clay on either side was like a gaping wound. Sabra shrank from it. She longed for the green of Kansas. The Oklahoma sky was not blue but steel color, and all through the day it was a brazen sheet of glittering tin over their heads. Its glare seared the eyeballs.

It was a hard trip for the child. He was by turns unruly and listless. He could not run about, except when they stopped to make camp. Sabra, curiously enough, had not the gift of amusing him as Yancey had, or even Isaiah. Isaiah told him tales that were Negro folklore, handed down by word of mouth through the years. Like the songs he sang, these were primitive accounts of the sorrows and the tribulations of a wronged people and their inevitable reward in after life.

"An' de angel say to him, he say, 'Mose, come on up on dis 'ya throne an' eat 'case yo' hongry, an' drink 'case yo' parch, and res' yo' weary an' achin' feet . . .'"

But when he rode with his father he heard thrilling tales. If it was just before his bedtime, after their early supper had been eaten, Yancey invariably began his story with the magic words, "It was on just such a night as this . . ."

There would follow a legend of buried treasure. Spanish conquistadores wandered weary miles over plains and prairie

43

and desert, led, perhaps, by the false golden promises of some captured Indian eager to get back to the home of his own tribe far away. Like all newly settled countries, there were here hundreds of such tales. The sparsely settled land was full of them. The poorer the class the more glittering the treasure. These people, wresting a meager living from the barren plains, consoled themselves with tales of buried Spanish gold; of jewels. No hairy squatter or nester in his log cabin with his bony parchment-skinned wife and litter of barelegged brats but had some tale of long-sought treasure. Cim heard dozens of these tales as they dragged their way across the red clay of Oklahoma, as they forded rivers, passed little patches of blackjack or cottonwood. He was full of them. They became as real to him as the rivers and trees themselves.

During the day Yancey told him stories of the Indians. He taught him the names of the Five Civilized Tribes, and Cim remembered the difficult Indian words and repeated them— Cherokee, Choctaw, Creek, Seminole, and Chickasaw. He heard the Indian story, not in terms of raids, scalpings, tomahawk, and tom-tom, but as the saga of a tricked and wronged people. Yancey Cravat needed only a listener. That that listener was four, and quite incapable of comprehending the significance of what he heard, made no difference to Cravat. He told the boy the terrific story of the Trail of Tears—of the Cherokee Nation, a simple and unnomadic people, driven from their homes in Georgia, like cattle across hundreds of miles of plain and prairie to die by the thousands before they reached the Oklahoma land that had been allotted to them, with two thousand troops under General Winfield Scott to urge on their flagging footsteps.

"Why did they make the Indians go away?"

"They wanted the land for themselves."

"Why?"

"It had marble, and gold and silver and iron and lead, and great forests. So they took all this away from them and drove them out. They promised them things and then broke their promise."

Sabra was horrified at Cim's second-hand recital of this saga. He told her all about it as he later sat on the seat beside her. "Uncle Sam is a mean bad man. He took all the farms and the gold and the silver and the buff'loes away from the Indians and made them go away and they didn't want to go and so they went and they died."

He knew more about David Payne than about Columbus. He was more familiar with Quanah Parker, the Comanche,

44

with Elias Boudinot and General Stand Waitie, his brother, both full-blooded Cherokees, than he was with the names of Lincoln and Washington.

Sabra, in her turn, undertook to wipe this impression from the boy's mind. "Indians are bad people. They take little boys from their mammas and never bring them back. They burn down people's houses, and hurt them. They're dirty and lazy, and they steal."

She was unprepared for the hysterical burst of protest that greeted this. The boy grew white with rage. "They're not. You're a liar. I hate you. I won't ride with you."

He actually prepared to climb down over the wagon wheel. She clutched at him with one hand, shook him smartly, cuffed him. He kicked her. She stopped the team, wound the reins, took him over her knee and spanked him soundly. He announced, through his tears, that he was going to run away and join the Indians and never come back. If she could have known that his later life was to be shaped by Yancey's tales and this incident, certainly her protests would have been even more forceful than they were.

"Why can't you talk to him about something besides those dirty thieving Indians? There's enough to teach him about the history of his country, I should think. George Washington and Jefferson Davis and Captain John Smith . . ."

"The one who married Pocahontas, you mean?"

"I declare, Yancey, sometimes I wonder if——"

"What?"

"Oh—nothing."

But often the days were gay enough. They fell into the routine, adjusted themselves to the discomfort. At first Sabra had been so racked with the jolting of the wagon that she was a cripple by night. Yancey taught her how to relax; not to brace herself against the wagon's jolting but to sway easily with it. By the second day her young body had accustomed itself to the motion. She actually began to enjoy it, and at the journey's end missed it as a traveler at sea misses the roll and dip of a ship. By this time she had the second-best gray cheviot open at the throat and her hair in a long black braid. She looked like a schoolgirl. She had got out the sunbonnet which one of the less formidable Venables had jokingly given her at parting, and this she wore to shield her eyes from the pitiless glare of sky and plain. The gray straw bonnet, with its puff of velvet and its bird, reposed in its box in the back of the wagon. The sight of her in that prairie wilderness engaged in the domestic task of beating up a bowl of biscuit dough struck no one as being incongruous. The bread supply was early exhausted. She baked in a little portable tin oven that Yancey had fitted out for her.

As for Yancey himself, Sabra had never known him so happy. He was tireless, charming, varied. She herself was fascinated by his tales of hidden mines, of Spanish doubloons, of iron chests plowed up by some gaunt homesteader's hand plow hitched to a stumbling mule. Yancey roared snatches of cowboy songs:

> When I was young I was a reckless lad,
> Lots of fun with the gals I had,
> I took one out each day fur a ride,
> An' I always had one by my side.
> I'd hug 'em an' kiss 'em just fur fun,
> An' I've proposed to more'n one,
> If there's a gal here got a kiss for me,
> She'll find me as young as I used to be.
>
> Hi rickety whoop ti do,
> How I love to sing to you.
> Oh, I could sing an' dance with glee,
> If I was as young as I used to be.

Once they saw him whip a rattlesnake to death with his wagon whip. They had unhitched the horses to water them. Yancey, whip in hand, had taken them down to the muddy stream, Cim leaping and shouting at his side. His two guns, in their holsters, lay on the ground with the belt which he had just now unstrapped from about his waist. Sabra saw the thick coil, the wicked head. Perhaps she sensed it. She screamed horribly, stood transfixed. The boy's face was a mask of fright. Yancey lashed out once with his whip, the thing struck out, he lashed again, again, again, in a kind of fury. She turned away, sickened. The whip kept up its whistle, its snap. The coiled thing lay in ribbons. Isaiah though ashen with fright, still had to be forcibly restrained from prowling among the mass for the rattlers which, with some combination of sunset and human saliva, were supposed to be a charm against practically every misfortune known to man. Cim had nightmares all that night and awoke screaming.

Once they saw the figure of a solitary horseman against the sunset sky. Inexplicably the figure dismounted, stood a moment, mounted swiftly and vanished.

"What was that?"

46

"That was an Indian."

"How could you tell?"

"He dismounted on the opposite side from a white man."

That night it was Sabra who did not sleep. She held the boy tight in her arms. Every snap of a twig, every stamp of a horse's hoof caused her to start up in terror.

Yancey tried in vain to reassure her. "Indian? What of it? Indians aren't anything to be scared of. Not any more."

She remembered something that Mother Bridget had said. "They're no different. They haven't changed since Joshua."

"Since what?" He was very sleepy.

"Joshua."

He could make nothing of this. He was asleep again, heavily, worn out with the day's journey.

The wind, at certain periods of the year, blows almost without ceasing in Oklahoma. And when it rains the roads become slithering bogs of greased red dough, so that a wagon will sink and slide at the same time. They had two days of rain during which they plodded miserably, inch by inch. Cim squalled, Isaiah became just a shivering black lump of misery, and Sabra thought of her dimity-hung bed back home in Wichita; of the garden in the cool of the evening; of the family gathered in the dining room; of the pleasant food, the easy talk, the luxurious ease. "Lak yo' breakfus' in bed, Miss Sabra? Mizzly mo'nin'."

At Pawnee Yancey saw fresh deer tracks. He saddled a horse and was off. They had, before this, caught bass in the streams, and Yancey had shot prairie chicken and quail, and Sabra had fried them delicately. But this was their first promise of big game. Sabra felt no fear at being left alone with the two children. It was mid-afternoon. She was happy, peaceful. There was about this existence a delightful detachment. Her prim girlhood, which, because she had continued to live in her parents' household, had lasted into her marriage, was now behind her. Ahead of her lay all manner of unknown terrors and strangeness, but here in the wilderness she was secure. She ruled her little world. Her husband was hers, alone. Her child, too. The little black boy Isaiah was as much her slave as though the Emancipation Proclamation had never been. Here, in the wide freedom of the prairie, she was, temporarily at least, suspended out of the reach of human interference.

Now she welcomed this unexpected halt. She and Isaiah carried water from the creek and washed a few bits of clothes and hung them to dry. She bathed Cim. She heated water for herself and bathed gratefully. She set Isaiah to gathering fuel for the evening meal, while Cim played in the shade of the clump of scrub oak. She was quite serene. She listened for the sound of horse's hoofs that would announce Yancey's triumphant return. She could hear Cim as he played under the trees, crooning to himself some snatch of song that Yancey had taught him. Vaguely she began to wonder if Yancey should not have returned by now. She brushed her hair thoroughly, enjoying the motion, throwing it over her head and bending far forward in that contortionistic attitude required by her task. After she had braided it she decided to leave it in a long thick plait down her back. Audaciously she tied it with a bright red ribbon, smiling to think of what Yancey would say. She tidied the wagon. She was frankly worried now. Nothing could happen. Of course nothing could happen. And in another part of her mind she thought that any one of a dozen dreadful things could happen. Indians. Why not? Some wild thing in the woods. Broken bones. A fall from his horse. He might lose his way. Suppose she had to spend the night alone here on the prairie with the two children. Here was the little clump of scrub oaks. The land just beyond showed a series of tiny hillocks that rolled gently away toward the horizon—rolled just enough to conceal what not of horror! A head perhaps even now peering craftily over the slope's edge to see what it could see.

In a sudden panic she stepped out of the wagon with the feeling that she must have her own human things near her— Cim, Isaiah—to talk to. Cim was not there playing with his bits of stone and twigs. He had gone off with Isaiah to gather fuel, though she had forbidden it. Isaiah, his long arms full of dead twigs and small branches, was coming toward the wagon now. Cim was not with him.

"Where's Cim?"

He dropped his load, looked around. "I lef' him playin' by hisself right hyah when Ah go fetch de wood. Ain' he in de wagon?"

"No. No."

"Might be he crep' in de print wagon."

"Wagon?" She ran to the other wagon, peered inside, called. He was not there.

Together they looked under the wagons, behind the trees. Cim! Cim! Cimarron Cravat, if you are hiding I shall punish you if you don't come out this minute. A shrill note of terror crept into her voice. She began to run up and down, calling him. She began to scream his name, her voice cracking grotesquely. Cim! Cim! She prayed as she ran, mumblingly. O God, help me find him. O God, don't let anything happen to him. Dear God, help me find him—Cim! Cim! Cim!

She had heard among pioneer stories that of the McAlastair wagon train crossing the continent toward California in '49. The Benson party had got separated perhaps a half day's journey from the front section when scouts brought news of Indians on the trail. Immediately they must break camp and hurry on to join the section ahead for mutual protection. In the midst of the bustle and confusion it was discovered that a child—a boy of three—was missing. The whole party searched at first confidently, then frenziedly, then despairingly. The parents of the missing child had three other small children and another on the way. Every second's delay meant possible death to every other member of the party. They must push on. They appealed to the mother. "I'll go on," she said, and the wagon train wound its dusty way across the plains. The woman sat ashen faced, stony, her eyes fixed in a kind of perpetual horror. She never spoke of the child again.

O God! whimpered Sabra, running this way and that. O God! Oh, Cim! Cim!

She came to a little mound that dipped suddenly and unexpectedly to a draw. And there, in a hollow, she came upon him, seated before a cave in the side of the hill, the front and roof ingeniously timbered to make a log cabin. One might pass within five feet of it and never find it. Four men were seated about the doorstep outside the rude cabin. Cim was perched on the knee of one of them, who was cracking nuts for him. They were laughing and talking and munching nuts and having altogether a delightful time of it. Sabra's knees suddenly became weak. She was trembling. She stumbled as she ran toward him. Her face worked queerly. The men sprang up, their hands at their hips.

"The man is cracking nuts for me," remarked Cim, sociably, and not especially glad to see her.

The man on whose knee he sat was a slim young fellow with a sandy mustache and a red handkerchief knotted cowboy fashion around his throat. He put the boy down gently as Sabra came up, and rose with a kind of easy grace.

"You ran away—you—we hunted every—Cim——" she stammered, and burst into tears of mingled anger and relief.

The slim young man seemed the spokesman, though the other three were obviously older than he.

"Why, I'm real sorry you was distressed, ma'am. We was going to bring the boy back safe enough. He wandered down here lookin' for his pa, he said." He was standing with one hand resting lightly, tenderly, on Cim's head, and looking down at Sabra with a smile of utter sweetness. His was the soft-spoken, almost caressing voice of the Southwestern cowman and ranger. At this Sabra's anger, born of fright, vanished. Besides, he was so young—scarcely more than a boy.

"Well," she explained, a little sheepishly, "I was worried. . . . My husband went off on the track of a deer . . . hours ago . . . he hasn't come back . . . then when Cim . . . I came out and he was gone. . . . I was so—so terribly . . ."

She looked very wan and schoolgirlish in her prim gray dress and with her hair in a braid tied with a bright red ribbon, and her tear-stained cheeks.

One of the men who had strolled off a little way with the appearance of utmost casualness returned to the group in time to hear this. "He'll be back any minute now," he announced. "He didn't get no deer."

"But how do you know?"

The soft-spoken young man shot a malignant look at the other, and the older man looked suddenly abashed. Sabra's question went unanswered. "Won't you sit and rest yourself, ma'am?" suggested the spokesman. The words were hospitable enough, yet there was that in the boy's tone which conveyed to Sabra the suggestion that she and Cim had better be gone. She took Cim's hand. Now that her fright was past she thought she must have looked very silly running down the draw with her tears and her pigtail and her screaming. She thanked them, using a little Southern charm and Southern drawl, which she often legitimately borrowed from the ancestral Venables for special occasions such as this.

"I'm ve'y grateful to you-all," she now said. "You've been mighty kind. If you would just drop around to our camp I'm sure my husband would be delighted to meet you."

The young man smiled more sweetly than ever, and the others looked at him, an inexplicable glint of humor in their weather-beaten faces.

"I sure thank you, ma'am. We're movin' on, my friends here and me. Pronto. Floyd, how about you getting a piece of deer meat for the lady, seeing she's been cheated of her supper. Now, if you and the little fella don't mind sittin' up behind and before, why, I'll take you back a ways. You probably run fu'ther than you expected, ma'am, scared as you was." She had, as a matter of fact, in her terror, run almost half a mile from camp.

He mounted first. His method of accomplishing this was

something of a miracle. At one moment the horse was standing ready and he was at its side. The next there was a flash, and he was on its back. It was like an optical illusion in which he seemed to have been drawn to the saddle as a needle flies to the magnet. Cim he drew up to the pommel, holding him with one hand; Sabra, perched on the horse's rump, clung with both arms round the lad's slim waist. Something of a horsewoman, she noticed his fine Mexican saddle, studded with silver. From the sides of the saddle hung hair-covered pockets whose bulge was the outline of a gun. A slicker such as is carried by those who ride the trails made a compact ship-shape roll behind the saddle. The horse had a velvet gait, even with this triple load. Sabra found herself wishing that this exhilarating ride might go on for miles. Suddenly she noticed that the young rider wore gloves. The sight of them made her vaguely uneasy, as though some memory had been stirred. She had never seen a plainsman wearing gloves. It was absurd, somehow.

A hundred feet or so from the camp he reined in his horse abruptly, half turned in his saddle, and with his free hand swung Sabra gently to the ground, leaning far from his saddle and keeping a firm hold on Cim and reins as he did so. He placed the child in her upraised arms, wheeled, and was gone before she could open her lips to frame a word of thanks. The piece of deer meat, neatly wrapped, lay on the ground at her feet. She stood staring after the galloping figure, dumbly. She took Cim's hand. Together they ran toward the camp. Isaiah had a fire going, a pot of coffee bubbling. His greeting to Cim was sternly admonitory. Ten minutes later Yancey galloped in, empty handed.

"What a chase he led me! Twice I thought I had him. I'd have run him into Texas if I hadn't thought you'd be——"

Sabra, for the first time since her marriage, felt superior to him; was impatient of his tale of prowess. She had her own story to tell, spiced with indignation. She was not interested in his mythical deer. She had an actual piece of fresh deer meat to cook for their supper.

". . . and just when I was ready to die with fright, there he was, talking to those four men, and sitting on the knee of one of them as though he'd known him all his life eating nuts. . . . Anything might have happened to him and to me while you were off after your old deer."

Yancey seemed less interested in the part that she and Cim had played in the adventure than in the appearance and

51

behavior of the four men in the draw, and especially the charming young man who had so gallantly brought them back.

"Thin faced, was he? And a youngster? About nineteen or twenty? What else?"

"Oh, a low voice, and kind of sweet, as though he sang tenor. And his teeth——"

Yancey interrupted. "Long, weren't they? The two at the side, I mean. Like a wolf's?"

"Yes. How did you—— Do you know him?"

"Sort of," Yancey answered, thoughtfully.

Sabra was piqued. "It was lucky for us it was someone who knows you, probably. Because you don't seem to care much about what happened to us—what might have happened."

"You said you wanted to go a-pioneering."

"Well?"

"This is it. Stir that fire, Isaiah. Sabra, get that deer meat a-frizzling that your friend gave you. Because we're moving on."

"Now? To-night? But it's late. I thought we were camping here for the night."

"We'll eat and get going. Moonlight to-night. I don't just like it here. There's been a lot of time lost this afternoon. We'll push on. In another day or so, with luck, we'll be in Osage, snug and safe."

They ate hurriedly. Yancey seemed restless, anxious to be off.

They jolted on. Cim slept, a little ball of weariness, in the back of the wagon. Isaiah drowsed beside Sabra, and she herself was half asleep, the reins slack in her hands. The scent of the sun-warmed prairie came up to her, and the pungent smell of the sagebrush. The Indians had swept over this plain in hordes; and buffalo by the millions. She wondered if the early Spaniards, in their lust for gold, had trod this ground —perhaps this very trail. Coronado, De Soto, Narvaez. She had seen pictures of them, these dark-skinned élégantes in their cumbersome trappings of leather and heavy metal, tramping the pitiless plains of this vast Southwest, searching like children for cities of gold. . . . The steady clop-clop of the horses' feet, the rattle of the wagon, the squeak of the wheels, the smell of sunbaked earth . . .

She must have dozed off, for suddenly the sun's rays were sharply slanted, and she shivered with the cool of the prairie night air. Voices had awakened her. Three horsemen had dashed out of a little copse and stood in the path of Yancey's lead wagon. They were heavily armed. Their hands rested on their guns. Their faces were grim. They wore the mournful mustaches of the Western plainsman, their eyes were the eyes of men accustomed to great distances; their gaze was searing. All three wore the badge of United States marshals, but there was about them something that announced this even before the eye was caught by their badge of office. The leader addressed Yancey, his voice mild, even gentle.

"Howdy."

"Howdy."

"Where you bound for, pardner?"

"Osage."

The questioner's hand rested lightly on the butt of the six-shooter at his waist. "What might your name be?"

"Cravat—Yancey Cravat."

The spokesman's face lighted up with the slow, incredulous smile of a delighted child. "I'll be doggoned!" He turned his slow grin on the man at his right, on the man at his left. "Yancey Cravat!" he said again, as though they had not heard. "I sure am pleased to make your acquaintance. Heard about you till I feel like I knew you."

"Why, thanks," replied Yancey, unusually modest and laconic. Sabra knew then that Yancey was playing one of his rôles. He would talk as they talked. Be one of them.

"Aimin' to make quite a stay in Osage?"

"Aim to live there."

"Go on! I've a notion to swear you in as Deputy Marshal right now, darned if I ain't. Citizens like you is what we need, and no mistake. Lawy'in'?"

"I'm planning to take up my law practice in Osage, yes," Yancey answered, "and start a newspaper as well."

The three looked a little perturbed at this. They glanced at each other, then at Yancey, then away, uncomfortably. "Oh, newspaper, huh?" There was little enthusiasm in the marshal's voice. "Well, we did have a newspaper there for a little while in Osage, 'bout a week."

"A daily?"

"A weekly."

There was something sinister in this. "What became of it?"

"Well, seems the editor—name of Pegler—died."

There was a little silence. Sabra gathered up her reins and brought her team alongside Yancey's, the better to hear. The three mustached ones acknowledged her more formal presence by briefly touching their hat brims with the fore-finger of the hand that had rested on their guns.

"Who killed him?"

A little shadow of pained surprise passed over the features of the marshal. "He was just found dead one morning on the banks of the Canadian. Bullet wounds. But bullets is all pretty much alike, out here. He might 'a' killed himself, plumb discouraged."

The silence fell again. Yancey broke it. "The first edition of the *Oklahoma Wigwam* will be off the press two weeks from to-morrow."

He gathered up the reins as though to end this chance meeting, however agreeable. "Well, gentlemen, good-evening. Glad to have met you."

The three did not budge. "What we stopped to ask you," said the spokesman, in his gentle drawl, "was, did you happen to glimpse four men anywhere on the road? They're nesting somewheres in here, the Kid and his gang. Stole four horses, robbed the bank at Red Fork, shot the cashier, and lit out for the prairie. Light complected, all of 'em. The Kid is a slim young fella, light hair, red handkerchief, soft spoken, and rides with gloves on. But then you know what he's like, Cravat, well's I do."

Yancey nodded in agreement. "Everybody's heard of the Kid. No, sir, I haven't seen him. Haven't seen anybody the last three days but a Kaw on a pony and a bunch of dirty Cheyennes in a wagon. Funny thing, I never yet knew a bad man who wasn't light complected—or, anyway, blue or gray eyes."

"Oh, say, now!" protested the marshal, stroking his sandy mustache.

"Fact. You take the Kid, and the James boys, and Tom O'Phalliard, and the whole Mullins gang."

"How about yourself? You're pretty good with the gun, from all accounts. And black as a crow."

Yancey lifted his great head and the heavy lids that usually drooped over the gray eyes and looked at the marshal. "That's so," said the other, as though in agreement at the end of an argument. "I reckon it goes fur killers and fur killers of killers. . . . Well, boys, we'll be lopin'. Good luck to you."

"Good luck to *you!*" responded Yancey, politely.

The three whirled their steeds spectacularly, raised their right hands in salute; the horses pivoted on their hind legs prettily; Cim crowed with delight. They were off in a cloud of red dust made redder by the last rays of the setting sun.

Yancey gathered up his reins. Sabra stared at him in bewildered indignation. "But the person who shields a criminal is just as bad as the criminal himself, isn't he?"

Yancey looked back at her around the side of his wagon top. His smile was mischievous, sparkling, irresistible. "Don't be righteous, Sabra. It's middle class—and a terrible trait in a woman."

Late next day, just before sunset, after pushing on relentlessly through the blistering sun of midday, Yancey pointed with his wagon whip to something that looked like a wallow of mud dotted with crazy shanties and tents. Theatrically he picked Cim up in his arms so that the child, too, might see. But he spoke to Sabra.

"There it is," he said. "That's our future home."

Sabra looked. And her brain seemed to have no order or reason about it, for she could think only of the green nun's veiling trimmed with ruchings of pink which lay so carefully folded, with its modish sleeves all stuffed out with soft paper, in the trunk under the canvas of the wagon.

Six

LONG before the end of that first nightmarish day in Osage, Sabra had confronted her husband with blazing eyes. "I won't bring up my boy in a town like this!"

It had been a night and a day fantastic with untoward happenings. Their wagons had rumbled wearily down the broad main street of the settlement—a raw gash in the prairie. All about, on either side, were wooden shacks, and Indians and dried mud and hitching posts and dogs and crude wagons like their own. It looked like pictures Sabra had seen of California in '49. They had supped on ham and eggs, fried potatoes, and muddy coffee in a place labeled Ice Cream and Oyster Parlor. They spent that first night in a rooming house above one of the score of saloons that enlivened the main street—Pawhuska Avenue, it was called. It was a longish street, for the Osage town settlers seemed to have felt the need of huddling together for company in this wilderness. The street stopped abruptly at either end and became suddenly prairie.

"Pawhuska Avenue," said a tipsy sign tacked on the front of a false-front pine shack. Yancey chose this unfortunate time to impart a little Indian lore to Cim, wide eyed on the wagon seat beside his mother.

"That's Osage," he shouted to the boy. "Pawhu—that means hair. And scah, that means white. White Hair. Pawhuska—White Hair—was an old Osage Chief——"

"Yancey Cravat!" Sabra called in a shout that almost equaled his own, and in a tone startlingly like one of Felice Venable's best (she was, in fact, slightly hysterical, what with weariness and disappointment and fear), "Yancey Cravat, will you stop talking Indian history and find us a place to eat and sleep! Where's your sense? Can't you see he's ready to drop, and so am I?"

The greasy food set before them in the eating house sickened her. She shrank from the slatternly bold-faced girl who slammed the dishes down in front of them on the oil-cloth-covered table. At this same table with them—there was only one, a long board accommodating perhaps twenty—sat red-faced men talking in great rough voices, eating with a mechanical and absent-minded thoroughness, shoveling potatoes, canned vegetables, pie into their mouths with knives. Cim was terribly wide awake and noisily unruly, excited by the sounds and strangeness about him.

"I'm an Indian!" he would yell, making a great clatter with his spoon on the table. "Ol' White Hair! Wa-wa-wa-wa-wa-wa-wa!" Being reprimanded, and having the spoon forcibly removed from his clutching fingers, he burst into tears and howls.

Sabra had taken him up to the bare and clean enough little room which was to be their shelter for the night. From wide-eyed wakefulness Cim had become suddenly limp with sleep. Yancey had gone out to see to the horses, to get what information he could about renting a house, and a shack for the newspaper. A score of plans were teeming in his mind.

"You'll be all right," he had said. "A good night's sleep and everything'll look rosy in the morning. Don't look so down in the mouth, honey. You're going to like it."

"It's horrible! It's—and those men! Those dreadful men."

" 'For my part, I had rather be the first man among these fellows than the second man in Rome.' " Yancey struck an attitude.

Sabra looked at him dully. "Rome?"

"Plutarch, my sweet." He kissed her; was gone with a great flirt of his coat tails. She heard his light step clattering down the flimsy wooden stairs. She could distinguish his beautiful vibrant voice among the raucous speech of the other men below.

The boy was asleep in a rude box bed drawn up beside theirs. Black Isaiah was bedded down somewhere in a little kennel outside. Sabra sank suspiciously down on the doubtful mattress. The walls of the room were wafer thin; mere pine slats with cracks between. From the street below came women's shrill laughter, the sound of a piano hammered horribly. Horses clattered by. Voices came up in jocose greeting; there were conversations and arguments excruciatingly prolonged beneath her window.

"I was sellin' a thousand beef steers one time—holdin' a herd of about three thousand—and me and my foreman, we was countin' the cattle as they come between us. Well, the steers was wild long-legged coasters—and run! Say, they come through between us like scairt wolves, and I lost the count . . ."

"Heard where the Mullins gang rode in there this morning and cleaned up the town—both banks—eleven thousand in one and nineteen thousand in the other, and when they come out it looked like the whole county'd rallied against 'em. . . ."

"Say, he's a bad hombre, that fella. Got a poisoned tongue, like a rattlesnake. . . . Spades trump?"

"No, hearts. Say, I would of known how to handle him. One time we was campin' on Amarillo Creek . . ."

A loud knock at the door opposite Sabra's room. The knock repeated. Then a woman's voice, metallic, high. *"Quien es? Quién es?"* The impatient rattle of a door knob, and a man's gruff voice.

A long-drawn wail in the street below, "Oh, Joe! He-e-ere's your mule!" followed by a burst of laughter.

Yet somehow she had fallen asleep in utter exhaustion, only to be awakened by pistol shots, a series of blood-curdling yells, the crash and tinkle of broken glass. Then came screams of women, the sound of horses galloping. She lay there, cowering. Cim stirred in his bed, sighed deeply, slept again. She was too terrified to go to the window. Her shivering seemed to shake the bed. She wanted to waken the child for comfort, for company. She summoned courage to go to the window; peered fearfully out into the dim street below. Nothing. No one in the street. Yancey's bleeding body was not lying in the road; no masked men. Nothing again but the clink of glasses and plates; the tinny piano, the slap of cards.

She longed with unutterable longing, not for the sweet security of her bed back in Wichita—that seemed unreal

57

now—but for those nights in the wagon on the prairie with no sound but the rustle of the scrub oaks, the occasional stamp of horses' hoofs on dry clay, the rippling of a near-by stream. She looked at her little gold watch, all engraved with a bird and a branch and a waterfall and a church spire. It was only nine.

It was midnight when Yancey came in. She sat up in bed in her high-necked, long-sleeved nightgown. Her eyes, in her white face, were two black holes burned in a piece of paper.

"What was it? What was it?"

"What was what? Why aren't you asleep, sugar?"

"Those shots. And the screaming. And the men hollering."

"Shots?" He was unstrapping his broad leather belt with its twin six-shooters whose menacing heads peered just above their holsters. He wore it always now. It came, in time, to represent for her a sinister symbol of all the terrors, all the perils that lay waiting for them in this new existence. "Why, sugar, I don't recollect hearing any—— Oh—that!" He threw back his great head and laughed. "That was just a cowboy, feeling high, shooting out the lights over in Strap Turket's saloon. On his way home and having a little fun with the boys. Scare you, did it?"

He came over to her, put a hand on her shoulder. She shrugged away from him, furious. She pressed her hand frantically to her forehead. It was cold and wet. She was panting a little. "I won't bring my boy up in a town like this. I won't. I'm going back. I'm going back home, I tell you."

"Wait till morning, anyhow, won't you, honey?" he said, and took her in his arms.

Next morning was, somehow, magically, next morning, with the terrors of the night vanished quite. The sun was shining. For a moment Sabra had the illusion that she was again at home in her own bed at Wichita. Then she realized that this was because she had been awakened by a familiar sound. It was the sound of Isaiah's voice somewhere below in the dusty yard. He was polishing Yancey's boots, spitting on them industriously and singing as he rubbed. His husky sweet voice came up to her as she lay there.

Lis'en to de lambs, all a-cryin'
Lis'en to de lambs, all a-cryin'
Lis'en to de lambs, all a-cryin',
Ah wanta go to heab'n when ah die.
Come on, sister, wid yo' ups an' downs,
Wanta go to heab'n when ah die,

58

> *De angels waitin' fo' to gib yo' a crown,*
> *Wanta go to heab'n when ah die.*

Lugubrious though the words were, Sabra knew he was utterly happy.

There was much to be done—a dwelling to be got somehow —a place in which to house the newspaper plant. If necessary, Yancey said, they could live in the rear and set up the printing and law office in the front. Almost everyone who conducted a business in the town did this. "Houses are mighty scarce," Yancey said, making a great masculine snorting and snuffling at the wash bowl as they dressed. "It's take what you can get or live in a tent. I heard last night that Doc Nisbett's got a good house. Five rooms, and he'll furnish us with water. There're a dozen families after it, and Doc's as independent as a hog on ice."

Sabra rather welcomed this idea of combining office and home. She would be near him all day. As soon as breakfast was over she and Yancey fared forth, leaving Cim in Isaiah's care (under many and detailed instructions from Sabra). She had put on her black grosgrain silk with the three box pleats on each side, trimmed with the passementerie and jet buttons—somewhat wrinkled from its long stay in the trunk— and her modish hat with the five ostrich plumes and the pink roses that had cost twelve dollars and fifty cents in Wichita, and her best black buttoned kid shoes and her black kid gloves. In the tightly basqued black silk she was nineteen inches round the waist and very proud of it. Her dark eyes, slightly shadowed now, what with weariness, excitement, and loss of sleep, were enormous beneath the brim of the romantic black plumed hat.

Yancey, seeing her thus attired in splendor after almost a fortnight of the gray cheviot, struck an attitude of dazzlement. Blank verse leaped to his ready lips. " 'But who is this, what thing of land or sea,—female of sex it seems—that so bedeck'd, ornate, and gay, comes this way sailing, like a stately ship of Tarsus, bound for th' isles of Javan or Gadire, with all her bravery on. . . .' "

"Oh, now, Yancey, don't talk nonsense. It's only my second-best black grosgrain."

"You're right, my darling. Even Milton has no words for such beauty."

"Do hurry, dear. We've so much to do."

With his curling locks, his broad-brimmed white sombrero, his high-heeled boots, his fine white shirt, the ample skirts of his Prince Albert spreading and swooping with the vigor of his movements, Yancey was an equally striking figure, though perhaps not so unusual as she, in this day and place.

The little haphazard town lay broiling in the summer sun. The sky that Sabra was to know so well hung flat and glaring, a gray-blue metal disk, over the prairie.

"Well, Sabra honey, this isn't so bad!" exclaimed Yancey, and looked about him largely. " 'Now Morning saffron-robed arose from the streams of Ocean to bring light to gods and men.' "

"Ocean!" echoed Sabra, the literal. "Mighty little water I've seen around here—unless you call that desert prairie the ocean."

"And so it is, my pet. That's very poetic of you. The prairie's an ocean of land." He seemed enormously elated—jubilant, almost. His coat tails switched; he stepped high in his fine Texas star boots. She tucked her hand in her handsome husband's arm. The air was sweet, and they were young, and it was morning. Perhaps it was not going to be so dreadful, after all.

Somehow, she had yet no feeling that she, Sabra Cravat, was part of this thing. She was an onlooker. The first thing she noticed, as she stepped into the dust of the street in her modish dress and hat, caused her heart to sink. The few women to be seen scuttling about wore sunbonnets and calico—the kind of garments in which Sabra had seen the women back home in Wichita hanging up the Monday wash to dry on the line in the back yard. Here they came out of butcher's shop or grocery store with the day's provisions in their arms; a packet of meat, tins of tomatoes or peaches, unwrapped. After sharp furtive glances at Sabra, they vanished into this little pine shack or that. Immediately afterward there was great agitation among the prim coarse window curtains in those dwellings boasting such elegance.

"But the others—the other kind of women——" Sabra faltered.

Yancey misunderstood. "Plenty of the other kind in a town like this, but they aren't stirring this time of day."

"Don't be coarse, Yancey. I mean ladies like myself—that I can talk to—who'll come calling—that is——"

He waved a hand this way and that. "Why, you just saw some women folks, didn't you?"

"Those!"

"Well, now, honey, you can't expect those ladies to be

wearing their best bib and tucker mornings to do the house-work in. Besides, most of the men came without their women folks. They'll send for them, and then you'll have plenty of company. It isn't every woman who'd have the courage you showed, roughing it out here. You're the stuff that Rachel was made of, and the mother of the Gracchi."

Rachel was, she knew, out of the Bible; she was a little hazy about the Gracchi, but basked serene in the knowledge that a compliment was intended.

There was the absurdly wide street—surely fifty feet wide —in this little one-street town. Here and there a straggling house or so branched off it. But the life of Osage seemed to be concentrated just here. There were tents still to be seen serving as dwellings. Houses and stores were built of un-painted wood. They looked as if they had been run up over-night, as indeed they had. They stared starkly out into the wide-rutted red clay road, and the muddy road glared back at them, and the brazen sky burned with fierce intensity down on both, with never a tree or bit of green to cheer the spirit or rest the eye. Tied to the crude hitching posts driven well into the ground were all sorts of vehicles: buckboards, crazy carts, dilapidated wagons, mule drawn; here and there a top buggy covered with the dust of the prairie; and every-where, lording it, those four-footed kings without which life in this remote place could not have been sustained— horses of every size and type and color and degree. Indian ponies, pintos, pack horses, lean long-legged range horses, and occasionally a flashing-eyed creature who spurned the red clay with the disdainful hoof of one whose ancestors have known the mesas of Spain. Direct descendants, these, of the equine patricians who, almost four hundred years before, had been brought across the ocean by Coronado or Moscos-co to the land of the Seven Cities of Gold.

There were the sounds of the hammer and the saw, the rattle of chains, the thud of hoofs, all very sharp and distinct, as though this mushroom town were pulling itself out of the red clay of the prairie by its own boot straps before one's very eyes. Crude and ugly though the scene was that now spread itself before Sabra and Yancey, it still was not squalid. It had vitality. You sensed that behind those bare boards peo-ple were planning and stirring mightily. There was life in the feel of it. The very names tacked up over the store fronts had bite and sting. Sam Pack. Mott Bixler. Strap Buckner. Ike Hawes. Clint Hopper. Jim Click.

Though they had come to town but the night before, it

61

seemed to her that a surprising number of people knew Yancey and greeted him as they passed down the street. "H'are you, Yancey! Howdy, ma'am." Loungers in doorways stared at them curiously. Cowboys loping by gave her a long hard look that still had in it something of shyness—a boyish look, much like that with which the outlaws had greeted her down in the draw on the prairie when they learned that she was Cim's mother.

It struck Sabra suddenly with a little shock of discovery that the men really were doing nothing. They lounged in doorways and against hitching posts and talked; you heard their voices in animated conversation within saloon and store and office; they cantered by gracefully, and wheeled and whirled and cantered back again. She was to learn that many of these men were not builders but scavengers. The indomitable old '49ers were no kin of these. They were, frequently, soft, cruel, furtive, and avaricious. They had gathered here to pick up what they could and move on. Some were cowmen, full of resentment against a government that had taken the free range away from them and given it over to the homesteaders. Deprived of their only occupation, many of these became outlaws. Equipped with six-shooters, a deadly aim, and horsemanship that amounted to the miraculous, they took to the Gyp Hills, or the Osage, swooping down from their hidden haunts to terrorize a town, shoot up a bank, hold up a train, and dash out again, leaving blood behind them. They risked their lives for a few hundred dollars. Here was a vast domain without written laws, without precedent, without the customs of civilization; part of a great country, yet no part of its government. Here a horse was more valuable than a human life. A horse thief, caught, was summarily hanged to the nearest tree; the killer of a man often went free.

Down the street these two stepped in their finery, the man swaggering a little as a man should in a white sombrero and with a pretty woman on his arm; the woman looking about her interestedly, terrified at what she saw and determined not to show it. If two can be said to make a procession, then Yancey and Sabra Cravat formed quite a parade as they walked down Pawhuska Avenue in the blaze of the morning sun. Certainly they seemed to be causing a stir. Lean rangers in buckboards turned to stare. Loungers in doorways nudged each other, yawping. Cowboys clattering by whooped a greeting. It was unreal, absurd, grotesque.

"Hi, Yancey! Howdy, ma'am."

Past the Red Dog Saloon. A group in chairs tilted up against the wall or standing about in high-heeled boots and sombreros greeted Yancey now with a familiarity that astonished Sabra. "Howdy, Cim! Hello, Yancey!"

"He called you Cim!"

He ignored her surprised remark. Narrowly he was watching them as he passed. "Boys are up to something. If they try to get funny while you're here with me . . ."

Sabra, glancing at the group from beneath her shielding hat brim, did see that they were behaving much like a lot of snickering schoolboys who are preparing to let fly a bombardment of snowballs. There was nudging, there was whispering, an air of secret mischief afoot.

"Why are they—what do you think makes them——" Sabra began, a trifle nervously.

"Oh, they're probably fixing up a little initiation for me," Yancey explained, his tone light but his eye wary. "Don't get nervous. They won't dare try any monkey-shines while you're with me."

"But who are they?" He evaded her question. She persisted. "Who are they?"

"I can't say for sure. But I suspect they're the boys that did Pegler dirt."

"Pegler? Who is—oh, isn't that the man—the editor—the one who was found dead—shot dead on the banks of the—— Yancey! Do you mean they did it!"

"I don't say they did it—exactly. They know more than is comfortable, even for these parts. I was inquiring around last night, and everybody shut up like a clam. I'm going to find out who killed Pegler and print it in the first number of the *Oklahoma Wigwam*."

"Oh, Yancey! Yancey, I'm frightened!" She clung tighter to his arm. The grinning mirthless faces of the men on the saloon porch seemed to her like the fanged and snarling muzzles of wolves in a pack.

"Nothing to be frightened of, honey. They know me. I'm no Pegler they can scare. They don't like my white hat, that's the truth of it. Dared me last night down at the Sunny Southwest Saloon to wear it this morning. Just to try me out. They won't have the guts to come out in the open——"

The sentence never was finished. Sabra heard a curious buzzing sound past her ear. Something sang—zing! Yancey's white sombrero went spinning into the dust of the road.

Sabra's mouth opened as though she were screaming, but

63

the sounds she would have made emerged, feebly, as a croak.

"Stay where you are," Yancey ordered, his voice low and even. "The dirty dogs." She stood transfixed. She could not have run if she had wanted to. Her legs seemed suddenly no part of her—remote, melting beneath her, and yet pricked with a thousand pins and needles. Yancey strolled leisurely over to where the white hat lay in the dust. He stooped carelessly, his back to the crowd on the saloon porch, picked up the hat, surveyed it, and reached toward his pocket for his handkerchief. At that movement there was a rush and a scramble on the porch. Tilted chairs leaped forward, heels clattered, a door slammed. The white-aproned proprietor who, tray in hand, had been standing idly in the doorway, vanished as though he had been blotted out by blackness. Of the group only three men remained. One of these leaned insolently against a porch post, a second stood warily behind him, and a third was edging prudently toward the closed door. There was nothing to indicate who had fired the shot that had sent Yancey's hat spinning.

Yancey, now half turned toward them, had taken his fine white handkerchief from his pocket, had shaken out its ample folds with a gesture of elegant leisure, and, hat in hand, was flicking the dust from his headgear. This done he surveyed the hat critically, seemed to find it little the worse for its experience unless, perhaps, one excepts the two neat round holes that were drilled, back and front, through the peak of its crown. He now placed it on his head again with a gesture almost languid, tossed the fine handkerchief into the road, and with almost the same gesture, or with another so lightning quick that Sabra's eye never followed it, his hand went to his hip. There was the crack of a shot. The man who was edging toward the door clapped his hand to his ear and brought his hand away and looked at it, and it was darkly smeared. Yancey still stood in the road, his hand at his thigh, one slim foot, in its fine high-heeled Texas star boot, advanced carelessly. His great head was lowered menacingly. His eyes, steel gray beneath the brim of the white sombrero, looked as Sabra had never before seen them look. They were terrible eyes, merciless, cold, hypnotic. She could only think of the eyes of the rattler that Yancey had whipped to death with the wagon whip on the trip across the prairie.

"A three-cornered piece, you'll find it, Lon. The Cravat sheep brand."

flaring skirts, and a poker hand of cards which later she learned was a royal flush, all handsomely embossed on the patent leather cuffs of the boots). She realized, in a flash of pure terror, that he was making straight for her. She stood, petrified. He came nearer, he stood before her, he threw his arms like steel bands about her, he kissed her full on the lips, released her, leaped on his horse, and was off with a blood-curdling yelp and a clatter and a whirl of dust.

She thought that she was going to be sick, there, in the road. Then she began to run, fleetly but awkwardly, in her flounced and bustled silken skirts. Hefner's Furniture Store. Hefner's Furniture Store. Hefner's Furniture Store. She saw it at last. Hefner's Furniture and Undertaking Parlors. A crude wooden shack, like the rest. She ran in. Yancey, Yancey! Everything looked dim to her bewildered and sun-blinded eyes. Someone came toward her. A large moist man, in shirt sleeves. Hefner, probably. My husband. My husband, Yancey Cravat. No. Sorry, ma'am. Ain't been in, I know of. Anything I can do for you, ma'am?

She blurted it, hysterically. "A man—a cowboy—I was walking along—he jumped off his horse—he—I never saw him b——he kissed me—there on the street in broad daylight—a cowboy—he kissed——"

"Why, ma'am, don't take on so. Young fella off the range, prob'ly. Up from Texas, more'n likely, and never did see a gorgeous critter like yourself, if you'll pardon my mentioning it."

Her voice rose in her hysteria. "You don't understand! He kissed me. He k-k-k-k——" racking sobs.

"Now, now, lady. He was drunk, and you kind of went to his head. He'll ride back to Texas, and you'll be none the worse for it."

At this calloused viewpoint of a tragedy she broke down completely and buried her head on her folded arms atop the object nearest at hand. Her slim body shook with her sobs. Her tears flowed. She cried aloud like a child.

But at that a plaintive but firm note of protest entered Mr. Hefner's voice.

"Excuse me, ma'am, but that's velvet you're crying on, and water spots velvet something terrible. If you'd just lean on something else . . . ."

She raised herself from the object on which she had collapsed, weeping, and looked at it with brimming eyes that widened in horror as she realized that she had showered her tears on that pride of Hefner's Furniture and Undertaking establishment, the newly arrived white velvet coffin (child's size) intended for show window purposes alone.

Seven

FROM Doc Nisbett, Yancey received laconic information to the effect that the house had been rented by a family whose aquatic demands were more modest than Sabra's. Sabra was inconsolable, but Yancey did not once reproach her for her mistake. It was characteristic of him that he was most charming and considerate in crises which might have been expected to infuriate him. "Never mind, sugar. Don't take on like that. We'll find a house. And, anyway, we're here. That's the main thing. God, when I think of those years in Wichita!"

"Why, Yancey! I thought you were happy there."

" 'A prison'd soul, lapped in Elysium.' Almost five years in one place—that's the longest stretch I've ever done, honey. Five years, back and forth like a trail horse; walking down to the *Wigwam* office in the morning, setting up personal and local items and writing editorials for a smug citizenry interested in nothing but the new waterworks. Walking back to dinner at noon, sitting on the veranda evenings, looking at the vegetables in the garden or the Venables in the house until I couldn't tell vegetables from Venables and began to think, by God, that I was turning into one or the other myself."

He groaned with relief, stretched his mighty arms, shook himself like a great shaggy lion. In all this welter of red clay and Indians and shirt sleeves and tobacco juice and drought he seemed to find a beauty and an exhilaration that eluded Sabra quite. But then Sabra, after those first two days, had ceased to search for a reason for anything. She met and accepted the most grotesque, the most fantastic happenings. When she looked back on the things she had done and the things she had said in the first few hours of her Oklahoma experience it was as though she were tolerantly regarding the naïvetés of a child. Ten barrels of water a day! She knew now that water, in this burning land, was a precious thing to be measured out like wine. Life here was an anachronism, a great crude joke. It was hard to realize that while the rest of the United States, in this year of 1889, was living a conventionally civilized and primly Victorian existence, in which plumbing, gaslight, trees, gardens, books, laws, millinery, Sunday churchgoing, were taken for granted, here in this Oklahoma country life had been set back according to the frontier standards of half a century earlier. Literally she was pioneering in a wilderness surrounded but untouched by civilization.

Yancey had reverted. Always—even in his staidest Wichita incarnation—a somewhat incredibly romantic figure, he now was remarkable even in this town of fantastic humans gathered from every corner of the brilliantly picturesque Southwest. His towering form, his curling locks, his massive head, his vibrant voice, his dashing dress, his florid speech, his magnetic personality drew attention wherever he went. On the day following their arrival Yancey had taken from his trunk a pair of silver-mounted ivory-handled six-shooters and a belt and holster studded with silver. She had never before seen them. She had not known that he possessed these grim and gaudy trappings. His white sombrero he had banded with a rattlesnake skin of gold and silver, with glass eyes, a treasure also produced from the secret trunk, as well as a pair of gold-mounted spurs which further enhanced the Texas star boots. Thus bedecked for his legal and editorial pursuits he was by far the best dressed and most spectacular male in all the cycloramic Oklahoma country. He had always patronized a good tailor, and because the local talent was still so limited in this new community he later sent as far as San Antonio, Texas, when his wardrobe needed replenishing.

Sabra learned many astounding things in these first few days, and among the most terrifying were the things she learned about the husband to whom she had been happily married for more than five years. She learned, for example, that this Yancey Cravat was famed as the deadliest shot in all the deadly shooting Southwest. He had the gift of being able to point his six-shooters without sighting, as one would point with a finger. It was a direction-born gift in him and an enviable one in this community. He was one of the few who could draw and fire two six-shooters at once with equal speed and accuracy. His hands would go to his hips with a lightning gesture that yet was so smooth, so economical that the onlooker's eye scarcely followed it. He could hit his mark as he walked, as he ran, as he rode his horse. He practised a great deal. From the back door of their cabin Sabra and Cim and rolling-eyed Isaiah used to stand watching him. He sometimes talked of wind and trajectory. You had to make allowance mathematically, he said, for this ever-

71

blowing Oklahoma wind. Sabra was vaguely uneasy. Wichita had not been exactly effete, and Dodge City, Kansas, was notoriously a gunplay town. But here no man walked without his six-shooters strapped to his body. On the very day of her harrowing encounter with Doc Nisbett and the cowboy, Sabra, her composure regained, had gone with Yancey to see still another house owner about the possible renting of his treasure. The man was found in his crude one-room shack which he used as a combination dwelling and land office. He and Yancey seemed to know each other. Sabra was no longer astonished to find that Yancey, twenty-four hours after his arrival, appeared to be acquainted with everyone in the town. The man glanced up at them from the rough pine table at which he was writing.

"Howdy, Yancey!"

"Howdy, Cass!"

Yancey, all grace, performed an introduction. The lean, leather-skinned house owner wiped his palm on his pants' seat in courtly fashion and, thus purified, extended a hospitable hand to Sabra. Yancey revealed to him their plight.

"Well, now, say, that's plumb terr'ble, that is. Might be I can help you out—you and your good lady here. But say, Yancey, just let me step out, will you, to the corner, and mail this here letter. The bag's goin' any minute now."

He licked and stamped the envelope, rose, and took from the table beside him his broad leather belt with its pair of holstered six-shooters, evidently temporarily laid aside for comfort while writing. This he now strapped quickly about his waist with the same unconcern that another man would use in slipping into his coat. He merely was donning conventional street attire for the well-dressed man of the locality. He picked up his sheaf of envelopes and stepped out. In three minutes he was back, and affably ready to talk terms with them.

It was, perhaps, this simple and sinister act, more than anything she had hitherto witnessed, that impressed Sabra with the utter lawlessness of this new land to which her husband had brought her.

This house, so dearly held by the man called Cass, turned out to be a four-room dwelling inadequate to their needs, and they were in despair at the thought of being obliged to wait until a house could be built. Then Yancey had a brilliant idea. He found a two-room cabin made of rough boards. This was hauled to the site of the main house, plastered, and —added to it—provided them with a six-room combination dwelling, newspaper plant, and law office. There was all the splendor of sitting room, dining room, bedroom, and kitchen to live in. One room of the small attached cabin was a combination law and newspaper office. The other served as composing room and print shop. The Hefner Furniture and Undertaking Parlors provided them with furniture—a large wooden bedstead to fit Sabra's mattress and spring; a small bed for Cim; tables, chairs—the plainest of everything. The few bits of furnishing and ornament that Sabra had brought with her from Wichita were fortunately—or unfortunately —possessed of the enduring beauty of objects which have been carefully made by hands exquisitely aware of line, texture, color, and further enhanced by the rich mellow patina that comes with the years. Her pieces of silver, of china, of fine linen were as out of place in this roughly furnished cabin of unpainted lumber as a court lady in a peasant's hovel. In two days Sabra was a housewife established in her routine as though she had been at it for years. A pan of biscuits in the oven of the wood-burning kitchen stove; a dress pattern of calico, cut out and ready for basting, on the table in the sitting room.

Setting up the newspaper plant and law office was not so simple. Yancey, for example, was inclined to write his first editorial entitled Whither Oklahoma? before the hand press had been put together. He was more absorbed in the effect of the sign tacked up over the front of the shop than he was in the proper mechanical arrangement of the necessary appliances inside. THE OKLAHOMA WIGWAM, read the sign in block letters two feet high, so that the little cabin itself was almost obscured. Then, beneath, in letters scarcely less impressive: YANCEY CRAVAT, PROP. AND EDITOR. ATTORNEY AT LAW. NOTARY.

The placing of this sign took the better part of a day, during which time all other work was suspended. While the operation was in progress Yancey crossed the road fifty times, ostensibly to direct matters from a proper vantage point of criticism, but really to bask in the dazzling effect of the bold fat black letters. As always in the course of such proceedings on the part of the laboring male there was much hoarse shouting, gesticulation, and general rumpus. To Sabra, coming to the door from time to time, dish towel or ladle in hand, the clamor seemed out of all proportion to the results achieved. She thought (privately) that two women could have finished the job in half the time with one tenth the fuss. She still was far too feminine, tactful, and in love with her husband to say so. Cim enjoyed the whole thing enormously, as did his black satellite, bodyguard, and playmate, Isaiah. They capered, shouted, whooped, and added much to the din.

Yancey, from across the road—"Lift her up a little higher that end!"

"What say?" from the perspiring Jesse Rickey, his assistant.

"That end—up! NO! UP! I said, UP!"

"Well, which end, f'r Chris' sakes, right or left?"

"Right! RIGHT! God Almighty, man, don't you know your right from your left?"

"Easy now. E-e-e-esy! Over now. Over! There! That's—no—yeh—now head her a little this way. . . ."

"How's that?"

"Oh, my land's sakes alive!" thought Sabra, going back to her orderly kitchen. "Men make such a lot of work of nothing."

It was her first admission that the male of the species might be fallible. A product of Southern training, even though a daily witness, during her girlhood, to the dominance of her matriarchal mother over her weak and war-shattered father, she had been bred to the tradition that the male was always right, always to be deferred to. Yancey, still her passionate lover, had always treated her, tenderly, as a charming little fool, and this rôle she had meekly—even gratefully—accepted. But now suspicion began to rear its ugly head. These last three weeks had shown her that the male was often mistaken, as a sex, and that Yancey was almost always wrong as an individual. But these frightening discoveries she would not yet admit even to herself. Also that he was enthralled by the dramatics of any plan he might conceive, but that he often was too impatient of its mechanics to carry it through to completion.

"Yancey, this case of type's badly pied." Jesse Rickey, journeyman printer and periodic drunkard, was responsible for this misfortune, having dropped a case, face down, in the dust of the road while assisting Yancey in the moving. "It'll have to be sorted before you can get out a paper."

"Oh, Rickey'll tend to that. I've got a lot of important work to do. Editorials to write, news to get, lot of real estate transfers—and I'm going to find out who killed Pegler and print it in the first issue if it takes the last drop of blood in me."

"Oh, please don't. What does it matter! He's dead. Maybe

he did shoot himself. And besides, you've got Cim and me to think of. You can't let anything happen to you."

"Let that Yountis gang get away with a thing like that and anything *is* likely to happen to me; the same thing that happened to him. No, sir! I'll show them, first crack, that the *Oklahoma Wigwam* prints all the news, all the time, knowing no law but the Law of God and the government of these United States! Say, that's a pretty good slogan. Top of the page, just above the editorial column."

In the end it was she who sorted the case of pied type. The five years of Yancey's newspaper ownership in Wichita had familiarized her, almost unconsciously, with many of the mechanical aspects of a newspaper printing shop. She even liked the smell of printer's ink, of the metal type, of the paper wet from the hand press. She found that the brass and copper thin spaces, used for setting up ads, had no proper container, and at a loss to find one she hit upon the idea of using a muffin tin until a proper receptacle could be found. It never was found, and the muffin tin still served after a quarter of a century had gone by. She was, by that time, sentimental about it, and superstitious.

The hand press was finally set up, and the little job press, and the case rack containing the type. The rollers were in place, and their little stock of paper. Curiously enough, though neither Yancey nor Sabra was conscious of it, it was she who had directed most of this manual work and who had indeed actually performed much of it, with Isaiah and Jesse Rickey to help her. Yancey was off and up the street every ten minutes. Returning, he would lose himself in the placing of his law library, his books of reference, and his favorite volumes, for which he contended there was not enough shelf room in the house proper. He had brought along boxes of books stowed away in the covered wagons. If the combined book wealth contained in all the houses, offices, and shops of the entire Oklahoma country so newly settled could have been gathered in one spot it probably would have been found to number less than this preposterous library of the paradoxical Yancey Cravat. Glib and showy though he was with his book knowledge Yancey still had in these volumes of his the absorption of the true book lover. He gave more attention to the carpenter who put up these crude bookshelves than he had bestowed upon the actual coupling of the two cabins when first they had moved in. The books he insisted on placing himself, picking them up, one by one, and losing himself now in this page, now in that, so that at the end of

75

the long hot afternoon he had accomplished nothing. Blackstone and Kent (ineffectual enough in this lawless land) were shocked to find themselves hobnobbing side by side with Childe Harold and the Decameron. Culpepper's Torts nestled cosily between the shameless tale of the sprightly Wife of Bath and Yancey's new and joyously discovered copy of Fitzgerald's Omar Khayyám.

Lost to all else he would call happily in to Sabra as she bent over the case rack, her cheek streaked with ink, her fingers stained, her head close to Jesse Rickey's bleary-eyed one as she sorted type or filled the muffin tin with the metal thin spaces: "Sabe! Oh, Sabe—listen to this." He would clear his throat. " 'Son of Nestor, delight of my heart, mark the flashing of bronze through the echoing halls, and the flashing of gold and of amber and of silver and of ivory. Such like, methinks, is the court of Olympian Zeus within, for the world of things that are here; wonder comes over me as I look thereon.' . . . God, Sabra, it's as fine as the Old Testament. Finer!"

" 'The world of things that are here,' " echoed Sabra, not bitterly, but with grave common sense. "Perhaps if you'd pay more attention to those, and less to your nonsense in books about gold and silver and ivory, we might get settled."

But he was ready with a honeyed reply culled from the same book so dear to his heart and his grandiloquent tongue. " 'Be not wroth with me hereat, goddess and queen.' "

The goddess and queen pushed her hair back from her forehead with a sooty hand, leaving still another smudge of printer's ink upon that worried surface.

Jesse Rickey, the printer (known, naturally, to his familiars as "Gin" Rickey, owing to his periods of intemperance) and black Isaiah were, next to Sabra, most responsible for the astounding fact that the Cravat family finally was settled in house and office. The front door, which was the office entrance, faced the wide wallow of the main street. The back and the side doors of the dwelling looked out on a stretch of Oklahoma red clay, littered with the empty tin cans that mark any new American settlement, and especially one whose drought is relieved by the thirst-quenching coolness of tinned tomatoes and peaches. Perhaps the canned tomato, as much as anything, made possible the settling of the vast West and Southwest. In the midst of this clay and refuse, in a sort of shed-kennel, lived little Isaiah; rather, he slept there, like a faithful dog, for all day long he was about the house and the printing office, tireless, willing, invaluable. He belonged to

Sabra, body and soul, as completely as though the Civil War had never been. A little servant of twelve, born to labor, he became as dear to Sabra, as accustomed, as one of her own children, despite her Southern training and his black skin. He dried the dishes, a towel tied round his neck; he laid the table; he was playmate and nursemaid for Cim; he ran errands, a swift and splay-footed Mercury; he was a born reporter, and in the course of his day's scurrying about the town on this errand or that brought into Sabra's kitchen more items of news and gossip (which were later transferred to the newspaper office) than a whole staff of trained newspaper men could have done. He was so little, so black, so lithe, so harmless looking, that his presence was, more often than not, completely overlooked. The saloon loungers, cowboys, rangers, and homesteaders in and about the town alternately spoiled and plagued him. One minute they were throwing him dimes in the dust for his rendition of his favorite song:

King Jesus come a-ridin' on a milk-white steed,
Wid a rainbow on his shoulder.

The next moment they were making his splay-feet dance frenziedly as the bullets from their six-shooters plopped playfully all about him and his kinky hair seemed to grow straight and dank with terror.

Sabra, in time, taught him to read, write, and figure. He was quick to learn, industrious, lovable. He thought he actually belonged to her. Cim was beginning to learn the alphabet, and as Sabra bent over the child, Isaiah, too, would bring his little stool out of its corner. Perched on it like an intelligent monkey he mastered the curlycues in their proper sequence. He cleared the unsightly back yard of its litter of tin cans and refuse. Together he and Sabra even tried to plant a little garden in this barren sanguine clay. More than anything else, Sabra missed the trees and flowers. In the whole town of almost ten thousand inhabitants there were two trees: stunted jack oaks. Sometimes she dreamed of lilies of the valley—the translucent, almost liquid green of their stems and leaves, the perfumed purity of their white bells.

All this, however, came later. These first few days were filled to overflowing with the labor of making the house habitable and the office and plant fit for Yancey's professional pursuits. Already his talents as a silver-tongue were being sought in defense of murderers, horse thieves, land grab-

77

bers, and more civil offenders in all the surrounding towns and counties. It was known that the average jury was wax in his hands. Once started on his plea it was as though he were painting the emotions that succeeded each other across the faces of the twelve (or less, depending on the number available in the community) good men (or good enough) and true. A tremolo tone—their eyes began to moisten, their mouth muscles to sag with sympathy; a wave of the hand, a lilt of the golden voice—they guffawed with mirth. Even a horse thief, that blackest of criminals in this country, was said to have a bare chance for his life if Yancey Cravat could be induced to plead for him—and provided always, of course, that the posse had not dealt with the offender first.

Yancey, from the time he rose in the morning until he went to bed late at night, was always a little over-stimulated by the whisky he drank. This, together with a natural fearlessness, an enormous vitality, and a devouring interest in everybody and everything in this fantastic Oklahoma country, gained him friends and enemies in almost equal proportion.

In the ten days following their arrival in Osage, his one interest seemed to be the tracing of the Pegler murder—for he scoffed at the idea that his predecessor's death was due to any other cause.

He asked his question everywhere, even in the most foolhardy circumstances, and watched the effect of his question. Pegler had been a Denver newspaper man; known, respected, decent. Yancey had sworn to bring his murderers to justice.

Sabra argued with him, almost hysterically, but in vain. "You didn't do anything about helping them catch the Kid, out there on the prairie, when they were looking for him, and you knew where he was—or just about—and he had killed a man, too, and robbed a bank, and I don't know what all."

"That was different. The Kid's different," Yancey answered, unreasonably and infuriatingly.

"Different! How different? What's this Pegler to you! They'll kill you, too—they'll shoot you down—and then what shall I do?—Cim—Cim—and I here, alone—Yancey, darling—I love you so—if anything should happen to you———" She waxed incoherent.

"Listen, honey. Hush your crying and listen. Try to understand. The Kid's a terror. He's a bad one. But it isn't his fault. The government at Washington made him an outlaw."

"Why, Yancey Cravat, what are you talking about? Don't you ever say a thing like that before Cim."

"The Kid's father rode the range before there were fences or railroads in Kansas, and when this part of the country was running wild with longhorn cattle that had descended straight from the animals that the Spaniards had brought over four centuries ago. The railroads began coming in. The settlers came with it, from the Gulf Coast, up across Texas, through the Indian Territory to the end of steel at Abilene, Kansas. The Kid was brought up to all that. Freighters, bull whackers, mule skinners, hunters, and cowboys—that's all he knew. Into Dodge City, with perhaps nine months' pay jingling in his pocket. I'll bet neither the Kid nor his father before him ever saw a nickel or a dime. They wouldn't have bothered with such chicken feed. Silver dollars were the smallest coin they knew. They worked for it, too. I've seen seventy-five thousand cattle at a time waiting shipment to the East, with lads like the Kid in charge. The Kid's grandfather was a buffalo hunter. The range was the only life they wanted. Along comes the government. What happens?"

"What?" breathed Sabra, as always enthralled by one of Yancey's arguments, forgetting quite that she must oppose this very plea.

"They take the range away from the cattle men and cow-boys—the free range that never belonged to them really, but that they had come to think of as theirs through right of use. Squatters come in, Sooners, too, and Nesters, and then the whole rush of the Opening. The range is cut up into town sites, and the town into lots, before their very eyes. Why, it must have sickened them—killed them almost—to see it."

"But that's progress, Yancey. The country's got to be settled."

"This was different. There's never been anything like this. Settling a great section of a country always has been a matter of years—decades—centuries, even. But here they swept over it in a day. You know that as well as I do. Wilderness one day; town sites the next. And the cowboys and rangers having no more chance than chips in a flood. Can't you see it? Shanties where the horizon used to be; grocery stores on the old buffalo trails. They went plumb locoed, I tell you. They couldn't fight progress, but they could get revenge on the people who had taken their world away from them and cut it into little strips and dirtied it."

"You're taking the part of criminals, of murderers, of

79

bad men! I'm ashamed of you! I'm afraid of you! You're as bad as they are."

"Now, now, Sabra. No dramatics. Leave that for me. I'm better at it. The Kid's bad, yes. They don't come worse than he. And they'll get him, eventually. But he never kills unless he has to. When he robs a bank or holds up a train it's in broad daylight, by God, with a hundred guns against him. He runs a risk. He doesn't shoot in the dark. The other fellow always has a chance. It's three or four, usually, against fifty. He was brought up a reckless, lawless, unschooled youngster. He's a killer now, and he'll die by the gun, with his boots on. But the man who fathered him needn't be ashamed of him. There's no yellow in the Kid."

For one dreadful sickening second something closed with iron fingers around Sabra Cravat's heart and squeezed it, and it ceased to beat. White faced, her dark eyes searched her husband's face. Wichita whispers. Kansas slander. But that face was all exaltation, like the face of an evangelist, and as pure. His eyes were glowing. The iron fingers relaxed.

"But Pegler. The men who killed Pegler. Why are they so much worse——"

"Skunks. Dirty jackals hired by white-livered politicians."

"But why? Why?"

"Because Pegler had the same idea I have—that here's a chance to start clean, right from scratch. Live and let live. Clean politics instead of the skulduggery all around; a new way of living and of thinking, because we've had a chance to see how rotten and narrow and bigoted the other way has been. Here everything's fresh. It's all to do, and we can do it. There's never been a chance like it in the world. We can make a model empire out of this Oklahoma country, with all the mistakes of the other pioneers to profit by. New England, and California, and the settlers of the Middle West—it got away from them, and they fell into the rut. Ugly politics, ugly towns, ugly buildings, ugly minds." He was off again. Sabra, all impatience, stopped him.

"But Pegler. What's that got to do with Pegler?" She hated the name. She hated the dead man who was stalking their new life and threatening to destroy it.

"I saw that one copy of his paper. He called it the *New Day*—poor devil. And in it he named names, and he outlined a policy and a belief something like—well—along the lines I've tried to explain to you. He accused the government of robbing the Indians. He accused the settlers of cheating them. He told just how they got their whisky, in spite of its being forbidden, and how their monthly allotment was pinched out of their foolish fingers————"

"Oh, my heavens, Yancey! Indians! You and your miserable dirty Indians! You're always going on about them as if they mattered! The sooner they're all dead the better. What good are they? Filthy, thieving, lazy things. They won't work. You've said so yourself. They just squat there, rotting."

"I've tried to explain to you," Yancey began, gently. "White men can't do those things to a helpless————"

"And so they killed him!" Sabra cried, irrelevantly. "And they'll kill you, too. Oh, Yancey—please—please—I don't want to be a pioneer woman. I thought I did, but I don't. I can't make things different. I liked them as they were. Comfortable and safe. Let them alone. I don't want to live in a model empire. Darling! Darling! Let's just make it a town like Wichita . . . with trees . . . and people being sociable . . . not killing each other all the time . . . church on Sunday . . . a school for Cim. . . ."

The face she adored was a mask. The ocean-gray eyes were slate-gray now, with the look she had seen and dreaded—cold, determined, relentless.

"All right. Go back there. Go back to your trees and your churches and your sidewalks and your Sunday roast beef and your whole goddamned, smug, dead-alive family. But not me! Me, I'm staying here. And when I find the man who killed Pegler I'll face him with it, and I'll publish his name, and if he's alive by then I'll bring him to justice and I'll see him strung up on a tree. If I don't it'll be because I'm not alive myself."

"Oh, God!" whimpered Sabra, and sank, a limp bundle of misery, into his arms. But those arms were, suddenly, no haven, no shelter. He put her from him, gently, but with iron firmness, and walked out of the house, through the newspaper office, down the broad and sinister red road.

Eight

YANCEY put his question wherever he came upon a little group of three or four lounging on saloon or store porch or street corner. "How did Pegler come to die?" The effect of the question always was the same. One minute they were standing sociably, gossiping, rolling cigarettes; citizenry at ease in their shirt sleeves. Yancey would stroll up with his light, graceful step, his white sombrero with the two bullet holes in its crown, his Prince Albert, his fine high-heeled boots. He would ask his question. As though by magic the group dispersed, faded, vanished.

He visited Coroner Hefner, of Hefner's Furniture Store and Undertaking Parlor. That gentleman was seated, idle for the moment, in his combination office and laboratory. "Listen, Louie. How did Pegler come to die?"

Hefner's sun-kissed and whisky-rouged countenance became noticeably less roseate. His pale blue pop-eyes stared at Yancey in dismay. "Are you going around town askin' that there question, or just me?"

"Oh—around."

Hefner leaned forward. He looked about him furtively. He lowered his voice. "Yancey, you and your missus, you bought your furniture and so on here in my place, and what's more, you paid cash for it. I want you as a customer, see, but not in the other branch of my business. Don't go round askin' that there question."

"Think I'd better not, h'm?"

"I know you better not."

"Why not?"

The versatile Hefner made a little gesture of despair, rose, vanished by way of his own back door, and did not return.

Yancey strolled out into the glaring sunshine of Pawhuska Avenue. Indians, Mexicans, cowboys, solid citizens lounged in whatever of shade could be found in the hot, dry, dusty street. On the corner stood Pete Pitchlyn talking to the Spaniard, Estevan Miro. They were the gossips of the town, these two. This Yancey knew. News not only of the town, but of the Territory—not alone of the Territory but of the whole brilliant burning Southwest, from Texas through New Mexico into Arizona, sieved through this pair. Miro not only knew: he sold his knowledge. The Spaniard made a gay splash of color in the drab prairie street. He wore a sash of purple wound round his middle in place of a belt and his neckerchief was of scarlet. His face was tiny, like the face of a child, and pointed; his hair was thick, blue-black, and lay in definite strands, coarse and glossy, like fine wire. His two upper incisor teeth were separated by, perhaps, the width of an eighth of an inch. He was very quiet, and his movements appeared slow because of their feline grace. Eternally he rolled cigarettes in the cowboy fashion, with exquisite deftness, manipulating the tobacco and brown paper magically between the thumb and two fingers of his right hand. The smoke of these he inhaled, consuming a cigarette in three voracious pulls. The street corner on which he lounged was ringed with limp butts.

Pete Pitchlyn, famous Indian scout of a bygone day, has grown pot-bellied and flabby, now that the Indians were rotting on their reservations and there was no more work for him to do. He was a vast fellow, his height of six feet three now balanced by his bulk. His wife, a full-blood Cherokee squaw, squatted on the ground in the shade of a near-by frame shack about ten feet away, as befits a wife whose husband is conversing with another male. On the ground all around her, like a litter of puppies tumbling about a bitch, were their half-breed children. Late in his hazardous career as a scout on the plains Pitchlyn had been shot in the left heel by a poisoned Indian arrow. It was thought he would surely die. This failing, it was then thought he would lose that leg. But a combination of unlimited whisky, a constitution made up of chilled steel, and a determination that those varmints should never kill him, somehow caused him not only to live but to keep the poison-ravaged leg clinging to his carcase. Stubbornly he had refused to have it amputated, and by a miracle it had failed to send its poison through the rest of that iron frame. But the leg had withered and shrunk until now it was fully twelve inches shorter than the sound limb. He refused to use crutches or the clumsy mechanical devices of the day, and got about with astonishing speed and agility. When he stood on the sound leg he was, with his magnificent breadth of shoulders, a giant of six feet three. But occasionally the sound leg tired, and he would rest it by slumping for a moment on the other. He then became a runt five feet high.

The story was told of him that when he first came to Osage in the rush of the Run he, with hundreds of others, sought the refreshment of the Montezuma Saloon, which hospice—a mere tent—had opened its bar and stood ready for business as the earliest homesteader drew his red-eyed sweating horse up before the first town site to which claim was laid in the settlement of Osage (at that time—fully a month before—a piece of prairie as bare and flat as the palm of your hand). The crowd around the rough pine slab of the hastily improvised bar was parched, wild eyed, clamorous. The bartenders, hardened importations though they were, were soon ready to drop with fatigue. Even in this milling mob the towering figure of Pete Pitchlyn was one to command attention. Above the clamor he ordered his drink—

83

three fingers of whisky It was a long time coming. He had had a hard day. He leaned one elbow on the bar, while shouts emerged as croaks from parched throats, and glasses and bottles whirled all about him. Dead tired, he shifted his weight from the sound right leg to the withered left, and conversed half-heartedly with the thirsty ones on this side and that. The harried bartender poured Pitchlyn's whisky, shoved it toward him, saw in his place only a wearily pensive little man whose head barely showed above the bar, and, outraged, his patience tried beyond endurance, yelled:

"Hey, you runt! Get out of there! Where's the son of a bitch who ordered this whisky?"

Like a python Pete Pitchlyn uncoiled to his full height and glared down on the bewildered bartender.

Crowded though it was, the drinks were on the house.

These two specimens of the Southwest it was that Yancey now approached, his step a saunter, his manner carefree, even bland. Almost imperceptibly the two seemed to stiffen, as though bracing themselves for action. In the old scout it evidenced itself in his sudden emergence from lounging cripple to statuesque giant. In the Spaniard you sensed, rather than saw, only a curiously rippling motion of the muscles beneath the smooth tawny skin, like a snake that glides before it really moves to go.

"Howdy, Pete!"

"Howdy, Yancey!"

He looked at the Spaniard. Miro eyed him innocently. *"Qué tal?"*

"Bien. Y tu?"

They stood, the three, wary, silent. Yancey balanced gayly from shining boot toe to high heel and back again. The Cherokee woman kept her sloe eyes on her man, as though, having received one signal, she were holding herself in readiness for another.

Yancey put the eternal question of the inquiring reporter. "Well, boys, what do you know?"

The two were braced for a query less airy. Their faces relaxed in an expression resembling disappointment. It was as when gunfire fails to explode. The Spaniard shrugged his shoulders, a protean gesture intended on this occasion to convey to the beholder the utter innocence and uneventfulness of the daily existence led by Estevan Miro. Pete Pitchlyn's eyes, in that ravaged face, were coals in an ash heap. It was not for him to be seen talking on the street corner with the man who was asking a fatal question—fatal not only to

84

the asker but to the one who should be foolhardy enough to answer it. He knew Yancey, admired him, wished him well. Yet there was little he dared say now before the reptilian Miro. Yancey continued, conversationally:

"I understand there's an element rarin' around town bragging that they're going to make Osage the terror of the Southwest, like Abilene and Dodge City in the old days; and the Cimarron." The jaws of Pete Pitchlyn worked rhythmically on the form of nicotine to which he was addicted. Estevan Miro inhaled a deep draught of his brand of poison and sent forth its wraith, a pale gray jet, through his nostrils. Thus each maintained an air of nonchalance to hide his nervousness. "I'm interviewing citizens of note," continued Yancey, blandly, "on whether they think this town ought to be run on that principle or on a Socratic one that the more modern element has in mind." He lifted his great head and turned his rare gaze full on the little Spaniard. His gray eyes, quizzical, mocking, met the black eyes, and the darker ones shifted. "Are you at all familiar with the works of Socrates —'Socrates . . . whom well inspir'd the oracle pronounced wisest of men'?"

Again Estevan Miro shrugged. This time the gesture was exquisitely complicated in its meaning, even for a low-class Spaniard. Slight embarrassment was in it, some bewilderment, and a grain—the merest fleck—of something as nearly approaching contempt as was possible in him for a man whom he feared.

"Yancey," said Pete Pitchlyn, deliberately, "stick to your lawy'in'."

"Why?"

"Anybody's got the gift of gab like you have is wastin' their time doin' anything else."

"Oh, I wouldn't say that," Yancey replied, all modesty. "Running a newspaper keeps me in touch with folks. I like it. Besides, the law isn't very remunerative in these parts. Running a newspaper's my way of earning a living. Of course," he continued brightly, as an afterthought, "there have been times when running a newspaper has saved the editor the trouble of ever again having to earn a living." The faces of the two were blank as a sponged slate. Suddenly—"Come on, boys. Who killed Pegler?"

Pete Pitchlyn, his Cherokee squaw, and the litter of babies dispersed. It was magic. They faded, vanished. It was as though the woman had tossed her young into a pouch, like a kangaroo. As for the cripple, he might have been a centipede. Yancey and the Spaniard were left alone on the sunny street corner. The face of Miro now became strangely pinched. The eyes were inky slits. He was summoning all his little bravado, pulling it out of his inmost depths.

"I know something. I have that to tell you," he said in Spanish, his lips barely moving.

Yancey replied in the same tongue, "Out with it."

The Spaniard did not speak. The slits looked at Yancey. Yancey knew that already he must have been well paid by someone to show such temerity when his very vitals were gripped with fear. "You know something, h'm? Well, Miro, *más vale saber que haber*." With which bit of philosophy he showed Miro what a Westerner can do in the way of a shrug; and sauntered off.

Miro leaped after him in one noiseless bound, like a cat. He seemed now to be more afraid of not revealing that which he had been paid to say than of saying it. He spoke rapidly, in Spanish. His hard *r* sounds drummed like hail on a tin roof. "I say only that which was told to me. The words are not mine. They say, 'Are you a friend of Yancey Cravat?' I say, 'Yes.' They say then, 'Tell your friend Yancey Cravat that wisdom is better than wealth. If he does not keep his damn mouth shut he will die.' The words are not mine."

"Thanks," replied Yancey, thoughtfully, speaking in English now. Then with one fine white hand he reached out swiftly and gave Miro's scarlet neckerchief a quick strong jerk and twist. The gesture was at once an insult and a threat. "Tell them——" Suddenly Yancey stopped. He opened his mouth, and there issued from it a sound so dreadful, so unearthly as to freeze the blood of any within hearing. It was a sound between the gobble of an angry turkey cock and the howl of a coyote. Throughout the Southwest it was known that this terrible sound, famed as the gobble, was Cherokee in origin and a death cry among the Territory Indians. It was known, too, that when an Indian gobbled it meant sudden destruction to any or all in his path.

The Spaniard's face went a curious dough gray. With a whimper he ran, a streak of purple and scarlet and brown, round the corner of the nearest shack, and vanished.

Unfortunately, Yancey could not resist the temptation of dilating to Sabra on this dramatic triumph. The story was, furthermore, told in the presence of Cim and Isaiah, and illustrated—before Sabra could prevent it—with a magnificent rendering of the blood-curdling gobble. They were seated at noonday dinner, with Isaiah slapping briskly back and forth between stove and table. Sabra's fork, half way to her mouth, fell clattering on her plate. Her face blanched. Her appetite was gone. Cim, tutored by that natural Thespian and mimic, black Isaiah, spent the afternoon attempting faithfully to reproduce the hideous sound, to the disastrous end that Sabra, nerves torn to shreds, spanked him soundly and administered a smart cuff to Isaiah for good measure. Luckily, the full import of the sinister Indian gobble was lost on her, else she might have taken even stronger measures.

It was all like a nightmarish game, she thought. The shooting, the carousing, the brawls and high altercations; the sounds of laughter and ribaldry and drinking and song that issued from the flimsy cardboard false-front shacks that lined the preposterous street. Steadfastly she refused to believe that this was to be the accepted order of their existence. Yancey was always talking of a new code, a new day; live and let live. He was full of wisdom culled from the Old Testament, with which he pointed his remarks. " 'The fathers have eaten sour grapes, and the children's teeth are set on edge,' " when Sabra reminded him of this or that pleasant Wichita custom. But Sabra prepared herself with a retort, and was able, after some quiet research, to refute this with:

" 'Stand ye in the ways, and see, and ask for the old paths, where is the good way, and walk therein.' There! Now perhaps you'll stop quoting the Bible at me every time you want an excuse for something you do."

"The devil," retorted Yancey, "can cite Scripture for his purpose." But later she wondered whether by this he had intended a rather ungallant fling at her own quotation or a sheepish excuse for his own.

She refused to believe, too, that this business of the Pegler shooting was as serious as Yancey made it out to be. It was just one of his whims. He would, she told herself, publish something or other about it in the first edition of the *Oklahoma Wigwam*. Yancey stoutly maintained it was due off the press on Thursday. Privately, Sabra thought that this would have to be accomplished by a miracle. This was Friday. A fortnight had gone by. Nothing had been done. Perhaps he was exaggerating the danger as well as the importance of all this Pegler business. Something else would come up to attract his interest, arouse his indignation, or outrage his sense of justice.

She was overjoyed when, that same day, a solemn deputation of citizens, three in number, *de rigueur* in sombreros and six-shooters, called on Yancey in his office (where, by some chance, he happened momentarily to be) with the amazing request that he conduct divine service the following Sunday morning. Osage was over a month old. The women folks, they said, in effect, thought it high time that some contact be established between the little town sprawled on the prairie and the Power supposedly gazing down upon it from beyond the brilliant steel-blue dome suspended over it. Beneath the calico and sunbonnets despised of Sabra on that first day of her coming to Osage there apparently glowed the same urge for convention, discipline and the old order that so fired her to revolt. She warmed toward them. She made up her mind that, once the paper had gone to press, she would don the black silk and the hat with the plumes and go calling on such of the wooden shacks as she knew had fostered this meeting. Then she recollected her mother's training and the stern commands of fashion. The sunbonnets had been residents of Osage before she had arrived. They would have to call first. She pictured, mentally, a group of Mother Hubbards balanced stylishly on the edge of her parlor chairs, making small talk in this welter of Southwestern barbarism.

She got out a plaid silk tie for Cim. "Church meeting!" she exclaimed, joyously. Here, at last, was something familiar; something on which she could get a firm foothold in this quagmire. Yancey temporarily abandoned his journalistic mission in order to make proper arrangements for Sunday's meeting. There was, certainly, no building large enough to hold the thousands who, surprisingly enough, made up this settlement spawned overnight on the prairie. Yancey, born entrepreneur, took hold with the enthusiasm that he always displayed in the first spurt of a new enterprise. Already news of the prospective meeting had spread by the mysterious means common to isolated settlements. Nesters, homesteaders, rangers, cowboys for miles around somehow got wind of it. Saddles were polished, harnesses shined, calicoes washed and ironed, faces scrubbed. Church meeting.

Yancey turned quite naturally to the one shelter in the town adequate to the size of the crowd expected. It was the gambling tent that stood at the far north end of Pawhuska Avenue, flags waving gayly from its top in the brisk Oklahoma wind. For the men it was the social center of Osage. Faro, stud poker, chuckaluck diverted their minds from the stern business of citizenship and saved them the trouble of counting their ready cash on Saturday night. Sunday was, of course, the great day in the gambling tent. Rangers, cowboys, a generous sprinkling of professional bad men from the near-by hills and plains, and all the town women who were not respectable flocked to the tent on Sunday for recreation, society, and excitement. Shouts, the tinkle of glass, the sound of a tubercular piano playing Champagne Charley assailed the ears of the passers-by. The great canvas dome, measuring ninety by one hundred and fifty feet, was decorated with flags and bunting; cheerful, bright, gay.

It was a question whether the owner and dealer would be willing to sacrifice any portion of Sunday's brisk trade for the furtherance of the Lord's business, even though the goodwill of the townspeople were to be gained thereby. After all, he might argue, it was not this element that kept a faro game going.

Yancey, because of his professional position and his well-known power to charm, was delegated to confer with that citizen *du monde,* Mr. Grat Gotch, better known as Arkansas Grat, proprietor and dealer of the gambling tent. Mr. Gotch was in. Not only that, it being mid-afternoon and a slack hour for business, he was superintending the placing of a work of art recently purchased by him and just arrived via the Missouri, Kansas & Texas Railroad, familiarly known throughout the Territory, by a natural process of elision, as the Katy. The newly acquired treasure was a picture, done in oils of a robust and very pink lady of full habit who, apparently having expended all her energy upon the arrangement of her elaborate and highly modern coiffure, was temporarily unable to proceed further with her toilette until fortified by refreshment and repose. To this end she had flung herself in a complete state of nature (barring the hairpins) down on a convenient couch where she lolled at ease, her lips parted to receive a pair of ripe red cherries which she held dangling between thumb and forefinger of a hand whose little finger was elegantly crooked. Her eyes were not on the cherries but on the beholder, of whom she was, plainly, all unaware.

As a tent naturally boasts no walls, it was impossible properly to hang this *objet d'art*, and it was being suspended by guy ropes from the tent top so that it dangled just in front of the bar, as it properly should, flanked by mirrors. Arkansas Grat had pursued his profession in the bonanza days of Denver, San Francisco, White Oaks, and Dodge City. In these precocious cities his artistic tastes had been developed. He knew that the eye, as well as the gullet, must have refreshment in hours of ease. A little plump man, Grat, with a round and smiling countenance, strangely unlined. He looked like an old baby.

He now, at Yancey's entrance, called his attention to the newly acquired treasure, expressing at the same time his admiration for it.

"Ain't she," he demanded, "a lalapaloosa!"

Yancey surveyed the bright pink lady. He had come to ask a favor of Grat, but he would not sell his artistic soul for this mess of pottage.

"It's a calumny," he announced, with some vehemence, "on nature's fairest achievement."

The word was not contained in Mr. Gotch's vocabulary. He mistook Yancey's warmth of tone for enthusiasm. "That's right," he agreed, in triumphant satisfaction. "I was sayin' to the boys only this morning when she come."

Yancey ordered his drink and invited Gotch to have one with him. Arkansas Grat was not one of those abstemious characters frequently found in fiction who, being dispensers of alcoholic refreshment, never sample their own wares. Over the whisky Yancey put his case.

"Listen, Grat. The women folks have got it into their heads that there ought to be a church service Sunday, now that Osage is over a month old, with ten thousand inhabitants, and probably the metropolis of the great Southwest in another ten years. They want the thing done right. I'm chosen to conduct the meeting. There's no building in town big enough to hold the crowd. What I want to know is, can we have the loan of your tent here for about an hour Sunday morning for the purpose of divine worship?"

Arkansas Grat set down his glass, made a sweeping gesture with his right hand that included faro tables, lolling cherry eater, bar, piano, and all else that the tent contained.

"Divine worship! Why, hell, yes, Yancey," he replied, graciously.

They went to work early Sunday. So as not to mar the numbers they covered the faro and roulette tables with twenty-two-foot boards. Such of the prospective congregation as came early would use these for seats. There were, too, a few rude benches on which the players usually sat. The remainder must stand. The meeting was to be from eleven to twelve. As early as nine o'clock they began to arrive. They seemed to spring out of the earth. The horizon spewed up little hurrying figures, black against the brilliant Oklahoma sky. They came from lonely cabins, dugouts, tents. Ox carts, wagons, buggies, horsemen, mule teams. They were starving for company. It wasn't religion they sought; it was the stimulation that comes of meeting their kind in the mass. They brought picnic baskets and boxes, prepared for a holiday. The cowboys were gorgeous. They wore their pink and purple shirts, their five-gallon hats, their gayest neckerchiefs, their most ornate high-heeled boots. They rode up and down before the big tent, their horses curveting and stepping high. "Whoa there! Don't crowd the cattle! . . . You figgerin' on gettin' saved, Quince? . . . Yessir, I'm here for the circus and I'm stayin' for the concert and grand olio besides. . . . Say, you're too late, son. Good whisky and bad women has ruined you."

The town seemed alive with blanketed Indians.

They squatted in the shade of the wooden shacks. They walked in from their near-by reservations, or rode their mangy horses, or brought in their entire families—squaw, papoose, two or three children of assorted sizes, dogs. The family rarely was a large one. Sabra had once remarked this.

"They don't have big families, do they? Two or three children. You'd think savages like that—I mean——"

Yancey explained. "The Indian is a cold race—passionless, or almost. I don't know whether it's the food they eat —their diet—or the vigorous outdoor life they've lived for centuries, or whether they're a naturally sterile race. Funny. No hair on their faces—no beards. Did you ever see an Indian festival dance?"

"Oh, no! I've heard they——"

"They work themselves up, you know, at those dances. Insidious music, mutilations, hysteria—all kinds of orgies to get themselves up to pitch."

Sabra had shuddered with disgust.

This Sunday morning they flocked in by the dozens, with their sorry nags and their scabrous dogs. The men were decked in all their beads and chains with metal plaques. They camped outside the town, at the end of the street.

Sabra, seeing them, told herself sternly that she must remember to have a Christian spirit, and they were all God's children; that these red men had been converted. She didn't believe a word of it. "They're just where they were before Joshua," Mother Bridget had said.

Rangers, storekeepers, settlers. Lean squatters with their bony wives and their bare-legged, rickety children, as untamed as little wolves.

Sabra superintended the toilettes of her men folk from Yancey to Isaiah. She herself had stayed up the night before

91

to iron his finest shirt. Isaiah had polished his boots until they glittered. Sabra sprinkled a drop of her own cherished cologne on his handkerchief. It was as though they were making ready a bridegroom.

He chided her, laughing, "My good woman, do you realize that this is no way to titivate for the work of delivering the Word of God? Sackcloth and ashes is, I believe, the prescribed costume." He poured and drank down three fingers of whisky, the third since breakfast.

Cim cavorted excitedly in his best suit, with the bright plaid silk tie and the buttoned shoes, tasseled at the top. The boy, Sabra thought as she dressed him, grew more and more like Yancey, except that he seemed to lack his father's driving force, his ebullience. But he was high spirited enough now, so that she had difficulty in dressing him.

"I'm going to church!" he shouted, his voice shrill. "Hi, Isaiah! Blessed be the name of the Lawd Amen hall'ujah glory be oh my fren's come and be save hell fire and brimstone——"

"Cimarron Cravat, stop that this minute or you'll have to stay home." Evidently he and Isaiah, full of the Sunday meeting, had been playing church on Saturday afternoon. This was the result of their rehearsal.

Yancey's sure dramatic instinct bade him delay until he could make an effective entrance. A dozen times Sabra called to him, as he sat in the front office busy with paper and pencil. This was, she decided, his sole preparation for the sermon he would be bound to deliver within the next hour. Later she found in the pocket of his sweeping Prince Albert the piece of paper on which he had made these notes. The paper was filled with those cabalistic whorls, crisscrosses, parallel lines and skulls with which the hand unconsciously gives relief to the troubled or restless mind. One word he had written on it, and then disguised it with meaningless marks—but not quite. Sabra, studying the paper after the events of the morning, made out the word "Yountis."

At last he was ready. As they stepped into the road they saw that stragglers were still hurrying toward the tent. Sabra had put on, not her second-best black grosgrain, but her best, and the hat with the plumes, none of which splendor she had worn since that eventful first day. She and Yancey stepped sedately down the street, with Cim's warm wriggling fingers in her own clasp. Sabra was a slimly elegant little figure in her modish black; Yancey, as always, a dashing one; Cim's clothes were identical with those being worn, perhaps, by a million little boys all over the United States, now on their unwilling way to church. Isaiah, on being summoned from his little kennel in the back yard, had announced that his churchgoing toilette was not quite completed, urged them to proceed without him, and promised to catch up with them before they should have gone a hundred feet.

They went on their way. It occurred neither to Sabra nor to Yancey that there was anything bizarre or even unusual in their thus proceeding, three well-dressed and reasonably conventional figures, toward a gambling tent and saloon which, packed to suffocation with the worst and the best that a frontier town has to offer, was for one short hour to become a House of God.

"Are you nervous, Yancey dear?"

"No, sugar. Though I will say I'd fifty times rather plead with a jury of Texas Panhandle cattlemen for the life of a professional horse thief than stand up to preach before this gang of——" He broke off abruptly. "What's everybody laughing at and pointing to?" Certainly passers-by were acting strangely. Instinctively Sabra and Yancey turned to look behind them. Down the street, perhaps fifty paces behind them, came Isaiah. He was strutting in an absurd and yet unmistakably recognizable imitation of Yancey's stride and swing. Around his waist was wound a red calico sash, and over that hung a holstered leather belt so large for his small waist that it hung to his knees and bumped against them at every step. Protruding from the holsters one saw the ugly heads of what seemed at first glance to be two six-shooters, but which turned out, on investigation by the infuriated Mrs. Cravat, to be the household monkey wrench and a bar of ink-soaked iron which went to make up one of the printing shop metal forms. On his head was a battered—an unspeakable—sombrero which he must have salvaged from the back-yard débris. But this was not, after all, the high point of his sartorial triumph. He had found somewhere a pair of Yancey's discarded boots. They were high heeled, slim, star trimmed. Even in their final degradation they still had something of the elegance of cut and material that Yancey's footgear always bore. Into these wrecks of splendor Isaiah had thrust, as far as possible, his own great bare splay feet. The high heels toppled. The arched insteps split under the pressure. Isaiah teetered, wobbled, walked now on his ankles as the treacherous heel betrayed him; now on his toes. Yet he managed, by the very power of his dramatic

93

gift, to give to the appreciative onlooker a complete picture of Yancey Cravat in ludicrous—in grotesque miniature.

He advanced toward them, in spite of his pedestrian handicaps, with an appalling imitation of Yancey's stride. Sabra's face went curiously sallow, so that she was, suddenly, Felice Venable, enraged. Yancey gave a great roar of laughter, and at that Sabra's blazing eyes turned from the ludicrous figure of the black boy to her husband. She was literally panting with fury. Her idol, her god, was being mocked.

"You—laugh! . . . Stop. . . ."

She went in a kind of swoop of rage toward the now halting figure of Isaiah. Though Cim's hand was still tightly clutched by her own she had quite forgotten that he was there so that, as she flew toward the small mimic, Cim was yanked along as a cyclone carries small objects in its trail by the very force of its own velocity. She reached him. The black face, all eyes now (and those all whites), looked up at her, startled, terrorized. She raised her hand in its neat black kid glove to cuff him smartly. But Yancey was too quick for her. Swiftly as she had swooped upon Isaiah, Yancey's leap had been quicker. He caught her hand halfway in its descent. His fingers closed round her wrist in an iron grip.

"Let me go!" For that instant she hated him.

"If you touch him I swear before God I'll not set foot inside the tent. Look at him!"

The black face gazed up at him. In it was worship, utter devotion. Yancey, himself a born actor, knew that in Isaiah's grotesque costume, in his struttings and swaggerings, there had been only that sincerest of flattery, imitation of that which was adored. The eyes were those of a dog, faithful, hurt, bewildered.

Yancey released Sabra's wrist. He turned his brilliant winning smile on Isaiah. He put out his hand, removed the mangy sombrero from the child's head, and let his fine white hand rest a moment on the woolly poll.

Isaiah began to blubber, his fright giving way to injury. "Ah didn't go fo' to fret nobody. You-all was dress up fine fo' ch'ch meetin' so I crave to dress myself up Sunday style——"

"That's right, Isaiah. You look finer than any of us. Now listen to me. Do you want a real suit of Sunday clothes?"

The white teeth now vied with the rolling eyes. "Sunday suit fo' me to wear! Fo' true!"

"Listen close, Isaiah. I want you to do something for me.

Something big. I don't want you to go to the church meeting." Then, as the black boy's expressive face, all smiles the instant before, became suddenly doleful: "Isaiah, listen hard. This is something important. Everybody in town's at the church meeting. Jesse Rickey's drunk. The house and the newspaper office are left alone. There are people in town who'd sooner set fire to the newspaper plant and the house than see the paper come out on Thursday. I want you to go back to the house and into the kitchen, where you can see the back yard and the side entrance, too. Patrol duty, that's what I'm putting you on."

"Yes, *suh*, Mr. Yancey!" agreed Isaiah. "Patrol." His dejected frame now underwent a transformation as it stiffened to fit the new martial role.

"Now listen close. If anybody comes up to the house—they won't come the front way, but at the back, probably, or the side—you take this—and shoot." He took from beneath the Prince Albert a gun which, well on the left, under the coat, was not visible as were the two six-shooters that he always carried at his belt. It was a six-shooter of the kind known as the single action. The trigger was dead. It had been put out of commission. The dog—that part of the mechanism by which the hammer was held cocked and which was released at the pulling of the trigger—had been filed off. It was the deadliest of Southwestern weapons, a six-shooter whose hammer, when pulled back by the thumb, would fall again as soon as released. No need for Isaiah's small forefinger to wrestle with the trigger.

"Oh, Yancey!" breathed Sabra, in horror. She made as though to put Cim behind her—to shield him with her best black grosgrain silk from sight of this latest horror of pioneer existence. "Yancey! He's a child!" Now it was she who was protecting the black boy from Yancey. Yancey ignored her.

"You remember what I told you last week," he went on, equably. "When we were shooting at the tin can on the fence post in the yard. Do it just as you did it then—draw, aim, and shoot with the one motion."

"Yes, *suh*, Mr. Yancey! I kill 'em daid."

"You'll have a brand-new suit of Sunday clothes next week, remember, and boots to go with it. Now, scoot!"

Isaiah turned on the crazy high-heeled boots. "Take them off!" screamed Sabra. "You'll kill yourself. The gun. You'll stumble!"

But he flashed a brilliant, a glorified smile at her over his shoulder and was off, a ludicrous black Don Quixote miraculously keeping his balance; the boots slapping the deep dust of the road now this way, now that.

All Sabra's pleasurable anticipation in the church meeting had fled. "How could you give a gun to a child like that! You'll be giving one to Cim, here, next. Alone in the house, with a gun."

"It isn't loaded. Come on, honey. We're late."

For the first time in their married life she doubted his word absolutely. He strode along toward the tent. She hurried at his side. Cim trotted to keep up with her, his hand in hers.

"What did you mean when you said there were people who would set fire to the house? I never heard of such . . . Did you really mean that someone . . . or was it an excuse to send Isaiah back because of the way he looked?"

"That was it."

For the second time she doubted him. "I don't believe you. There's something going on—something you haven't told me. Yancey, tell me."

"I haven't time now. Don't be foolish. I just don't like the complexion of—I just thought that maybe this meeting was the idea of somebody who isn't altogether inspired by a desire for a closer communion with God. Just occurred to me. I don't know why. Good joke on me, if it's true."

"I'm not going to the meeting. I'm going back to the house." She was desperate. Her house was burning up, Isaiah was being murdered. Her linen, the silver in the DeGrasse pattern, the cake dish, the green nun's veiling.

"You're coming with me." He rarely used this tone toward her.

"Yancey! Yancey, I'm afraid to have you stand up there, before all those people. I'm afraid. Let's go back. Tell them you're sick. Tell them I'm sick. Tell them——"

They had reached the tent. The flap was open. A roar of talk came to them from within. The entrance was packed with lean figures smoking and spitting. "Hi, Yancey! How's the preacher? Where's your Bible, Yancey?"

"Right here, boys." And Yancey reached into the capacious skirt of his Prince Albert to produce in triumph the Word of God. "Come in or stay out, boys. No loafing in the doorway." With Sabra on his arm he marched through the close-packed tent. "They've saved two seats for you and Cim down front—or should have. Yes, there they are."

Sabra felt faint. She had seen the foxlike face of Lon Yountis in the doorway. "That man," she whispered to

Yancey. "He was there. He looked at you as you passed by—he looked at you so——"

"That's fine, honey. Better than I hoped for. Nothing I like better than to have members of my flock right under my eye."

Nine

RANGED along the rear of the tent were the Indians. Osages, Poncas, Cherokees, Creeks. They had come from miles around. The Osages wore their blankets, striped orange, purple, green, scarlet, blue. The bucks wore hats—battered and dirty sombreros set high up on their heads. The thin snaky braids of their long black hair hung like wire ropes over their shoulders and down their breasts. Though they wore, for the most part, the checked gingham shirt of the white man there was always about them the gleam of metal, the flash of some brightly dyed fabric, the pattern of colored beads. The older women were shapeless bundles, with the exception of those of the Osage tribe. The Osage alone had never intermarried with the Negro. Except for intermingled white blood, the tribe was pure. The Indian children tumbled all about. The savages viewed the proceedings impassively, their faces bronze masks in which only the eyes moved. Later, on their reservations, with no white man to see and hear, they would gossip like fishwives; they would shake with laughter; they would retail this or that absurdity which, with their own eyes, they had seen the white man perform. They would slap their knees and rock with mirth.

"Great jokers, the Indians," Yancey had once said, offhand, to Sabra. She had felt sure that he was mistaken. They were sullen, taciturn, grave. They did not speak; they grunted. They never laughed.

Holding Cim's hand tightly in her own, Sabra, escorted by Yancey, found that two chairs had been placed for them. Other fortunate ones sat perched on the saloon bar, on the gambling tables, on the benches, on upturned barrels. The rest of the congregation stood. Sabra glanced shyly about her. Men—hundreds of men. They were strangely alike, all those faces; young-old, weather-beaten, deeply seamed, and, for the most part, beardless. The Plains had taken them early, had scorched them with her sun, parched them with her drought, buffeted them with her wind, stung them with

97

her dust. Sabra had grown accustomed to these faces during the past two weeks. But the women—she was not prepared for the women. Calico and sunbonnets there were in plenty; but the wives of Osage's citizenry had taken this first opportunity to show what they had in the way of finery; dresses that they had brought with them from Kansas, from Texas, from Arkansas, from Colorado, carefully laid away in layers of papers which in turn were smoothed into pasteboard boxes or into trunks. Headgear trembled with wired roses. Cheviot and lady's-cloth and henrietta graced shoulders that had known only cotton this month past. Near her, and occupying one of the seats evidently reserved for persons of distinction, was a woman who must be, Sabra thought, about her own age; perhaps twenty or twenty-one, fair, blue eyed, almost childlike in her girlish slimness and purity of contour. She was very well dressed in a wine-color silk-warp henrietta, bustled, very tightly basqued, and elaborate with fluting on sleeves and collar. Dress and bonnet were city made and very modish. From Denver, Sabra thought, or Kansas City, or even Chicago. Sabra further decided, with feminine unreason, that her nose was the most exquisite feature of the kind she had ever seen; that her fair skin could not long endure this burning, wind-deviled climate and that the man beside her, who looked old enough to be her father, must be, after all, her husband. It was in the way he spoke to her, gazed at her, touched her. Yancey had pointed him out one day. She remembered his name because it had amused her at the time: Waltz, Evergreen Waltz. He was a notorious Southwest gambler, earned his living by the cards, and was supposed to be the errant son of the former governor of some state or other—she thought it was Texas. The girl looked unhappy; and beneath that, rebellious.

Still, the sight of this lovely face, and of the other feminine faces looking out from at least fairly modish and decent straw bonnets and toques, gave Sabra a glow of reassurance. Immediately this was quenched at the late, showy, and dramatic entrance, just before Yancey took his place, of a group of women of whom Sabra had actually been unaware. As a matter of fact, the leader of this spectacular group, whose appearance caused a buzz and stir throughout the tent, had arrived in Osage only the day before, accompanied by a bevy of six young ladies. The group had stepped off the passenger coach of the Katy at the town of Wahoo arrayed in such cinder-strewn splendor as to cause the depot loafers to reel. The Katy had not yet been brought as far as

Osage. It terminated at Wahoo, twenty-two miles away. The vision, in her purple grosgrain silk, with a parasol to match, and two purple plumes in her hat, with her six gayly bedecked companions had mounted a buckboard amid much shrill clamor and many giggles and a striking display of ankle. In this crude vehicle, their silks outspread, their astounding parasols unfurled, they had bumped their way over the prairie to the town. Osage, since that first mad day of its beginning, had had its quota of shady ladies, but these had been raddled creatures, driftwood from this or that deserted mining camp or abandoned town site, middle aged, unsavory, and doubtless slightly subnormal mentally.

These were different. The leader, a handsome black-haired woman of not more than twenty-two or -three, had taken for herself and her companions such rooms as they could get in the town. Osage gazed on the parasols, bedazzled. Within an hour it was known that the woman claimed the name of Dixie Lee. That she was a descendant of decayed Southern aristocracy. That her blooming companions boasted such fancy nomenclature as Cherry de St. Maurice, Carmen Brown, Belle Mansero, and the like. That the woman, shrewd as a man and sharp as a knife, had driven a bargain whereby she was to come into possession, at a stiff price, of the building known as the Elite Rooming House and Café, situated at the far end of Pawhuska Avenue, near the gambling tent; and that she contemplated building a house of her own, planned for her own peculiar needs, if business warranted. Finally, she brought the news, gained God knows how or where, that the Katy was to be extended to Osage and perhaps beyond it. Thus harlotry, heretofore a sordid enough slut in a wrapper and curling pins, came to Osage in silks and plumes, with a brain behind it and a promise of prosperity in its gaudy train.

Dixie Lee, shrewd saleswoman, had been quick to learn of Sunday's meeting, and quicker still to see the advantage of this opportunity for a public advertisement of her business. So now, at Osage's first church meeting, in marched the six, with Dixie Lee at their head making a seventh. They rustled in silks. The air of the close-packed tent became as suffocating with scent as a Persian garden at sunset. Necks were craned; whispers became a buzz; seats were miraculously found for these representatives of a recognized social order, as for visiting royalty. The dazzling tent top, seeming to focus rather than disseminate the glare of the Oklahoma sun, cast its revealing spotlight upon painted cheeks and beaded lashes. The nude and lolling lady of the cherries in Grat Gotch's newly acquired art treasure stared down at them, open-mouthed, with the look of one who is surprised and vanquished by an enemy from her own camp. The hardworking worthy wives of Osage, in their cheviots and their faded bonnets and cotton gloves, suddenly seemed sallow, scrawny, and almost spectacularly unalluring.

All this Sabra beheld in a single glance, as did the entire congregation. Only the Indians, standing or squatting in a row at the back, like an Egyptian frieze against the white of the tent, remained unagitated, remote. Yancey, having lifted Cim into the chair next his mother, looked up at the entrance of this splendid procession.

"God Almighty!" he said. His tone was as irreverent as the words were sacred. A dull flush suffused his face, a thing so rare in him as to startle Sabra more than the words he had uttered or the tone in which he had said them.

"What is it? Yancey! What's wrong?"

"That's the girl."

"What girl?"

"That one—Dixie Lee—she's the girl in the black tights and the skullcap . . . in the Run . . . on the thoroughbred . . ." he was whispering.

"Oh, no!" cried Sabra, aloud. It was wrung from her. Those near by stared.

So this was the church meeting toward which she had looked with such hope, such happy assurance. Harlots, pictures of nude women, Indians, heat, glare, her house probably blazing at this moment, Isaiah weltering in his own gore, Lon Yountis's sinister face sneering in the tent entrance. And now this woman, unscrupulous, evil, who had stolen Yancey's quarter section from him by a trick.

Yancey made his way through the close-packed crowd, leaped to the top of the roulette table which was to be his platform, flung his broad-brimmed white sombrero dexterously to the outjutting base of a suspended oil lamp, where it spun and then clung, cocked rakishly; and, lifting the great lolling head, swept the expectant congregation with his mysterious, his magnetic eyes.

Probably never in the history of the Christian religion had the Word of God been preached by so romantic and dashing a figure. His long black locks curled on his shoulders; the fine eyes glowed; the Prince Albert swayed with his graceful movements; his six-shooters, one on each side, bulged reassuringly in their holsters.

100

His thrilling voice sounded through the tent, stilling its buzz and movement.

"Friends and fellow citizens, I have been called on to conduct this opening meeting of the Osage First Methodist, Episcopal, Lutheran, Presbyterian, Congregational, Baptist, Catholic, Unitarian Church. In the course of my career as a lawyer and an editor I have been required to speak on varied occasions and on many subjects. I have spoken in defense of my country and in criticism of it; I have been called on to defend and to convict horse thieves, harlots, murderers, samples of which professions could doubtless be found in any large gathering in the Indian Territory to-day. I name no names. I point no finger. Whether for good or for evil, the fact remains that any man or woman, for whatever purpose, found in this great Oklahoma country to-day is here because in his or her veins, actuated by motives lofty or base, there is the spirit of adventure. I ask with Shakespeare, 'Why should a man, whose blood is warm within, sit like his grandsire cut in alabaster?' Though I know the Bible from cover to cover, and while many of its passages and precepts are graven on my heart and in my memory, this, fellow citizens of Osage, is the first time that I have been required to speak the Word of God in His Temple." He glanced around the gaudy, glaring tent. "For any shelter, however sordid, however humble—no offense, Grat—becomes, while His Word is spoken within it, His Temple. Suppose, then, that we unite in spirit by uniting in song. We have, you will notice, no hymn books. We will therefore open this auspicious occasion in the brief but inevitably glorious history of the city of Osage by singing—uh—what do you all know boys, anyway?"

There was a moment's slightly embarrassing pause. The hard-bitten faces of the motley congregation stared blankly up at Yancey. Yancey, self-possessed, vibrant, looked warmly down on them. He raised an arm in encouragement. "Come on, boys! Name it! Any suggestions, ladies and gentlemen?"

"How about Who Were You At Home? just for a starter," called out a voice belonging to a man with a shining dome-shaped bald head and a flowing silky beard, reddish in color. He was standing near the rear of the tent. It was Shanghai Wiley, up from Texas; owner of more than one hundred thousand long-horn cattle and of the Rancho Palacios, on Tres Palacios Creek. He was the most famous cattle singer in the whole Southwest, besides being one of its richest cattle and land owners. Possessed of a remarkably high sweet

101

tenor voice that just escaped being a clear soprano, he had been known to quiet a whole herd of restless cattle on the verge of a mad stampede. It was an art he had learned when a cowboy on the range. Many cowboys had it, but none possessed the magic soothing quality of Shanghai's voice. It was reputed to have in it the sorcery of the superhuman. It was told of him that in a milling herd, their nostrils distended, their flanks heaving, he had been seen to leap from the back of one maddened steer to another, traveling the moving mass that was like a shifting sea, singing to them in his magic tenor, stopping them just as they were about to plunge into the Rio Grande.

Yancey acknowledged this suggestion with a grateful wave of the hand. "That's right, Shanghai. Thanks for speaking up. A good song, though a little secular for the occasion, perhaps. But anyway, you all know it, and that's the main thing. Kindly favor us with the pitch, will you, Shanghai? Will the ladies kindly join in with their sweet soprano voices? Now, then, all together!"

It was a well-known song in the Territory where, on coming to this new and wild country, so many settlers with a checkered—not to say plaid—past had found it convenient to change their names.

The congregation took it up feelingly, almost solemnly:

Who were you at home?
Who were you at home?
God alone remembers
Ere you first began to roam.
Jack or Jo or Bill or Pete,
Anyone you chance to meet,
Sure to hit it just as neat,
Oh, who were you at home?

"Now, all together! Again!"

Somebody in the rear suddenly produced an accordion, and from the crowd perched on the saloon bar came the sound of a jew's harp. The chorus now swelled with all the fervor of song's ecstasy. They might have been singing Onward, Christian Soldiers. Through it all, high and clear, sounded Shanghai Wiley's piercing tenor, like brasses in a band, and sustaining it from the roulette table platform the 'cello of Yancey Cravat's powerful, rich barytone.

Oh, WHO were you at home?
WHO were you at HOME?

They had not risen to sing for the reason that most of the congregation was already standing, and the few who were seated were afraid to rise for fear that their seats would be snatched from under them.

Sabra had joined in the singing, not at first, but later, timidly. It had seemed, somehow, to relieve her. This, she thought, was better. Perhaps, after all, this new community was about to make a proper beginning. Yancey, she thought, looked terribly handsome, towering there on the roulette table, his eyes alight, his slim foot, in its shining boot, keeping time to the music. She began to feel prim and good and settled at last.

"Now, then," said Yancey, all aglow, "the next thing in order is to take up the collection before the sermon."

"What for?" yelled Pete De Vargas.

Yancey fixed him with a pitying gray eye. "Because, you Spanish infidel, part of a church service is taking up a collection. Southwest Davis, I appoint you to work this side of the house. Ike Bixler, you take that side. The collection, fellow citizens, ladies and gentlemen—and you, too, Pete—is for the new church organ."

"Why, hell, Yancey, we ain't even got a church!" bawled Pete again, aggrieved.

"That's all right, Pete. Once we buy an organ we'll have to build a church to put it in. Stands to reason. Members of the congregation, anybody putting in less than two bits will be thrown out of the tent by me. Indians not included."

The collection was taken up, in two five-gallon sombreros, the contents of which, as they passed from one hairy sunburned paw to the next, were watched with eagle eyes by Southwest Davis and Ike Bixler, and, in fact, by the entire gathering. The sombreros were then solemnly and with some hesitation brought to the roulette table pulpit for Yancey's inspection.

"Mr. Grat Gotch, being used to lightning calculations in the matter of coins, will kindly count the proceeds of the collection."

Arkansas Grat, red-faced and perspiring, elbowed his way to the pulpit and made his swift and accurate count. He muttered the result to Yancey. Yancey announced it publicly. "Fellow citizens, the sum of the first collection for the new church organ for the Osage church, whose denomination shall be nameless, is the gratifying total of one hundred and thirty-three dollars and fifty-five cents.—Heh, wait a minute, Grat! Fifty-five—did you say fifty-five cents?"

"That's right, Yancey."

Yancey's eye swept his flock. "Some miserable tight-fisted skinflint of a—— But maybe it was a Ponca or an Osage, by mistake."

"How about a Cherokee, Yancey!" came a taunting voice from somewhere in the rear.

"No, not a Cherokee, Sid. Recognized your voice by the squeak. A Cherokee—as you'd know if you knew anything at all—you and Yountis and the rest of your outfit—is too smart to put anything in the contribution box of a race that has robbed him of his birthright." He did not pause for the titter that went round. He now took from the rear pocket of the flowing Prince Albert the small and worn little Bible. "Friends! We've come to the sermon. What I have to say is going to take fifteen minutes. The first five minutes are going to be devoted to a confession by me to you, and I didn't expect to make it when I accepted the job of conducting this church meeting. Walt Whitman—say, boys, there's a poet with red blood in him, and the feel of the land, and a love of his fellow beings!—Walt Whitman has a line that has stuck in my memory. It is: 'I say the real and permanent grandeur of these states must be their religion.' That's what Walt says. And that's the text I intended to use for the subject of my sermon, though I know that the Bible should furnish it. And now, at the eleventh hour, I've changed my mind. It's from the Good Book, after all. I'll announce my text, and then I'll make my confession, and following that, any time left will be devoted to the sermon. Any lady or gent wishing to leave the tent will kindly do so now, before the confession, and with my full consent, or remain in his or her seat until the conclusion of the service, on pain of being publicly held up to scorn by me in the first issue of my newspaper, the *Oklahoma Wigwam,* due off the press next Thursday. Anyone wishing to leave the tent kindly rise now and pass as quietly as may be to the rear. Please make way for all departing—uh—worshipers."

An earthquake might have moved a worshiper from his place in that hushed and expectant gathering: certainly no lesser cataclysm of nature. Yancey waited, Bible in hand, a sweet and brilliant smile on his face. He waited quietly, holding the eyes of the throng in that stifling tent. A kind of power seemed to flow from him to them, drawing them, fixing them, enthralling them. Yet in his eyes, and in the great head raised now as it so rarely was, there was that which sent a warning pang of fear through Sabra. She, too, felt his magnetic draw, but mingled with it was a dreadful terror—a stab of premonition. The little pitted places in the skin of forehead and cheeks were somehow more noticeable. Twice she had seen his eyes look like that.

Yancey waited yet another moment. Then he drew a long breath. "My text is from Proverbs. 'There is a lion in the way; a lion is in the streets.' Friends, there is a lion in the streets of Osage, our fair city, soon to be Queen of the Great Southwest. A lion is in the streets. And I have been a liar and a coward and an avaricious knave. For I pretended not to have knowledge which I have; and I went about asking for information of this lion—though I would change the word lion to jackal or dirty skunk if I did not feel it to be sacrilege to take liberties with Holy Writ—when already I had proof positive of his guilt—proof in writing, for which I paid, and about which I said nothing. And the reason for this deceit of mine I am ashamed to confess to you, but I shall confess it. I intended to announce to you all today that I had this knowledge, and I meant to announce to you from this pulpit—" he glanced down at the roulette table—"from this platform—that I would publish this knowledge in the columns of the *Oklahoma Wigwam* on Thursday, hoping thereby to gain profit and fame because of the circulation which this would gain for my paper, starting it off with a bang!" At the word "bang," uttered with much vehemence, the congregation of Osage's First Methodist, Episcopal, Lutheran, etc., church jumped noticeably and nervously. "Friends and fellow citizens, I repent of my greed and of my desire for self-advancement at the expense of this community. I no longer intend to withhold, for my own profit, the name of the jackal in a lion's skin who, by threats of sudden death, has held this town abjectly terrorized. I stand here to announce to you that the name of that skunk, that skulking fiend and soulless murderer who shot down Jack Pegler when his back was turned—that coward and poltroon—" he was gesturing with his Bible in his hand, brandishing it aloft—"was none other than——"

He dropped the Bible to the floor as if by accident, in his rage. As he stooped for it, on that instant, there was the crack of a revolver, a bullet from a six-shooter in the rear of the tent sang past the spot where his head had been, and there appeared in the white surface of the tent a tiny circlet of blue that was the Oklahoma sky. But before that dot of blue appeared Yancey Cravat had raised himself halfway from the hips, had fired from the waist without, seemingly, pausing to take aim. His thumb flicked the hammer. That was all. The crack of his six-shooter was, in fact, so close on the heels of that first report that the two seemed almost simultaneous. The congregation was now on its feet, en masse, its back to the roulette table pulpit. Its eyes were on one figure; its breath was suspended. That figure—a man—was seen to perform some curious antics. He looked, first of all, surprised. With his left hand he had gripped one of the taut tent ropes, and now, with his hand still grasping the hempen line, his fingers slipping gently along it, as though loath to let go, he sank to the floor, sat there a moment, as if in meditation, loosed his hand's hold of the rope, turned slightly, rolled over on one side and lay there, quite still.

"—Lon Yountis," finished Yancey, neatly concluding his sentence and now holding an ivory-mounted six-shooter in right and left hand.

Screams. Shouts. A stampede for the door. Then the voice of Yancey Cravat, powerful, compelling, above the roar. He sent one shot through the dome of the tent to command attention. "Stop! Stand where you are! The first person who stampedes this crowd gets a bullet. Shut that tent flap, Jesse, like I told you to this morning. Louie Hefner, remove the body and do your duty."

"Okeh, Yancey. It's self-defense and justifiable homicide."

"I know it. Louie, . . . Fellow citizens! We will forego the sermon this morning, but next Sabbath, if requested, I shall be glad to take the pulpit again, unless a suitable and ordained minister of God can be procured. The subject of my sermon for next Sabbath will be from Proverbs XXVI, 27: 'Whoso diggeth a pit shall fall therein' . . . This church meeting, brethren and sisters, will now be concluded with prayer." There was a little thudding, scuffling sound as a heavy, inert burden was carried out through the tent flap into the noonday sunshine. His six-shooters still in his hands, Yancey Cravat bowed his magnificent buffalo head—but not too far—and sent the thrilling tones of his beautiful voice out into the agitated crowd before him.

". . . bless this community, O Lord. . . ."

Ten

MOURNFULLY, and in accordance with the custom of the community, Yancey carved a notch in the handsome ivory and silver-mounted butt of his six-shooter. It was then for the first time that Sabra, her eyes widening with horror, noticed that there were five earlier notches cut in the butts of Yancey's two guns—two on one, three on the other. This latest addition brought the number up to six.

Aghast, she gingerly investigated further. She saw that the two terrifying weapons were not worn completely encased in the holster but each was held within it by an ingenious steel clip, elastic and sensitive as a watch spring. This spring gripped the barrel securely and yet so lightly that the least effort would set it free. Yancey could pull his gun and thumb the hammer with but one motion, instead of two. The infinitesimal saving of time had saved his life that day.

"Oh, Yancey, you haven't killed six men!"

"I've never killed a man unless I knew he'd kill me if I didn't."

"But that's murder!"

"Would you have liked to see Yountis get me?"

"Oh, darling, no! I died a thousand deaths while you were standing there. That terrible prayer, when I thought surely someone else would shoot you. But wasn't there some other way? Did you have to kill him? Like that?"

"Why, no, honey. I could have let him kill me."

"Cim has seen his own father shoot a man and kill him."

"Better than seeing a man shoot and kill his own father."

There was nothing more that she could say on this subject. But still another question was consuming her.

"That woman. That woman. I saw you talking to her, right on the street, in broad daylight to-day, after the meeting. All that horrible shooting—all those people around you —Cim screaming—and then to find that woman smirking and talking. Bad enough if you'd never seen her before. But she stole your land from you in the Run. You stood there, actually talking to her. Chatting."

"I know. She said she had made up her mind that day of the Run to get a piece of land, and farm it, and raise cattle. She wanted to give up her way of living. She's been at it since she was eighteen. Now she's twenty-six. Older than she looks. She comes of good stock. She was desperate."

"What she doing here, then!"

"Before the month was up she saw she couldn't make it go. One hundred and sixty acres. Then the other women homesteaders found out about her. It was no use. She sold out for five hundred dollars, added to it whatever money she had saved, and went to Denver."

"Why didn't she stay there?"

"Her business was overcrowded there. She got a tip that the railroad was coming through here. She's a smart girl. She got together her outfit, and down she came."

"You talk as though you admired her! That—that—" Felice Venable's word came to her lips—"that hussy!"

"She's a smart girl. She's a—" he hesitated, as though embarrassed—"in a way she's a—well, in a way, she's a good girl."

Sabra's voice rose to the pitch of hysteria.

"Don't you quote your Bible at me, Yancey Cravat! You with your Lukes and your Johns and your Magdalenes! I'm sick of them."

The first issue of the *Oklahoma Wigwam* actually appeared on Thursday, as scheduled. It was a masterly mixture of reticence and indiscretion. A half column, first page, was devoted to the church meeting. The incident of the shooting was not referred to in this account. An outsider, reading it, would have gathered that all had been sweetness and light. On an inside column of the four-page sheet was a brief notice:

It is to be regretted that an unimportant but annoying shooting affray somewhat marred the otherwise splendid and truly impressive religious services held in the recreation tent last Sunday, kindness of the genial and popular proprietor, Mr. Grat Gotch. A ruffian, who too long had been infesting the streets of our fair city of Osage, terrorizing innocent citizens, and who was of the contemptible ilk that has done so much toward besmirching the dazzling fame of the magnificent Southwest, took this occasion to create a disturbance, during which he shot, with intent to kill, at the person presiding. It was necessary to reply in kind. The body, unclaimed, was interred in Boot Hill, with only the prowling jackals to mourn him, their own kin. It is hoped that his nameless grave will serve as a warning to others of his class.

Having thus modestly contained himself in the matter of the actual shooting, Yancey let himself go a little on the editorial page. His editorials, in fact, for a time threatened the paper's news items. Sabra and Jesse Rickey had to convince him that the coming of the Katy was of more interest to prospective subscribers than was the editorial entitled, Lower than the Rattlesnake. He was prevailed upon to cut it slightly, though under protest.

The rattlesnake has a bad reputation. People accuse him of a great many mean things, and it cannot be denied that the world would be better off if his species were exterminated. Nine times out of ten his bite is fatal, and many homes have been saddened because of his venomous attacks. But the rattlesnake is a gentleman and a scholar beside some snakes. He always gives warning. It is the snake that takes you unawares that hurts the worst. . . .

Thus for a good half column.

Sabra, reading the damp galley proof, was murmurous with admiration. "It's just wonderful! But, Yancey, don't you think we ought to have more news items? Gossip, sort of. I don't mean gossip, really, but about people, and what they're doing, and so on. Those are the things I like to read in a newspaper. Of course men like editorials and important things like that. But women——"

"That's right, too," agreed Jesse Rickey, looking up, ink smeared, from his case. "Get the women folks to reading the paper."

Sabra was emerging slowly from her rôle of charming little fool. By degrees she was to take more and more of a hand in the assembling of the paper's intimate weekly items, while Yancey was concerned with cosmic affairs. Indeed, had it not been for Sabra and Jesse Rickey that first issue of the *Oklahoma Wigwam* might never have appeared, for the front office of the little wooden shack that served as newspaper plant was crowded, following that eventful Sunday, with congratulatory committees, so that it seemed stuffed to suffocation with sombreros, six-shooters, boots, tobacco, and repetitious talk.

"Yessir, Yancey, that was one of the quickest draws I ever see. . . . And you was on to him all the time, huh? Sa-a-ay, you're a slick one, all right. They don't come no slicker. . . . The rest of the gang has took to the Hills, I understand. That shows they're scairt, because they got a feud with the Kid and his outfit, and the Kid sees 'em he'll drop 'em like a row of gobblers at a turkey shootin'. Yessir, Yancey, you're the kind of stuff this country needs out here. First thing you know you'll be Governor of the Territory. How's that, boys! Come on out and have a drink to the future new Governor, the Honorable Yancey Cravat!"

The group moved in a body across the dusty street into the Sunny Southwest Saloon, from whence came further and more emphatic sounds of approbation.

Sabra, in her checked gingham kitchen apron, was selecting fascinating facts from the stock of ready-print brought with them from Wichita, fresh supplies of which they would receive spasmodically by mail or express via the Katy or the Santa Fé.

SWIMMING BRIDES
Girls inhabiting the Island of Himla, near Rhodes, are not allowed to marry until they have brought up a specified number of sponges, each taken from a certain depth. The people of the Island earn their living by the sponge fishery.

STRENGTH OF THE THUMB
The thumb is stronger than all the other fingers together.

COMPRESSED AIR FOR MINE HAULAGE
During the last ten years a great many mines have replaced animal haulage with compressed air motors.

As the printing plant boasted only a little hand press, the two six-column forms had to be inked with a hand roller. Over this was placed the damp piece of white print paper. Each sheet was done by hand. The first issue of the *Oklahoma Wigwam* numbered four hundred and fifty copies, and before it was run off, Yancey, Jesse Rickey, Sabra, Isaiah—every member of the household except little Cim—had taken a turn at the roller. Sabra's back and arm muscles ached for a week.

Yancey made vigorous protest. "What! Ink on the white wonder of dear Juliet's hand! Out, damned spot! See here, honey. This will never do. My sweet Southern jasmine working over a miserable roller! I'd rather never get out a paper, I tell you."

"It looks as if you never would, anyway." The sweet Southern jasmine did not mean to be acid; but the events of the past two or three weeks were beginning to tell on her nerves. The ready-print contained the opening chapters of a novel by Bertha M. Clay in which beauty and virtue triumphed over evil. An installment of this would appear weekly. The second half of it was missing. But Sabra sagely decided that this fragment, for a time at least, would compensate the feminine readers of the *Oklahoma Wigwam* for the preponderance of civic and political matter and the scarcity of social and personal items. She made up her mind that she would conquer her shyness and become better acquainted with some of those cheviots and straw bonnets seen at the Sunday church meeting.

Yancey and Jesse Rickey seemed to have some joke between them. Sabra, in her kitchen, could hear them snickering like a couple of schoolgirls. They were up to some mischief. Yancey was possessed of the rough and childlike notion of humor that was of the day and place.

"What are you boys up to?" she asked him at dinner.

He was all innocence. "Nothing. Not a thing! What a suspicious little puss you're getting to be."

The paper came out on Thursday afternoon, as scheduled. Sabra was astonished and a little terrified to see the occasion treated as an event, with a crowd of cowboys and local citizens in front of the house, pistols fired, whoops and yells, and Yancey himself, aided by Jesse Rickey, handing out copies as if they had cost nothing to print. Perhaps twenty-five of these were distributed, opened eagerly, perused by citizens leaning against the porch posts, and by cowboys on horseback, before Sabra, peeking out of the office window, saw an unmistakable look of surprise—even of shock—on their faces and heard Cass Bixby drawl, "Say, Yancey, that's a hell of a name for a newspaper."

She sent Isaiah out to get hold of a copy. He came back with it, grinning. It was a single sheet. The *Oklahoma Galoot*. Motto: Take It or Leave It. Beneath this a hastily assembled and somewhat pied collection of very personal items, calculated to reveal the weaknesses and foibles of certain prominent citizens now engaged in perusing the false sheet.

The practical joke being revealed and the *bona fide* paper issued, this was considered a superb triumph for Yancey, and he was again borne away to receive the congratulatory toasts of his somewhat sheepish associates.

It was a man's town. The men enjoyed it. They rode, gambled, swore, fought, fished, hunted, drank. The antics of many of them seemed like those of little boys playing robber's cave under the porch. The saloon was their club, the

111

brothel their social rendezvous, the town women their sweethearts. Literally there were no other young girls of marriageable age; for the men and women who had come out here were, like Sabra and Yancey, married couples whose ages ranged between twenty and forty. It was no place for the very young, the very old, or even the middle-aged. Through it all wove the Indians, making a sad yet colorful pattern. The Osage reservation was that nearest the town of Osage. There now was some talk of changing the name of the town because of this, but it never was done. It had been named in the rush of the Run. The Osages, unlike many of the other Territory Plains tribes, were a handsome people— tall broad shouldered, proud. The women carried themselves well, head up, shoulders firm, their step leisurely and light. Their garments were mean enough, but over them they wore the striped blanket of the tribe, orange and purple and scarlet and blue, dyed with the same brilliant lasting dyes that Mother Bridget had used in Sabra's coverlet. They came in from the Reservation on foot; sometimes a family rattled along the red clay road that led into town, huddled in a wagon, rickety, mud spattered. Sometimes a buck rode a scrofulous horse, his lean legs hugging its sorry flanks. The town treated them with less consideration than the mongrel curs that sunned themselves in the road. They bought their meager supplies with the stipend that the government allowed them; the men bought, stole, or begged whisky when they could, though fire water was strictly forbidden them, and to sell or give it to an Indian was a criminal offense. They lolled or squatted in the sun. They would not work. They raised a little corn which, mixed with lye, they called soffica. This mess, hot or cold, was eaten with a spoon made from the horn of a cow. Sabra hated them, even feared them, though Yancey laughed at her for this. Cim was forbidden by her to talk to them. This after she discovered that Yancey had taken him out to visit the Reservation one afternoon. Here, then, was the monstrous society in which Sabra Cravat now found herself. For her, and the other respectable women of the town, there was nothing but their housework, their children, their memories of the homes they had left.

And so the woman who was, after all, the most intelligent among them, set about creating some sort of social order for the good wives of the community. All her life Sabra had been accustomed to the open-handed hospitality of the South. The Venable household in Wichita had been as nearly as possible a duplicate of the Mississippi mansion which had housed generations of Sabra's luxury-loving and open-handed ancestors. Hordes of relatives came and went. Food and drink were constantly being passed in abundance. White muslin dresses and blue sashes whirled at the least provocative tinkle of the handsome old square piano with its great blobs of grapevine carving. Friends drove up for midday dinner and stayed a week. Felice Venable's musical drawl was always tempting the sated guest to further excesses. "I declare, Cousin Flora May, you haven't eaten enough to keep a bird alive. Angie'll think you don't fancy her cooking. . . . Lacy, just another quail. They're only a mouthful. . . . Mittie, pass the currant jell."

Grimly Sabra (and, in time, the other virtuous women of the community) set about making this new frontier town like the old as speedily as possible. Yancey, almost single handed, tried to make the new as unlike the old as possible. He fought a losing fight from the first. He was muddled; frequently insincere; a brilliant swaggerer. He himself was not very clear as to what he wanted, or how to go about getting it. He only knew that he was impatient of things as they were; that greed, injustice, and dishonesty in office were everywhere; that here, in this wild and virgin land, was a chance for a Utopian plan. But he had no plan. He was sentimental about the under dog; overgallant to women; emotional, quick-tempered, impulsive, dramatic, idealistic. And idealism does not flourish in a frontier settlement. Yancey Cravat, with his unformed dreams—much less the roistering play boys of saloon and plain and gambling house—never had a chance against the indomitable materialism of the women.

Like Sabra, most of the women had brought with them from their homes in Nebraska, in Arkansas, in Missouri, in Kansas, some household treasure that in their eyes represented elegance or which was meant to mark them as possessed of taste and background. A chair, a bed, a piece of silver, a vase, a set of linen. It was the period of the horrible gimcrack. Women all over the country were covering wire bread toasters with red plush, embroidering sulphurous yellow chenille roses on this, tying the whole with satin ribbons and hanging it on the wall to represent a paper rack (to be used on pain of death). They painted the backsides of frying pans with gold leaf and daisies, enhanced the handles of these, too, with bows of gay ribbon and, the utilitarian duckling thus turned into a swan, hung it on

113

the wall opposite the toaster. Rolling pins were gilded or sheathed in velvet. Coal scuttles and tin shovels were surprised to find themselves elevated from the kitchen to the parlor, having first been subjected to the new beautifying process. Sabra's house became a sort of social center following the discovery that she received copies of *Harper's Bazaar* with fair regularity. Felice Venable sometimes sent it to her, prompted, no doubt, by Sabra's rather guarded account of the lack of style hints for the person or for the home in this new community. Sabra's social triumph was complete when she displayed her new draped jars, done by her after minute instructions found in the latest copy of *Harper's*. She then graciously printed these instructions in the *Oklahoma Wigwam*, causing a flurry of excitement in a hundred homes and mystifying the local storekeepers by the sudden demand for jars.

As everything [the fashion note announced, haughtily] is now draped, we give an illustration [Sabra did not—at least in the limited columns of the *Wigwam*] of a china or glass jar draped with India silk and trimmed with lace and ribbon, the decoration entirely concealing any native hideousness in the shape or ornamentation of the jar. Perfectly plain jars can also be draped with a pretty piece of silk and tied with ribbon bows or ornamented with an odd fragment of lace and thereby makes a pretty ornament at little or no cost.

Certainly the last four words of the hint were true.

With elegancies such as these the womenfolk of Osage tried to disguise the crudeness and bareness of their glaring wooden shacks. Usually, there was as well a plush chair which had survived the wagon journey; a tortured whatnot on which reposed painted seashell and the *objets d'art* above described; or, on the wall, a crayon portrait or even an oil painting of some stern and bewhiskered or black-silk and fichued parent looking down in surprised disapproval upon the ructions that comprised the daily activities of this town. From stark ugliness the house interiors were thus transformed into grotesque ugliness, but the Victorian sense of beauty was satisfied. The fact was that these women were hungry for the feel of soft silken things; their eyes, smarting with the glare, the wind, the dust, ached to rest on that which was rich and soothing; their hands, roughened by alkali water, and red dust, and burning sun and wind, dwelt lovingly on these absurd scraps of silk and velvet, snipped from

114

an old wedding dress, from a bonnet, from finery that had found its way to the scrap bag.

Aside from the wedding silver and linen that she had brought with her, the loveliest thing that Sabra possessed was the hand-woven blue coverlet that Mother Bridget had given her. It made a true and brilliant spot of color in the sitting room, where it lay neatly folded at the foot of the sofa, partly masking the ugliness of that utilitarian piece of furniture. This Sabra did not know. As silk patchwork quilts, made in wheel and fan patterns, and embroidered in spider webs of bright-colored threads were quite the fashion, the blue coverlet was looked on with considerable disrespect. Thirty years later, its color undimmed, Sabra contributed it temporarily to an exhibition of early American handiwork held in the Venetian room of the Savoy-Bixby Hotel, and it was cooed and ah'd over by all the members of Osage's smart set. They said it was quaint and authentic and very native and a fine example of pioneer handicraft and Sabra said yes indeed, and told them of Mother Bridget. They said she must have been quaint, too. Sabra said she was.

Slowly, in Sabra's eyes, the other women of the town began to emerge from a mist of drabness into distinct personalities. There was one who had been a school teacher in Cairo, Illinois. Her husband, Tracy Wyatt, ran the spasmodic bus and dray line between Wahoo and Osage. They had no children. She was a sparse and simpering woman of thirty-nine, who talked a good deal of former trips to Chicago during which she had reveled in the culture of that effete city. Yancey was heard learnedly discoursing to her on the subject of Etruscan pottery, of which he knew nothing. The ex-school teacher rolled her eyes and tossed her head a good deal.

"You don't know what a privilege it is, Mr. Cravat, to find myself talking to someone whose mind can soar above the sordid life of this horrible town."

Yancey's ardent eyes took on their most melting look. "Madam, it is you who have carried me with you to your heights. 'In youth and beauty wisdom is but rare!' " It was simply his way. He could not help it.

"Ah, Shakespeare!" breathed Mrs. Wyatt, bridling.

"Shakespeare—hell!" said Yancey to Sabra, later. "She doesn't know Pope when she hears him. No woman ought to pretend to be intelligent. And if she is she ought to have the intelligence to pretend she isn't. And this one looks like Cornelia Blimber, to boot."

"Cornelia? . . ."

"A schoolmarm in Dickens's *Dombey and Son*. A magnificent book, honey. I want you to read it. I want Cim to read it by the time he's twelve. I've got it somewhere here on the shelves." He was searching among the jumble of books. Five minutes later he was deep in a copy of Plutarch which he had bewailed as lost.

Sabra persisted. "But why did you make her think she was so smart and attractive when you were talking to her?"

"Because she is so plain, darling."

"It's just that you can't bear not to have everybody think you're fascinating."

She never read *Dombey and Son*, after all. She decided that she preferred exchanging recipes and discussing the rearing of children with the other women to the more intellectual conversation of Mrs. Wyatt.

It was Sabra who started the Philomathean Club. The other women clutched at the idea. It was part of their defense against these wilds. After all, a town that boasted a culture club could not be altogether lost. Sabra had had no experience with this phase of social activity. The languorous yet acid Felice Venable had always scorned to take part in any civic social life that Wichita knew. Kansas, even then, had had its women's clubs, though they were not known by this title. The Ladies' Sewing Circle, one was called; the Twentieth Century Culture Society; the Hypatias.

Felice Venable, approached as a prospective member, had refused languidly.

"I just naturally hate sewing," she had drawled, looking up from the novel she was reading. "And as for culture! Why, the Venables and the Marcys have had it in this country for three hundred years, not to speak of England and France, where they practically started it going. Besides, I don't believe in women running around to club meetings. They'll be going into politics next."

Sabra timidly approached Mrs. Wyatt with her plan to form a woman's club, and Mrs. Wyatt snatched at it with such ferocity as almost to make it appear her own idea. Each was to invite four women of the town's élite. Ten, they decided, would be enough as charter members.

"I," began Mrs. Wyatt promptly, "am going to ask Mrs. Louie Hefner, Mrs. Doc Nisbett——"

"Her husband's horrid! I hate him. I don't want her in my club." The ten barrels of water still rankled.

"We're not asking husbands, my dear Mrs. Cravat. This is a ladies' club."

"Well, I don't think the wife of any such man could be a lady."

"Mrs. Nisbett," retorted Mrs. Wyatt, introducing snobbery into that welter of mud, Indians, pine shacks, drought, and semi-barbarism known as Osage, Indian Territory, "was a Krumpf, of Ouachita, Arkansas."

Sabra, descendant of the Marcys and the Venables, lifted her handsome black eyebrows. Privately, she decided to select her four from among the less vertebrate and more ebullient of Osage's matrons. Culture was all very well, but the thought of mingling once every fortnight with nine versions of the bony Mrs. Wyatt or the pedigreed Mrs. Nisbett (née Krumpf) was depressing. She made up her mind that next day, after the housework was done, she would call on her candidates, beginning with that pretty and stylish Mrs. Evergreen Waltz. Sabra had inherited a strain of frivolity from Felice Venable. At supper that evening she told Yancey of her plans.

"We're going to take up literature, you know. And maybe early American history."

"Why, honey, don't you know you're making it?"

This she did not take seriously. "And then current events, too."

"Well, the events in this town are current enough. I'll say that for them. The trick is to catch them as they go by. You girls'll have to be quick." She told him of her four prospective members.

"Waltz's wife!" Surprise and amusement, too, were in his voice, but she was too full of her plans to notice. Besides, Yancey often was mystifyingly amused at things that seemed to Sabra quite serious. "Why, that's fine, Sabra. That's fine! That's the spirit!"

"I noticed her at church meeting last Sunday. She's so pretty, it rests me to look at her, after all these—not that they're—I don't mean they're not very nice ladies. But after all, even if it's a culture club, someone nearer my own age would be much more fun."

"Oh, much," Yancey agreed, still smiling. "That's what a town like this should be. No class distinctions, no snobbery, no highfalutin notions."

"I saw her washing hanging on the line. Just by accident. You can tell she's a lady. Such pretty underthings, all trimmed with embroidery, and there were two embroidery petticoats

117

all flounced and every bit as nice as the ones Cousin Belle French Vian made for me by hand, for my trousseau."

"I'm not surprised." Yancey was less loquacious than usual. But then, men were not interested in women's clothes.

"She looks kind of babyish and lonely, sitting there by the window sewing all day. And her husband's so much older, and a cripple, too, or almost. I noticed he limps quite badly. What's his trouble?"

"Shot in the leg."

"Oh." She had already learned to accept this form of injury as a matter of course. "I thought I'd ask her to prepare a paper for the third meeting on Mrs. Browning's 'Aurora Leigh.' I could lend her yours to read up on, if you don't mind, just in case she hasn't got it."

Yancey thought it unlikely.

Mrs. Wyatt's house was one of the few in Osage which were used for dwelling purposes alone. No store or office occupied the front of it. Tracy Wyatt's bus and dray line certainly could not be contained in a pine shack intended for family use. Mrs. Wyatt had five rooms. She was annoyingly proud of this, and referred to it on all possible occasions.

"The first meeting," she said, "will be held at my house, of course. It will be so much nicer."

She did not say nicer than what, but Sabra's face set itself in a sort of mask of icy stubbornness. "The first meeting of the Philomathean Society will be held at the home of the Founder." After all, Mrs. Wyatt's house could not boast a screen door, as Sabra's could. It was the only house in Osage that had one. Yancey had had Hefner order it from Kansas City. The wind and the flies seemed to torture Sabra. It was so unusual a luxury that frequently strangers came to the door by mistake, thinking that here was the butcher shop, which boasted the only other screen door in the town.

"I'll serve coffee and doughnuts," Sabra added, graciously. "And I'll move to elect you president. I"—this not without a flick of malice—"am too busy with my household and my child and the newspaper—I often assist my husband editorially—to take up with any more work."

The paper on Mrs. Browning's "Aurora Leigh" never was written by the pretty Mrs. Evergreen Waltz. Three days later Sabra, chancing to glance out of her sitting-room window, saw the crippled and middle-aged gambler passing her house, and in spite of his infirmity he was walking with great speed —running, almost. In his hand was a piece of white paper—

a letter, Sabra thought. She hoped it was not bad news. He had looked, she thought, sort of odd and wild.

Evergreen Waltz, after weeks of tireless waiting and watching, had at last intercepted a letter from his young wife's lover. As he now came panting up the street the girl sat at the window, sewing. The single shot went just through the center of the wide white space between her great babyish blue eyes. They found her with the gold initialed thimble on her finger, and the bit of work on which she had been sewing, now brightly spotted with crimson, in her lap.

"Why didn't you tell me that when she married him she was a girl out of a—out of a—house!" Sabra demanded, between horror and wrath.

"I thought you knew. Women are supposed to have intuition, or whatever they call it, aren't they? All those embroidered underthings on the line in a town where water's scarce as champagne—scarcer. And then 'Aurora Leigh.'"

She was thoroughly enraged by now. "What, for pity's sake, has 'Aurora Leigh' got to do with her!"

He got down the volume. "I thought you'd been reading it yourself, perhaps." He opened it. "'Dreams of doing good for good-for-nothing people.'"

Eleven

SABRA'S second child, a girl, was born in June, a little more than a year after their coming to Osage. It was not as dreadful an ordeal there in those crude surroundings as one might have thought. She refused to send for her mother; indeed, Sabra insisted that Felice Venable be told nothing of the event until after her granddaughter had wailed her way into the Red Man's country. Yancey had been relieved at Sabra's decision. The thought of his luxury-loving and formidable mother-in-law with her flounced dimities and her high-heeled slippers in the midst of this Western wallow to which he had brought her daughter was a thing from which even the redoubtable Yancey shrank. Curiously enough, it was not the pain, the heat, nor the inexpert attention she received that most distressed Sabra. It was the wind. The Oklahoma wind tortured her. It rattled the doors and windows; it whirled the red dust through the house; its hot breath was on her agonized face as she lay there; if allowed its own way it leaped through the rooms, snatching

119

the cloth off the table, the sheets off the bed, the dishes off the shelves.

"The wind!" Sabra moaned. "The wind! The wind! Make it stop." She was a little delirious. "Yancey! With your gun. Shoot it. Seven notches. I don't care. Only stop it."

She was tended, during her accouchement, by the best doctor in the county and certainly the most picturesque man of medicine in the whole Southwest, Dr. Don Valliant. Like thousands of others living in this new country, his past was his own secret. He rode to his calls on horseback, in a black velveteen coat and velveteen trousers tucked into fancy leather boots. His soft black hat, rivaling Yancey's white one, intensified the black of his eyes and hair. It was known that he often vanished for days, leaving the sick to get on as best they could. He would reappear as inexplicably as he had vanished; and it was noticed then that he was worn looking and his horse was jaded. It was no secret that he was often called to attend the bandits when one of their number, wounded in some outlaw raid, had taken to their hiding place in the Hills. He was tender and deft with Sabra, though between them he and Yancey consumed an incredible quantity of whisky during the racking hours of her confinement. At the end he held up a caterwauling morsel of flesh torn from Sabra's flesh—a thing perfect of its kind, with an astonishing mop of black hair.

"This is a Spanish beauty you have for a daughter, Yancey. I present to you Señorita Doña Cravat."

And Donna Cravat she remained. The town, somewhat scandalized, thought she had been named after Dr. Don himself. Besides, they did not consider Donna a name at all. The other women of the community fed their hunger for romance by endowing their girl children with such florid names as they could conjure up out of their imagination or from the novels they read between dish washings. The result was likely to range from the pathetic to the ridiculous. Czarina McKee; Emmeretta Folsom; Gazelle Slaughter; Maurine Turket; Cassandra Sipes; Jewel Riggs.

The neighborhood wives showered the Cravat household with the customary cakes, pies, meat loaves, and bowls of broth. Black Isaiah was touching, was wonderful. He washed dishes, he mopped floors, he actually cooked as though he had inherited the art from Angie, his vast black mother, left behind in Wichita. One of Sabra's gingham kitchen aprons, checked blue and white, was always hitched up under his arms, and beneath this utilitarian yet coquettish garment his great bare feet slapped in and out as he did the work of the household. He was utterly fascinated by the new baby. "Looka dat! She know me! Hi, who yo' rollin' yo' eyes at, makin' faces!" He danced for her, he sang Negro songs to her, he rocked her to sleep. He was, as Donna grew older, her nursemaid, pushing her baby buggy up and down the dusty street, and later still her playmate as well as Cim's.

When Sabra Cravat arose from that bed something in her had crystallized. Perhaps it was that, for the first time in a year, she had had hours in which to rest her tired limbs; perhaps the ordeal itself worked a psychic as well as a physical change in her; it might have been that she realized she must cut a new pattern in this Oklahoma life of theirs. The boy Cim might surmount it; the girl Donna never. During the hours through which she had lain in her bed in the stifling wooden shack, mists seemed to have rolled away from before her eyes. She saw clearly. She felt light and terribly capable—so much so that she made the mistake of getting up, dizzily donning slippers and wrapper, and tottering into the newspaper office where Yancey was writing an editorial and shouting choice passages of it into the inattentive ear of Jesse Rickey, who was setting type in the printing shop.

". . . the most stupendous farce ever conceived by the mind of man in a civilized country. . . ."

He looked up to see in the doorway a wraith, all eyes and long black braids. "Why, sugar! What's this? You can't get up!"

She smiled rather feebly. "I'm up. I felt so light, so——"

"I should think you would. All that physic."

"I feel so strong. I'm going to do so many things. You'll see. I'm going to paper the whole house. Rosebuds in the bedroom. I'm going to plant two trees in the front. I'm going to start another club—not like the Philomathean—I think that's silly now—but one to make this town . . . no saloons . . . women like that Dixie Lee . . . going to have a real hired girl as soon as the newspaper begins to . . . feel so queer . . . Yancey . . ."

As she began to topple, Yancey caught the Osage Joan of Arc in his arms.

Incredibly enough, she actually did paper the entire house, aided by Isaiah and Jesse Rickey. Isaiah's ebony countenance splashed with the white paste mixture made a bizarre effect, a trifle startling to anyone coming upon the scene unawares. Also Jesse Rickey's inebriate eye, which so often resulted in many grotesque pied print lines appearing in unexpected and inconvenient places in the *Oklahoma Wigwam* columns, was none too dependable in the matching of rosebud patterns. The result, in spots, was Burbankian, with roses grafted on leaves and tendrils emerging from petals. Still, the effect was gay, even luxurious. The Philomathean Club, as one woman, fell upon wall paper and paste pot, as they had upon the covered jars in Sabra's earlier effort at decoration. Within a month Louie Hefner was compelled to install a full line of wall paper to satisfy the local demand.

Slowly, slowly, the life of the community, in the beginning so wild, so unrelated in its parts, began to weave in and out, warp and woof, to make a pattern. It was at first faint, almost undiscernible. But presently the eye could trace here a motif, there a figure, here a motif, there a figure. The shuttle swept back, forward, back, forward.

"It's almost time for the Jew," Sabra would say, looking up from her sewing. "I need some number forty sewing-machine needles."

And then perhaps next day, or the day after, Cim, playing in the yard, would see a familiar figure, bent almost double, gnomelike and grotesque, against the western sky. It was Sol Levy, the peddler, the Alsatian Jew. Cim would come running into the house, Donna, perhaps, trotting at his heels. "Mom, here comes the Jew!"

Sabra would fold up her work, brush the threads from her apron; or if her hands were in the dough she would hastily mold and crimp her pie crust so as to be ready for his visit.

Sol Levy had come over an immigrant in the noisome bowels of some dreadful ship. His hair was blue-black and very thick, and his face was white in spite of the burning Southwest sun. A black stubble of beard intensified this pallor. He had delicate blue-veined hands and narrow arched feet. His face was delicate, too, and narrow, and his eyes slanted ever so little at the outer corners, so that he had the faintly Oriental look sometimes seen in the student type of his race. He belonged in crowded places, in populous places, in the color and glow and swift drama of the bazaars. God knows how he had found his way to this vast wilderness. Perhaps in Chicago, or in Kansas City, or Omaha he had heard of this new country and the rush of thousands for its land. And he had bummed his way on foot. He had started to peddle with an oilcloth-covered pack on his back. Through the little hot Western towns in summer. Through the bitter cold Western towns in winter. They turned the dogs on him. The children cried, "Jew! Jew!" He was only a boy, disguised with that stubble of beard. He would enter the yard of a farmhouse or a dwelling in a town such as Osage. A wary eye on the dog. Nice Fido. Nice doggie. Down, down! Pins, sewing-machine needles, rolls of gingham and calico, and last, craftily, his Hamburg lace. Hamburg lace for the little girls' petticoats, for the aprons of the lady of the house; the white muslin apron edged with Hamburg lace, to be donned after the midday dinner dishes were done, the house set to rights, her hair tidied with a wet comb, the basket of mending got out, or the roll of strips for the rag rug, to be plaited in the precious hours between three and five. He brought news, too.

"The bridge is out below Gray Horse. . . . The Osages are having a powwow at Hominy. All night they kept me awake with their drums, those savages. . . . The Kid and his gang held up the Santa Fé near Wetoka and got thirty-five thousand dollars; but one of them will never hold up a train again. A shot in the head. Verdigris Bob, they call him. A name! They say the posse almost caught the Kid himself because this Vedrigris Bob when he finds he is dying he begs the others to leave him and go on, but first they must stop to take his boots off. His boots he wants to have off, that murderer, to die a respectable man! The Kid stops to oblige him, and the posse in ten more minutes would have caught him, too. A feather in that sheriff's cap, to catch the Kid! . . . A country! My forefathers should have lived to see me here!"

His beautiful, civilized face, mobile as an actor's, was at once expressive of despair and bitter amusement. His long slender hands were spread in a gesture of wondering resignation.

Later he bought a horse—a quadruped possessed unbelievably of the power of locomotion—a thing rheumy-eyed, cadaverous, high rumped, like a cloth horse in a pantomime. Sol Levy was always a little afraid of it; timorous of those great square white teeth, like grave-stones. He came of a race of scholars and traders. Horses had been no part of their experience. He had to nerve himself to wait on it, to give it the feed bag, an occasional apple or lump of sugar. With the horse and rickety wagon he now added kitchenware to his stock, coarse china, too; bolts of woollen cloth; and, slyly, bright colored silks and muslin flowers and ribbons. Dixie Lee and her girls fell upon these with feverish fingers and shrill cries, like children. He spread his wares for them silently. Sometimes they teased him, these pretty morons; they hung on his meager shoulders, stroked his beard. He regarded them remotely, almost sadly.

"Come on, Solly!" they said. "Why don't you smile? Don't you never have no fun? I bet you're rich. Jews is all rich. Ain't that the truth, Maude?"

His deep-sunk eyes looked at them. *Schicksas*. They grew uncomfortable under his gaze, then sullen, then angry. "Go on, get the hell out of here! You got your money, ain't you? Get, sheeny!"

He sometimes talked to Dixie Lee. There existed between these two a strange relation of understanding and something resembling respect. Outcasts, both of them, he because of his race, she because of her calling. "A smart girl like you, what do you want in such a business?"

"I've got to live, Solly. God knows why!"

"You come from a good family. You are young yet, you are smart. There are other ways."

"Ye-e-e-s? I guess I'll take up school teaching. Tell a lot of snotty-nosed brats that two and two make four and get handed eleven dollars at the end of the month for it. I tried a couple of things. Nix, nix!"

In a year or two he opened a little store in Osage. It was, at first, only a wooden shack containing two or three rough pine tables on which his wares were spread. He was the town Jew. He was a person apart. Sometimes the cowboys deviled him; or the saloon loungers and professional bad men. They looked upon him as fair game. He thought of them as savages. Yancey came to his rescue one day in the spectacular fashion he enjoyed. Seated at his desk in the *Wigwam* office Yancey heard hoots, howls, catcalls, and then the crack and rat-a-tat-tat of a fusillade. The porch of the Sunny Southwest Saloon was filled with grinning faces beneath sombreros. In the middle of the dusty road, his back against a Howe scale, stood Sol Levy. They had tried to force him to drink a great glass of whisky straight. He had struggled, coughed, sputtered; had succeeded in spitting out the burning stuff. They had got another. They were holding it up from their vantage point on the porch. Their six-shooters were in their hands. And they were shooting at him—at his feet, at his head, at his hands, expertly, devilish-ly, miraculously, never hitting him, but always careful to come within a fraction of an inch. He had no weapon. He would not have known how to use it if he had possessed one. He was not of a race of fighters.

"Drink it!" the yells were high and less than human. "You're a dead Jew if you don't. Dance, gol darn you! Dance for your drink!"

The bullets spat all about him, sang past his ears, whipped up the dust about his feet. He did not run. He stood there, facing them, frozen with fear. His arms hung at his sides. His face was deathly white. They had shot off his hat. He was bareheaded. His eyes were sunken, suffering, stricken. His head lolled a little on one side. His thick black locks hung dank on his forehead. At that first instant of seeing him as he rushed out of his office, Yancey thought, subconsciously, "He looks like—like——" But the resemblance eluded him then. It was only later, after the sickening incident had ended, that he realized of Whom it was that the Jew had reminded him as he stood there, crucified against the scale.

Yancey ran into the road. It is impossible to say how he escaped being killed by one of the bullets. He seemed to leap into the thick of them like a charmed thing. As he ran he whipped out his own ivory-handled guns, and at that half the crowd on the saloon porch made a dash for the door and were caught in it and fell sprawling, and picked themselves up, and crawled or ran again until they were inside. Yancey stood beside Sol Levy, the terrible look in his eyes, the great head thrust forward and down, like a buffalo charging. Here was a scene to his liking.

"I'll drill the first son of a bitch that fires another shot. I will, so help me God! Go on, fire now, you dirty dogs. You filthy loafers. You stinking spawn of a rattlesnake!"

He was, by now, a person in the community—he was, in fact, the person in the town. The porch loafers looked sheepish. They sheathed their weapons, or twirled them, sulkily.

"Aw, Yancey, we was foolin'!"

"We was only kiddin' the Jew. . . . Lookit him, the white-livered son of a gun. Lookit—Holy Doggie, look at him! He's floppin'."

With a little sigh Sol Levy slid to the dust of the road and lay in a crumpled heap at the foot of the Howe scale. It was at that moment, so curiously does the human mind work, that Yancey caught that elusive resemblance. Now he picked the man up and flung him over his great shoulder as he would a sack of meal.

"Yah!" hooted the jokesters, perhaps a little shamefaced now.

Yancey, on his way to his own house so near by, made first a small detour that brought him to the foot of the tobacco-stained saloon porch steps. His eyes were like two sword blades flashing in the sun.

"Greasers! Scum of the Run! Monkey skulls!"

His limp burden dangling over his shoulder, he now strode through the *Wigwam* office, into the house, and laid him gently down on the sitting-room couch. Revived, Sol Levy stopped to midday dinner with the Cravats. He sat, very white, very still, in his chair and made delicate pretense of eating. Sabra, because Yancey asked her to, though she was mystified, had got out her DeGrasse silver and a set of her linen. His long meager fingers dwelt lingeringly on the fine hand-wrought stuff. His deep-sunk haunting eyes went from Sabra's clear-cut features, with the bold determined brows, to Yancey's massive head, then to the dazzling freshness of the children's artless countenances.

"This is the first time that I have sat at such a table in two years. My mother's table was like this, in the old country. My father—peace to his soul!—lighted the candles. My mother—sainted—spread the table with her linen and her precious thin silver. Here in this country I eat as we would not have allowed a beggar to eat that came to the door for charity."

"This Oklahoma country's no place for you, Sol. It's too rough, too hard. You come of a race of dreamers."

The melancholy eyes took on a remote—a prophetic look. There was, suddenly, a slight cast in them, as though he were turning his vision toward something the others could not see. "It will not always be like this. Wait. Those savages to-day will be myths, like the pictures of monsters you see in books of prehistoric days."

"Don't worry about those dirty skunks, Sol. I'll see that they leave you alone from now on."

Sol Levy smiled a little bitter smile. His thin shoulders lifted in a weary shrug. "Those barbarians! My ancestors were studying the Talmud and writing the laws the civilized world now lives by when theirs were swinging from tree to tree."

Twelve

IN THE three and a half years of her residence in Osage Sabra had yielded hardly an inch. It was amazing. It was heroic. She had set herself certain standards, and those she had maintained in spite of almost overwhelming opposition. She had been bred on tradition. If she had yielded at all it was in minor matters and because to do so was expedient. True, she could be seen of a morning on her way to the butcher's or the grocer's shielded from the sun by one of the gingham sunbonnets which in the beginning she had despised. Certainly one could not don a straw bonnet, velvet or flower trimmed, to dart out in a calico house dress for the purchase of a pound and a half of round steak, ten cents worth of onions, and a yeast cake.

Once only in those three years had she gone back to Wichita. At the prospect of the journey she had been in a fever of anticipation for days. She had taken with her Cim and Donna. She was so proud of them, so intent on outfitting them with a wardrobe sufficiently splendid to set off their charms, that she neglected the matter of her own costuming and found herself arriving in Wichita with a trunk containing the very clothes with which she had departed from it almost four years earlier. Prominent among these was the green nun's veiling with the pink ruchings. She had had little enough use for it in these past years or for the wine-colored silk-warp henrietta.

"Your skin!" Felice Venable had exclaimed at sight of her daughter. "Your hands! Your hair! As dry as a bone! You look a million. What have you done to yourself?"

Sabra remembered something that Yancey once had said about Texas. Mischievously she paraphrased it in order to shock her tactless mother. "Oklahoma is fine for men and horses, but it's hell on women and oxen."

The visit was not a success. The very things she had expected to enjoy fell, somehow, flat. She missed the pace, the exhilarating uncertainty of the Oklahoma life. The teacup conversation of her girlhood friends seemed to lack tang and meaning. Their existence was orderly, calm, accepted. For herself and the other women of Osage there was everything still to do. There lay a city, a county, a whole vast Territory to be swept and garnished by an army of sunbonnets. Paradoxically enough, she was trying to implant in the red clay of Osage the very forms and institutions that now bored her in Wichita. Yet it was, perhaps, a very human trait. It was illustrated literally by the fact that she was, on her return, more thrilled to find that the scrawny elm, no larger than a baby's arm, which she had planted outside the doorway in Osage, actually had found some moisture for its thirsty roots, and was now feebly vernal, than she had been at sight of the cool glossy canopy of cedar, arbor vitae, sweet locust, and crêpe myrtle that shaded the Kansas garden. She took a perverse delight in bringing the shocked look to the faces of her Wichita friends, and to all the horde of Venables and Marcys and Vians that swarmed up from the South to greet the pioneer. Curiously enough, it was not the shooting affrays and Indian yarns that ruffled them so much as her stories of the town's social life.

". . . rubber boots to parties, often, because when it rains we wade up to our ankles in mud. We carry lanterns when we go to the church sociables. . . . Mrs. Buckner's sister came to visit her from St. Joseph, Missouri, and she remarked that she had noticed that the one pattern of table silver seemed to be such a favorite. She had seen it at all the little tea parties that had been given for her during her visit. Of course it was my set that had been the rounds. Everybody borrowed it. We borrow each other's lamps, too, and china, and even linen."

At this the Venables and Marcys and Vians and Goforths looked not only shocked but stricken. Chests of lavender-scented linen, sideboards flashing with stately silver, had always been part of the Venable and Marcy tradition.

Then the children. The visiting Venables insisted on calling Cim by his full name—Cimarron. Sabra had heard it so rarely since the day of his birth that she now realized, for the first time, how foolish she had been to yield to Yancey's whim in the naming of the boy. Cimarron. Spanish; wild, or unruly. The boy had made such an obstreperous entrance into the world, and Yancey had shouted, in delight, "Look at him! See him kick with his feet and strike out with his fists! He's a wild one. Heh, Cimarron! *Peceno Gitano.*"

Cousin Jouett Goforth or Cousin Dabney Venable said, pompously, "And now, Cimarron, my little man, tell us about the big red Indians. Did you ever fight Indians, eh, Cimarron?" The boy surveyed them from beneath his long lashes, his head lowered, looking for all the world like his father.

Cimarron was almost eight now. If it is possible for a boy of eight to be romantic in aspect, Cimarron Cravat was that. His head was not large, like Yancey's, but long and fine, like Sabra's—a Venable head. His eyes were Sabra's, too, dark and large, but they had the ardent look of Yancey's gray ones, and he had Yancey's absurdly long and curling lashes, like a beautiful girl's. His mannerisms— the head held down, the rare upward glance that cut you like a sword thrust when he turned it full on you—the swing of his walk, the way he gestured with his delicate hands—all these were Yancey in startling miniature.

His speech was strangely adult. This, perhaps, because of his close association with his elders in those first formative years in Osage. Yancey had delighted in talking to the boy; in taking him on rides and drives about the broad burning countryside. His skin was bronzed the color of his father's. He looked like a little patrician Spaniard or perhaps (the Venables thought privately) part Indian. Then, too, there had been few children of his age in the town's beginning. Sabra had been, at first, too suspicious of such as there were. He would, probably, have seemed a rather unpleasant and priggish little boy if his voice and manner had not been endowed miraculously with all the charm and magnetism that his father possessed in such disarming degree.

He now surveyed his middle-aged cousins with the concentrated and disconcerting gaze of the precocious child.

"Indians," he answered, with great distinctness, "don't fight white men any more. They can't. Their—uh—spirit is broken." Cousin Dabney Venable, who still affected black stocks (modified), now looked slightly apoplectic. "They only fought in the first place because the white men took their buff'loes away from them, that they lived on and ate and traded the skins and that was all they had; and their land away from them."

"Well," exclaimed Cousin Jouett Goforth, of the Louisiana Goforths, "this is quite a little Redskin you have here, Cousin Sabra."

"And," continued Cimarron, warming to his subject, "look at the Osage Indians where my father took me to visit the reservation near where we live. The white people made them move out of Missouri to Kansas because they wanted their land, and from there to another place—I forget— and then they wanted that, too, and they said, 'Look, you go and live in the Indian Territory where we tell you,' and it's all bare there, and nothing grows in that place—it's called the Bad Lands—unless you work and slave and the Osages they were used to hunting and fishing not farming, so they are just starving to death and my father says some day they will get their revenge on the white——"

Felice Venable turned her flashing dark gaze on her daughter.

"Aha!" said Cousin Jouett Goforth.

Cousin Dabney Venable, still the disgruntled suitor, brought malicious eyes to bear on Sabra. "Well, well, Cousin Sabra! Look out that you don't have a Pocahontas for a daughter-in-law some fine day."

Sabra was furious, though she tried in her pride to conceal it. "Oh, Cim has just heard the talk of the men around the newspaper office—the Indian agent, Mr. Heeney, sometimes drops in on his trips to Osage—they're talking now of having the Indian Agent's office transferred to Osage, though Oklahoma City is fighting for it—Yancey has always been very much stirred by the wretched Indians—Cim has heard him talking."

Cim sensed that he had not made the desired effect on his listeners. "My father says," he announced, suddenly, striding up and down the room in absurd and unconscious imitation of his idol—one could almost see the Prince Albert coat tails switching—"my father says that some day an Indian will be President of the United States, and then you bet you'll all be sorry you were such dirty skunks to 'em."

The eyes of the visiting Venables swung, as one orb, from the truculent figure of the boy to the agitated face of the mother.

"My poor child!" came from Felice Venable in accents of rage rather than pity. She was addressing Sabra.

Sabra took refuge in hauteur. "You wouldn't understand. Our life there is so different from yours here. Yancey's Indian editorials in the *Wigwam* have made a sensation. They were spoken of in the Senate at Washington." Felice dismissed all Yancey's written works with a wave of her hand. "In fact," Sabra went on—she who hated Indians and all their ways—"in fact, his editorials on the subject have been so fearless and free that he has been in danger of his life from the people who have been cheating the Indians. It has been even more dangerous than when he tracked down the murderer of Pegler."

"Pegler," repeated the Venables, disdainfully, and without the slightest curiosity in their voices.

Sabra gave it up. "You don't understand. The only thing you care about is whether the duck runs red ot not."

Even little Donna was not much of a success. The baby was an eerie little elf, as plain as the boy was handsome. She resembled her grandmother, Felice Venable, without a trace of that redoubtable matron's former beauty. But she had that almost indefinable thing known as style. At the age of two she wore with undeniable chic the rather clumsy little garments that Sabra had so painstakingly made for her; and when she was dressed, for the first time, in one of the exquisitely hemstitched, tucked and embroidered white frocks that her grandmother had wrought for her, that gifted though reluctant needlewoman said, tartly, "Thank God, she's got style, at least. She'll have to make out with that."

All in all, Sabra found herself joyously returning to the barren burning country to which, four years earlier, she had gone in such dread and terror. She resented her mother's do-this, do-that. She saw Felice Venable now, no longer as a power, an authority in all matters of importance, but as a sallow old lady who tottered on heels that were too high and who, as she sat talking, pleated and unpleated with tremulous fingers the many ruffles of her white dimity wrapper. The matriarch had lost her crown. Sabra was matriarch now of her own little kingdom; and already she was planning to extend that realm beyond and beyond its present confines into who knows what vastness of demesne.

She decided that she must take the children more than ever in hand. No more of this talk of Indians, of freedom, or equality of man. She did not realize (it being long before the day of psychology as applied so glibly to the training of children) that she was, so far as Cim was concerned, years too late. At eight his character was formed. She had taught him the things that Felice Venable had taught her—stand up straight; eat your bread and butter; wash your hands; say how do you do to the lady; one and one are two; somebody has been eating *my* porridge, said the little wee bear. But Yancey had taught him poetry far beyond his years, and accustomed his ears to the superb cadences of the Bible; Yancey had told him, bit by bit, and all unconsciously, the saga of the settling of the great Southwest.

"Cowboys wear big sombreros to shield their faces from the rain and the sun when they're riding the range, and the snow from dripping down their backs. He wears a handkerchief knotted at the back of the neck and hanging down in front so that he can wipe the sweat and dust from his face with it, and then there it is, open, drying in the wind; and in a dust storm he pulls it over his mouth and nose, and in a blizzard it keeps his nose and chin from freezing. He wears chaps, with the hairy side out, to keep his legs warm in winter and to protect them from being torn by chaparral and cactus thorns in summer. His boots are high heeled to keep his feet from slipping in the stirrups when he has to work standing in the saddle, and because he can sink them in the sod when he's off his horse and roping a plunging bronc. He totes a six-shooter to keep the other fellow from shooting."

The child's eyes were enormous, glowing, enthralled. Yancey told him the story of the buffalo; he talked endlessly of the Indians. He even taught him some words of Comanche, which is the court language of the Indian. He put him on a horse at the age of six. A sentimentalist and a romantic, he talked to the boy of the sunset; of Spanish gold; of the wild days of the Cimarron and the empire so nearly founded there. The boy loved his mother dutifully, and as a matter of course, as a child loves the fount of food, of tender care, of shelter. But his father he worshiped, he adored.

Sabra's leave-taking held one regret, one pain. Mother Bridget had died two weeks before Sabra arrived in Wichita. It was not until she learned this sad news that Sabra realized how tremendously she had counted on telling her tale of Osage to the nun. She would have understood. She would have laughed at the story of the ten barrels of water; of the wild cowboy's kiss in the road; she would have sympathized with Sabra's terror during that Sunday church meeting. She had known that very life a half century ago, there in Kansas. Sabra, during her visit, did not go to the Mission School. She could not.

She had meant, at the last, to find occasion to inform her mother and the minor Venables that it was she who ironed Yancey's fine white linen shirts. But she was not a spiteful woman. And she reflected that this might be construed as a criticism of her husband.

So, gladly, eagerly, Sabra went back to the wilds she once had despised.

Thirteen

BEFORE the Katy pulled in at the Osage station (the railroad actually had been extended, true to Dixie Lee's prediction, from Wahoo to Osage and beyond) Sabra's eyes were searching the glaring wooden platform. Len Orson, the chatty and accommodating conductor, took Donna in his arms and stood with her at the foot of the car steps. His heavy gold plated watch chain, as broad as a cable, with its concomitant Masonic charm, elk's tooth, gold pencil and peach pit carved in the likeness of an ape, still held Donna enthralled, though she had snatched at it whenever he passed their seat or stood to relate the gossip of the Territory to Sabra. She was hungry for news, and Len was a notorious fishwife. Now, as she stepped off the train, Sabra's face wore that look of radiant expectancy characteristic of the returned traveler, confident of a welcome.

"Well, I guess I know somebody'll be pretty sorry to see you," Len said, archly. He looked about for powerful waiting arms in which to deposit Donna. The engine bell clanged, the whistle tooted. His kindly and inquisitive blue eyes swept the station platform. He plumped Donna, perforce, into Sabra's strangely slack arms, and planted one foot, in its square-toed easy black shoe, onto the car step in the nick of time, the other leg swinging out behind him as the train moved on.

Yancey was not there. The stark red-painted wooden station sat blistering in the sun. Yancey simply was not there. Not only that, the station platform, usually graced by a score of vacuous faces and limp figures gathered to witness the exciting event of the Katy's daily arrival and departure, was bare. Even the familiar figure of Pat Leary, the station agent, who always ran out in his shirt sleeves to wrestle such freight or express as was left on the Osage platform, could not be seen. From within the ticket office came the sound of his telegraph instrument. Its click was busy; was frantic. It chattered unceasingly in the hot afternoon stillness.

Sabra felt sick and weak. Something was wrong. She left her boxes and bags and parcels on the platform where Len Orson had obligingly dumped them. Half an hour before their arrival in Osage she had entrusted the children to the

care of a fellow passenger while she had gone to the wash-
room to put on one of the new dresses made in Wichita
and bearing the style cachet of Kansas City: green, with
cream colored ruchings at the throat and wrists, and a leg-
horn hat with pink roses. She had anticipated the look in
Yancey's gray eyes at sight of it. She had made the children
spotless and threatened them with dire things if they sullied
their splendor before their father should see them.

And now he was not there.

With Donna in her arms and Cim at her heels she hurried toward the sound of the clicking. And as she went her
eyes still scanned the dusty red road that led to the station,
for sight of a great figure in a white sombrero, its coat
tails swooping as it came.

She peered in at the station window. Pat Leary was bent
over his telegraph key. A smart tight little Irishman who had
come to the Territory with the railroad section crew when
the Katy was being built. Station agent now, and studying
law at night.

"Mr. Leary! Mr. Leary! Have you seen Yancey?" He looked
up at her absently, his hand still on the key. Click . . .
click . . . clickclickclickety—clicketyclickclick.

"Wha' say?"

"I'm Mrs. Cravat. I just got off the Katy. Where's my
husband? Where's Yancey?"

He clicked on a moment longer; then wiped his wet
forehead with his forearm protected by the black sateen
sleevelet. "Ain't you heard?"

"No," whispered Sabra, with stiff lips that seemed no part
of her. Then, in a voice rising to a scream, "No! No! No!
What? Is he dead?"

The Irishman came over to her then, as she crouched
at the window. "Oh, no, ma'am. Yancey's all right. He ain't
hurt to speak of. Just a nick in the arm—and left arm at
that."

"Oh, my God!"

"Don't take on. You goin' to faint or——?"

"No. Tell me."

"I been so busy. . . . Yancey got the Kid, you know.
Killed him. The whole town's gone crazy. Pitched battle
right there on Pawhuska Avenue in front of the bank, and
bodies layin' around like a battlefield. I'm sending it out.
I ain't got much time, but I'll give you an idea. Biggest
thing that's happened in the history of the Territory—or the
whole Southwest, for that matter. Shouldn't wonder if they'd

134

make Yancey President. Governor, anyway. Seems Yancey was out hunting up in the Hills last Thursday——"

"Thursday! But that's the day the paper comes out."

"Well, the *Wigwam* ain't been so regular since you been away." She allowed that to pass without comment. "Up in the Hills he stumbles on Doc Valliant, drunk, but not so drunk he don't recognize Yancey. Funny thing about Doc Valliant. He can be drunker'n a fool, but one part of his brain stays clear as a diamond. I seen him take a bullet out of Luke Slaughter once and sew him up when he was so drunk he didn't know his right hand from his left, or where he was at, but he done it. What? Oh, yeh—well, he tells Yancey, drunk as he is, that he's right in the camp where the Kid and his gang is hiding out. One of them was hurt bad in that last Santa Fé hold-up at Cimarron. Like to died, only they sent for Doc, and he come and saved him. They got close to thirty thousand that trick, and it kind of went to their head. Valliant overheard them planning to ride in here to Osage, like to-day, and hold up the Citizens' National in broad daylight like the Kid always does. They was already started. Well, Yancey off on his horse to warn the town, and knows he's got to detour or he'll come on the gang and they'll smell a rat. Well, say, he actually did meet 'em. Came on 'em, accidental. The Kid sees him and grins that wolf grin of his and sings out, 'Yancey, you still runnin' that paper of yourn down at Osage?' Yancey says, 'Yes.' 'Well, say,' he says, 'how much is it?' Yancey says a dollar a year. The Kid reaches down and throws Yancey a shot sack with ten silver dollars in it. 'Send me the paper for ten years,' he says. 'Where to?' Yancey asks him. Well, say, the Kid laughs that wolf laugh of his again and he says, 'I never thought of that. I'll have to leave you know later.' Well, Yancey, looking as meek and mealy-mouthed as a baby, he rides his way, he's got a little book of poems in his hand and he's reading as he rides, or pretending to, but first chance he sees he cuts across the Hills, puts his horse through the gullies and into the draws and across the scrub oaks like he was a circus horse or a centipede or something. He gets into Osage, dead tired and his horse in a lather, ten minutes before the Kid and his gang sweeps down Pawhuska Avenue, their six-shooters barking like a regiment was coming, and makes a rush for the bank. But the town is expecting them. Say! Blood!"

Sabra waited for no more. She turned. And as she turned she saw coming down the road in a cloud of dust a grotesque scarecrow, all shanks and teeth and rolling eyes. Black Isaiah.

"No'm, Miss Sabra, he ain't hurt—not what yo' rightly call hurt. No, ma'am. Jes'a nip in de arm, and he got it slung in a black silk hank'chief and looks right sma't hand-some. They wouldn't let him alone noways. Ev'ybody in town they shakin' his hand caze he shoot the shot dat kill de Kid. An' you know what he do then, Miss Sabra? He kneel down an' he cry like a baby. . . . Le' me tote dis yere valise. Ah kin tote Miss Donna, too. My, she sho' growed!"

The newspaper office, the print shop, her parlor, her kitchen, her bedroom, were packed with men in boots, spurs, sombreros; men in overalls; with women; with children. Mrs. Wyatt was there—the Philomatheans as one wom-an were there; Dixie Lee, actually; everyone but—sinisterly —Louie Hefner.

"Well, Mis' Cravat, I guess you must be pretty proud of him! . . . This is a big day for Osage. I guess Oklahoma City knows this town's on the map now, all right. . . . You missed the shootin', Mis' Cravat, but you're in time to help Yancey celebrate. . . . Say, the Santa Fé alone offered five thousand dollars for the capture of the Kid, dead or alive. Yancey gets it, all right. And the Katy done the same. And they's a government price on his head, and the Citizens' National is making up a purse. You'll be ridin' in your own carriage, settin' in silks, from now."

Yancey was standing at his desk in the *Wigwam* office. His back was against the desk, as though he were holding this crowd at bay instead of welcoming them as congratula-tory guests. His long locks hung limp on his shoulders. His face was white beneath the tan, like silver under lacquer. His great head lolled on his chest. His left arm lay in a black and scarlet silk sling made of one of his more piratical handkerchiefs.

He looked up as she came in, and at the look in his face she forgave him his neglect of her; forgave him the house full of what Felice Venable would term riffraff and worse; his faithlessness to the *Wigwam*. Donna, tired and frightened, had set up a wail. Cim, bewildered, had gone on a rampage. But as Yancey took a stumbling step toward her she had only one child, and that one needed her. She thrust Donna again into Isaiah's arms; left Cim whirling among the throng; ran toward him. She was in his great arms, but it was her arms that seemed to sustain him.

"Sabra. Sugar. Send them away. I'm so tired. Oh, God, I'm so tired."

Next day they exhibited the body of the Kid in the new plate glass show window of Hefner's Furniture Store and Undertaking Parlors. All Osage came to view him, all the county came to view him; they rode in on trains, on horses, in wagons, in ox carts for miles and miles around. The Kid. The boy who, in his early twenties, had sent no one knew how many men to their death—whose name was the symbol for terror and daring and merciless marauding throughout the Southwest. Even in the East—in New York—the name of the Kid was known. Stories had been written about him. He was, long before his death, a mythical figure. And now he, together with Clay McNulty, his lieutenant, lay side by side, quite still, quite passive. The crowd was so dense that it threatened Louie Hefner's window. He had to put up rope barriers to protect it, and when the mob surged through these he stationed guards with six-shooters, and there was talk of calling out the militia from Fort Tipton. Sabra said it was disgusting, uncivilized. She forbade Cim to go within five hundred yards of the place—kept him, in fact, virtually a prisoner in the yard. Isaiah she could not hold. His lean black body could be seen squirming in and out of the crowds; his ebony face, its eyes popping, was always in the front row of the throng gloating before Hefner's window. He became, in fact, a sort of guide and unofficial lecturer, holding forth upon the Kid, his life, his desperate record, the battle in which he met his death in front of the bank he had meant to despoil.

"Well, you got to hand it to him," the men said, gazing their fill. "He wasn't no piker. When he held up a train or robbed a bank or shot up a posse it was always in broad daylight, by God. Middle of the day he'd come riding into town. No nitro-glycerin for him, or shootin' behind fence posts and trees in the dark. Nosiree! Out in the open, and takin' a bigger chance than them that was robbed. Ride! Say, you couldn't tell which was him and which was horse. They was one piece. And shoot! It wa'n't shootin'. It was magic. They say he's got half a million in gold cached away up in the Hills."

For weeks, for months, the hills were honeycombed with prowlers in search of this buried treasure.

Sabra did a strange, a terrible thing. Yancey would not go near the grisly window. Sabra upheld him; denounced the gaping crowd as scavengers and ghouls. Then, suddenly, at the last minute, as the sun was setting blood red across the prairie, she walked out of the house, down the road, as if impelled, as if in a trance, like a sleep walker, and stood before Hefner's window. The crowd made way for her respectfully. They knew her. This was the wife of Yancey Cravat, the man whose name appeared in headlines in every newspaper throughout the United States, and even beyond the ocean.

They had dressed the two bandits in new cheap black suits of store clothes, square in cut, clumsy, so that they stood woodenly away from the lean hard bodies. Clay McNulty's face had a faintly surprised look. His long sandy mustaches drooped over a mouth singularly sweet and resigned. But the face of the boy was fixed in a smile that brought the lips in a sardonic snarl away from the wolf-like teeth. He looked older in death than he had in life, for his years had been too few for lines such as death's fingers usually erase; and the eyes, whose lightning glance had pierced you through and through like one of the bullets from his own dreaded six-shooters, now were extinguished forever behind the waxen shades of his eyelids.

It was at the boy that Sabra looked; and having looked she turned and walked back to the house.

They gave them a decent funeral and a burial with everything in proper order, and when the minister refused to read the service over these two sinners Yancey consented to do it and did, standing there with the fresh-turned mounds of red Oklahoma clay sullying his fine high-heeled boots, and the sun blazing down upon the curling locks of his uncovered head.

" 'Whoso sheddeth man's blood, by man shall his blood be shed. . . . His hand will be against every man, and every man's hand against him. . . . The words of his mouth were smoother than butter, but war was in his heart. . . . Fools make mock at sin. . . .' "

They put up two rough wooden slabs, marking the graves. But souvenir hunters with little bright knives soon made short work of those. The two mounds sank lower, lower. Soon nothing marked this spot on the prairie to differentiate it from the red clay that stretched for miles all about it.

They sent to Yancy, by mail, in checks, and through solemn committees in store clothes and white collars, the substantial money rewards that, for almost five years, had been offered by the Santa Fé road, the M.K. & T., the government itself, and various banks, for the capture of the Kid, dead or alive.

Yancey refused every penny of it. The committees, the townspeople, the county, were shocked and even offended. Sabra, tight lipped, at last broke out in protest.

"We could have a decent house—a new printing press—Cim's education—Donna——"

"I don't take money for killing a man," Yancey repeated, to each offer of money. The committees and the checks went back as they had come.

Fourteen

SABRA noticed that Yancey's hand shook with a perceptible palsy before breakfast, and that this was more than ever noticeable as that hand approached the first drink of whisky which he always swallowed before he ate a morsel. He tossed it down as one who, seeking relief from pain, takes medicine. When he returned the glass to the table he drew a deep breath. His hand was, miraculously, quite steady.

More and more he neglected the news and business details of the *Wigwam*. He was restless, moody, distrait. Sabra remembered with a pang of dismay something that he had said on first coming to Osage. "God, when I think of those years in Wichita! Almost five years in one place—that's the longest stretch I've ever done."

The newspaper was prospering, for Sabra gave more and more time to it. But Yancey seemed to have lost interest, as he did in any venture once it got under way. It was now a matter of getting advertisements, taking personal and local items, recording the events in legal, real estate, commercial, and social circles. Mr. and Mrs. Abel Dagley spent Sunday in Chuckmubbee. The Rev. McAlestar Couch is riding the Doakville circuit.

Even in the courtroom or while addressing a meeting of townspeople Yancey sometimes would behave strangely. He would stop in the midst of a florid period. At once a creature savage and overcivilized, the flaring lamps, the hot, breathless atmosphere, the vacuous white faces looming up at him like balloons would repel him. He had been known to stalk out, leaving them staring. In the courtroom he was an alarming figure. When he was defending a local county or Territorial case they flocked from miles around to hear

139

him, and the crude pine shack that was the courtroom would be packed to suffocation. He towered over any jury of frontiersmen—a behemoth in a Prince Albert coat and fine linen, his great shaggy buffalo's head charging menacingly at his opponent. His was the florid hifalutin oratory of the day, full of sentiment, hyperbole, and wind. But he could be trenchant enough when needs be; and his charm, his magnetic power, were undeniable, and almost invariably he emerged from the courtroom victorious. He was not above employing tricks to win his case. On one occasion, when his client was being tried for an affair of gunplay which had ended disastrously, the jury, in spite of all that Yancey could do, turned out to be one which would be, he was certain, heavily for conviction. He deliberately worked himself up into an appearance of Brobdingnagian rage. He thundered, he roared, he stamped, he wept, he acted out the events leading up to the killing and then, while the jury's eyes rolled and the weaker among them wiped the sweat from their brows, he suddenly whipped his two well known and deadly ivory-handled and silver six-shooters from their holsters in his belt. "And this, gentlemen, is what my client did." He pointed them. But at that, with a concerted yelp of pure terror the jury rose as one man and leaped for the windows, the doors, and fled.

Yancey looked around, all surprise and injured innocence. The jury had disbanded. According to the law, a new jury had to be impaneled. The case was retried. Yancey won it.

Sabra saw more and more to the editing and to the actual printing of the *Oklahoma Wigwam*. She got in as general houseworker and helper an Osage Indian girl of fifteen who had been to the Indian school and who had learned some of the rudiments of household duties: cleaning, dishwashing, laundering, even some of the simpler forms of cookery. She tended Donna, as well. Her name was Arita Red Feather, a quiet gentle girl who went about the house in her calico dress and moccasins and had to be told everything over again, daily. Isaiah was beginning to be too big for these duties. He was something of a problem in the household. At the suggestion that he be sent back to Wichita he set up a howling and wailing and would not be consoled until both Sabra and Yancey assured him that he might remain with them forever. So he now helped Arita Red Feather with the heavier housework; did odd jobs about the printing shop; ran errands; saw that Donna kept from under horses' hoofs; he could even beat up a pan of good light biscuits in a pinch. When Jesse Rickey was too drunk to stand at the type case and Yancey was off on some legal matter, he slowly and painstakingly helped Sabra to make possible the weekly issue of the *Oklahoma Wigwam*. Arita Red Feather's dialect became a bewildering thing in which her native Osage, Sabra's refined diction, and Isaiah's Southern Negro accent were rolled into an almost unintelligible jargon. "I'm gwine wash um clothes big rain water extremely nice um make um clothes white fo' true."

"That's fine!" Sabra would say. Then, an hour later, "Oh, Arita, don't you remember I've told you a hundred times you put the bluing in *after* they're rubbed, not before?"

Arita's dead black Indian eyes, utterly devoid of expression, would stare back at her.

Names of families of mixed Indian and white blood appeared from time to time in the columns of the *Wigwam*, for Sabra knew by now that there were in the Territory French-Indian families who looked upon themselves as aristocrats. This was the old French St. Louis, Missouri, background cropping up in the newly opened land. The early French who had come to St. Louis, there to trade furs and hides with the Osages, had taken Indian girls as squaws. You saw, sprinkled among the commonplace nomenclature of the frontier, such proud old names as Bellieu, Revard, Revelette, Tayrien, Perrier, Chouteau; and their owners had the unmistakable coloring and the bearing of the Indian. These dark-skinned people bore, often enough, and ridiculously enough, Irish names as well, for the Irish laborers who had come out with pickax and shovel and crowbar to build the Territory railroads had wooed and married the girls of the Indian tribes. You saw little Indian Kellys and Flahertys and Riordans and Caseys.

All this was bewildering to Sabra. But she did a man's job with the paper, often against frightening odds, for Yancey was frequently absent now, and she had no one but the wavering Jesse Rickey to consult. There were times when he, too, failed her. Still the weekly appeared regularly, somehow.

Grandma Rosey, living eleven miles northwest of town, is very ill with the la grippe. Mrs. Rosey is quite aged and fears are entertained for her recovery.

Preaching next Sunday morning and evening at the Presbyterian church by Rev. J. H. Canby. Come and hear the new bell.

Mrs. Wicksley is visiting with the Judge this week.

A movement is on foot to fill up the sink holes on Pawhuska Avenue. The street in its present state is a disgrace to the community.

C. H. Snack and family expect to leave next week for an extended visit with Mrs. Snack's relatives in southeastern Kansas. Mr. Snack disposed of his personal property at public sale last Monday. Our loss is Kansas's gain.

(A sinister paragraph this. You saw C. H. Snack, the failure, the defeated, led back to Kansas there to live the life of the nagged and unsuccessful husband tolerated by his wife's kin.)

Sabra, in a pinch, even tried her unaccustomed hand at an occasional editorial, though Yancey seldom failed her utterly in this department. A rival newspaper set up quarters across the street and, for two or three months, kept up a feeble pretense of existence. Yancey's editorials, during this period, were extremely personal.

The so-called publishers of the organ across the street have again been looking through glasses that reflect their own images. A tree is known by its fruit. The course pursued by the *Dispatch* does not substantiate its claim that it is a Republican paper.

The men readers liked this sort of thing. It was Yancey who brought in such items as:

Charles Flasher, wanted for murder, forgery, selling liquor without a license and breaking jail at Skiatook, was captured in Oklahoma City as he was trying to board a train in the Choctaw yards.

But it was Sabra who held the women readers with her accounts of the veal loaf, cole slaw, baked beans, and angel-food cake served at the church supper, and the somewhat touching decorations and costumes worn at the wedding of a local or county belle.

If, in the quarter of a century that followed, every

trace of the settling of the Oklahoma country had been lost, excepting only the numbers of the *Oklahoma Wigwam*, there still would have been left a clear and inclusive record of the lives, morals, political and social and economic workings of this bizarre community. Week by week, month by month, the reader could have noticed in its columns whatever of progress was being made in this fantastic slice of the Republic of the United States.

It was the day of the practical joke, and Yancey was always neglecting his newspaper and his law practice to concoct, with a choice group of conspirators, some elaborate and gaudy scheme for the comic downfall of a fellow citizen or a newcomer to the region. These jokes often took weeks for their successful consummation. Frequently they were founded on the newcomer's misapprehension concerning the Indians. If this was the Indian Territory, he argued, not unreasonably, it was full of Indians. He had statistics. There were 200,000 Indians in the Territory. Indians meant tomahawks, scalping, burnings, raidings, and worse. When the local citizens assured him that all this was part of the dead past the tenderfoot quoted, sagely, that there was no good Indian but a dead Indian. Many of the jokes, then, hinged on the mythical bad Indian. The newcomer was told that there was a threatened uprising; the Cheyennes had been sold calico—bolts and bolts of it—with the stripes running the wrong way. This, it was explained, was a mistake most calculated to madden them. The jokesters armed themselves to the teeth. Six-shooters were put in the clammy, trembling hand of the tenderfoot. He was told that the nights were freezing cold. He was led to a near-by field that was man-high with sunflowers and cautioned not to fire unless he heard the yells of the maddened savages. There, shaking and sweating in overcoat, overshoes, mufflers, ear muffs, and leggings, he cowered for hours while all about him (at a safe distance) he heard the horrid, blood-curdling yells of the supposed Indians. His scalp, when finally he was rescued, usually was found to be almost lifted of its own accord.

Next day, Yancey would spend hours writing a humorous account of this Indian uprising for the Thursday issue of the *Wigwam*. The drinks were on the newcomer. That ceremony also took hours.

O jest unseen, inscrutable, invisible,
As a nose on a man's face, or a weathercock on a steeple.

Thus Yancey's article would begin with a quotation from his favorite poet.

"Oh, Yancey darling, sometimes I think you're younger than Cim."

"What would you like me to be, honey? A venerable Venable? 'A man whose blood is very snow-broth; one who never feels the wanton stings and motions of the sense'?"

Sabra, except for Yancey's growing restlessness, was content enough. The children were well; the paper was prospering; she had her friends; the house had taken on an aspect of comfort; they had added another bedroom; Arita Red Feather and Isaiah together relieved her of the rougher work of the household. She was, in a way, a leader in the crude social life of the community. Church suppers; sewing societies; family picnics.

One thing rankled deep. Yancey had been urged to accept the office of Territorial delegate to Congress (without vote) and had refused. All sorts of Territorial political positions were held out to him. The city of Guthrie, Capital of the Territory, wooed him in vain. He laughed at political position, rejected all offers of public nature. Now he was being offered the position of Governor of the Territory. His oratory, his dramatic quality, his record in many affairs, including the Pegler murder and the shooting of the Kid, had spread his fame even beyond the Southwest.

"Oh, Yancey!" Sabra thought of the Venables, the Marcys, the Vians, the Goforths. At last her choice of a mate was to be vindicated. Governor!

But Yancey shook his great head. There was no moving him. He would go on the stump to make others Congressmen and Governors, but he himself would not take office. "Palavering to a lot of greasy office seekers and panhandlers! Dancing to the tune of that gang in Washington! I know the whole dirty lot of them."

Restless. Moody. Irritable. Riding out into the prairies to be gone for days. Coming back to regale Cim with stories of evenings spent on this or that far-off Reservation, smoking and talking with Chief Big Horse of the Cherokees, with Chief Buffalo Hide of the Chickasaws, with old Black Kettle of the Osages.

But he was not always like this. There were times when his old fiery spirit took possession. He entered the fight for the statehood of Oklahoma Territory, and here he encountered opposition enough even for him. He was for the consolidation of the Oklahoma Territory and the Indian Territory under single statehood. The thousands who were opposed to the Indians—who looked upon them as savages totally unfit for citizenship—fought him. A year after their coming to Oklahoma the land had been divided into two territories—one owned and occupied by the Indian Tribes, the other owned by the whites. Here the Cravats lived, on the border line. And here was Yancey, fighting week after week, in the editorial and news columns of the *Oklahoma Wigwam*, for the rights of the Indians; for the consolidation of the two halves as one state. Yet, unreasonably enough, he sympathized with the Five Civilized Tribes in their efforts to retain their tribal laws in place of the United States Court laws which were being forced upon them. He made a thousand bitter enemies. Many of the Indians themselves were opposed to him. These were for separate statehood for the Indian Territory, the state to be known as Sequoyah, after the great Cherokee leader of that name.

Sabra, who at first had paid little enough heed to these political problems, discovered that she must know something of them as protection against those times (increasingly frequent) when Yancey was absent and she must get out the paper with only the uncertain aid of Jesse Rickey.

She dared not, during these absences of Yancey, oppose outright his political and Territorial stand. But she edged as near the line as she could, for her hatred of the Indians was still deep and (she insisted) unconquerable. She even published—slyly—the speeches and arguments of the Double Statehood party leaders, stating simply that these were the beliefs of the opposition. They sounded very reasonable and convincing as the *Wigwam* readers perused them.

Sabra came home one afternoon from a successful and stirring meeting of the Twentieth Century Philomathean Culture Club (the two had now formed a pleasing whole) at which she had read a paper entitled, Whither Oklahoma? It had been received with much applause on the part of Osage's twenty most exclusive ladies, who had heard scarcely a word of it, their minds being intent on Sabra's new dress. She had worn it for the first time at the club meeting, and it was a bombshell far exceeding any tumult that her paper might create.

Her wealthy Cousin Bella French Vian, visiting the World's Fair in Chicago, had sent it from Marshall Field's store. It consisted of a blue serge skirt, cut wide and flaring at the hem but snug at the hips; a waist-length blue serge Eton jacket trimmed with black soutache braid; and a garment called a shirtwaist to be worn beneath the jacket. But astounding—revolutionary—as all this was, it was not the thing that caused the eyes of feminine Osage to bulge with envy and despair. The sleeves! The sleeves riveted the attention of those present, to the utter neglect of Whither Oklahoma? The balloon sleeve now appeared for the first time in the Oklahoma Territory, sponsored by Mrs. Yancey Cravat. They were bouffant, enormous; a yard of material at least had gone into each of them. Every woman present was, in her mind, tearing to rag strips, bit by bit, every gown in her own scanty wardrobe.

Sabra returned home, flushed, elated. She entered by way of the newspaper office, seeking Yancey's approval. Curtseying and dimpling she stood before him. She wanted him to see the new costume before she must thriftily take it off for the preparation of supper. Yancey's comment, as she pirouetted for his approval, infuriated her.

"Good God! Sleeves! Let the squaws see those and they'll be throwing away their papoose boards and using the new fashion for carrying their babies, one in each sleeve."

"They're the very latest thing in Chicago. Cousin Bella French Vian wrote that they'll be even fuller than this, by autumn."

"By autumn," echoed Yancey. He held in his hand a slip of paper. Later she knew that it was a telegram—one of the few telegraphic messages which the *Wigwam's* somewhat sketchy service received. He was again completely oblivious of the new costume, the balloon sleeves. "Listen, sugar. President Cleveland's just issued a proclamation setting September sixteenth for the opening of the Cherokee Strip."

"Cherokee Strip?"

"Six million, three hundred thousand acres of Oklahoma land to be opened for white settlement. The government has bought it from the Cherokees. It was all to be theirs—all Oklahoma. Now they're pushing them farther and farther out."

"Good thing," snapped Sabra, still cross about the matter of Yancey's indifference to her costume. Indians. Who cared! She raised her arms to unpin her hat.

Yancey rose from his desk. He turned his rare full gaze on her, his handsome eyes aglow. "Honey, let's get out of this. Clubs, sleeves, church suppers—God! Let's get our hundred and sixty acre allotment of Cherokee Strip land and start a ranch—raise cattle—live in the open—ride—this town life is no good—it's hideous."

146

Her arms fell, leaden, to her side. "Ranch? Where?"

"You're not listening. There's to be a new Run. The Cherokee Strip Opening. You know. You wrote news stories about it only last week, before the opening date had been announced. Let's go, Sabra. It's the biggest thing yet. The 1889 Run was nothing compared to it. Sell the *Wigwam*, take the children, make the Run, get our hundred and sixty, start a ranch, stock up with cattle and horses, build a ranch house and patio; in the saddle all day——"

"Never!" screamed Sabra. Her face was distorted. Her hands were clutching the air, as though she would tear to bits this plan of his for the future. "I won't. I won't go. I'd rather die first. You can't make me."

He came to her, tried to take her in his arms, to pacify her. "Sugar, you won't understand. It's the chance of a lifetime. It's the biggest thing in the history of Oklahoma. When the Territory's a state we'll own forever one hundred and sixty acres of the finest land anywhere. I know the section I want."

"Yes. You know. You know. You knew the last time, too. You let that slut—that hussy—take it away from you —or you gave it to her. Go and take her with you. You'll never make me go. I'll stay here with my children and run the paper. Mother! Cim! Donna!"

She had a rare and violent fit of hysterics, after which Yancey, aided clumsily by Arita Red Feather, divested her of the new finery, quieted the now screaming children, and finally restored to a semblance of supper-time order the household into which he had hurled such a bomb. Felice Venable herself, in her heyday, could not have given a finer exhibition of Marcy temperament. It was intended, as are all hysterics (no one ever has hysterics in private), to intimidate the beholder and fill him with remorse. Yancey was properly solicitous, tender, charming as only he could be. From the shelter of her husband's arms Sabra looked about the cosy room, smiled wanly upon her children, bade Arita Red Feather bring on the belated supper. "That," thought Sabra to herself, bathing her eyes, smoothing her hair, and coming pale and wistful to the table, her lip quivering with a final effective sigh, "settles that."

But it did not. September actually saw Yancey making ready to go. Nothing that Sabra could say, nothing that she could do, served to stop him. She even negotiated for a little strip of farm land outside the town of Osage and managed to get Yancey to make a payment on it, in the hope that this would keep him from the Run. "If it's land you want you can stay here and farm the piece at Tuskamingo. You can raise cattle on it. You can breed horses on it."

Yancey shook his head. He took no interest in the farm. It was Sabra who saw to the erection of a crude little farmhouse, arranged for the planting of such crops as it was thought that land would yield. It was very near the Osage Reservation land and turned out, surprisingly enough, doubtless owing to some mineral or geological reason (they knew why, later), to be fertile, though the Osage land so near by was barren and flinty.

"Farm! That's no farm. It's a garden patch. D'you think I'm settling down to be a potato digger and chicken feeder, in a hayseed hat and manure on my boots!"

September, the month of the opening of the vast Cherokee Strip, saw him well on his way. Cim howled to be taken along, and would not be consoled for days.

Sabra's farewell was intended to be cold. Her heart, she told herself, was breaking. The change that these last four years had made in her never was more apparent than now.

"You felt the same way when I went off to the first Run," Yancey reminded her. "Remember? You carried on just one degree less than your mother. And if I hadn't gone you'd still be living in the house in Wichita, with your family smothering you in Southern fried chicken and advice." There was much truth in this, she had to admit. She melted; clung to him.

"Yancey! Yancey!"

"Smile, sugar. Wait till you see Cim and Donna, five years from now, riding the Cravat acres."

After all, a hundred other men in Osage were going to make the Cherokee Strip Run. The town—the whole Territory—had talked of nothing else for months.

She dried her eyes. She even managed a watery smile. He was making the Run on a brilliant, wild-eyed mare named Cimarron, with a strain of Spanish in her for speed and grace, and a strain of American mustang for endurance. He had decided to make the trip from Osage to the Cherokee Outlet on horseback by easy stages so as to keep the animal in condition, though the Santa Fé and the Rock Island roads were to run trains into the Strip. He made a dashing, a magnificent figure as he sat the strong, graceful animal that now was pawing and pirouetting to be off. Though a score of others were starting with him, it was Yancey that the town turned out to see. He rode in his white sombrero, his fine white shirt, his suit with the Prince Albert coat, his glittering high-heeled Texas star boots with the gold-plated spurs. The start was made shortly after sunrise so as to make progress before the heat of the day. But a cavalcade awoke them before dawn with a rat-a-tat-tat of six-shooters and a blood-curdling series of cowboy yips. The escort rode with Yancey and the others for a distance out on the Plains. Sabra, at the last minute, had the family horse hitched to the buggy, bundled Cim and Donna in with her, and—Isaiah hanging on behind, somehow—the prim little vehicle bumped and reeled its way over the prairie road in the wake of the departing adventurers.

At the last Sabra threw the reins to Isaiah, sprang from the buggy, ran to Yancey as he pulled up his horse. He bent far over in his saddle, picked her up in one great arm, held her close while he kissed her long and hard.

"Sabra, come with me. Let's get clear away from this."

"You've gone crazy! The children!"

"The children, too. All of us. Come on. Now." His eyes were blazing. She saw that he actually meant it. A sudden premonition shook her.

"Where are you going? Where are you going?"

He set her down gently and was off, turned halfway in his saddle to face her, his white sombrero held aloft in his hand, his curling black locks tossing in the Oklahoma breeze.

Five years passed before she saw him again.

Fifteen

DIXIE LEE'S girls were riding by on their daily afternoon parade. Sabra recognized their laughter and the easy measured clatter of their horses' hoofs before they came into view. She knew it was Dixie Lee's girls. Somehow, the virtuous women of Osage did not laugh much though Sabra did not put this thought into words, even in her mind. She glanced up now as they drove by. She was seated at her desk by the window in the front office of the *Oklahoma Wigwam*. Their plumes, their parasols, their brilliant-hued dresses made a gay garden of color in the monotony of Pawhuska Avenue. They rode in open phaëtons, but without the usual top, so that they had only their parasols to shade their brightly painted faces from the ardent Southwest sun. The color of the parasols and plumes and dresses was changed from day to day, but they always were done in ensemble effect. One day the eyes of Osage's male population were dazzled (and its female population's eyes affronted) by a burst of rosy splendor shading from pale pink to scarlet. The next day they would shade from palest lavender to deepest purple. The next, from delicate lemon to orange; the day following they ran the gamut of green. They came four by four, and usually one in each carriage handled the reins, though occasionally a Negro driver occupied the front seat alone. They were not boisterous. Indeed, they conducted themselves in seemly enough fashion except perhaps for the little bursts of laughter and for the fact that they were generous with the ankles beneath the ruffled skirts. Often they carried dolls in their arms. Sometimes—rarely—they called to each other. Their voices were high and curiously unformed, like the voices of little children, and yet with a metallic note in them.

"Madge, looka! When we get to the end of Pawhuska we'll race you to Coley's Gulch and back." These afternoon races became almost daily sporting events, and the young bloods of Osage got into the habit of stationing themselves along the road to bet on the pale pink plumes or the deep rose plumes.

"Heh, go it, Clemmie! Whip him up, Carmen. Give him the whip! Come on! Whoop-ee! Yi!" Plumes whirling, parasols bobbing, skirts flying, shrill shouts and screams of laughter from the edge of town. But on the return drive their behavior was again seemly enough, their cheeks flushed with a natural color beneath the obvious red.

Sabra's face darkened now as she saw them driving slowly by. Dixie Lee never drove with them. Sabra knew where she was this afternoon. She was down in the back room of the Osage First National Bank talking business to the President, Murch Rankin. The business men of the town were negotiating for the bringing of the packing house and a plough works and a watch factory to Osage. Any one of these industries required a substantial bonus. The spirit of the day was the boom spirit. Boom the town of Osage. Dixie Lee was essentially a commercial woman—shrewd, clear headed. She had made a great success of her business. It was one of the crude town's industries, and now she, as well as the banker, the hardware man, the proprietor of the furniture store, the meat market, the clothing store, contributed her share toward coaxing new industries to favor Osage. That way lay prosperity.

Dixie Lee was a personage in the town. Visitors came to her house now from the cities and counties round about. She had built for herself and her thriving business the first brick structure in the wooden town; a square, solid, and imposing two-story house, its bricks formed from the native Oklahoma red clay. Cal Bixby had followed close on it with the Bixby Block on Pawhuska Avenue, but Dixie Lee had led the way. She had commissioned Louie Hefner to buy her red velvet and gold furniture and her long gilt-framed mirrors, her scarlet deep-pile carpet—that famous velvet-pile carpet in which Shanghai Wiley, that bearded, cultured, and magnetic barbarian, said he sank so deep that for a terrified moment he fell into a panic, being unable to tell which was red carpet and which his own flowing red beard. Dixie herself had gone East for her statues and pictures. The new house had been opened with a celebration the like of which had never been seen in the Southwest. Sabra Cravat, mentioning no names, had had an editorial about it in which the phrases "insult to the fair womanhood of America" and "orgy rivaling the Bacchanalian revels of history" (Yancey's library stood her in good stead these days) figured prominently. Both the Philomathean Society and the Twentieth Century Culture Club had, for the duration of one meeting at least, deserted literature and culture for the discussion of the more vital topic of Dixie Lee's new mansion.

It was—this red brick brothel—less sinister than these good and innocent women suspected. Dixie Lee, now a woman of thirty or more, ruled it with an iron hand. Within it obtained certain laws and rules of conduct so rigid as to be almost prim. In a crude, wild, and nearly lawless country the brick mansion occupied a strange place, filled a want foreign to its original purpose. It was, in a way, a club, a rendezvous, a salon. For hundreds of men who came there it was all they had ever known of richness, of color, of luxury. The red and gold, the plush and silk, the perfume, the draperies, the white arms, the gleaming shoulders sank deep into their hard-bitten senses, long starved from years on wind-swept ranches, plains dust bedeviled, prairies baked barren by the fierce Southwest sun. Here they lolled, sunk deep in rosy comfort, while they talked Territory politics, swapped yarns of the old cattle days, played cards, drank wines which tasted like sweet prickling water to their whisky-scarred palates. They kissed these women, embraced them fiercely, thought tenderly of many of them, and frequently married them; and these women, once married, settled down contentedly to an almost slavish domesticity.

A hard woman, Dixie Lee; a bad woman. Sabra was morally right in her attitude toward her. Yet this woman, as well as Sabra, filled her place in the early life of the Territory.

Now, as the laughter sounded nearer and the equipages came within her view, Sabra, seated at her desk in the newspaper office, put down the soft pencil with which she had been filling sheet after sheet of copy paper. She wrote easily now, with no pretense to style, but concisely and with an excellent sense of news values. The *Oklahoma Wigwam* had flourished in these last five years of her proprietorship. She was thinking seriously of making it a daily instead of a weekly; of using the entire building on Pawhuska Avenue for the newspaper plant and building a proper house for herself and the two children on one of the residence streets newly sprung up—streets that boasted neatly painted houses and elm and cottonwood trees in the front yards.

Someone came up the steps of the little porch and into the office. It was Mrs. Wyatt. She often brought club notices and social items to the *Wigwam:* rather fancied herself as a writer; a born woman's club corresponding secretary.

"Well!" she exclaimed now, simply, but managing to put enormous bite and significance into the monosyllable. Her glance followed Sabra's. Together the two women, tight lipped, condemnatory, watched the gay parade of Dixie Lee's girls go by.

The flashing company disappeared. A whiff of patchouli floated back to the two women standing by the open window. Their nostrils lifted in disdain. The sound of the horses' hoofs grew fainter.

"It's a disgrace to the community"—Mrs. Wyatt's voice took on its platform note—"and an insult to every wife and mother in the Territory. There ought to be a law."

Sabra turned away from the window. Her eyes sought the orderly rows of books, bound neatly in tan and red—Yancey's law books, so long unused now, except, perhaps, for occasional newspaper reference. Her face set itself in lines of resolve. "Perhaps there is."

It had taken almost three of those five years to bring those lines into Sabra Cravat's face. They were not, after all, lines. Her face was smooth, her skin still fresh in spite of dust and alkali water and sun and wind. It was, rather, that a certain hardening process had taken place—a crystallization. Yancey had told her, tenderly, that she was a charming little fool, and she had believed it—though perhaps with subconscious reservations. It was not until he left her, and the years rolled round without him, that she developed her powers. The sombrero had ridden gayly away. The head under the sun-bonnet had held itself high in spite of hints, innuendoes, gossip.

A man like Yancey Cravat—spectacular, dramatic, impulsive—has a thousand critics, scores of bitter enemies. As the weeks had gone by and Yancey failed to return—had failed to write—rumor, clouded by scandal, leaped like prairie fire from house to house in Osage, from town to town in the Oklahoma Country, over the Southwest, indeed. All the old stories were revived, and their ugly red tongues licked a sordid path through the newly opened land.

They say he is living with the Cherokee squaw who is really his wife.

They say he was seen making the Run in the Kickapoo Land Opening in 1895.

They say he killed a man in the Cherokee Strip Run and was caught by a posse and hung.

They say he got a section of land, sold it at a high figure, and was seen lording it around the bar of the Brown Palace Hotel in Denver, in his white sombrero and his Prince Albert coat.

They say Dixie Lee is his real wife, and he left her when she was seventeen, came to Wichita, and married Sabra Venable; and he is the one who has set Dixie up in the brick house.

They say he drank five quarts of whisky one night and died and is buried in an unmarked grave in Horse-shoe Ranch, where the Doolin gang held forth.

They say he is really the leader of the Doolin gang.

They say. They say. They say.

It is impossible to know how Sabra survived those first terrible weeks that lengthened into months that lengthened into years. There was in her the wiry endurance of the French Marcys; the pride of the Southern Venables. Curiously enough, in spite of all that had happened to her she still had that virginal look—that chastity of lip, that clearness of the eye, that purity of brow. Men come back to the women who look as Sabra Cravat looked, but the tempests of men's love pass them by.

153

She told herself that he was dead. She told the world that he was dead. She knew, by some deep and unerring instinct, that he was alive. Donna had been so young when he left that he now was all but wiped from her memory. But Cim, strangely enough, spoke of Yancey Cravat as though he were in the next room. "My father says . . ." Sometimes, when Sabra saw the boy coming toward her with that familiar swinging stride, his head held down and a little thrust forward, she was wrenched by a physical pang of agony that was almost nausea.

She ran the paper competently; wrung from it a decent livelihood for herself and the two children. When it had no longer been possible to keep secret from her parents the fact of Yancey's prolonged absence, Felice Venable had descended upon her prepared to gather to the family bosom her deserted child and to bring her, together with her offspring, back to the parental home. Lewis Venable had been too frail and ill to accompany his wife, so Felice had brought with her the more imposing among the Venables, Goforths, and Vians who chanced to be visiting the Wichita house at the time of her departure. Osage had looked upon these stately figures with much awe, but Sabra's reception of them had been as coolly cordial as her rejection of their plans for her future was firm.

"I intend to stay right here in Osage," she announced, quietly, but in a tone that even Felice Venable recognized as inflexible, "and run the paper, and bring up my children as their father would have expected them to be brought up."

"Their father!" Felice Venable repeated, in withering accents.

The boy Cimarron, curiously sensitive to sounds and moods, stood before his grandmother, his head thrust forward, his handsome eyes glowing. "My father is the most famous man in Oklahoma. The Indians call him Buffalo Head."

Felice Venable pounced on this. "If that's what you mean by bringing them up as their father . . ."

The meeting degenerated into one of those family bickerings. "I do wish, Mamma, that you wouldn't repeat everything I say and twist it by your tone into something poisonous."

"*I* say! I can't help it if the things you say sound ridiculous when they are repeated. I simply mean——"

"I don't care what you mean. I mean to stay here in

Osage until Yancey—until——" She never finished that sentence.

The Osage society notes became less simple. From bare accounts of quiltings, sewing bees, and church sociables they blossomed into flowery imitations of the metropolitan dailies' descriptions of social events. Refreshments were termed elegant. Osage matrons turned from the sturdy baked beans, cole slaw, and veal loaf of an earlier day to express themselves in food terms culled from the pictures in the household magazines. They heard about fruit salads. They built angel-food cakes whose basis was the whites of thirteen eggs, and their husbands, at breakfast, said, "What makes these scrambled eggs so yellow?" Countrified costumes were described in terms of fashion. The wilted prairie flowers that graced weddings and parties were transformed into rare hothouse blooms by the magic touch of the *Oklahoma Wigwam* hand press. Sabra cannily published all the brilliant social news items that somewhat belatedly came her way via the ready-print and the paper's scant outside news service.

Newport. Oct. 4—One of the most brilliant weddings which Newport has seen for many years was solemnized in old Trinity Church to-day. The principals were Miss Georgina Harwood and Mr. Harold Blake, both members of families within the charmed circle of the 400. The bride wore a gown of ivory satin with draperies and rufflings of rarest point lace, the lace veil being caught with a tiara of pearls and diamonds. After the ceremony a magnificent collation . . .

The feminine population of Osage—of the county—felt that it had seen the ivory satin, the point lace, the tiara of pearls and diamonds, as these splendors moved down the aisle of old Trinity on the person of Miss Georgina Harwood of Newport. They derived from it the vicarious satisfaction that a dieting dyspeptic gets from reading the cook book.

Sabra was, without being fully aware of it, a power that shaped the social aspect of this crude Southwestern town. The Ladies of the new Happy Hour Club, on her declining to become a member, pleading lack of time and press of work (as well she might) made her an honorary member, resolved to have her influential name on their club roster, somehow. They were paying unconscious tribute to Oklahoma's first feminist. She still ran the paper single handed, with the aid of Jesse Rickey, the most expert printer in the Southwest (when sober), and as good as the average when drunk.

Sabra, serene in the knowledge that the attacked could do little to wreak vengeance on a woman, printed stories and statements which for boldness and downright effrontery would have earned a male editor a horse-whipping. She publicly scolded the street loafers who, in useless sombreros and six-shooters and boots and spurs, relics of a bygone day, lolled limply on Pawhuska Avenue corners, spitting tobacco juice into the gutter. Sometimes she borrowed Yancey's vigorous and picturesque phraseology. She denounced a local politician as being too crooked to sleep in a round-house, and the phrase stuck, and in the end defeated him. Law, order, the sanctity of the home, prunes, prisms. Though the Gyp Hills and the Osage Hills still were as venomous with outlaws as the Plains were with rattlesnakes; though the six-shooter still was as ordinary a part of the Oklahoma male costume as boots or trousers; though outlawry still meant stealing a horse rather than killing a man; though the Territory itself had been settled and peopled, in thousands of cases, by men who had come to it, not in a spirit of adventure, but from cowardice, rapacity, or worse. Sabra Cravat and the other basically conventional women of the community were working unconsciously, yet with a quiet ferocity, toward that day when one of them would be able to say, standing in a doorway with a stiff little smile:

"Awfully nice of you to come."

"Awfully nice of you to ask me," the other would reply.

When that day came, Osage would no longer need to feel itself looked down upon by Kansas City, Denver, Chicago, St. Louis, and San Francisco.

Slowly, slowly, certain figures began to take on the proportions of personalities. No one had arisen in the Territory to fill Yancey Cravat's romantic boots. Pat Leary was coming on as a Territory lawyer, with an office in the Bixby Block and the railroads on which he had worked as section hand now consulting him on points of Territorial law. In his early railroad days he had married an Osage girl named Crook Nose. People shook their heads over this and said that he regretted it now, and that a lawyer could never hope to get on with this marital millstone round his neck.

There still was very little actual money in the Territory. People traded this for that. Sabra often translated subscriptions to the *Oklahoma Wigwam*—and even advertising space —into terms of fresh vegetables, berries, wild turkey, quail, prairie chickens, dress lengths and shoes and stockings for the children.

Sol Levy's store, grown to respectable proportions now, provided Sabra with countless necessities in return for the advertisement which, sent through the country via the *Oklahoma Wigwam*, urged its readers to Trade at Sol Levy's. Visit the Only Zoo in the Territory. This invitation, a trifle bewildering to the uninitiated, was meant to be taken literally. In the back of his store Sol Levy kept a sizable menagerie. It had started through one of those chance encounters. A gaunt and bearded plainsman had come into the store one day with the suggestion that the proprietor trade a pair of pants for a bear cub. The idea had amused Sol Levy; then he had glanced out into the glare of Pawhuska Avenue and had seen the man's ocherous wife, his litter of spindling children, huddled together in a crazy wagon attached by what appeared to be ropes, strings, and bits of nail and wire, to horses so cadaverous that his amusement was changed to pity. He gave the man the pants, stockings for the children, and—the sentimentalist in him—a piece of bright-colored cotton stuff for the woman.

The bear cub, little larger than a puppy, had been led gingerly into the welter of packing cases, straw, excelsior, and broken china which was the Levy Mercantile Company's back yard, and there tied with a piece of rope which he immediately bit in two. Five minutes later a local housewife, deep in the purchase of a dress length of gingham, and feeling something rubbing against her stout calves, looked down to see the bear cub sociably gnawing his way through her basket of provisions, carelessly placed on the floor by her side.

One week later the grateful ranger brought in a pair of catamounts. A crude wire cage was built. There were added coyotes, prairie dogs, an eagle. The zoo became famous, and all the town came to see it. It brought trade to the Mercantile Company, and free advertising. It was the nucleus for the zoo which, fifteen years later, Sol Levy shyly presented to the Osage City Park, and which contained every wild thing that the Southwest had known, from the buffalo to the rattlesnake.

In a quiet, dreamy way Sol Levy had managed to buy a surprising amount of Osage real estate by now. He owned the lot on which his store stood, the one just south of it, and, among other pieces, the building and lot which comprised the site of the *Wigwam* and the Cravat house. In the year following Yancey's departure Sabra's economic survival was made possible only through the almost shamefaced generosity of this quiet, sad-eyed man.

"I've got it all down in my books," Sabra would say, proudly. "You know that it will all be paid back some day."

He began in the *Oklahoma Wigwam* a campaign of advertising out of all proportions to his needs, and Sabra's debt to him began to shrink to the vanishing point. She got into the habit of talking to him about her business problems, and he advised her shrewdly. When she was utterly discouraged he would say, not triumphantly, but as one who states an irrefutable and not particularly happy fact:

"Some day, Mrs. Cravat, you and I will look back on this and we will laugh—but not very loud."

"How do you mean—laugh?"

The little curious cast came into his eyes. "Oh—I will be very rich, and you will be very famous. And Yancey——"

"Yancey!" The word was wrenched from her like a cry.

"They will tell stories about Yancey until he will grow into a legend. He will be part of the history of the Southwest. They will remember him and write about him when all these mealy-faced governors are dead and gone and forgotten. They will tell the little children about him, and they will dispute about him—he did this, he did that; he was like this, he was like that. You will see."

Sabra thought of her own children, who knew so little of their father. Donna, a thin secretive child of almost seven now, with dark, straight black hair and a sallow skin like Yancey's; Cim, almost thirteen, moody, charming, imaginative. Donna was more like her grandmother Felice Venable than her own mother; Cim resembled Yancey so strongly in mood, manner, and emotions as to have almost no trace of Sabra. She wondered, with a pang, if she had failed to impress herself on them because of her absorption in the town, in the newspaper, in the resolve to succeed. She got out a photograph of Yancey that she had hidden away because to see it was to feel a stab of pain, and had it framed, and hung it on the wall where the children could see it daily. He was shown in the familiar costume—the Prince Albert, the white sombrero, the six-shooters, the boots, the spurs, the long black locks curling beneath the hat brim, the hypnotic eyes startling you with their arresting gaze, so that it was as if he were examining you rather than that you were seeing his likeness in a photograph. One slim foot, in its high-heeled boot, was slightly advanced, the coat tails flared, the whole picture was somehow endowed with a sense of life and motion.

"Your father——" Sabra would begin, courageously, resolved to make him live again in the minds of the children. Donna was not especially interested. Cim said, "I know it," and capped her story with a tale of his own in which Yancey's feat of derring-do outrivaled any swashbuckling escapade of D'Artagnan.

"Oh, but Cim, that's not true! You mustn't believe stories like that about your father."

"It is true. Isaiah told me. I guess he ought to know." And then the question she dreaded. "When are Isaiah and Father coming back?"

She could answer, somehow, evasively, about Yancey, for her instinct concerning him was sure and strong. But at the fate that had overtaken the Negro boy she cowered, afraid even to face the thought of it. For the thing that had happened to the black boy was so dreadful, so remorseless that when the truth of it came to Sabra she felt all this little world of propriety, of middle-class Middle West convention that she had built up about her turning to ashes under the sudden flaring fire of hidden savagery. She tried never to think of it, but sometimes, at night, the hideous thing took possession of her, and she was swept by such horror that she crouched there under the bedclothes, clammy and shivering with the sweat of utter fear. Her hatred of the Indians now amounted to an obsession.

It was in the fourth year of Yancey's absence that, coming suddenly and silently into the kitchen from the newspaper office, where she had been busy as usual, she saw Arita Red Feather twisted in a contortion in front of the table where she had been at work. Her face was grotesque, was wet, with agony. It was the agony which only one kind of pain can bring to a woman's face. The Indian girl was in the pangs of childbirth. Even as she saw her Sabra realized that something about her had vaguely disturbed her in the past few weeks. Yet she had not known, had not dreamed of this. The loose garment which the girl always wore—her strong natural slenderness—the erect dignity of her Indian carriage—the stoicism of her race—had served to keep secret her condition. She had had, too, Sabra now realized in a flash, a way of being out of the room when her mistress was in it; busy in the pantry when Sabra was in the kitchen; busy in the kitchen when Sabra was in the dining room; in and out like a dark, swift shadow.

"Arita! Here. Come. Lie down. I'll send for your father —your mother." Her father was Big Knee, well known and something of a power in the Osage tribe. Of the tribal officers he was one of the eight members of the Council and as such was part of the tribe's governing body.

Dreadful as the look on Arita Red Feather's face had been, it was now contorted almost beyond recognition. "No! No!" She broke into a storm of pleading in her own tongue. Her eyes were black pools of agony. Sabra had never thought that one of pure Indian blood would thus give way to any emotion before a white person.

She put the girl to bed. She sent Isaiah for Dr. Valliant, who luckily was in town and sober. He went to work quietly, efficiently, aided by Sabra, making the best of such crude and hasty necessities as came to hand. The girl made no outcry. Her eyes were a dull, dead black; her face was rigid. Sabra, passing from the kitchen to the girl's bedroom with hot water, cloths, blankets, saw Isaiah crouched in a corner by the wood box. He looked up at her mutely. His face was a curious ash gray. As Sabra looked at him she knew.

The child was a boy. His hair was coarse and kinky. His nose was wide. His lips were thick. He was a Negro child. Doc Valliant looked at him as Sabra held the writhing red-purple bundle in her arms.

"This is a bad business."

"I'll send for her parents. I'll speak to Isaiah. They can marry."

"Marry! Don't you know?"

Something in his voice startled her. "What?"

"The Osages don't marry Negroes. It's forbidden."

"Why, lots of them have. You see Negroes who are Indians every day. On the street."

"Not Osages. Seminoles, yes. And Creeks, and Choctaws, and even Chickasaws. But the Osages, except for intermarriage with whites, have kept the tribe pure."

This information seemed to Sabra to be unimportant and slightly silly. Purity of the tribe, indeed! Osages! She resolved to be matter of fact and sensible now that the shocking event was at hand, waiting to be dealt with. She herself felt guilty, for this thing had happened in her own house. She should have foreseen danger and avoided it. Isaiah had been a faithful black child in her mind, whereas he was, in reality, a man grown.

Dr. Valliant had finished his work. The girl lay on the bed, her dull black eyes fixed on them; silent, watchful, hopeless. Isaiah crouched in the kitchen. The child lay now in Sabra's arms. Donna and Cim were, fortunately, asleep, for it was now long past midnight. The tense excitement past, the whole affair seemed to Sabra sordid, dreadful. What would the town say? What would the members of the Philomathean Club and the Twentieth Century Culture Club think?

Doc Valliant came over to her and looked down at the queer shriveled morsel in her arms. "We must let his father see him."

Sabra shrank. "Oh, no!"

He took the baby from her and turned toward the kitchen. "I'll do it. Let me have a drink of whisky, will you, Sabra? I'm dead tired."

She went past him into the dining room, without a glance at the Negro boy cowering in the kitchen. Doc Valliant followed her. As she poured a drink of Yancey's store of whisky, almost untouched since he had left, she heard Valliant's voice, very gentle, and then the sound of Isaiah's blubbering. All the primness in her was outraged. Her firm mouth took on a still straighter line. Valliant took the child back to the Indian girl's bed and placed it by her side. He stumbled with weariness as he entered the dining room where Sabra stood at the table. As he reached for the drink Sabra saw that his hand shook a little as Yancey's used to do in that same gesture. She must not think of that. She must not think of that.

"There's no use talking now, Doctor, about what the Osages do or don't do that you say is so pure. The baby's born. I shall send for the old man—what's his name?— Big Knee. As soon as Arita can be moved he must take her home. As for Isaiah, I've a notion to send him back to Kansas, as I wanted to do years ago, only he begged so to stay, and Yancey let him. And now this."

Doc Valliant had swallowed the whisky at a gulp—had thrown it down his throat as one takes medicine to relieve pain. He poured another glass. His face was tired and drawn. It was late. His nerves were not what they had been, what with drink, overwork, and countless nights without sleep as he rode the country on his black horse, his handsome figure grown a little soft and sagging now. But he still was a dashing sight when he sat the saddle in his black corduroys and his soft-brimmed black hat.

He swallowed his second drink. His face seemed less drawn, his hand steadier, his whole bearing more alert. "Now listen, Sabra. You don't understand. You don't understand the Osages. This is serious."

Sabra interrupted quickly. "Don't think I'm hard. I'm not condemning her altogether, or Isaiah, either. I'm partly to blame. I should have seen. But I am so busy. Anyway, I can't have her here now, can I? With Isaiah. Even you . . ."

He filled his glass. She wished he would stop drinking; go home. She would sit up the night with the Indian girl. And in the morning—well, she must get someone in to help. They would know, sooner or later.

He was repeating rather listlessly what he had said. "The Osages have kept the tribe absolutely free of Negro blood. This is a bad business."

Her patience was at an end. "What of it? And how do you know? How do you know?"

"Because they remove any member of the tribe that has had to do with a Negro."

"Remove!"

"Kill. By torture."

She stared at him. He was drunk, of course. "You're talking nonsense," she said crisply. She was very angry.

"Don't let this get around. They might blame you. The Osages. They might——I'll just go and take another look at her."

The girl was sleeping. Sabra felt a pang of pity as she gazed down at her. "Go to bed—off with you," said Doc Valliant to Isaiah. The boy's face was wet, pulpy with tears and sweat and fright. He walked slackly, as though exhausted.

"Wait." Sabra cut him some bread from the loaf, sliced a piece of meat left from supper. "Here. Eat this. Everything will be all right in the morning."

The news got round. Perhaps Doc Valliant talked in drink. Doubtless the girl who came in to help her. Perhaps Isaiah, who after a night's exhausted sleep had suddenly become proudly paternal and boasted loudly about the house (and no doubt out of it) of the size, beauty, and intelligence of the little lump of dusky flesh that lay beside Arita Red Feather's bed in the very cradle that had held Donna when an infant. Arita Red Feather was frantic to get up. They had to keep her in bed by main force. She had not spoken a dozen words since the birth of the child.

On the fourth day following the child's birth Sabra came

into Arita Red Feather's room early in the morning and she was not there. The infant was not there. Their beds had been slept in and now were empty. She ran straight into the yard where Isaiah's little hut stood. He was not there. She questioned the girl who now helped with the housework and who slept on a couch in the dining room. She had heard nothing, seen nothing. The three had vanished in the night.

Well, Sabra thought, philosophically, they have gone off. Isaiah can make out, somehow. Perhaps he can even get a job as a printer somewhere. He was handy, quick, bright. He had some money, for she had given him, in these later years, a little weekly wage, and he had earned a quarter here, a half dollar there. Enough, perhaps, to take them by train back to Kansas. Certainly they had not gone to Arita's people, for Big Knee, questioned, denied all knowledge of his daughter, of her child, of the black boy. He behaved like an Indian in a Cooper novel. He grunted, looked blank, folded his arms, stared with dead black, expressionless eyes. They could make nothing of him. His squaw, stout, silent, only shook her head; pretended that she neither spoke nor understood English.

Then the rumor rose, spread, received credence. It was started by Pete Pitchlyn, the old Indian guide and plainsman who sometimes lived with the Indians for months at a time on their reservations, who went with them on their visiting jaunts, hunted, fished, ate with them, who was married to a Cherokee, and who had even been adopted into the Cherokee tribe. He had got the story from a Cherokee who in turn had had it from an Osage. The Osage, having managed to lay hands on some whisky, and becoming very drunk, now told the grisly tale for the first time.

There had been an Osage meeting of the Principal Chief, old Howling Wolf; the Assistant Chief; the eight members of the Council, which included Big Knee, Arita's father. There the news of the girl's dereliction had been discussed, her punishment gravely decided upon, and that of Isaiah.

They had come in the night and got them—the black boy, the Indian girl, the infant—by what means no one knew. Arita Red Feather and her child had been bound together, placed in an untanned and uncured steer hide, the hide was securely fastened, they were carried then to the open, sun-baked, and deserted prairie and left there, with a guard. The hide shrank and shrank and shrank in the burning sun, closer and closer, day by day, until soon there was no movement within it.

Isaiah, already half dead with fright, was at noonday securely bound and fastened to a stake. Near by, but not near enough quite to touch him, was a rattlesnake so caught by a leather thong that, strike and coil and strike as it might, it could not quite reach, with its venomous head, the writhing, gibbering thing that lay staring with eyes that protruded out of all semblance to human features. But as dusk came on the dew fell, and the leather thong stretched a little with the wet. And as twilight deepened and the dew grew heavier the leather thong holding the horrible reptile stretched more and more. Presently it was long enough.

Sixteen

"REMEMBER the *Maine!* To hell with Spain!" You read this inflaming sentiment on posters and banners and on little white buttons pinned to coat lapels or dress fronts. There were other buttons and pennants bearing the likeness of an elderly gentleman with a mild face disguised behind a martial white mustache; and thousands of male children born within the United States in 1898 grew up under the slight handicap of the christened name of Dewey. The *Oklahoma Wigwam* bristled with new words: Manila Bay—Hobson—Philippines. Throughout the Southwest sombreros suddenly became dust-colored army hats with broad, flat brims and peaked crowns. People who, if they had thought of Spain at all, saw it in the romantic terms of the early Southwest explorers—Coronado, De Soto, Moscosco—and, with admiration for these intrepid and mistaken seekers after gold, now were told that they must hate Spain and the Spanish and kill as many little brown men living in the place called the Philippines as possible. This was done as dutifully as could be, but with less than complete enthusiasm.

Rough Riders! That was another matter. Here was something that the Oklahoma country knew and understood— tall, lean, hard young men who had practically been born with a horse under them and a gun in hand; riders, hunters, dead shots; sunburned, keen eyed, daredevil. Their uniforms, worn with a swagger, had about them a dashing something that the other regiments lacked. Their hat crowns were dented, not peaked, and the brims were turned romantically up at one side and caught with the insignia of the Regiment—the crossed sabers. And their lieutenant-colonel and leader was that energetic, toothy young fellow who was making something of a stir in New York State—Roosevelt, his name was. Theodore Roosevelt.

Osage was shaken by chills and fever; the hot spasms of patriotism, the cold rigors of virtue. One day the good wives of the community would have a meeting at which they arranged for a home-cooked supper, with coffee, to be served to this or that regiment. Their features would soften with sentiment, their bosoms heave with patriotic pride. Next day, eyes narrowed, lips forming a straight line, they met to condemn Dixie Lee and her ilk, and to discuss ways and means for ridding the town of their contaminating presence.

The existence of this woman in the town had always been a festering sore to Sabra. Dixie Lee, the saloons that still lined Pawhuska Avenue, the gambling houses, all the paraphernalia of vice, were anathema lumped together in the minds of the redoubtable sunbonnets. A new political group had sprung up, ostensibly on the platform of civic virtue. In reality they were tired of seeing all the plums dropping into the laps of the early-day crew, made up of such strong-arm politicians as had been the first to shake the Territorial tree. In the righteous ladies of the Wyatt type they saw their chance for a strong ally. The saloons and the gamblers were too firmly intrenched to be moved by the reform element: they had tried it. Sabra had been urged to help. In the columns of the *Oklahoma Wigwam* she had unwisely essayed to conduct a campaign against Wick Mongold's saloon, in whose particularly lawless back room it was known that the young boys of the community were in the habit of meeting. With Cim's future in mind (and as an excuse) she wrote a stirring editorial in which she said bold things about shielding criminals and protecting the Flower of our Southwest's Manhood. Two days later a passer-by at seven in the morning saw brisk flames licking the foundations of the *Oklahoma Wigwam* office and the Cravat dwelling behind it. The whole had been nicely soaked in coal oil. But for the chance passer-by, Sabra, Cim, Donna, newspaper plant, and house would have been charred beyond recognition. As the town fire protection was still of the scantiest, the alarmed neighbors beat out the fire with blankets wet in the near-by horse trough. It was learned that a Mexican had been hired to do the job for twenty dollars. Mongold skipped out.

After an interval reform turned its attention to that always vulnerable objective known then as the Scarlet Woman. Here it met with less opposition. Almost five years after Yancey's departure it looked very much as though Dixie Lee and her fine brick house and her plumed and parasoled girls would soon be routed by the spiritual broomsticks and sunbonnets of the purity squad.

It was characteristic that at this moment in Osage's history, when the town was torn, now by martial music, now by the call of civic virtue, Yancey Cravat should have chosen to come riding home; and not that alone, but to come riding home in full panoply of war, more dashing, more romantic, more mysterious than on the day he had ridden away.

It was eight o'clock in the morning. The case of Dixie Lee (on the charge of disorderly conduct) was due to come up at ten in the local court. Sabra had been at her desk in the *Wigwam* office since seven. One ear was cocked for the sounds that came from the house; the other was intent on Jesse Rickey's erratic comings and goings in the printing shop just next the office.

"Cim! Cim Cravat! Will you stop teasing Donna and eat your breakfast. Miss Swisher's report said you were late three times last month, and all because you dawdle while you dress, you dawdle over breakfast, you dawdle—— Jesse! Oh, Jesse! The Dixie Lee case will be our news lead. Hold two columns open. . . ."

Horse's hoofs at a gallop, stopping spectacularly in front of the *Wigwam* office in a whirl of dust. A quick, light step. That step! But it couldn't be. Sabra sprang to her feet, one hand at her breast, one hand on the desk, to steady herself. He strode into the office. For five years she had pictured him returning to her in dramatic fashion; in his white sombrero, his Prince Albert, his high-heeled boots. For five years she had known what she would say, how she would look at him, in what manner she would conduct herself toward him—toward this man who had deserted her without a word, cruelly. In an instant, at sight of him, all this left her mind, her consciousness. She was in his arms with an inarticulate cry, she was weeping, her arms were about him, the buttons of his uniform crushed her breasts. His uniform. She realized then, without surprise, that he was in the uniform of the Oklahoma Rough Riders.

It is no use saying to a man who has been gone for five years, "Where have you been?" Besides, there was not time. Next morning he was on his way to the Philippines. It was not until he had gone that she realized her failure actually to put this question that had been haunting her for half a decade.

Cim and Donna took him for granted, as children do. So did Jesse Rickey, with his mind of a child. For that matter, Yancey took his own return for granted. His manner was nonchalant, his spirits high, his exuberance infectious. He set the pitch. There was about him nothing of the delinquent husband.

He now strode magnificently into the room where the children were at breakfast, snatched them up, kissed them. You would have thought he had been gone a week.

Donna was shy of him. "Your daughter's a Venable, Mrs. Cravat," he said, and turned to the boy. Cim, slender, graceful, taller than he seemed because of that trick of lowering his fine head and gazing at you from beneath his too-long lashes, reached almost to Yancey's broad shoulders. But he had not Yancey's heroic bulk, his vitality. The Cravat skull structure was contradicted by the narrow Venable face. The mouth was oversensitive, the hands and feet too exquisite, the smile almost girlish in its wistful sweetness. " 'Gods! How the son degenerates from the sire!' "

"Yancey!" cried Sabra in shocked protest. It was as though the five years had never been.

"Do you want to see my dog?" Cim asked.

"Have you got a pony?"

"Oh, no."

"I'll buy you one this afternoon. A pinto. Here. Look."

He took from his pocket a little soft leathern pouch soiled and worn from much handling. It was laced through at the top with a bit of stout string. He loosed this, poured the bag's contents onto the breakfast table; a little heap of shining yellow. The three stood looking at it. Cim touched it with one finger.

"What is it?"

Yancey scooped up a handful of it and let it trickle through his fingers. "That's gold." He turned to Sabra. "It's all I've got to show, honey, for two years and more in Alaska."

"Alaska!" she could only repeat, feebly. So that was it.

"I'm famished. What's this? Bacon and eggs?" He reached for a slice of bread from the plate on the table, buttered it lavishly, clapped a strip of coldish bacon on top of that, and devoured it in eager bites. Sabra saw then, for the first time, that he was thinner; there were hollow shadows in the pock-marked cheeks; there was a scarcely perceptible sag to the massive shoulders. There was something about his hand. The forefinger of the right hand was gone. She felt suddenly faint, ill. She reeled a little and stumbled, As always, he sprang toward her. His lips were against her hair.

"Oh, God! How I've missed you, Sabra, sugar!"

"Yancey! The children!" It was the prim exclamation of a woman who had forgotten the pleasant ways of dalliance. Those five years had served to accentuate her spinsterish qualities; had made her more and more powerful; less human; had slowed the machinery of her emotional equipment. A man in the house. A possessive male, enfolding her in his arms; touching her hair, her throat with urgent fingers. She was embarrassed almost. Besides, this man had neglected her, deserted her, had left his children to get on as best they could. She shrugged herself free. Anger leaped within her. He was a stranger.

"Don't touch me. You can't come home like this—after years—after years——"

"Ah, Penelope!"

She stared. "Who?"

" 'Strange lady, surely to thee above all womankind the Olympians have given a heart that cannot be softened. No other woman in the world would harden her heart to stand thus aloof from her husband, who after travail and sore had come to her . . . to his own country.' "

"You and your miserable Milton!"

He looked only slightly surprised and did not correct her.

One by one, and then in groups and then in crowds, the neighbors and townspeople began to come in—the Wyatts, Louie Hefner, Cass Peery, Mott Bixler, Ike Hawes, Grat Gotch, Doc Nisbett—the local politicians, the storekeepers, their wives. They came out of curiosity, though they felt proper resentment toward this strange—this baffling creature who had ridden carelessly away, leaving his wife and children to fend for themselves, and now had ridden as casually back again. They would have stayed away if they could, but his enchantment was too strong. Perhaps he represented, for them, the thing they fain would be or have. When Yancey, flouting responsibility and convention, rode away to be gone for mysterious years, a hundred men, bound by ties of work and wife and child, escaped in spirit with him; a hundred women, faithful wives and dutiful mothers, thought of Yancey as the elusive, the romantic, the desirable male.

Well, they would see how she had met it, and take their cue from her. A smart woman, Sabra Cravat. Throw him out, likely as not, and serve him right. But at sight of Yancey Cravat in his Rough Rider uniform of khaki, U.S.V. on the collar, the hat brim dashingly caught up on the left side with the insignia of crossed sabers, they were snared again in the mesh of his enchantment. The Rough Riders. Remember the *Maine*, to hell with Spain! There'll Be a Hot Time in the Old Town To-night. He became a figure symbolic of the war, of the Oklahoma country, of the Territory, of the Southwest—impetuous, romantic, adventuring.

"Hi, Yancey! Well, say, where you been, you old son of a stampedin' steer!"

"Howdy, Cimarron! Where at's your white hat?"

"You and this Roosevelt get goin' in this war, I guess the Spaniards'll wish Columbus never been born."

And Yancey, in return, "Hello, Clint! Howdy, Sam! Well, damn' if it isn't you, Grat! H'are you, Ike, you old hoss thief!"

The great figure towered even above these tall plainsmen; the fine eyes glowed; the mellifluous voice worked its magic. The renegade was a hero; the outcast had returned a conqueror.

Alaska. Oklahoma had not been so busy with its own growing pains that it had failed to hear of Alaska and the Gold Rush. "Alaska! Go on, you wasn't never in Alaska! Heard you'd turned Injun. Heard you was buried up in Boot Hill along of the Doolins."

He got out the little leather sack. While they gathered round him he poured out before their glistening eyes the shining yellow heap of that treasure with which the whole history of the Southwest was intertwined. Gold. The hills and the plains had been honeycombed for it; men had hungered and fought and parched for it; had died for it; had been killed for it; had sacrificed honor, home, happiness in the hope of finding it. And here was the precious yellow stuff from far-off Alaska trickling through Yancey Cravat's slim white fingers.

"Damn it all, Yancey, some folks has all the luck."

And so he stood, this Odysseus, and wove for them this new chapter in his saga. And they listened, and wondered, and believed and were stirred with envy and admiration and the longing for like adventure. He talked, he laughed, he gesticulated, he strode up and down, and they never missed the flirt of the Prince Albert coat tails, for there were brass buttons and patch pockets and gold embroidery and the glitter of crossed sabers to take their place.

"Luck! Call it luck, do you, Mott, to be frozen, starved, lost, snow-blinded! One whole winter shut up alone in a one-room cabin with the snow piled to the roof-top and no living soul to talk to for months. Luck to have your pardner that you trusted cheat you out of your claim and rob you of your gold in the bargain! All but this handful. I was going to see Sabra covered in gold like an Aztec princess."

The eyes of listening Osage swung to the prim blue serge figure of the cheated Aztec princess, encountered the level gaze, the unsmiling lips; swung back again hastily to the dashing, the martial figure of the lately despised wanderer.

A tale of another world; a story of a land so remote from the brilliant scarlet and orange of the burning South-west country that the very sound of the words he used in describing it fell with a strange cadence on the ears of the eager listeners. And as always when Yancey was telling the tale, he filled his hearers with a longing for the place he described; a longing that was like a nostalgia for something they had never known. Well, folks, winters at fifty below zero. Two hours of bitter winter sunshine, and then blackness. Long splendid summer days in May and June, with twenty hours of sunshine and four hours of twilight. Sabra, listening with the others, found this new vocabulary as strange, as terrifying, as the jargon of the Oklahoma country had been to her when first she had encountered it years ago.

Yukon. Chilkoot Pass. Skagway. Kuskokwim. Klondike. Moose. Caribou. Huskies. Sledges. Nome. Sitka. Blizzards. Snow blindness. Frozen fingers. Pemmican. Cold. Cold. Cold. Gold. Gold. Gold. To the fascinated figures crowded into the stuffy rooms of this little frame house squatting on the sun-baked Oklahoma prairie he brought, by the magic of his voice and his eloquence the relentless movement of the glaciers, the black menace of icy rivers, the waste plains of blinding, treacherous snow. Two years of this, he said; and looked ruefully down at the stump that had been his famous trigger finger.

They, too, looked. Two years. Two years, and he had been gone five. That left three unaccounted for, right enough. The old stories seeped up in their minds. Their eyes, grown accustomed to the uniform, were less dazzled now. They saw the indefinable break that had come to the magnificent figure—not a break, really, but a loosening, a lowering of the resistance such as comes to steel that has been too often in the flaming furnace. You looked at the massive shoulders —they did not droop. The rare glance still pierced you like a sword thrust. The buffalo head, lowered, menaced you; lifted, thrilled you. Yet something had vanished.

"Where'd you join up, Yancey?"

"San Antonio. Leonard Wood's down there—Colonel Wood now—and young Roosevelt, Lieutenant Colonel. He's been drilling the boys. Most of them born on a horse and weaned on a Winchester. We're better equipped than the regulars that have been at it for years. Young Roosevelt's to thank for that. They were all for issuing us winter clothing, by God, to wear through a summer campaign in the tropics—those nincompoops in Washington—and they'd have done it if it hadn't been for him."

Southwest Davis spoke up from the crowd. "That case, you'll be leaving right soon, won't you? Week or so."

"Week!" echoed Yancey, and looked at Sabra. "I go back to San Antonio to-morrow. The regiment leaves for Tampa next day."

He had not told her before. Yet she said nothing, gave no sign. She had outfaced them with her pride and her spirit for five years; she would give them no satisfaction now. Five years. One day. San Antonio—Tampa—Cuba—the Philippines—War. She gave no sign. Curiously, the picture that was passing in her mind was this: she saw herself, as though it were someone she had known in the dim, far past, standing in the cool, shady corridor of the Mission School in Wichita. She saw, through the open door, the oblong of Kansas sunshine and sky and garden; there swept over her again that wave of nostalgia she had felt for the scene she was leaving; she was shaken by terror of this strange Indian country to which she was going with her husband.

". . . but here in this land, Sabra, my girl, the women, they've been the real hewers of wood and drawers of water. You'll want to remember that."

Sabra remembered it now, well enough.

Slowly the crowd began to disperse. The men had their business; the women their housework. Wives linked their arms through those of husbands, and the gesture was one of perhaps not entirely unconscious cruelty, accompanied as it was by a darting glance at Sabra.

"Rough Rider uniform, sack of gold, golden voice, and melting eye," that glance seemed to say. "You're welcome to all the happiness you can get from those. Security, permanence, home, husband—I wouldn't change places with you."

"Come on, Yancey!" shouted Strap Buckner. "Over to the Sunny Southwest and have a drink. We got a terrible lot of drinking to do, ain't we, boys? Come on, you old longhorn. We got to drink to you because you're back and because you're going away."

"And to the war!" yelled Bixler.

"And the Rough Riders!"

"And Alaska!"

Their boots clattered across the board floor of the newspaper office. They swept the towering figure in its khaki uniform with them. He turned, waved his hat at her. "Back in a minute, honey." They were gone.

Sabra turned to the children, Cim and Donna, flushed, both, with the unwonted excitement; out of hand. Her face set itself with that look of quiet resolve. "Half the morning's gone. But I want you to go along to school, anyway. Now, none of that! It's no use your staying around here. The paper must be got out. Jesse'll be no good to me the rest of the day. It's easy to see that. I'll write a note to your teachers. . . . Run along now. I must go to court."

She actually had made up her mind that she would see the day through as she had started it. The Dixie Lee case, seething for weeks, was coming to a crisis this morning—this very minute. She would be late if she did not hasten. She would not let the work of months go for nothing because this man—this stranger had seen fit to stride into her life for a day.

She pinned on her hat, saw that her handbag contained pencil and paper, hurried into the back room that was printing shop, composing room, press room combined. She had been right about Jesse Rickey. That consistently irresponsible one was even now leaning a familiar elbow on the polished surface of the Sunny Southwest bar as he helped toast the returned wanderer or the departing hero or the war in the semi-tropics, or the snows of Alaska "—or God knows what!" concluded Sabra, in her mind.

Cliff Means, the ink-smeared printer's devil who, at fifteen, served as Jesse Rickey's sole assistant in the mechanical end of the *Wigwam* office, looked up from his case rack as Sabra entered.

"It's all right, Mis' Cravat. I got the head all set up like you said. 'Vice Gets Death Blow. Reign of Scarlet Woman Ends. Judge Issues Ban.' Even if Jesse don't—even if he ain't—why, you and me can set up the story this afternoon so we can start the press goin' for Thursday. We ain't been late with the paper yet, have we?"

172

"Out on time every Thursday for five years," Sabra said, almost defiantly.

Suddenly, sharp and clear, Yancey's voice calling her from the office porch, from the front office, from the print-shop doorway; urgent, perturbed. "Sabra! Sabra! Sabra!"

He strode into the back shop. She faced him. Instinctively she knew. "What's this about Dixie Lee?" His news-trained eye leaped to the form. He read the set-up head, upside down, expertly. "When's this case come up?"

"Now."

"Who's defending her?"

"Nobody in town would touch the case. They say she got a lawyer from Denver. He didn't show up. He knew better than to take her money."

"Prosecuting?"

"Pat Leary."

Without a word he turned. She caught him at the door, gripped his arm. "Where are you going?"

"Court."

"What for? What for?" But she knew. She actually interposed her body between him and the street door then, as though physically to prevent him from going. Her face was white. Her eyes stared enormous.

"You can't take the case of that woman."

"Why not?"

"Because you can't. Because I've been fighting her. Because the *Wigwam* has come out against all that she stands for."

"Why, Sabra, honey, where are you thinking of sending her?"

"Away. Away from Osage."

"But where?"

"I don't know. I don't care. Things have changed since you went away. Went away and left me."

"Nothing's changed. It's all the same. Dixie's been stoned in the market place for two thousand years and more. Driving her out is not going to do it. You've got to drive the devil out of——"

"Yancey Cravat, are you preaching to me? You who left your wife and children to starve, for all you cared! And now you come back and you take this creature's part against every respectable woman in Osage—against me!"

"I know it. I can't help it, Sabra."

"I'll tell you what I think," cried Sabra—the Sabra Cravat who had been evolved in the past five years. "I think you're

173

crazy! They've all said so. And now I know they are right."

"Maybe so."

"If you dare to think of disgracing me by defending her. And your children. I've fought her for months in the paper. A miserable creature like that! Your own wife—a laughing stock—for a—a——"

"The Territory's rotten. But, by God, every citizen's still got the legal right to fight for existence!" He put her gently aside.

She went mad. She became a wildcat. She tried to hold him. She beat herself against him. It was like an infuriated sparrow hurling itself upon a mastodon. "If you dare! Why did you come back? I hate you. What's she to you? I say you won't. I'd rather see you dead. I'd kill you first. That scum! That filth! That harlot!"

Her dignity was gone. He lifted her, scratching, kicking, clawing, set her gently down in the chair in front of her desk. The screen slammed. His quick, light step across the porch, down the stair. Crumpled, tearstained, wild as she was, and with her hat on one side she reached automatically for her pencil, a pad of copy paper, and wrote a new head. Vice Again Triumphs Over Justice. Then, with what composure she could summon, she sped down the dusty road to where the combination jail and courthouse—a crude wooden building—sat broiling in the sun.

Because of the notoriety of the defendant the inadequate little courtroom would have been crowded enough in any case. But the news of Yancey's abrupt departure from the Sunny Southwest Saloon—and the reason for it—had spread from house to house through the little town with the rapidity of a forest fire leaping from tree to tree. Mad Yancey Cravat's latest freak. Men left their offices, their stores; women their cooking, their cleaning. The courtroom, stifling, fly infested, baked by the morning sun, was packed beyond endurance. The crowd perched on the window sills, stood on boxes outside the windows, suffocated in the doorway, squatted on the floor. The jury so hastily assembled, Pat Leary in a solemn suit of black, Dixie Lee with her girls, even Judge Sipes himself seemed in momentary danger of being trampled by the milling mob. It was a travesty of a courtroom. The Judge nervously champing his cud of tobacco, the corners of his mouth stained brown; Pat Leary neat, tight, representing law and order in his glittering celluloid collar; Dixie Lee, with a sense of the dramatic, all in black, her white cheeks unrouged, her dark abundant hair in neat smooth bands under the prim brim of her toque. But her girls were in full panoply of plumes. It was rather exhilarating to see them in that assemblage of drab respectability.

The jury was a hard-faced lot for the most part. Plucked from the plains or the hills; halting of speech, slow of mind, quick on the trigger. Two or three in overalls; one or two in the unaccustomed discomfort of store clothes. The rest in the conventional boots, corduroys or jeans, and rough shirt. A slow, rhythmic motion of the jaw was evidence that a generous preliminary bite of plug served as a precaution to soothe the nerves and steady the judgment.

This legal farce had already begun before Yancey made his spectacular entrance.

Seventeen

"CASE of the Territory of Oklahoma versus Dixie Lee!" (So they had made it a Territorial case. . . .) "Counsel for the Territory of Oklahoma!" Pat Leary stood up. ". . . for the defense." No one. The close-packed courtroom was a nightmare of staring eyes and fishlike mouths greedily devouring Dixie Lee's white, ravaged face. Oddly enough, compared to these, she seemed pure, aloof, exquisite. "The defendant having failed to provide herself with counsel, it is my duty, according to the laws of the gover'ment of the United States and the Territory of Oklahoma to appoint counsel for the defendant." He shifted his quid, the while his cunning, red-rimmed eyes roved solemnly through the crowd seeking the shyster, Gwin Larkin. A stir in the close-packed crowd; a murmur. "I hereby appoint——" The murmur swelled. "Order in the court!"

"Your Honor!"

Towering above the crowd, forging his way through like some relentless force of nature, came the great buffalo head, the romantic Rough Rider hat with its turned-up brim caught by the crossed sabers; the massive khaki-clad figure. It was dramatic, it was melodramatic, it was ridiculous. It was superb. The fish faces turned their staring eyes and their gasping mouths away from the white-faced woman and upon him. Here was the kind of situation that the Southwest loved

175

and craved; here was action, here was blood-and-thunder, here was adventure. Here, in a word, was Cimarron.

He stood before the shoddy judge. He swept off his hat with a gesture that invested it with plumes. "If it please Your Honor, I represent the defendant, Dixie Lee."

No Territorial judge, denying Yancey Cravat, would have dared to face that crowd. He cast another glance round— a helpless, baffled one, this time—waved the approaching Gwin Larkin back with a feeble gesture, and prepared to proceed with the case according to the laws of the Territory. Certainly the look that he turned on Sabra Cravat as she entered a scant ten minutes later, white faced, resolute, and took her place as representative of the press, was one of such mingled bewilderment and reproach as would have embarrassed anyone less utterly preoccupied than the editor and publisher of the *Oklahoma Wigwam*.

Objection on the part of the slick Pat Leary. Overruled, perforce, by the Judge. A shout from the crowd. Order! Bang! Another shout. Law in a lawless community not yet ten years old; a community made up, for the most part, of people whose very presence there meant impatience of the old order, defiance of the conventions. Ten minutes earlier they had been all for the cocky little Leary, erstwhile station agent; eager to cast the first stone at the woman in the temple. Now, with the inexplicable fickleness of the mob, the electric current of sympathy flowed out from them to the woman to be tried, to the man who would defend her. Hot and swift and plenty of action—that was the way the Southwest liked its justice.

Pat Leary. Irish, ambitious, fiery. His temper, none too even at best, had been lost before he ever rose. The thought of Yancey ahead of him, the purity brigade behind him, spurred him to his frantic, his disorderly charge.

His years as section hand on the railroad had equipped him with a vocabulary well suited to scourge this woman in black who sat so quietly, so white faced, before him, for all the crowd to see. Adjective on adjective; vituperation; words which are considered obscenity outside the Bible and the courtroom.

". . . all the vicious influences, your Honor, with which our glorious Territory is infested, can be laid at this woman's leprous door. . . . A refuge for the evil, for the diseased, for the criminal . . . waxed fat and sleek in her foul trade, on the money that should have been spent to help build up, to ennoble this fair Southwest land of ours . . . scavenger

. . . vilest of humans . . . disgrace to the fair name of woman. . . ." Names, then, that writhed from his tongue like snakes.

A curious embarrassment seized the crowd. There were many in the packed room who had known the easy hospitality of Dixie's ménage; who had eaten at her board, who had been broken in Grat Gotch's gambling place and had borrowed money from Dixie to save themselves from rough frontier revenge. She had plied her trade and taken the town's money and given it out again with the other merchants of the town. The banker could testify to that; the mayor; this committee; that committee. Put Dixie Lee's name down for a thousand. Part of the order of that disorderly, haphazard town.

Names. Names. Names. The dull red of resentment deepened the natural red of their sunburned faces. The jurors shifted in their places. A low mutter, ominous, like a growl, sounded its distant thunder. Blunt. Sharp. Ruthless. Younger than Yancey, less experienced, he still should have known better. These men of the inadequate jury, these men in the courtroom crowd, had come of a frontier background, had lived in the frontier atmosphere. In their rough youth, and now, women were scarce, with the scarcity that the hard life predicated. And because they were scarce they were precious. No woman so plain, so hard, so undesirable that she did not take on, by the very fact of her sex, a value far beyond her deserts. The attitude of a whole nation had been touched by this sentimental fact which was, after all, largely geographic. For a full century the countries of Europe, bewildered by it, unable to account for it, had laughed at this adolescent reverence of the American man for the American woman.

Here was Pat Leary, jumping excitedly about, mouthing execrations, when he himself, working on the railroads ten years before, had married an Indian girl out of the scarcity of girls in the Oklahoma country. Out of the corner of his eye, as he harangued, he saw the great lolling figure of Yancey Cravat. The huge head was sunk on the breast; the eyelids were lowered. Beaten, Pat Leary thought. Defeated, and he knows it. Cravat, the wind bag, the wife deserter. He finished in a burst of oratory so ruthless, so brutal that he had the satisfaction of seeing the painful, unaccustomed red surge thickly over Dixie Lee's pale face from her brow down to where the ladylike white turnover of her high collar met the line of her throat.

177

The pompous little Irishman seated himself, chest out, head high, eye roving the crowd and the bench, lips open with self-satisfaction. A few more cases like this and maybe they'd see there was material for a Territory governor right here in Osage.

The crowd shifted, murmured, gabbled. Yancey still sat sunk in his chair as though lost in thought. The gabble rose, soared. "He's given it up," thought Sabra, exulting. "He sees how it is."

The eyes of the crowd so close packed in that suffocating little courtroom were concentrated on the inert figure lolling so limply in its chair. Perhaps they were going to be cheated of their show after all.

Slowly the big head lifted, the powerful shoulders straightened, he rose, he seemed to rise endlessly, he walked to Judge Sipes's crude desk with his light, graceful stride. The lids were still cast down over the lightning eyes. He stood a moment, that singularly sweet and winning smile wreathing his lips. He began to speak. The vibrant voice, after Leary's shouts, was so low pitched that the crowd held its breath in order to hear.

"Your Honor. Gentlemen of the Jury. I am the first to bow to achievement. Recognition where recognition is due—this, gentlemen, has ever been my way. May I, then, before I begin my poor plea in defense of this lady, my client, most respectfully call your attention to that which, in my humble opinion, has never before been achieved, much less duplicated, in the whole of the Southwest. Turn your eye to the figure which has so recently and so deservedly held your attention. Gaze once more upon him. Regard him well. You will not look upon his like again. For, gentlemen, in my opinion this gifted person, Mr. Patrick Leary, is the only man in the Oklahoma Territory—in the Indian Territory—in the whole of the brilliant and glorious Southwest—nay, I may even go so far as to say the only man in this magnificent country, the United States of America!—of whom it actually can be said that he is able to strut sitting down."

The puffed little figure in the chair collapsed, then bounded to its feet, red faced, gesticulating. "Your Honor! I object!"

But the rest was lost in the gigantic roar of the delighted crowd.

"Go it, Yancey!"

"That's the stuff, Cimarron!"

Here was what they had come for. Doggone, there was nobody like him, damn if they was!

Even to-day, though more than a quarter of a century has gone by, there still are people in Oklahoma who have kept a copy, typed neatly now from records made by hand, of the speech made that day by Yancey Cravat in defense of the town woman, Dixie Lee. Yancey Cravat's Plea for a Fallen Woman, it is called; and never was a speech more sentimental, windy, false, and utterly moving. The slang words hokum and bunk were not then in use, but even had they been they never would have been applied, by that appreciative crowd, at least, to the flowery and impassioned oratory of the Southwest Silver Tongue, Yancey Cravat.

Cheap, melodramatic, gorgeous, impassioned. A quart of whisky in him; an enthralled audience behind him; a white-faced woman with hopeless eyes to spur him on; the cry of his wronged and righteous wife still sounding in his ears—Booth himself, in his heyday, never gave a more brilliant, a more false performance.

"Your Honor! Gentlemen of the Jury! You have heard with what cruelty the prosecution has referred to the sins of this woman, as if her condition was of her own preference. A dreadful—a vicious—a revolting picture has been painted for you of her life and surroundings. Tell me—tell me—do you really think that she willingly embraced a life so repellent, so horrible? No, gentlemen! A thousand times, no! This girl was bred in such luxury, such refinement, as few of us have known. And just as the young girl was budding into womanhood, cruel fate snatched all this from her, bereft her of her dear ones, took from her, one by one, with a terrible and fierce rapidity, those upon whom she had come to look for love and support. And then, in that moment of darkest terror and loneliness, came one of our sex, gentlemen. A wolf in sheep's clothing. A fiend in the guise of a human. False promises. Lies. Deceit so palpable that it would have deceived no one but a young girl as innocent, as pure, as starry eyed as was this woman you now see white and trembling before you. One of our sex was the author of her ruin, more to blame than she. What could be more pathetic than the spectacle she presents? An immortal soul in ruin. The star of purity, once glittering on her girlish brow, has set its seal, and forever. A moment ago you heard her reviled, in the lowest terms a man can employ toward a woman, for the depths to which she has sunk, for the company she keeps, for the life she leads.

Yet where can she go that her sin does not pursue her? You would drive her out. But where? Gentlemen, the very promises of God are denied her. Who was it said, 'Come unto me all ye that are heavy laden, and I will give you rest'? She is indeed heavy laden, this trampled flower of the South, but if at this instant she were to kneel down before us all and confess her Redeemer, where is the Church that would receive her, where the community that would take her in? Scorn and mockery would greet her; those she met of her own sex would gather their skirts the more closely to avoid the pollution of her touch. Our sex wrecked her once pure life. Her own sex shrinks from her as from a pestilence. Society has reared its relentless walls against her. Only in the friendly shelter of the grave can her betrayed and broken heart ever find the Redeemer's promised rest. The gentleman who so eloquently spoke before me told you of her assumed names, of her sins, of her habits. He never, for all his eloquence, told you of her sorrows, her agonies, her hopes, her despairs. But I could tell you. I could tell you of the desperate day—the red-letter day in the banner of the great Oklahoma country—when she tried to win a home for herself where she could live in decency and quiet. . . . When the remembered voices of father and mother and sisters and brothers fall like music on her erring ears . . . who shall tell what this heavy heart, sinful though it may seem to you and to me . . . understanding, pity, help, like music on her erring soul . . . oh, gentlemen . . . gentlemen . . ."

But by this time the gentlemen, between emotion and tobacco juice, were having such difficulty with their Adam's apples as to make a wholesale strangling seem inevitable. The beautiful flexible voice went on, the hands wove their enchantment, the eyes held you in their spell. The pompous figure of little Pat Leary shrank, dwindled, disappeared before their mind's eye. The harlot Dixie Lee, in her black, became a woman romantic, piteous, appealing. Sabra Cravat, her pencil flying over her paper, thought grimly:

"It isn't true. Don't believe him. He is wrong. He has always been wrong. For fifteen years he has always been wrong. Don't believe him. I shall have to print this. How lovely his voice is. It's like a knife in my heart. I mustn't look at his eyes. His hands—what was that he said?—I must keep my mind on . . . music on her erring soul . . . oh, my love . . . I ought to hate him . . . I do hate him. . . ."

Dixie Lee's head drooped on her ravaged breast. Even

180

her plumed satellites had the wit to languish like crushed lilies and to wipe their eyes with filmy handkerchiefs the while they sniffled audibly.

It was finished. Yancey walked to his seat, sat as before, the great buffalo head lowered, the lids closed over the compelling eyes, the beautiful hands folded, relaxed.

The good men and true of the jury filed solemnly out through the crowd that made way for them. As solemnly they crossed the dusty road and repaired to a draw at the roadside, where they squatted on such bits of rock or board as came to hand. Solemnly, briefly, and with utter disregard of its legal aspect, they discussed the case—if their inarticulate monosyllables could be termed discussion. The courtroom throng, scattering for refreshment, had barely time to down its drink before the jury stamped heavily across the road and into the noisome courtroom.

". . . find the defendant, Dixie Lee, not guilty."

Eighteen

IT WAS as though Osage and the whole Oklahoma country now stopped and took a deep breath. Well it might. Just ahead of it, all unknown, waited years of such clangor and strife as would make the past years seem uneventful in comparison. Ever since the day of the Run, more than fifteen years ago, it had been racing helter-skelter, devil take the hindmost; shooting into the air, prancing and yelping out of sheer vitality and cussedness. A rough roof over its head; coarse food on its table; a horse to ride; a burning drink to toss down its throat; border justice; gyp water; a girl to hug; mud roads to the edge of the sun-baked prairie, and thereafter no road; grab what you need; fight for what you want—the men who had come to the wilderness of the Oklahoma country had expected no more than this; and this they had got. A man's country it seemed to be, ruled by men for men. The women allowed them to think so. The word feminism was unknown to the Sabra Cravats, the Mrs. Wyatts, the Mrs. Hefners, the Mesdames Turket and Folsom and Sipes. Prim, good women and courageous, banded together by their goodness and by their common resolve to tame the wilderness. Their power was the more tremendous because they did not know they had it. They never once said, during those fifteen years, "We women will

181

do this. We women will change that." Quietly, indomitably, relentlessly, without even a furtive glance of understanding exchanged between them, but secure in their common knowledge of the sentimental American male, they went ahead with their plans.

The Philomathean Club. The Twentieth Century Culture Club. The Eastern Star. The Daughters of Rebekah. The Venus Lodge.

"Ha-ha!" and "Ho-ho!" roared their menfolk. "What do you girls do at these meetings of yours? Swap cooking receipts and dress patterns?"

"Oh, yes. And we talk."

"I bet you do. Say, you don't have to tell any man that. Talk! Time about ten of you women folks start gabblin' together I bet you get the whole Territory settled—politics, Injuns, land fights, and all."

"Just about."

Yancey had come home from the Spanish-American War a hero. Other men from Osage had been in the Philippines. One had even died there (dysentery and ptomaine from bad tinned beef). But Yancey was the town's Rough Rider. He had charged up San Juan Hill with Roosevelt. Osage, knowing Yancey and never having seen Roosevelt, assumed that Yancey Cravat—the Southwest Cimarron—had led the way, an ivory-and-silver-mounted six-shooter in either hand, the great buffalo head lowered with such menace that the little brown men had fled to their jungles in terror.

His return had been the occasion for such a celebration as the town had never known and never would know again, they assured each other, between drinks, until the day when statehood should come to the Territory. He returned a captain, unwounded, but thin and yellow, with the livery look that confirmed the stories one had heard of putrid food, typhoid, dysentery, and mosquitoes more deadly, in this semi-tropical country, than bullets or cannon.

Poisoned and enfeebled though he was, his return seemed to energize the crude little town. Wherever he might be he lived in a swirl of events that drew into its eddy all that came within its radius. Hi, Yancey! Hi, Clint! He shed the khaki and the cocked hat and actually appeared again in the familiar white sombrero, Prince Albert, and high-heeled boots. Osage breathed a sigh of satisfaction. His dereliction was forgiven, the rumors about him forgotten—or allowed to subside, at least. Again the editorial columns of the *Oklahoma Wigwam* blazed with hyperbole.

It was hard for Sabra to take second place (or to appear to take second place) in the office of the *Wigwam*. She had so long ruled there alone. Her word had been law to the wavering Jesse Rickey and to the worshiping Cliff Means. And now to say, "You'd better ask Mr. Cravat."

"He says leave it to you. He's went out."

Yancey did a good deal of going out. Sabra, after all, still did most of the work of the paper without having the satisfaction of dictating its policy. A linotype machine, that talented iron monster, now chattered and chittered and clanked in the composing room of the *Wigwam*. It was the first of its kind in the Oklahoma country. Very costly and uncannily human, Sabra never quite got over her fear of it. The long arm reached down with such leisurely assurance, snatched its handful of metal, carried it over, descended, dropped it. It opened its capacious maw to be fed bars of silvery lead which it spat forth again in the shape of neat cakes of type. Its keys were like grinning teeth. It grunted, shivered, clumped, spoke—or nearly.

"I never come near it," Sabra once admitted, "that I don't expect the thing to reach down with its iron arm and clap me on the shoulder and clatter, 'Hello, Sabra!'"

She was proud of the linotype machine, for it had been her five years at the head of the *Wigwam* that had made it possible. It was she who had gone out after job printing contracts; who had educated the local merchants to the value of advertising. Certainly Yancey, prancing and prating, had never given a thought to these substantial foundations on which the entire business success of the paper rested. They now got out with ease the daily *Wigwam* for the Osage townspeople and the weekly for county subscribers. Passing the windows of the *Wigwam* office on Pawhuska Avenue you could hear the thump and rattle of the iron monster. Between them Jesse Rickey and Cliff Means ran the linotype. Often they labored far into the night on job work, and the late passer-by would see the little light burning in the printing shop and hear the rattle and thump of the machine. In a pinch Sabra herself could run it. Yancey never went near it, and, strangely enough, young Cim had a horror of it, as he had of most things mechanical. After one attempt at the keyboard, during which he had hopelessly jammed the machine's delicate insides, he was forbidden ever to go near it again. For that matter, Cim had little enough taste for the newspaper business. He pied type at the case rack. He had no news sense. He had neither his father's gift for mingling with people and winning their confidence nor his mother's more orderly materialistic mind. He had much of Yancey Cravat's charm, and something of the vagueness of his grandfather, old Lewis Venable (dead these two years), but combining the worst features of both.

"Stop dreaming!" Sabra said to him, often and often. "What are you dreaming about?"

She had grown to love the atmosphere of the newspaper office and resented the boy's indifference to it. She loved the very smell of it—the mixed odor of hot metal, printer's ink, dust, white paper, acid, corncob pipe, and cats.

"Stop dreaming!" Yancey, hearing her thus admonishing Cim, whirled on her in one of his rare moments of utter rage. "God a'mighty, Sabra! That's what Ann Hathaway said to Shakespeare. Don't you women know that 'Dreams grow holy put in action; work grows fair through starry dreaming'? Leave the boy alone! Let him dream! Let him dream!"

"One starry dreamer in a family is enough," Sabra retorted, tartly.

Five years had gone by—six years since Yancey's return. Yet, strangely enough, Sabra never had a feeling of security. She never forgot what he had said about Wichita. "Almost five years in one place. That's the longest stretch I've ever done, honey." Five years. And this was well into the sixth. He had plunged head first into the statehood fight, into the Indian Territory situation. The anti-Indian faction was bitterly opposed to the plan for combining the Oklahoma Territory and the Indian Territory under the single state of Oklahoma. Their slogan was The White Man's State for the White Man.

"Who brought the Indian here to the Oklahoma country in the first place?" shouted Yancey in the editorial columns of the *Wigwam*. "White men. They hounded them from Missouri to Arkansas, from Arkansas to southern Kansas, then to northern Kansas, to northern Oklahoma, to southern Oklahoma. You white men sold them the piece of arid and barren land on which they now live in squalor and misery. It isn't fit for a white man to live on, or the Indians wouldn't be living on it now. Deprived of their tribal laws, deprived of their tribal rites, herded together in stockades like wild animals, robbed, cheated, kicked, hounded from place to place, give them the protection of the country that has taken their country away from them. Give them at least the right to become citizens of the state of Oklahoma."

He was obsessed by it. He traveled to Washington in the

hope of lobbying for it, and made quite a stir in that formal capital with his white sombrero, his Prince Albert, his Texas star boots, his great buffalo head, his charm, his grace, his manner. Roosevelt was characteristically cordial to his old campaign comrade. Washington ladies were captivated by the flowery speeches of this romantic, this story-book swaggerer out of the Southwest.

It was rumored on good authority that he was to be appointed the next Governor of the Oklahoma Territory.

"Oh, Yancey," Sabra said, "do be careful. Governor of the Territory! It would mean so much. It would help Cim in the future. Donna, too. Their father a governor." She thought, "Perhaps everything will be all right now. Perhaps all that I've gone through in the last ten years will be worth it, now. Perhaps it was for this. He'll settle down. . . . Mamma can't say now . . . and all the Venables and the Vians and the Goforths and the Greenwoods. . . ." She had had to endure their pity, even from a distance, all these years.

The rumor took on substance. My husband, Yancey Cravat, Governor of the Territory of Oklahoma. And then, when statehood came, as it must in the next few years, perhaps Governor of the state of Oklahoma. Why not!

At which point Yancey blasted any possibility of his appointment to the governorship by hurling a red-hot editorial into the columns of the *Wigwam*. The gist of it was that the hundreds of thousands of Indians now living on reservations throughout the United States should be allowed to live where they pleased, at liberty. The whites of the Oklahoma Territory and the Indian Territory, with an Indian population of about one hundred and twenty thousand of various tribes—Poncas, Cherokees, Chickasaws, Creeks, Osages, Kiowas, Comanches, Kaws, Choctaws, Seminoles, and a score of others—read, emitted a roar of rage, and brandishing the paper ran screaming into the streets, cursing the name of Yancey Cravat.

Sabra had caught the editorial in the wet proof sheet. Her eye leaped down its lines.

Herded like sheep in a corral—no, like wild animals in a cage—they are left to rot on their reservations by a government that has taken first their land, then their self-respect, then their liberty from them. The land of the free! When the very people who first dwelt on it are prisoners! Slaves, but slaves deprived of the solace of work. What hope have they, what ambition, what object in living! Their spirit is broken. Their pride is gone.

185

Slothful, yes. Why not? Each month he receives his dole, his pittance. Look at the Osage Nation, now dwindled to a wretched two thousand souls. The men are still handsome, strong, vital; the women beautiful, dignified, often intelligent. Yet there they huddle in their miserable shanties like beaten animals eating the food that is thrown them by a great—a munificent—government. The government of these United States! Let them be free. Let the Red Man live a free man as the White Man lives. . . .

Much that he wrote was true, perhaps. Yet the plight of the Indian was not as pitiable as Yancey painted it. He cast over them the glamour of his own romantic nature. The truth was that they themselves cared little—except a few of their tribal leaders, more intelligent than the rest. They hunted a little, fished, slept, visited from tribe to tribe, the Poncas visiting the Osages, the Osages the Poncas, gossiping, eating, holding powwows. The men were great poker players, having learned the game from the white man, and spent hours at it.

They passed through the town of Osage in their brilliant striped blankets, sometimes walking, sometimes on sorry nags, sometimes in rickety wagons laden with pots, poles, rags, papooses, hounds. The townspeople hastily removed such articles as might please the pilfering fancy.

Sabra picked up the proof sheet, still damp from the press, and walked into Yancey's office. Her face was white, set.

"You're going to run this, Yancey?"

"Yes."

"You'll never be Governor of the Territory."

"Never."

She stood a moment, her face working. She crushed the galley proof in her hand so that her knuckles stood out, white.

"I've forgiven you many, many things, God knows, in the last ten years. I'll never forgive you for this. Never."

"Yes, you will, honey. Never is a long time. Not while I'm alive, maybe. But some day, a long time from now—though not so very long, maybe—you'll be able to turn back to the old files of the *Oklahoma Wigwam* and lift this editorial of mine right out of it, word for word, and run it as your own."

"Never. . . . Donna . . . Cim . . ."

"I can't live my children's lives for them, Sabra, honey.

They've got to live their own. I believe what I believe. This town is rotten—the Territory—the whole country. Rotten."

"You're a fine one to say what is or isn't rotten. You with your whisky and your Indians and your women. I despise you. So does everyone in the town—in the Territory."

" 'A prophet is not without honor, save in his own country and in his own home.' " A trifle sonorously.

She never really knew whether he had done this thing with the very purpose of making his governorship impossible. It was like him.

Curiously enough, the editorial, while it maddened the white population of the Territory, gained the paper many readers. The *Wigwam* prospered. Osage blossomed. The town was still rough, crude, wide open, even dangerous. But it began to take on an aspect of permanence. It was no longer a camp; it was a town. It began to build schools, churches, halls. Arkansas Grat's gambling tent had long ago been replaced by a solid wooden structure, just as gambling terms of the West and the Southwest had slowly been incorporated into the language of daily use. I'm keeping cases on him . . . standing pat . . . bluffing . . . bucking the tiger. Terms filched from the gaming table; poker and faro and keno.

Sol Levy's store—the Levy Mercantile Company—had two waxen ladies in the window, their features only slightly affected by the burning Southwest sun. Yancey boomed Sol Levy for mayor of Osage, but he never had a chance. It was remarkable how the *Oklahoma Wigwam* persisted, though its position in most public questions was violently unpopular. Perhaps it, like Yancey, had a vitality and a charm that no one could withstand.

Athough Sol Levy was still the town Jew, respected, prosperous, the town had never quite absorbed this Oriental. A citizen of years' standing, he still was a stranger. He mingled little with his fellow townsmen outside business hours. He lived lonesomely at the Bixby House and ate the notoriously bad meals served by Mrs. Bixby. He was shy of the town women though the Women of the Town found him kindly, passionate and generous. The business men liked him. They put him on committees. Occasionally Sabra or some other woman who knew him well enough would say, half playfully, half seriously, "Why don't you get married, Sol? A nice fellow like you. You'd make some girl happy."

Sometimes he thought vaguely of going to Wichita or

Kansas City or even Chicago to meet some nice Jewish girl there, but he never did. It never entered his head to marry a Gentile. The social life of the town was almost unknown to him. Sometimes if a big local organization—the Elks, the Odd Fellows, the Sons of the Southwest—gave a benefit dance, you would glimpse him briefly, in the early part of the evening, standing shyly against the wall or leaning half hidden in the doorway, a darkling, remote, curiously Oriental figure in the midst of these robust red-faced plainsmen and ex-cowmen.

"Come on, Sol, mix in! Grab off one of the girls and get to dancin', why don't you? What you scairt of?" But Sol remained aloof. He regarded the hot, sweaty, shouting dancers with a kind of interested bewilderment and wonder, much as the dancers themselves sometimes watched the Indians during one of the Festival Dances on the outlying reservations. On occasion he made himself politely agreeable to a stout matron well past middle age. They looked up at his tragic dark eyes; they noticed his slim ivory hand as it passed them a plate of cake or a cup of coffee. "He's real nice when you get to know him," they said. "For a Jew, that is."

Between him and Yancey there existed a deep sympathy and understanding. Yancey campaigned for Sol Levy in the mayoralty race—if a thing so one-sided could be called a race. The *Wigwam* extolled him.

Sol Levy, the genial proprietor of the Levy Mercantile Company, is the *Wigwam's* candidate for mayor. It behooves the people of Osage to do honor to one of its pioneer citizens whose career, since its early days, has been marked by industry, prosperity, generosity. He comes of a race of dreamers and doers. . . .

"Why, the very idea!" snorted the redoubtable virago, Mrs. Tracy Wyatt, whose husband was the opposing candidate. "A Jew for mayor of Osage! They'll be having an Indian mayor next. Mr. Wyatt's folks are real Americans. They helped settle Arkansas. And as for me, why, I can trace my ancestry right back to William Whipple, who was one of the signers of the Declaration of Independence."

Sol Levy never had a chance for public honor. He, in fact, did practically nothing to further his own possible election. He seemed to regard the whole matter with a remoteness slightly tinged with ironic humor. Yancey dropped into

Sol's store to bring him this latest pronouncement of the bristling Mrs. Wyatt. Sol was busy in the back of the store, where he was helping the boy unpack a new invoice of china and lamps just received, for the Levy Mercantile Company had blossomed into a general store of parts. His head was in a barrel, and when he straightened and looked up at the towering Yancey there were bits of straw and excelsior clinging to his shirt sleeves and necktie and his black hair.

"Declaration of Independence!" he exclaimed, thoughtfully. "Tell her one of my ancestors wrote the Ten Commandments. Fella name of Moses."

Yancey, roaring with laughter, used this in the *Wigwam,* and it naturally helped as much as anything to defeat the already defeated candidate.

Sometimes the slim, white-faced proprietor, with his friend Yancey Cravat, stood in the doorway of the store, watching the town go by. They said little. It was as though they were outsiders, looking on at a strange pageant.

"What the hell are you doing here in this town, anyway, Sol?" Yancey would say, as though musing aloud.

"And you?" Sol would retort. "A civilized barbarian."

The town went by—Indians, cowboys up from Texas, plainsmen, ranchers. They still squatted at the curb, as in the early days. They chewed tobacco and spat. The big sombrero persisted, and even the boots and spurs.

"Howdy, Yancey! Howdy, Sol! H'are you, Cim!"

There was talk of paving Pawhuska Avenue, but this did not come for years. The town actually boasted a waterworks. The *Wigwam* office still stood on Pawhuska, but it now occupied the entire house. Two years after Yancey's return they had decided to build a home on Kihekah Street, where there actually were trees now almost ten years old.

Sabra had built the house as she wanted it, though at first there had been a spirited argument about this. Yancey's idea had been, of course, ridiculous, fantastic. He said he wanted the house built in native style.

"Native! What in the world! A wickiup?"

"Well, a house in the old Southwest Indian style—almost pueblo, I mean. Or Spanish, sort of, made of Oklahoma red clay—plaster, maybe. Not brick. And low, with a patio where you can be out of doors and yet away from the sun. And where you can have privacy."

Sabra made short work of that idea. Or perhaps Yancey did not persist. He withdrew his plan as suddenly as he had presented it; shrugged his great shoulders as though the house no longer interested him.

Osage built its new houses with an attached front porch gaping socially out into the street. It sat on the front porch in its shirt sleeves and kitchen apron. It called from porch to porch, "How's your tomato plants doing? I see the Packses got out-of-town company visiting." It didn't in the least want privacy.

Sabra built a white frame house in the style of the day, with turrets, towers, minarets, cupolas, and scroll work. There was a stained glass window in the hall, in purple and red and green and yellow, which, confronting the entering caller, gave him the look of being suddenly stricken with bubonic plague. There were parlor, sitting room, dining room, kitchen on the first floor; four bedrooms on the second floor, and a bathroom, actually, with a full-size bathtub, a toilet, and a marble washstand with varicose veins. In the cellar there was a hot air furnace. In the parlor were brown brocade-and-velvet settee and stuffed chairs. In the sitting room was a lamp with a leaded glass shade in the shape of a strange and bloated flower—a Burbankian monstrosity, half water lily, half petunia.

"As long as we're building and furnishing," Sabra said, "it might as well be the best." She had gone about planning the house, and furnishing it, with her customary energy and capability. With it all she found time to do her work on the *Wigwam*—for without her the paper would have been run to the ground in six months. Osage had long since ceased to consider it queer that she, a woman, and the wife of one of its most prominent citizens, should go to work every morning like a man.

By ten every morning she had attended to her household, seen it started for the day, had planned the meals, ordered them on her way downtown, and was at her desk in the *Wigwam* office, sorting mail, reading exchanges, taking ads, covering news, writing heads, pasting up. Yancey's contributions were brilliant but spasmodic. The necessary departmental items—real estate transfers, routine court news, out-of-town district and county gleanings—bored him, though he knew well that they were necessary to the success of the paper. He left these to Sabra, among many other things.

Sabra, in common with the other well-to-do housewives of the community, employed an Indian girl as a house servant. There was no other kind of help available. After her hideous experience with Arita Red Feather she had been careful to get Indian girls older, more settled, though this was difficult. She preferred Osage girls. These married young, often before they had finished their studies at the Indian school.

Ruby Big Elk had been with Sabra now for three years. A curious, big, silent girl of about twenty-two—almost handsome—one of six children—a large family for an Osage. Sabra was somewhat taken aback, after the girl had been with her for some months, to learn that she already had been twice married.

"What became of your husbands, Ruby?"

"Died."

She had a manner that bordered on the insolent. Sabra put it down to Indian dignity. When she walked she scuffed her feet ever so little, and this, for some inexplicable reason, seemed to add insolence to her bearing. "Oh, do lift your feet, Ruby! Don't scuffle when you walk." The girl made no reply. Went on scuffling. Sabra discovered that she was lame; the left leg was slightly shorter than the right. She did not limp—or, rather, hid the tendency to limp by the irritating sliding sound. Her walk was straight, leisurely, measured. Sabra was terribly embarrassed; apologized to the Indian girl. The girl only looked at her and said nothing. Sabra repressed a little shiver. She had never got accustomed to the Indians.

Sabra was a bustler and a driver. As she went about the house in the morning, performing a dozen household duties before leaving for the *Wigwam* office, her quick tapping step drummed like hail on a tin roof. It annoyed her intensely, always, to see Ruby Big Elk making up the beds with that regal manner, or moving about the kitchen with the pace and air of a Lady Macbeth. The girl's broad, immobile face, her unspeaking eyes, her secret manner all worked a slow constant poison in Sabra. She spoke seldom; never smiled. When Sabra spoke to her about some household task she would regard her mistress with an unblinking gaze that was highly disconcerting.

"Did you understand about the grape jell, Ruby? To let it get thoroughly cool before you pour on the wax?"

Ruby would majestically incline her fine head, large, like a man's head. The word sinister came into Sabra's mind. Still, Sabra argued, she was good to the children, fed them well, never complained about the work. Sometimes—on rare occasions—she would dig a little pit in the back yard and build a slow hot smothered fire by some secret Indian process, and there, to the intense delight of young Cim, she would roast meats deliciously in the Indian fashion, crisp and sweet, skewered with little shafts of wood that she herself whittled down. Donna refused to touch the meat, as did Sabra. Donna shared her mother's dislike of the Indians —or perhaps she had early been impressed with her mother's feeling about them. Sometimes Donna, the spoiled, the pampered, the imperious (every inch her grandmother Felice Venable) would feel Ruby Big Elk's eye on her—that expressionless, dead black Indian eye. Yet back of its deadness, its utter lack of expression, there still seemed to lurk a cold contempt.

"What are you staring at, Ruby?" Donna would cry, pettishly. Ruby would walk out of the room with her slow scuffling step, her body erect, her head regal, her eyes looking straight ahead. She said nothing. "Miserable squaw!" Donna would hiss under her breath. "Gives herself the airs of a princess because her greasy old father runs the tribe or something."

Ruby's father, Big Elk, had in fact been Chief of the Osage tribe by election for ten years, and though he no longer held this highest office, was a man much looked up to in the Osage Nation. He had sent his six children and actually his fat wife to the Indian school, but he himself steadfastly refused to speak a word of English, though he knew enough of the language. He conversed in Osage, and when necessary used an interpreter. It was a kind of stubborn Indian pride in him. It was his enduring challenge to the white man. "You have not defeated me."

His pride did not, however, extend to more material things, and Sabra was frequently annoyed by the sight of the entire Big Elk family, the old ex-Chief, his squaw, and the five brothers and sisters, squatting in her kitchen doorway enjoying such juicy bits as Ruby saw fit to bestow upon them from the Cravat larder. When Sabra would have put a stop to this, Yancey intervened.

"He's a wise old man. If he had a little white blood in him he'd be as great as Quanah Parker was, or Sequoyah. Everything he says is wisdom. I like to talk with him. Leave him alone."

This did not serve to lessen Sabra's irritation. Often she returned home to find Yancey squatting on the ground with old Big Elk, smoking and conversing in a mixture of Osage and English, for Big Elk did not refuse to understand the

192

English language, even though he would not speak it. Yancey had some knowledge of Osage. Sabra, coming upon the two grunting and muttering and smoking and staring ahead into nothingness or (worse still) cracking some Indian joke and shaking with silent laughter, Indian fashion, was filled with fury. Nothing so maddened her.

It slowly dawned on Sabra that young Cim was always to be found lolling in the kitchen, talking to Ruby. Ruby, she discovered to her horror, was teaching Cim to speak Osage. A difficult language to the white, he seemed to have a natural aptitude for it. She came upon them, their heads close together over the kitchen table, laughing and talking and singing. Rather, Ruby Big Elk was singing a song with a curious rhythm, and (to Sabra's ear, at least) no melody. There was a pulsation of the girl's voice on sustained notes such as is sometimes produced on a violin when the same note is sounded several times during a single bow stroke. Cim was trying to follow the strange gutturals, slurs, and accents, his eyes fixed on Ruby's face, his own expression utterly absorbed, rapt.

"What are you doing? What is this?"

The Indian girl's face took on its customary expression of proud disdain. She rose. "Teach um song," she said; which was queer, for she spoke English perfectly.

"Well, I must say, Cimarron Cravat! When you know your father is expecting you down at the office——" She stopped. Her quick eye had leaped to the table where lay the little round peyote disk or mescal button which is the hashish of the Indian.

She had heard about it; knew how prevalent among the Indian tribes from Nebraska down to Mexico had become the habit of eating this little buttonlike top of a Mexican cactus plant. In shape a disk about an inch and a half in diameter and a quarter of an inch thick, the mescal or peyote gave the eater a strange feeling of lightness, dispelled pain and fatigue, caused visions of marvelous beauty and grandeur. The use of it had become an Indian religious rite.

Like a fury Sabra advanced to the table, snatched up the little round button of soft green.

"Peyote!" She whirled on Cim. "What are you doing with this thing?"

Cim's eyes were cast down sullenly. His hands in his pockets, he leaned against the wall, very limp, very bored, very infuriating and insolent.

193

"Ruby was just teaching me one of the Mescal Ceremony songs. Darned interesting. It's the last song. They sing it at sunrise when they're just about all in. Goes like this."

To Sabra's horror he began an eerie song as he stood there leaning against the kitchen wall, his eyes half closed.

"Stop it!" screamed Sabra. With the gesture of a tragedy queen she motioned him out of the kitchen. He obeyed with very bad grace, his going more annoying, in its manner, than his staying. Sabra followed him, silently. Suddenly she realized she hated his walk, and knew why. He walked with a queer little springing gait, on the very soles of his feet. It came over her that it always had annoyed her. She remembered that someone had laughingly told her what Pete Pitchlyn, the old Indian scout, lounging on his street corner, had said about young Cim:

"Every time I see that young Cimarron Cravat a-comin' down the street I expect to hear a twig snap. Walks like a story-book Injun."

In the privacy of the sitting room Sabra confronted her son, the bit of peyote still crushed in her hand.

"So you've come to this! I'm ashamed of you!"

"Come to what?"

She opened her hand to show the button of pulpy green crushed in her palm. "Peyote. A son of mine. I'd rather see you dead——"

"Oh, for heaven's sake, Mom, don't get Biblical, like Dad. To hear you a person would think you'd found me drugged in a Chinese opium den."

"I think I'd almost rather."

"It's nothing but a miserable little piece of cactus. And what was I doing but sitting in the kitchen listening to Ruby tell how her father——"

"I should think a man of almost eighteen could find some-

194

thing better to do than sit in a kitchen in the middle of the day talking to an Indian hired girl. Where's your pride!"

Cim's eyes were still cast down. He still lounged insolently, his hands in his pockets. "How about these stories you've told me all your life about the love you Southerners had for your servants and how old Angie was like a second mother to you?"

"Niggers are different. They know their place."

He raised the heavy eyelids then and lifted his fine head with the menacing look that she knew so well in his father. "You're right. They are different. In the first place, Ruby isn't an Indian hired girl. She is the daughter of an Osage chief."

"Osage fiddlesticks! What of it!"

"Ruby Big Elk is just as important a person in the Osage Nation as Alice Roosevelt is in Washington."

"Now, listen here, Cimarron Cravat! I've heard about enough. A lot of dirty Indians! Just you march yourself down to the *Wigwam* office, young man, and don't you ever again let me catch you talking in that disrespectful manner about the daughter of the President of the United States. And if I ever hear that you've eaten a bite of this miserable stuff"—she held out her hand, shaking a little, the mescal button crushed in her palm—"I'll have your father thrash you within an inch of your life, big as you are. As it is, he shall hear of this."

But Yancey, on being told, only looked thoughtful and a little sad. "It's your own fault, Sabra. You're bound that the boy shall live the life you've planned for him instead of the one he wants. So he's trying to escape into a dream life. Like the Indians. It's all the same thing."

"I don't know what you're talking about. I don't think you know, either."

"The Indians started to eat peyote after the whites had taken their religious and spiritual and decent physical life away from them. They had owned the plains and the prairies for centuries. The whites took those. The whites killed off the buffalo, whose flesh had been the Indians' food, and whose skins had been their shelter, and gave them bacon and tumbledown wooden houses in their place. The whites told them that the gods they had worshiped were commonplace things. The Sun was a dying planet—the Stars lumps of hot metal—the Rain a thing that could be regulated by tree planting—the Wind just a current of air that a man in Washington knew all about and whose travels he could prophesy by looking at a piece of machinery."

"And they ought to be grateful for it. The government's given them food and clothes and homes and land. They're a shiftless good-for-nothing lot and won't work. They won't even plant crops."

" 'Man cannot live by bread alone.' He has got to have dreams, or life is unendurable. So the Indian turned to the peyote. He finds peace and comfort and beauty in his dreams."

A horrible suspicion darted through Sabra. "Yancey Cravat, have you ever——"

He nodded his magnificent head slowly, sadly. "Many times. Many times."

Nineteen

CIM was nineteen, Donna fifteen. And now Sabra lived quite alone in the new house on Kihekah Street, except for a colored woman servant sent from Kansas. She ran the paper alone, as she wished it run. She ordered the house as she wished it. She very nearly ran the town of Osage. She was a power in the Territory. And Yancey was gone, Cim was gone, Donna was gone. Sabra had refused to compromise with life, and life had taken matters out of her hands.

Donna was away at an Eastern finishing school—Miss Dignum's on the Hudson. Yancey had opposed that, of course. It had been Sabra's idea to send Donna east to school.

"East?" Yancey had said. "Kansas City?"

"Certainly not."

"Oh—Chicago."

"I mean New York."

"You're crazy."

"I didn't expect you to approve. I suppose you'd like her to go to an Indian school. Donna's an unusual girl. She's not a beauty and never will be, but she's brilliant, that's what she is. Brilliant. I don't mean intellectual. You needn't smile. I mean that she's got the ambition and the insight and the foresight, too, of a woman of twice her age."

"I'm sorry to hear that."

"I'm not. She's like Mamma in many ways, only she's got lligence and drive. She doesn't get along with the girls —Maurine Turket and Gazelle Slaughter and Jewel

196

Riggs and Czarina McKee, and those. She's different. They go switching up and down Pawhuska Avenue. They'll marry one of these tobacco-chewing loafers and settle down like vegetables. Well, she won't. I'll see to that."

"Going to marry her off to an Eastern potentate—at fifteen?"

"You wait. You'll see. She knows what she wants. She'll get it, too."

"Sure it isn't you who know what you want her to want?"

But Sabra had sent her off to Miss Dignum's on a diet of prunes and prisms that even her high-and-mighty old grandmother Felice Venable approved.

Cim, walking the prairies beyond Osage with that peculiar light step of his, his eyes cast down; prowling the draws and sprawling upon the clay banks of the rivers that ran so red through the Red Man's Territory, said that he wanted to be a geologist. He spoke of the Colorado School of Mines. He worked in the *Wigwam* office and hated it. He could pi a case of type more quickly and completely than a drunken tramp printer. The familiar "shrdlu etaoin" was likely to appear in any column in which he had a hand. Even Jesse Rickey, his mournful mustaches more drooping than ever, protested to Yancey.

"She can't make a newspaper man out of that kid," he said. "Not in a million years. Newspaper men are born, not made. Cim, he just naturally hates news, let alone a newspaper office. He was born without a nose for news, like a fellow that's born without an arm, or something. You can't grow it if you haven't got it."

"I know it," said Yancey, wearily. "He'll find a way out."

For the first time a rival newspaper flourished in the town of Osage. The town was scarcely large enough to support two daily papers, but Yancey's political attitude so often was at variance with the feeling of the Territory politicians that the new daily, slipshod and dishonest though it was, and owned body and soul by Territorial interests, achieved a degree of popularity.

Sabra, unable to dictate the policy of the *Wigwam* with Yancey at its head, had to content herself with the management of its mechanical workings and with its increasingly important social and club columns. Osage swarmed with meetings, committees, lodges, Knights of This and Sisters of That. The Philomathean and the Twentieth Century clubs

197

began to go in for Civic Betterment, and no Osage merchant or professional man was safe from cajoling and unattractive females in shirtwaists and skirts and eyeglasses demanding his name signed to this or that petition (with a contribution. Whatever you feel that you can give, Mr. Hefner. Of course, as a leading business man . . .).

They planted shrubs about the cinder-strewn environs of the Santa Fé and the Katy depots. They agitated for the immediate paving of Pawhuska Avenue (it wasn't done). The Ladies of the Eastern Star. The Venus Lodge. Sisters of Rebekah. Daughters of the Southwest. They came into the *Wigwam* office with notices to be printed about lodge suppers and church sociables. Strangely enough, they were likely to stay longer and to chat more freely if Yancey and not Sabra were there to receive them. Sabra was polite but businesslike to her own sex encountered in office hours. But Yancey made himself utterly charming. He could no more help it than he could help breathing. It was almost functional with him. He made the stout, commonplace, middle-aged women feel that they were royal—and seductive. He flattered them with his fine eyes; he bowed them to the door; their eyeglasses quivered. He was likely, on their departure, to crumple their carefully worded notice and throw it on the floor. Sabra, though she made short work of the visiting Venuses and Rebekahs, ran their notice and, if necessary, carefully rewrote it.

"God A'mighty!" he would groan at noonday dinner. "The office was full of Wenuses this morning. Like a swarm of overstuffed locusts."

Sabra was at the head of many of these Betterment movements. Also if there could be said to be anything so formal as society in Osage, Sabra Cravat was the leader of it. She was the first to electrify the ladies of the Twentieth Century Culture Club by serving them Waldorf salad—that abominable mixture of apple cubes, chopped nuts, whipped cream, and mayonnaise. The club fell upon it with little cries and murmurs. Thereafter it was served at club meetings until Osage husbands, returning home to supper after a day's work, and being offered this salvage from the feast, would push it aside with masculine contempt for its contents and roar, "I can't eat this stuff. Fix me some bacon and eggs."

From this culinary and social triumph Sabra proceeded pineapple and marshmallow salad, the recipe for which been sent her by Donna in the East. Its indirect effects tal.

When it again became her turn to act as hostess to the members of the club she made her preparations for the afternoon meeting, held at the grisly hour of half-past two. Refreshments were invariably served at four. With all arrangements made, she was confronted by Ruby Big Elk with the astounding statement that this was a great Indian Festival Day (September, and the corn dances were on) and that she must go to the Reservation in time for the Mescal Ceremony.

"You can't go," said Sabra, flatly. Midday dinner was over. Yancey had returned to the office. Cim was lounging in the hammock on the porch. For answer Ruby turned and walked with her stately, irritating step into her own room just off the kitchen and closed the door.

"Well," shouted Sabra in the tones of Felice Venable herself, "if you do go you needn't come back." She marched out to the front porch, where the sight of the lounging Cim only aggravated her annoyance.

"This ends it. That girl has got to leave."

"What girl?"

"Ruby. Twenty women this afternoon, and she says she's going to the Reservation. They'll be here at half-past two." It was rather incoherent, but Cim, surprisingly enough, seemed to understand.

"But she told you a month ago."

"Told me what? How do you know?"

"Because she told me she told you, ever so long ago."

"Maybe she did. She never mentioned it again. I can't be expected to remember every time the Indians have one of their powwows. I told her she couldn't go. She's in there getting ready. Well, this ends it. She needn't come back."

She flounced into the kitchen. There stood a mild-mannered young Indian girl unknown to her.

"What do you want?"

"I am here," the girl answered, composedly, "to take Ruby Big Elk's place this afternoon. I am Cherokee. She told me to come." She plucked Ruby's blue and white checked gingham kitchen apron off the book behind the door and tied it around her waist.

"Well!" gasped Sabra, relieved, but still angry. Through the kitchen window she saw Cim hitching up the two pintos to the racy little yellow phaëton that Yancey had bought. She must run out and tell him before he left. He had seemed disturbed. She was glad he was clearing out. She liked having the men folks out of the way when afternoon company was due.

Ruby's door opened. The girl came out. Her appearance was amazing. She wore a dress of white doeskin hanging straight from shoulders to ankles, and as soft and pliable as velvet. The hem was fringed. Front, sleeves, collar were finely beaded in an intricate pattern that was more like embroidery than beading. On her feet were moccasins in ivory white and as exquisitely beaded as the dress. It was the robe of a princess. Her dark Indian eyes were alive. Her skin seemed to glow in contrast with the garment. The girl was, for the moment, almost beautiful.

"Hello, Theresa Jump. . . . This is Theresa Jump. She will do my work this day. I have told her. She knows about the pineapple and marshmallow salad." For a moment it seemed to Sabra that just the faintest shadow of amusement flitted over Ruby's face as she said this. But then, Sabra never had pretended to understand these Indians. "I will be back to-morrow morning."

She walked slowly out of the house by way of the kitchen door, across the yard with her slow insolent dragging step. A stab of suspicion cut Sabra. She flew to the back porch, stood there a moment. Ruby Big Elk walked slowly toward the barn. Cim drove out with the phaëton and pintos. He saw the Indian woman in her white doeskin dress. His eyes shone enormous. He lifted his head as though to breathe deeply. At that look in his face Sabra ran across the yard. One hand was at her breast, as though an Indian arrow had pierced her. Ruby had set one foot in its cream white moccasin on the buggy step. Cim held out his free hand.

Sabra reached them, panting. "Where are you going?"

"I am driving Ruby out to the Reservation."

"No, you're not. No, you're not." She put one hand in a futile gesture on the buggy wheel, as though to stop them by main force. She knew she must not lose her dignity before this Indian woman—before her son. Yet this thing was, to her way of thinking, monstrous.

Cim gathered up the reins, his eyes on the restive ponies. "I may stay to see some of the dancing and the Mescal Ceremony. Father says it's very interesting. Big Elk has invited me."

"Your father knows you're going? Like this?"

"Oh, yes." He cast a slight, an oblique glance at her hand on the wheel. Her hand dropped heavily to her side. He spoke to the horses. They were off. Ruby Big Elk looked straight ahead. She had uttered no word. Sabra turned and walked back to the house. The hot tears blinded her. She was choking. But her pride spoke, even then. You must not go the kitchen way. That Indian girl will see you. They are all alike. You must go around by the front way. Pretend it is nothing. Oh, God, what shall I do! All those women this afternoon. Perhaps I am making a fuss over nothing. Why shouldn't he take the Indian girl out to the Reservation and stop an hour or two to see the dances and the rites? . . . His face! His face when he saw her in that dress.

She bathed her eyes, powdered her nose, changed her dress, came into the kitchen, smiling. ". . . the pineapple cut into chunks about like this. Then you snip the marshmallow into it with the scissors. Mix whipped cream into your mayonnaise . . . a cherry on top . . . little thin sandwiches . . . damp napkin . . ." She went into the sitting room, adjusted a shade, plumped a pillow. The door bell rang. "Howdy-do, Mrs. Nisbett. . . . No, you're not. You're just on time. It's everybody else who's late." She thought, "Women are wonderful. No man could do what I am doing. Smiling and chatting when I am almost crazy." Her fine dark eyes were luminous. Her clear ivory skin was tinged now with a spot of red on either cheek. She looked very handsome.

Theresa Jump proved clumsy and unteachable. Sabra herself mixed and served the pineapple and marshmallow salad, and though this novelty proved a great success, the triumph of serving it was spoiled for Sabra. She bundled the girl off at six, after the dishes were done. Wearily she began to set the house to rights, but Yancey came home to a confusion of chairs and squashed pillows, a mingled odor of perfumery and coffee; a litter of cake crumbs, bits of embroidery silk, and crumpled tea napkins. His huge frame moving about the cluttered sitting room made these feminine remnants seem ridiculous. The disorder of the household irked him. Worst of all, Sabra, relieved now of her guests, was free to pour out upon him all the pent-up wrath, anxiety, and shock of the past few hours. Ruby. Cim. Theresa Jump. Peyote. Osages. If his own father allows such things—what will people say—no use trying to make something of yourself.

Yancey, usually so glib with quotations from this or that sonorous passage of poetry, said little. He did not even try to cajole her into a better humor with his flattery, his charm, his tenderness. His eyes were bloodshot, his hand more unsteady than usual. He had been drinking even more than was his wont, she knew that at once. By no means drunk (she had never seen him really drunk—no one had—he was seemingly incapable of reaching a visible state of drunkenness), he was in one of his fits of moody depression. The great shoulders sagged. The splendid head lolled on his breast. He seemed sunk in gloomy thought. She felt that he hardly heard what she was saying. She herself could eat nothing. She set a place for him at the dining-room table and plumped down before him a dish of the absurd salad, a cup of coffee, some cake, a plate of the left-over sandwiches, their edges curled dismally.

"What's this?" he said.

"Pineapple and marshmallow salad. With Ruby gone and all, I didn't get anything for your supper—I was so upset —all those women . . ."

He sat looking down at the slippery mass on his plate. His great arms were spread out on the table before him. The beautiful hands were opening and closing convulsively. So a mastodon might have looked at a worm. "Pineapple and marshmallow salad," he repeated, thoughtfully, almost wonderingly. Suddenly he threw back the magnificent head and began to laugh. Peal after peal of Herculean laughter. "Pineapple and marsh——" choking, the tears running down his cheeks. Sabra was angry, then frightened. For as suddenly as he had begun to laugh he became serious. He stood up, one hand on the table. Then he seemed to pull his whole body together like a tiger who is about to spring. He stood thus a moment, swaying a little. " 'Actum est de republica.' "

"What?" said Sabra, sharply.

"Latin, Latin, my love. Pineapple and marshmallow salad! 'It is all over with the Republic.' " She shrugged her shoulders impatiently. Yancey turned, stiffly, like a soldier, walked out of the room, flicked his white sombrero off the hall rack and put it on at the usual jaunty angle, went down the porch stair with his light, graceful step, to the sidewalk and up the street, the great head lowered, the arms swinging despondently at his sides.

Sabra went on with her work of tidying up the house. Her eyes burned, her throat was constricted. Men! Men! Cim off with that squaw. Yancey angry because she had given him this very feminine dish of left-overs. What was the use of working, what was the use of pride, what was the use of ambition for your children, your home, your town if this was all it amounted to? Her work done, she allowed herself the luxury of a deliberate and cleansing storm of tears.

Eight o'clock. She heated some of the afternoon coffee and drank it sitting at the kitchen table. She went out on the front porch. Darkness had come on. A hot September evening. The crickets squeaked and ground away in the weeds. She was conscious of an aching weariness in all her body, but she could not sleep. Her eyes felt as though they were being pulled apart by invisible fingers. She put her palms over them, to shut them, to cool them. Nine. Ten. Eleven. Twelve. She undressed, unpinned the braids of her thick hair, brushed it, plaited it for the night. All the time she was listening. Listening. One.

Suddenly she began to dress again with icy fumbling fingers. She did up her hair, put on her hat and a jacket. She closed the door behind her, locked it, slipped the key into the mail box. The *Wigwam* office. Yancey was not there. The office was dark. She shook the door, rattled the knob, peered in, unlocked it with the key in her handbag. Her heart was pounding, but she was not afraid of the darkness. A cat's eyes gleamed at her from the printing shop. She struck a light. No one. No one. The linotype machine grinned at her with its white teeth. Its iron arm and hand shook tauntingly at her in the wavering light. With a sudden premonition she ran to Yancey's desk, opened the drawer in which he kept his holster and six-shooters, now that Osage had become so effete as to make them an unessential article of dress. They were not there. She knew then that Yancey had gone.

Doc Valliant. She closed and locked the door after her, stepped out into the quiet blackness of Pawhuska Avenue. Doc Valliant. He would go with her. He would drive her out there. But his office and the room at the rear, which was his dwelling, gave forth no response. Gone out somewhere— a case. Down the rickety wooden steps of the two-story brick building. She stood a moment in the street, looking this way and that. She struck her palms together in a kind of agony of futility. She would go alone if she had a horse and buggy. She could rent one at the livery stable. But what would they think—those men at the livery stable? They were the gossips of the town. It would be all over Osage, all over the county. Sabra Cravat driving out into the prairie alone in the middle of the night. Something up. Well, she couldn't help that. She had to go. She had to get him

Toward the livery stable, past the Bixby House A quiet

little figure rose from the blackness of the porch where all through the day the traveling men and loafers sat with their chairs tilted back against the wall. The red coal of his cigar was an eye in the darkness.

"Sabra! What is this! What are you doing running around at this hour of the night?"

Sol Levy, sitting there in the Oklahoma night, a lonely little figure, sleepless, brooding. He had never before called her Sabra.

"Sol! Sol! Cim's out at the Reservation. Something's happened. I know. I feel it."

He did not scoff at this, as most men would. He seemed to understand her fear, her premonition, and to accept it with Oriental fatalism.

"What do you want to do?"

"Take me out there. Hitch up and drive me out there. Cim's got the buggy. He went out with her."

He did not ask where Yancey was. He asked nothing. "Go home," he said. "Wait on your porch. I will get my rig and come for you. They shouldn't see you. Do you want me to go home with you first?"

"No, no. I'm not afraid. I'm not afraid of anything."

Sol Levy had two very fine horses; really good animals. They won the races regularly at the local fairs. The little light rig with its smart rubber ties whirled behind them over the red dusty Oklahoma prairie roads. His slim hands were not expert with horses. He was a nervous, jerky driver. They left the town behind them, were swallowed up by the prairie. The Reservation was a full two hours distant. Sabra took off her hat. The night air rushed against her face, cooling it. A half hour.

"Let me drive, will you, Sol?"

Without a word he entrusted the reins to her strong, accustomed hands; the hands of one who had come of generations of horse lovers. The animals sensed the change. They leaped ahead in the darkness. The light buggy rocked and bounced over the rutted roads. Sol asked her nothing. They drove in silence. Presently she began to talk, disjointedly. Yet, surprisingly enough, he seemed intuitively to understand, to fill in the gaps with his own instinct and imagination. What she said sounded absurd; he knew it for tragedy.

". . . pineapple and marshamallow salad . . . hates that kind of thing . . . queer for a long time . . . moody . . . drinking . . . Ruby Big Elk . . . Cim . . . his face . . .

peyote . . . Mescal Ceremony . . . Osage . . . white doeskin dress . . . Theresa Jump . . ."

"I see," said Sol Levy, soothingly. "Sure. Well, sure. The boy will be all right. The boy will be all right. Well, Yancey—you know how he is—Yancey. Do you think he has gone away again? I mean—gone?"

"I don't know." Then, "Yes."

Three o'clock and after. They came in sight of the Osage Reservation, a scattered settlement of sterile farms and wooden shanties sprawled on the bare unlovely prairie.

Darkness. The utter darkness that precedes the dawn. Stillness, except for the thud of their horses' flying hoofs and the whir and bump of the buggy wheels. Then, as Sabra slowed them down, uncertainly, undecided as to what they might best do, they heard it—the weird wavering cadences of the Mescal song, the hail-like clatter of the gourd rattle shaken vigorously and monotonously; and beneath and above and around it all, reverberating, haunting, ominous, the beat of the buckskin drum. Through the still, cool night air of the prairie it came to them—to the overwrought woman, and to the little peaceful Jew. Barbaric sounds, wild, sinister. She pulled up the horses. They sat a moment listening. Listening. The drum. The savage sound of the drum.

Fear was gnawing at her vitals, wringing her very heart with clammy fingers, yet Sabra spoke matter-of-factly, her voice holding a hard little note because she was trying to keep it from quavering.

"He'll be in the Mescal tepee next to Big Elk's House. They built it there when he was Chief, and they still use it regularly for the ceremony. Yancey showed it to me once, when he drove me out here." She stopped and cleared her throat, for her voice was suddenly husky. She wondered, confusedly, if that sound was the drum or her own heart beating. She gave a little cracked laugh that bordered on hysteria. "A drum in the night. It sounds so terrible. So savage."

Sol Levy took the reins from her shaking fingers. "Nothing to be frightened about. A lot of poor ignorant Indians trying to forget their misery. Come." Perhaps no man ever made a more courageous gesture, for the little sensitive Jew was terribly frightened.

Uncertainly, in the blackness, they made their way toward the drum beat. Nearer and nearer, louder and louder. And yet all about, darkness, silence. Only that pulsing cry and rattle and beat pounding through the night like the tide. What if he is not there? thought Sabra.

Sol Levy pulled up in the roadway before the trampled yard that held the Mescal tepee, round, to typify the sun, built of wood, larger than any other building on the Reservation. The horses were frightened, restive. All about in the blackness you heard the stamp of other horses' hoofs, heard them crunching the dried herbage of the autumn prairie. With difficulty he groped his way to a stump that served as hitching post, tied the horses. As he helped Sabra down her knees suddenly bent, and he caught her as she sank. "Oh! It's all right. Stiff, I guess—from the ride." She leaned against him a moment, then straightened determinedly. He took her arm firmly. Together they made their way toward the tent-shaped wooden tepee.

Two great, silent blanketed figures at the door through which the fitful flame of the sacred fire flared. The figures did not speak. They stood there, barring the way. The little Jew felt Sabra's arm trembling in his hand. He peered up into the faces of the silent, immobile figures.

Suddenly, "Hello, Joe!" He turned to Sabra. "It's Joe Yellow Eyes. He was in the store only yesterday. Say, Joe, the lady here—Mrs. Cravat—she wants her son should come out and go home."

The blanketed figures stood silent.

Suddenly Sabra thought, "This is ridiculous."

She loosed her arm. She took a step forward, her profile sharp and clear in the firelight. "I am the woman of Yancey Cravat, the one you call Buffalo Head. If my son is in there I want to take him home now. It is time."

"Sure take um home," replied the blanket that Sol had addressed as Joe Yellow Eyes. He stood aside. Blinking, stumbling a little, Sol and Sabra entered the crowded Mescal tepee.

The ceremony was almost at an end. With daybreak it would be finished. Blinded by the light, Sabra at first could discern nothing except the central fire and the figure crouched before it. Yet her eyes went this way and that, searching for him. Gradually her vision cleared. The figures within the tepee paid no attention to those two white intruders. They stood there in the doorway, bewildered, terrified, brave.

In the center a crescent of earth about six inches high curved around a fire built of sticks so arranged that as the ashes fell they formed a second crescent within the other. A man squatted, tending this fire, watchfully, absorbedly. In the center of the crescent, upon a little star of sage twigs, lay the mescal, symbol of the rite. Facing them was the Chief, old Stump Horn, in the place of honor, the emblems of office in his hands—the rattle, the wand, the fan of eagle plumes. All about the tepee crouched or lay blanketed motionless figures. Some sat with heads bowed, others gazed fixedly upon the central mescal button. All had been eating the mescal or drinking a brew in which it had steeped. Now and then a figure would slowly draw the blanket over his head and sink back to receive the vision. And the song went on, the shaking of the gourd rattle, the beat-beat of the buckskin drum. The air of the room was stifling, the room itself scrupulously clean.

At intervals around the wall, and almost level with the dirt floor, were apertures perhaps sixteen inches square. A little wooden door was shut upon most of these. Near each lay figures limper, more spent ever than the other inert bodies. As Sabra and Sol stood, blinking, they learned the use of these openings. For suddenly nausea overcame one of the Indians crouched in the semicircle near the flame. The man crawled swiftly to one of the little doors, opened it, thrust head and shoulders out into the night air, relieved his body of the drug's overdose.

Sabra only turned her eyes away, searching, searching. Then she saw where the boy lay under his gay striped blanket. His face was covered, but she knew. She knew well how the slim body curled in its blankets, how it lay at night, asleep. This was a different sleep, but she knew. They went to him, picking their way over the crouching figures with the fixed trancelike gaze; the recumbent forms that lay so still. She turned back the blanket. His face was smiling, peaceful, lovely.

She thought, "This is the way I should look at him if he were dead." Then, "He is dead." The boy lay breathing quietly. All about the room was an atmosphere of reverie, of swooning bliss. If the Indians looked at all at Sabra, at the Jew, at their efforts to rouse the boy, it was with the eyes of sleep-walkers. Their lips were gently smiling. Sometimes they swayed a little. The sacred fire leaped orange and scarlet and gold. Old Stump Horn wielded his eagle feather fan, back and forth, back and forth. The quavering cadences of the Mescal song rose and fell to the accompaniment of the gourd rattle and the unceasing drum. The white man and woman, frail both, tugged and strained at the inert figure of the boy.

"Oh, God!" whimpered Sabra. "He's so heavy. What shall

we do?" They bent again, tugged with all their strength, lifted but could not carry him.

"We must drag him," Sol said, at last.

They took an arm each. So, dragging, tugging, past those rapt still forms, past those mazed smiling faces, they struggled with him to the door. The little beads of sweat stood out on her forehead, on her lip. She breathed in choking gasps. Her eyes were wide and staring and dreadful in their determination. The rattle. The drum beat. The high eerie song notes, wordless.

The blackness of the outer air; past the two towering motionless blanketed figures at the door. Dragging him along the earth, through the trampled weeds.

"We can't lift him into the buggy. We can't——" She ran back to the two at the door. She clasped her hands before the one called Joe Yellow Eyes. She lifted her white, agonized face to him. "Help me. Help me." She made a futile gesture of lifting.

The Indian looked at her a moment with a dead, unseeing gaze. Flecks of gold and red and yellow danced, reflected in the black pools of his eyes, and died there. Leisurely, wordless, he walked over to where the boy lay, picked him up lightly in his great arms as though he were a sack of meal, swung him into the buggy seat. He turned, then, and went back to his place at the door.

They drove back to the town of Osage. Cim's body leaned heavily, slackly against hers; his head lay in her lap, like a little boy's. One aching arm she held firmly about him to keep him from slipping to the floor of the buggy, so that finally it ceased to ache and became numb. The dawn came, and then the sunrise over the prairie, its red meeting the red of the Oklahoma earth, so that they drove through a fiery furnace.

She had been quiet enough until now, with a kind of stony quiet. She began to sob; a curious dry racking sound, like a hiccough.

"Now, now," said Sol Levy, and made a little comforting noise between tongue and teeth. "So bad it isn't. What did the boy do, he went out to see the sights on the Reservation and try what it was like to eat this dope stuff—this peyote. Say, when I was a boy I did lots worse."

She did not seem to pay much heed to this, but it must have penetrated her numbed brain at last, for presently she stopped the painful sobbing and looked down at his lovely smiling face in her lap, the long lashes, like a girl's, resting so fragilely on the olive cheek.

"He wanted to go. I wouldn't let him. Is it too late, Sol?"

"Go? Go where?"

"The Colorado School of Mines. Geology."

"Too late! That kid there! Don't talk foolish. September. This is the time to go. It just starts. Sure he'll go."

They drove through the yard, over Sabra's carefully tended grass, of which she was so proud, right to the edge of the porch steps, and so, dragging again and pulling, they got him in, undressed him; she washed his dust-smeared face.

"Well," said Sol Levy. "I guess I go and open the store and then have a good cup of coffee."

She put out her hand. Her lower lip was caught between her teeth, sharp and tight. Her face was distorted absurdly with her effort not to cry. But when he would have patted her grimed and trembling hand with his own, in a gesture of comforting, she caught his hand to her lips and kissed it.

The sound of the horses' hoofs died away on the still morning air. She looked down at Cim. She thought, I will take a bath, and then I will have some coffee, too. Yancey has gone again. Has left me. I know that. How do I know it? Well, nothing more can happen to me now. I have had it all, and I have borne it. Nothing more can happen to me now.

Twenty

FOR years Oklahoma had longed for statehood as a bride awaits the dawn of her wedding day. At last, "Behold the bridegroom!" said a paternal government, handing her over to the Union. "Here is a star for your forehead. Meet the family."

Then, at the very altar, the final words spoken, the pact sealed, the bride had turned to encounter a stranger—an unexpected guest, dazzling, breath-taking, embodying all her wildest girlish dreams.

"Bridegroom—hell!" yelled Oklahoma, hurling herself into the stranger's arms. "What's family to me! Go away! Don't bother me. I'm busy."

The name of the gorgeous stranger was Oil.

Oil. Nothing else mattered. Oklahoma, the dry, the wind-swept, the burning, was a sea of hidden oil. The red prairies, pricked, ran black and slimy with it. The work of years was undone in a day. The sunbonnets shrank back, aghast. Compared to that which now took place the early days following the Run in '89 were idyllic. They swarmed on Oklahoma from every state in the Union. The plains became black with little eager delving figures. The sanguine roads were choked with every sort of vehicle. Once more tent and shanty towns sprang up where the day before had been only open prairie staring up at a blazing sky. Again the gambling tent, the six-shooter, the roaring saloon, the dance hall, the harlot. Men fought, stole, killed, died for a piece of ground beneath whose arid surface lay who knew what wealth of fluid richness. Every barren sun-baked farm was a potential fortune; every ditch and draw and dried-up creek bed might conceal liquid treasure. The Wildcat Field—Panhandle—Cimarron—Crook Nose—Cartwright—Wahoo—Bear Creek—these became magic names; these were the Seven Cities of Cibola, rich beyond Coronado's wildest dream. Millions of barrels of oil burst through the sand and shale and clay and drenched the parched earth. Drill, pump, blast. Nitro-glycerin. Here she comes. A roar. Oklahoma went stark raving mad.

Sabra Cravat went oil mad with the rest of them. Just outside the town of Osage, for miles around, they were drilling. There was that piece of farm land she had bought years ago, when Yancey first showed signs of restlessness. She had thought herself shrewd to have picked up this fertile little oasis in the midst of the bare unlovely plain. She was proud of her bit of farm land with its plump yield of alfalfa, corn, potatoes, and garden truck. She knew now why it had been so prolific. By a whim of nature rich black oil lay under all that surrounding land, rendering it barren through its hidden riches. No taint of corroding oil ran beneath that tract of Cravat farm land, and because of this it lay there now, so green, so lush, with its beans, its squash, its ridiculous onions, taunting her, deriding her, like a mirage in the desert. Queerly enough, she had no better luck with her share in an oil lease for which she had paid a substantial sum—much more than she could afford to lose. Machinery, crew, days of drilling, weeks of drilling, sand, shale, salt. The well had come up dry—a duster.

That which happened to Sabra happened to thousands. The stuff was elusive, tantalizing. Here might be a gusher vomiting millions. Fifty feet away not so much as a spot of grease could be forced to the surface. Fortune seemed to take a delight in choosing strange victims for her pranks. Erv Wissler, the gawk who delivered the milk to Sabra's door each morning, found himself owner of a gusher whose outpourings yielded him seven thousand dollars a day. He could not grasp it. Seven dollars a day his mind might have encompassed. Seven thousand had no meaning.

"Why, Erv!" Sabra exclaimed, when he arrived at her kitchen door as usual, smelling of the barnyard. "Seven thousand dollars a day! What in the world are you going to do with it!"

Erv's putty features and all his loose-hung frame seemed to stiffen with the effort of his new and momentous resolve. "Well, I tell you, Mis' Cravat, I made up my mind I ain't going to make no more Sunday delivery myself. I'm a-going to hire Pete Lynch's boy to take the milk route Sundays."

Everyone in Osage knew the story of Ferd Sloat's wife when the news was brought to her that weeks of drilling on the sterile little Sloat farm had brought up a gusher. They had come running to her across the trampled fields with the news. She had stood there on the back porch of the shabby farmhouse, a bony drudge, as weather-beaten and unlovely as the house itself.

"Millions!" they shouted at her. "Millions and millions! What are you going to do?"

Ferd Sloat's wife had looked down at her hands, shriveled and gnarled from alkali water and rough work. She wiped them now on a corner of her gingham apron with a gesture of utter finality. Her meager shoulders straightened. The querulous voice took on a note of defiance.

"From now on I'm goin' to have the washin' done out."

In those first few frenzied weeks there was no time for scientific methods. That came later. Now, in the rush of it, they all but burrowed in the red clay with their finger nails. Men prowled the plains with divining rods, with absurd things called witch sticks, hoping thus to detect the precious stuff beneath the earth's surface.

For years the meandering red clay roads that were little more than trails had seen only occasional buggies, farm wagons, horsemen, an Indian family creeping along in a miserable cart or—rarely—an automobile making perilous progress through the thick dust in the dry season or the slippery dough in the wet. Now those same roads were choked, impassable. The frail wooden one-way bridges over creeks and draws sagged and splintered with the stream of traffic, but no one took the time to repair them. A torrent of vehicles of every description flowed without ceasing, night and day. Frequently the torrent choked itself with its own volume and then the thousands were piled there, locked, cursing, writhing, battling, on their way to the oil fields. From the Crook Nose field to Wahoo was a scant four miles; it sometimes took half a day to cover it in a motor car. Trucks, drays, wagons, rigs, Fords, buckboards. Every day was like the day of the Opening back in '89. Millionaire promoters from the East, engineers, prospectors, drillers, tool dressers, shooters, pumpers, roustabouts, Indians. Men in oil-soaked overalls that hadn't been changed for days. Men in London tailored suits and shirts from Charvet's. Only the ruthless and desperate survived. In the days of the covered wagon scarcely twenty years earlier those roads had been trails over the hot, dry plains marked by the bleaching skull of a steer or the carcass of a horse, picked clean by the desert scavengers and turned white and desolate to the blazing sky. A wagon wheel, a rusted rim, a split wagon tongue lay at the side of the trail, mute evidence of a traveler laboriously crawling his way across the prairie. Now the ditches by the side of these same roads were strewn with the bodies of wrecked and abandoned automobiles, their skeletons stripped and rotting, their lamps staring up at the sky like sightless eyes, testimony to the passing of the modern ravisher of that tortured region. Up and down the dust-choked roads, fenders ripped off like flies' wings, wheels interlocking, trucks overturned, loads sunk in the mud, plank bridges splitting beneath the strain. Devil take the hindmost. It was like an army push, but without an army's morale or discipline. Bear Creek boasted a killing a day and not a jail nor a courthouse for miles around. Men and women, manacled to a common chain, were marched like slave convicts down the road to the nearest temple of justice, a rough pine shack in a town that had sprung overnight on the prairie. There were no railroads where there had been no towns.

Boilers loaded on two wagons were hauled by twenty-mule-team outfits. Stuck in the mud as they inevitably were, only mules could have pulled the load out. Long lines of them choked the already impassable road. Wagons were heaped with the pipes through which the oil must be led; with lumber, hardware, rigs, tools, portable houses—all the vast paraphernalia of sudden wealth and growth in a frontier community.

Tough careless young boys drove the nitro-glycerin cars, a deadly job on those rough and crowded roads. It was this precious and dreadful stuff that shot the oil up out of the earth. Hard lads in corduroys took their chances and pocketed their high pay, driving the deathdealing wagons, singing as they drove, a red shirt tail tied to a pole flaunting its warning at the back of the load. Often an expected wagon would fail to appear. The workers on the field never took the trouble to trace it or the time to wait for it. They knew that somewhere along the road was a great gaping hole, with never a sizable fragment of wood or steel or bone or flesh anywhere for yards around to tell the tale they already knew.

Acres that had been carefully tended so that they might yield their scanty crop of cabbages, onions, potatoes were abandoned to oil, the garden truck rotting in the ground. Rawboned farmers and their scrawny wives and pindling brats, grown spectacularly rich overnight, walked out of their houses without taking the trouble to move the furniture or lock the door. It was not worth while. They left the sleazy curtains on the windows, the pots on the stove. The oil crew, clanking in, did not bother to wreck the house unless they found it necessary. In the midst of an inferno of oil rigs, drills, smoke, steam, and seeping oil itself the passer-by would often see a weather-beaten farmhouse, its windows broken, its front askew, like a beldame gone mad, gray hair streaming about her crazed face as she stared out at the pandemonium of oil hell about her.

The farmers moved into Osage, or Oklahoma City, or Wahoo. They bought automobiles and silk shirts and gewgaws, like children. The men sat on the front porch in shirt sleeves and stocking feet and spat tobacco juice into the fresh young grass.

Mile on mile, as far as the eye could see, were the skeleton frames of oil rigs outlined against the sky like giant Martian figures stalking across the landscape. Horrible new towns—Bret Harte wooden-front towns—sprang up overnight on the heels of an oil strike; towns inhabited by people who never meant to stay in them; stark and hideous houses thrown up by dwellers who never intended to remain in them; rude frontier crossroad stores stuffed with the necessities of frontier life and the luxuries of sudden wealth all jumbled together in a sort of mercantile miscegenation. The thump and clank of the pump and drill; curses, shouts; the clatter of thick dishes, the clink of glasses, the shrill laughter of women; fly-infested shanties. Oil, smearing itself over the prairies like a plague, killing the grass, blighting the trees, spreading over the surface of the creeks and rivers. Signs tacked to tree stumps or posts; For Ambulance Call 487. Sim Neeley Undertaker. Call 549. Call Dr. Keogh 735.

Oklahoma—the Red People's Country—lay heaving under the hot summer sun, a scarred and dreadful thing with the oil drooling down its face a viscid stream.

Tracy Wyatt, who used to drive the bus and dray line between Wahoo and Osage, standing up to the reins like a good-natured red-faced charioteer as the wagon bumped over the rough roads, was one of the richest men in Oklahoma—in the whole of the United States, for that matter. Wyatt. The Wyatt Oil Company. In another five years the Wyatt Oil Companies. You were to see their signs all over the world. The Big Boys from the East were to come to him, hat in hand, to ask his advice about this; to seek his favor for that. The sum of his daily income was fantastic. The mind simply did not grasp it. Tracy himself was, by now, a portly and not undignified looking man of a little more than fifty. His good-natured, rubicund face wore the grave slightly astonished look of a commonplace man who suddenly finds himself a personage.

Mrs. Wyatt, plainer, more horse-faced than ever in her expensive New York clothes, tried to patronize Sabra Cravat, but the Whipple blood was no match for the Marcy. The new money affected her queerly. She became nervous, full of spleen, and the Eastern doctors spoke to her of high blood pressure.

Sabra frankly envied these lucky ones. A letter from the adder-tongued Felice Venable to her daughter was characteristic of that awesome old matriarch. Sabra still dreaded to open her mother's letters. They always contained a sting.

All this talk of oil and millions and everyone in Oklahoma rolling in it. I'll be bound that you and that husband of yours haven't so much as enough to fill a lamp. Trust Yancey Cravat to get hold of the wrong piece of land. Well, at least you can't be disappointed. It has been like that from the day you married him, though you can't say your mother didn't warn you. I hope Donna will show more sense.

Donna, home after two years at Miss Dignum's on the Hudson, seemed indeed to be a granddaughter after Felice Venable's own heart. She was, in coloring, contour, manner, and outlook, so unlike the other Oklahoma girls—Czarina McKee, Gazelle Slaughter, Jewel Riggs, Maurine Turket—

as to make that tortured, wind-deviled day of her birth on the Oklahoma prairie almost nineteen years ago seem impossible. Even during her homecomings in the summer vacations she had about her an air of cool disdain together with a kind of disillusioned calculation very disconcerting to her former intimates, not to speak of her own family.

The other girls living in Osage and Oklahoma City and Guthrie and Wahoo were true products of the new raw Southwest country. They liked to dress in crude high colors —glaring pinks, cerise, yellow, red, vivid orange, magenta. They made up naïvely with white powder and big daubs of carmine paint on either cheek. The daughters of more wealthy parents drove their own cars in a day when this was considered rather daring for a woman. Donna came home tall, thin to the point of scrawniness in their opinion; sallow, unrouged, drawling, mysterious. She talked with an Eastern accent, ignored the letter *r*, said eyether and nyether and rih'ally and altogether made herself poisonously unpopular with the girls and undeniably stirring to the boys. She paid very little heed to the clumsy attentions of the Oklahoma home-town lads, adopting toward them a serpent-of-the-Nile attitude very baffling to these frank and open-faced prairie products.

Her school days finished, and she a finished product of those days, she now looked about her coolly, calculatingly. Her mother she regarded with a kind of affectionate amusement.

"What a rotten deal you've had, Sabra dear," she would drawl. "Really, I don't see how you've stood it all these years."

Sabra would come to her own defense, goaded by something strangely hostile in herself toward this remote, disdainful offspring. "Stood what?"

"Oh—you know. This being a pioneer woman and a professional Marcy and head-held-high in spite of a bum of a husband."

"Donna Cravat, if you ever again dare to speak like that of your father I shall punish you, big as you are."

"Sabra darling, how can you punish a grown woman? You might slap me, and I wouldn't slap you back, of course. But I'd be terribly embarrassed for you. As for Father— he is a museum piece. You know it."

"Your father is one of the greatest figures the Southwest has ever produced."

"Mm. Well, he's picturesque enough, I suppose. But I wish

215

he hadn't worked so hard at it. And Cim! There's a brother! A great help to me in my career, the men folks of this quaint family."

"I wasn't aware that you were planning a career," Sabra retorted, very much in the manner of Felice Venable. "Unless getting up at noon, slopping around in a kimono most of the day, and lying in the hammock reading is called a career by Dignum graduates. If it is, you're the outstanding success of your class."

"Darling, I adore you when you get viperish and Venable like that. Perhaps you influenced me in my early youth. That's the new psychology, you know. You used to tell me about Grandma trailing around in her white ruffled dimity wrappers and her high heels, never lifting a lily hand."

"At least your grandmother didn't consider it a career."

"Neither do I. This lovely flower-like head isn't so empty as you think, lolling in the front porch hammock. I know it's no use counting on Father, even when he's not off on one of his mysterious jaunts. What is he doing, anyway? Living with some squaw? . . . Forgive me, Mother darling. I didn't mean to hurt you. . . . Cim's just as bad, and worse, because he's weak and hasn't even Dad's phony ideals. You're busy with the paper. That's all right. I'm not blaming you. If it weren't for you we'd all be on the town—or back in Wichita living on Grandma in genteel poverty. I think you're wonderful, and I ought to try to be like you. But I don't want to be a girl reporter. Describing the sumptuous decorations of dandelions and sunflowers at one of Cassandra Sipes' parties."

Goaded by curiosity and a kind of wonder at this unnatural creature, Sabra must put her question: "What do you want to do, then?"

"I want to marry the richest man in Oklahoma, and build a palace that I'll hardly ever live in, and travel like royalty, and clank with emeralds. With my skin and hair they're my stone."

"Oh, emeralds, by all means," Sabra agreed, cuttingly. "Diamonds are so ordinary. And the gentleman that you consider honoring—let me see. From your requirements that would have to be Tracy Wyatt, wouldn't it?"

"Yes," replied Donna, calmly.

"You've probably overlooked Mrs. Wyatt. Of course, Tracey's only fifty-one, and you being nineteen, there's plenty of time if you'll just be patient." She was too amused to be really disturbed.

"I don't intend to be patient, Mamma darling."

Something in her hard, ruthless tone startled Sabra. "Donna Cravat, don't you start any of your monkey business. I saw you cooing and ah-ing at him the other day when we went over the Wyatts' new house. And I heard you saying some drivel about his being a man that craved beauty in his life, and that he should have it; and sneering politely at the new house until I could see him beginning to doubt everything in it, poor fellow. He had been so proud to show it. But I thought you were just talking that New York talk of yours."

"I wasn't. I was talking business."

Sabra was revolted, alarmed, and distressed, all at once. She gained reassurance by telling herself that this was just one of Donna's queer jokes—part of the streak in her that Sabra had never understood and that corresponded to the practical joker in Yancey. That, too, had always bewildered her. Absorbed in the workings of the growing, thriving newspaper the conversation faded to a dim and almost unimportant memory.

Sabra was sufficiently shrewd and level headed to take Sol Levy's sound advice. "You settle down to running your paper, Sabra, and you won't need any oil wells. You can have the best-paying paper and the most powerful in the Southwest. Bigger than Houston or Dallas or San Antonio. Because Osage is going to be bigger and richer than any of them. You mark what I say. Hardly any oil in the town of Osage, but billions of barrels of oil all around it. This town won't be torn to pieces, then. It'll grow and grow. Five years from now it'll look like Chicago."

"Oh, Sol, how can that be?"

"You'll see. There where the gambling tent stood with a mud hole in front of it a few years ago you'll see in another five years a skyscraper like those in New York."

She laughed at that.

Just as she had known that Yancey had again left her on that night of the Mescal ceremony, so now she sensed that he would come back in the midst of this new insanity that had seized all Oklahoma. And come back he did, from God knows where, on the very crest of the oil wave, and bringing with him news that overshadowed his return. He entered as he had left, with no word of explanation, and, as always, his entrance was so dramatic, so bizarre as to cause everything else to fade into the background.

He came riding, as always, but it was a sorry enough

nag that he bestrode this time; and his white sombrero was grimed and battered, the Prince Albert coat was spotted, the linen frayed, the whole figure covered with the heavy red dust of the trampled road. He must have ridden like an avenging angel, for his long black locks were damp, his eyes red rimmed. And when she saw this Don Quixote, so sullied, so shabby, her blood turned to water within her veins for pity.

She thought, it will always be like this as long as he lives, and each time he will be a little more broken, older, less and less the figure of splendor I married, until at last . . .

She only said, "Yancey," quietly.

He was roaring, he was reeling with Jovian laughter as he strode into the *Wigwam* office where she sat at her neat orderly desk just as she had sat on that day years before. For a dreadful moment she thought that he was drunk or mad. He flung his soiled white sombrero to the desk top, he swept her into his arms, he set her down.

"Sabra! Here's news for you. Jesse! Heh, Jesse! Where's that rum-soaked son of a printer's devil? Jesse! Come in here! God, I've been laughing so that I almost rolled off my horse." He was striding up and down as of old, his shabby coat tails spreading with the vigor of his movements, the beautiful hands gesticulating, the fine eyes—bloodshot now —still flashing with the fire that would burn until it consumed him.

"Oil, my children! More oil than anybody ever thought there was in any one spot in the world. And where! Where! On the Osage Indian Reservation. It came in an hour ago, like the ocean. It makes every other field look like the Sahara. There never was such a joke! It's cosmic—it's terrible. How the gods must be roaring. 'Laughter unquenchable among the blessed gods!' "

"Yancey dear, we're used to oil out here. It's an old story. Come now. Come home and have a hot bath and clean clothes." In her mind's eye she saw those fine white linen shirts of his all neatly stacked in the drawer as he had left them.

For answer he reached out with one great arm and swept a pile of exchanges, copy paper, galley proofs, and clippings off the desk, while with the other hand he seized the typewriter by its steel bar and plumped it to the floor with a force that wrung a protesting whine and zing from its startled insides. He had always scorned to use a typewriter. The black swathes of his herculean pencil bit deeper

218

into the paper's surface than any typewriter's metal teeth.

"Hot bath! Hot hell, honey! Do you realize what this means? Do you understand that two thousand Osage Indians, squatting in their rags in front of their miserable shanties, are now the richest nation in the world? In the world, I tell you. They were given that land—the barest, meanest desert land in the whole of the Oklahoma country. And the government of these United States said, 'There, you red dogs, take that and live on it. And if you can't live on it, then die on it.' God A'mighty, I could die myself with laughing. Millions and millions of dollars. They're spattering, I tell you, all over the Osage Reservation. There's no stopping that flow. Every buck and squaw on the Osage Reservation is a millionaire. They own that land, and, by God, I'm going to see that no one takes it away from them!"

"Oh, Yancey, be careful."

He was driving his pencil across the paper. "Send this out A.P. They tried to keep it dark when the flow came, but I'll show them. Sabra, kill your editorial lead, whatever it was. I'll write it. Make this your news lead, too. Listen. 'The gaudiest star-spangled cosmic joke that ever was played on a double-dealing government burst into fireworks to-day when, with a roar that could be heard for miles around, thousands of barrels of oil shot into the air on the miserable desert land known as the Osage Indian Reservation and occupied by those duped and wretched——!"

"We can't use that, I tell you."

"Why not?"

"This isn't the Cimarron. It's the state of Oklahoma. That's treason—that's anarchy——"

"It's the truth. It's history. I can prove it. They'll be down on those Osages like a pack of wolves. At least I'll let them know they're expected. I'll run the story, by God, as I want it run, and they can shoot me for it."

"And I say you won't. You can't come in here like that. I'm editor of this paper."

He turned quietly and looked at her, the great head jutting out, the eyes like cold steel. "Who is?"

"I am."

Without a word he grasped her wrist and led her out, across the old porch, down the steps and into the street. There, on Pawhuska Avenue, in the full glare of noonday, he pointed to the weather-worn sign that he himself, aided by Jesse Rickey, had hung there almost twenty years before.

She had had it painted and repainted. She had had it repaired. She had never replaced it with another.

THE OKLAHOMA WIGWAM

YANCEY CRAVAT PROPR. AND EDITOR

"When you take that down, Sabra honey, and paint your own name up in my place, you'll be the editor of this newspaper. Until you do that, I am."

As they stood there, she in her neat blue serge, he in his crumpled and shabby attire, she knew that she never would do it.

Twenty-one

YOUNG CIM came home from Colorado for the summer vacation, was caught up in the oil flood, and never went back. With his geological knowledge, slight as it was, and his familiarity with the region, he was shuttled back and forth from one end of the state to the other. Curiously enough Cim, like his father, was more an onlooker than a participant in this fantastic spectacle. The quality of business acumen seemed to be lacking in both these men; or perhaps a certain mad fastidiousness in them kept them from taking part in the feverish fight. A hint of oil in this corner, a trace of oil in that, and the thousands were upon it, pushing, scrambling, nose to the ground, down on all-fours like pigs in a trough. A hundred times Yancey could have bought an oil lease share for a song. Head lolling on his breast, lids lowered over the lightning eyes, he shrugged indifferent shoulders.

"I don't want the filthy muck," he said. "It stinks. Let the Indians have it. It's theirs. And the Big Boys from the East—let them sweat and scheme for it. They know where Oklahoma is now, all right."

His comings and goings had ceased to cause Sabra the keen agony of earlier days. She knew now that their existence, so long as Yancey lived, would always be made up of just such unexplained absences and melodramatic homecomings. She had made up her mind to accept the inevitable.

She did not mind that Yancey spent much time on the oil fields. He knew the men he called the Big Boys from the

East, and they often sought him out for his company, which they found amusing, and for a certain regional wisdom that they considered valuable. He despised them and spent most of his time with the pumpers and roustabouts, drillers and tool dressers and shooters—a hard-drinking, hard-talking, hard-fighting crew. In his white sombrero and his outdated Prince Albert and his high-heeled boots he was known as a picturesque character. Years of heavy drinking were taking their toll of the magnificent body and mind. The long locks showed streaks of gray.

Local townsmen who once had feared and admired him began to patronize him or to laugh at him, tolerantly. Many of them were rich now, counting their riches not in thousands but in millions. They had owned a piece of Oklahoma dirt, or a piece of a piece of dirt—and suddenly, through no act of theirs, it was worth its weight in diamonds. Pat Leary, the pugnacious little Irish lawyer who had once been a section hand in the early days of the building of the Santa Fé road, was now so rich through his vast oil holdings that his Indian wife, Crook Nose, was considered a quaint and picturesque note by the wives of Eastern operators who came down on oil business.

After the first shrill excitement of it Sabra Cravat relinquished the hope of making sudden millions as other luckier ones had done. Her land had yielded no oil; she owned no oil leases. It was a curious fact that Sabra still queened it in Osage and had actually become a power in the state. The paper was read, respected, and feared throughout the Southwest. It was said with pride by Osage's civic minded that no oil was rich enough to stain the pages of the *Oklahoma Wigwam*. Though few realized it, and though Sabra herself never admitted it, it was Yancey who had made this true. He neglected it for years together, but he always turned up in a crisis, whether political, economic, or social, to hurl his barbed editorials at the heads of the offenders, to sting with the poison of his ridicule. He championed the Indians, he denounced the oil kings, he laughed at the money grabbers, he exposed the land thieves. He was afraid of nothing. He would absent himself for six months. The *Wigwam* would run along smoothly, placidly. He would return, torch in hand, and again set fire to the paper until the town, the county, the state were ablaze. The Osages came to him with their legal problems, and he advised them soundly and took a minimum fee. He seemed always to sense an important happening from afar and to emerge,

221

growling like an old lion, from his hidden jungle lair, broken, mangy, but fighting, the fine eyes still alight, the magnificent head still as menacing as that of a buffalo charging. He had, on one occasion, come back just in time to learn of Dixie Lee's death.

Dixie had struck oil and had retired, a rich woman. She had closed her house and gone to Oklahoma City, and there she bought a house in a decent neighborhood and adopted a baby girl. She had gone to Kansas City for it, and though she had engaged a capable and somewhat bewildered nurse on that trip, Dixie herself carried the child home in her arms, its head close against the expensive satin bosom.

No one knew what means she had used to pull the wool over the eyes of the Kansas City authorities. She never could have done it in Oklahoma. She had had the child almost a year when the women of Osage got wind of it. They say she took it out herself in its perambulator daily, and perhaps someone recognized her on the street, though she looked like any plump and respectable matron now, in her rich, quiet dress and her pince nez, a little gray showing in the black, abundant hair.

Sabra Cravat heard of it. Mrs. Wyatt. Mrs. Doc Nisbett. Mrs. Pack.

They took the child away from her by law. Six months later Dixie Lee died; the sentimental said of a broken heart. It was Yancey Cravat who wrote her obituary:

Dixie Lee, for years one of the most prominent citizens of Osage and a pioneer in the early days of Oklahoma, having made the Run in '89, one of the few women who had the courage to enter that historic and terrible race, is dead.

She was murdered by the good women of Osage. . . .

The story was a nine-days' wonder, even in that melodramatic state. Sabra read it, white faced. The circulation of the *Wigwam* took another bound upward.

"Some day," said Osage, over its afternoon paper, "somebody is going to come along and shoot old Cimarron."

"I should think his wife would save them the trouble," someone suggested.

If Yancey's sporadic contributions increased the paper's circulation it was Sabra's steady drive that maintained it. It was a gigantic task to keep up with the changes that were sweeping over Osage and all of Oklahoma. Yet the columns of the *Wigwam* recorded these changes in its news columns, in its editorial pages, in its personal and local items and its advertisements, as faithfully as on that day of its first issue when Yancey had told them who killed Pegler. Perhaps it was because Sabra, even during Yancey's many absences, felt that the paper must be prepared any day to meet his scathing eye.

Strange items began to appear daily in the paper's columns —strange to the eye not interested in oil; but there was no such eye in Oklahoma, nor, for that matter, in the whole Southwest. Cryptic though these items might be to dwellers in other parts of the United States, they were of more absorbing interest to Oklahomans than front-page stories of war, romance, intrigue, royalty, crime.

> Indian Territory Illuminating Oil Company swabbed 42 barrels in its No. 3 Lizzie in the northwest corner of the southwest of the northwest of 11–8–6 after having plugged back to 4,268 feet and shooting with 52 quarts.
>
> The wildcat test of McComb two miles north of Kewoka which is No. 1 Sutton in the southwest corner of the southeast of the northeast of 35–2–9 was given a shot of 105 quarts in the sand from 1,867 feet and hole bridged. As it stands it is estimated good for 450 barrels daily.

The paper's ads reflected the change. The old livery stable, with its buggies and phaëtons, its plugs to be hired, its tobacco-chewing loungers, its odor of straw, manure, and axle grease, was swept away, and in its place was Fink's Garage and Auto Livery. Repairs of All Kinds. Buy a Stimson Salient Six. The smell of gasoline, the hiss of the hose, lean young lads with grease-grimed fingers, engine wise.

Come to the Chamber of Commerce Dinner. The Oklahoma City College Glee Club will sing.

Osage began to travel, to see the world. Their wanderings were no longer local. Where, two years ago, you read that Dr. and Mrs. Horace McGill are up from Concho to do their Christmas buying, you now saw that Mr. and Mrs. W. Fletcher Busby have left for a trip to Europe, Egypt, and the Holy Land. You knew that old Wick Busby had made his pile in oil and that Nettie Busby was out to see the world.

Most astounding of all were the Indian items, for now the *Oklahoma Wigwam* and every other paper in the county regularly ran news about those incredible people who in one short year had leaped from the Neolithic Age to Broadway.

The Osage Indians, a little more than two thousand in number, who but yesterday were a ragged, half-fed, and listless band, squatting wretchedly on the Reservation allotted them, waiting until time, sickness, and misery should blot them forever from the land, were now, by a miracle of nature, the richest nation in the world. The barren ground on which they had lived now yielded the most lavish oil flow in the state. Yancey Cravat's news story and editorial had been copied and read all over the country. A stunned government tried to bring order out of a chaos of riches. The two thousand Osages were swept off the Reservation to make way for the flood of oil that was transmuted into a flood of gold. They were transported to a new section called Wazhazhe, which is the ancient Indian word for Osage.

Agents appointed. Offices established. Millions of barrels of oil. Millions of dollars. Millions of dollars yearly to be divided somehow among two thousand Osage Indians, to whom a blanket, a bowl of soffica, a mangy pony, a bit of tobacco, a disk of peyote had meant riches. And now every full blood, half blood, or quarter blood Osage was put on the Indian Roll, and every name on the Indian Roll was entitled to a Head Right. Every head right meant a definite share in the millions. Five in a family—five head rights. Ten in a family—ten head rights. The Indian Agent's office was full of typewriters, files, pads, ledgers, neat young clerks all occupied with papers and documents that read like some fantastic nightmare. The white man's eye, traveling down the tidy list, with its story-book Indian names and its hard, cold, matter-of-fact figures, rejected what it read as being too absurd for the mind to grasp.

Clint Tall Meat	$523,000
Benny Warrior	$192,000
Ho ki ah se	$265,887
Long Foot Magpie	$387,942

The government bought them farms with their own oil money, and built big red brick houses near the roadside and furnished them in plush and pianos and linoleum and gas ranges and phonographs. You saw their powerful motor cars, dust covered, whirling up and down the red clay Oklahoma roads—those roads still rutted, unpaved, hazardous, for Oklahoma had had no time to attend to such matters. Fifty years before, whole bands of Osages on their wiry little ponies had traveled south in the winter and north in the summer to visit their Indian cousins. Later, huddled miserably on their Reservation, they had issued forth on foot or in wretched wagons to pay their seasonal visits and to try to recapture, by talk and song and dance and ritual, some pale ghost of their departed happiness. A shabby enough procession, guarded, furtive, smoldering.

But now you saw each Osage buck in his high-powered car, his inexpert hands grasping the wheel, his enormous sombrero—larger even than the white man's hat—flapping in the breeze that he made by his speed. In the back you saw the brilliance of feathers and blankets worn by the beady-eyed children and the great placid squaw crouched in the bottom of the car. The white man driving the same road gave these Indian cars a wide berth, for he knew they stopped for no one, kept the middle of the road, flew over bridges, draws, and ditches like mad things.

Grudgingly, for she still despised them, Sabra Cravat devoted a page of the *Wigwam* to news of the Osages, those moneyed, petted wards of a bewildered government. The page appeared under the title of Indian News, and its contents were more than tinged with the grotesque.

Long Foot Magpie and wife were week-end visitors of Plenty Horses at Watonga recently.

Grandma Standing Woman of near Hominy was a visitor at the home of Red Paint Woman.

Mr. and Mrs. Sampson Lame Bull have returned from Osage after accompanying Mrs. Twin Woman, who is now a patient in the Osage Hospital.

Albert Short Tooth and Robert White Eyes are batching it at the home of Mrs. Ghost Woman during her absence.

Laura Bird Woman and Thelma Eagle Nest of near here motored to Grey Horse to visit Sore Head but he was not at home.

Woodson Short Man and wife were shopping in Osage one day last week.

Red Bird Scabby has left the Reservation for a visit to Colorado Springs and Manitou.

Squaw Iki has returned recently after being a patient at the Concho Hospital for some time.

Joe Stump Horn and his wife Mrs. Long Dead are visiting Red Nose Scabby for a few days.

Sun Maker has given up the effort to find a first-class cook in Wazhazhe and is looking around in Osage.

The Osages were *Wigwam* subscribers. They read the paper, or had it read to them if they were of the older and less literate generation. Sabra was accustomed to seeing the doorway suddenly darkened by a huge blanketed form or to look up, startled, to behold the brilliant striped figure standing beside her desk in the business office. If Yancey chanced to be in the occasion became very social.

"How!"

"How!"

"Want um paper."

"All right, Short Tooth. Five dollars."

The blanketed figure would produce a wallet whose cheeks were plump to bursting with round silver dollars, for the Osage loved the sound and feel of the bright metal disks. Down on the desk they clinked.

The huge Osage stood then, waiting. Yancey knew what was wanted, as did Sabra.

"Me want see iron man. Make um name."

Whereupon Yancey or Sabra would conduct the visitor into the composing room. There were three linotype machines now, clanking and chattering away. Once Yancey had taken old Big Elk, Ruby's father, back there to see how the linotype turned liquid lead into printed words. He had had Jesse Rickey, at the linotype's keyboard, turn out old Big Elk's name in the form of a neat metal bar, together with the paper slip of its imprint.

There was no stopping it. The story of the iron monster that could talk and write and move spread like a prairie fire through Wazhazhe. Whole families subscribed separately for the *Oklahoma Wigwam*—bucks, squaws, girls, boys, papooses in arms. The iron monster had for them a fascination that was a mingling of admiration, awe, and fear. It was useless to explain that they need not take out a subscription in order to own one of these coveted metal bars. It had been done once. They always would do it that way. Sabra, if she happened to be in charge, always gave the five dollars to her pet charity, after trying in vain to refuse it when proffered. Yancey took it cheerfully and treated the boys at the new Sunny South Saloon, now a thing of splendor with its mahogany bar, its brass rail, its mirror, chandeliers, and flesh-tinted oil paintings.

Up and down the dusty Oklahoma roads at terrific speed, up and down Pawhuska Avenue, went the blanketed figures in their Packard and Pierce Arrow cars. The merchants of Osage liked to see them in town. It meant money freely spent on luxuries. The Osage Indian men were broad shouldered, magnificent, the women tall, stately. Now they grew huge with sloth and overfeeding. They ate enormously and richly. They paced Pawhuska Avenue with slow measured tread; calm, complete, grandly content. The women walked bareheaded, their brilliant blankets, striped purple and orange and green and red, wrapped about their shoulders and enveloping them from neck to heels. But beneath this you saw dresses of silk, American in make and style. On their feet were slippers of pale fine kid, high-heeled, or of patent-leather, ornamented with buckles of cut steel, shining and costly. The men wore the blanket, too, but beneath it they liked a shirt of silk brocade in gorgeous colors—bright green or purple or cerise—its tail worn outside the trousers, and the trousers often as not trimmed with a pattern of beadwork at the side. On their heads they wore huge sombreros trimmed with bands of snakeskin ornamented with silver. They hired white chauffeurs to drive their big sedan cars and sat back grandly after ordering them to drive round and round and round the main business block. Jewelry shops began to display their glistening wares in Osage, not so much in the hope of winning the favor of the white oil millionaire as the red. Bracelets, watches, gaudy rings and pins and bangles and beads and combs and buckles. Diamonds. These the Indians seemed instinctively to know about, and they bought them clear and blue-white and costly.

The Levy Mercantile Company had added a fancy grocery and market department to its three-story brick store. It was situated on the street floor and enhanced with a great plate-glass window. In this window Sol displayed a mouth-watering assortment of foods. Juicy white stalks of asparagus in glass, as large around as a man's two thumbs; great ripe olives, their purple-black cheeks glistening with oil; lobster, mushrooms, French peas, sardines, mountainous golden cheeses, tender broilers, peaches in syrup, pork roasts dressed in frills. Dozens of chickens, pounds of pork, baskets of delicacies were piled in the cars of homeward bound Osages. Often, when the food bills mounted too high, the Indian Agent at Wazhazhe threatened to let the bill go unpaid. He alone had the power to check the outpouring of Indian gold, and even he frequently was unable to cope with their mad extravagances.

"It's disgusting," Sabra Cravat said, again and again. "What are they good for? What earthly good are they? Ignorant savages who do nothing but eat and sleep and drive around in their ridiculous huge automobiles."

"Keep money in circulation," Sol Levy replied, for she often took him to task after seeing a line of Indian cars parked outside the Osage Mercantile Company's store.

"You ought to be ashamed of yourself."

"Now, now, Sabra. Not so grand, please. I don't do like dozens of other merchants here in town. Make out bills for goods they haven't bought and give them the money. Or charge them double on the bill that the Indian Agent sees, and return them the overcharge. They come in my store, they buy, they pay what the article is marked, and they get what they pay for. Inez Bull comes in and gets a silk step-in, or Sun Maker he buys twelve pounds of chicken and ten pounds of pork. I should tell them they can't have it! Let the President of the United States do it. The Big White Father."

Not only did Yancey agree with Sol, he seemed to find enormous satisfaction in the lavishness with which they spent their oil money; in the very absurdity of the things they bought.

"The joke gets better and better. We took their land away from them and exterminated the buffalo, then expected them to squat on the Reservations weaving baskets and molding pottery that nobody wanted to buy. Well, at least the Osages never did that. They're spending their money just as the white people do when they get a handful of it—chicken and plush and automobiles and phonographs and silk shirts and jewelry."

"Why don't they do some good with it?" Sabra demanded.

"What good's Wyatt doing? Or Nisbett, or old Buckner, or Ike Hawes, or their wives! Blowing it on houses and travel and diamonds and high-priced cars."

"The Osages could help the other tribes—poor Indian tribes that haven't struck oil."

"Maybe they will—when Bixby gives away his millions to down-and-out hotel keepers who are as poor as he was when he ran the Bixby House, back in the old days."

"Filthy savages!"

"No, honey. Just blanket Indians—horse Indians—Plains Indians, with about twenty-five millions of dollars a year gushing up out of the earth and splattering all around them. The wonder to me is that they don't die laughing and spoil their own good time."

Sometimes Sabra encountered old Big Elk and his vast

squaw and Ruby Big Elk, together with others of the family —a large one for an Osage—driving through Pawhuska Avenue. With their assembled head rights the family was enormously rich—one of the wealthiest on the Wazhazhe Reservation. When the Big Elks drove through the town it was a parade. No one car could have contained the family, though they would have scorned such economy even if it had been possible.

They made a brilliant Indian frieze in the modern manner. Old Big Elk and his wife, somewhat conservatively, lolled in a glittering Lincoln driven by a white chauffeur. Through the generous glass windows you saw the two fat bronze faces, the massive bodies, the brilliant colors of their blankets and chains and beads. One of the Big Elk boys drove a snow-white Pierce Arrow roadster that tore and shrieked like an avenging demon up and down the dusty road between Osage and Wazhazhe. Ruby herself, and a sister-in-law or so, and a brother, might follow in one of the Packards, while still another brother or sister preferred a Cadillac. If they walked at all it was to ascend with stately step the entrance to the Indian Agent's Office. The boys wore American dress, with perhaps an occasional Indian incongruity—beaded pants, a five-gallon hat with an eagle feather in it, sometimes moccasins. Ruby and her sisters and her sister-in-law wore the fine and gaudy blanket over their American dresses, they were hatless, and their long bountiful hair was done Indian fashion. The dress of old Big Elk and his wife was a gorgeous mixture of Indian and American, with the Indian triumphantly predominating. About the whole party, as in the case of any of the Osage oil families, there was an air of quiet insolence, of deep rich triumph.

Sabra always greeted them politely enough. "How do you do, Ruby," she would say. "What a beautiful dress." Ruby would say nothing. She would look at Sabra's neat business dress of dark blue or gray, at Sabra's plain little hat and sensible oxford ties. "Give my regards to your father and mother," Sabra would continue, blandly, but inwardly furious to find herself feeling uncomfortable and awkward beneath this expressionless Indian gaze. She fancied that in it there was something menacing, something triumphant. She wondered if Ruby, the oft-married, had married yet again. Once she asked young Cim about her, making her tone casual. "Do you ever see that girl who used to work here— Ruby, wasn't that it? Ruby Big Elk?"

Cim's tone was even more casual than hers. "Oh, yes.

We were working out Wazhazhe way, you know, on the Choteau field. That's near by."

"They're terribly rich, aren't they?"

"Oh, rotten. A fleet of cars and a regular flock of houses."

"It's a wonder that some miserable white squaw man hasn't married that big greasy Ruby for her head right. Mrs. Conn Sanders told me that one of the Big Elk boys was actually playing golf out at the Westchester Apawamis Club last Saturday. It's disgusting. He must know there's a rule against Indians. Mrs. Sanders reported him to the house committee."

"There's a rule, all right. But you ought to see the gallery when Standing Bear whams it out so straight and so far that he makes the pro look like a ping-pong player."

"How is he in a tomahawk contest?"

"Oh, Mother, you talk like Grandma when she used to visit here."

"The Marcys and the Venables didn't hobnob with dirty savages in blankets."

"Standing Bear doesn't wear his blanket when he plays golf," retorted Cim, coolly. "And he took a shower after he'd made the course in seven below par."

Donna came home from a bridge party one afternoon a week later, the creamy Venable pallor showing the Marcy tinge of ocherous rage. She burst in upon Sabra, home from the office.

"Do you know that Cim spends his time at the Big Elks' when we think he's out in the oil fields?"

Sabra met this as calmly as might be. "He's working near there. He told me he had seen them."

"Seen them! That miserable Gazelle Slaughter said that he's out there all the time. All the time, I tell you, and that he and Ruby drive around in her car, and he eats with them, he stays there, he——"

"I'll speak to your father. Cim's coming home Saturday. Gazelle is angry at Cim, you know that, because he won't notice her and she likes him."

She turned her clear appraising gaze upon this strange daughter of hers. She thought, suddenly, that Donna was like a cobra, with that sleek black head, that cold and slanting eye, that long creamy throat in which a pulse sometimes could be seen to beat and swell a little—the only sign of emotion in this baffling creature.

"I'll tell you what, Donna. If you'd pay a little less

attention to your brother's social lapses and a little more to your own vulgar conduct, perhaps it would be better."

Donna bestowed her rare and brilliant smile upon her forthright mother. "Now, now, darling! I suppose I say, 'What do you mean?' And you say, 'You know very well what I mean.'"

"You certainly do know what I mean. If you weren't my own daughter I'd say your conduct with Tracy Wyatt was that of a—a——"

"Harlot," put in Donna, sweetly.

"Donna! How can you talk like that? You are breaking my heart. Haven't I had enough? I've never complained, have I? But now—you——"

Donna came over to her and put her arms about her, as though she were the older woman protecting the younger. "It's all right, Mamma darling. You just don't understand. Life isn't as simple as it was when you were a frontier gal. I know what I want and I'm going to get it."

Sabra shrugged away from her; faced her with scorn. "I've seen you. I'm ashamed for you. You press against him like a—like a——" Again she could not say it. Another generation. "And that horse you ride. You say he loans it to you. He gave it to you. It's yours. What for?"

She was weeping.

"I tell you it's all right, Mamma. He did give it to me. He wants to give me lots of things, but I won't take them, yet. Tracy's in love with me. He thinks I'm young and beautiful and stimulating and wonderful. He's married to a dried-up, vinegary, bitter old hag who was just that when he married her, years ago. He's never known what love is. She has never given him children. He's insanely rich, and not too old, and rather sweet. We're going to be married. Tracy will get his divorce. Money does anything. It has taken me a year and a half to do it. I've never worked so hard in all my life. But it's going to be worth it. Don't worry, darling. Tracy's making an honest woman of your wayward daughter."

Sabra drew herself up, every inch the daughter of her mother, Felice Venable, née Marcy. "You are disgusting."

"Not really, if you just look at it without a lot of sentiment. I shall be happy, and Tracy, too. His wife will be unhappy, I suppose, for a while. But she isn't happy anyway, as it is. Better one than three. It'll work out. You'll see. Don't bother about me. It's Cim that needs looking after. He's got a streak of—of——" She looked at her mother. Did not finish the sentence. "When he comes home Saturday I wish you'd speak to him."

Twenty-two

BUT Cim did not come home on Saturday. On Saturday, at noon, when Sabra and Yancey drove from the office in their little utility car to the house on Kihekah Street for their noonday dinner they saw a great limousine drawn up at the curb. A chauffeur, vaguely familiar, lounged in front. The car was thick with the red dust of the country road.

A vague pang of premonition stabbed at Sabra's vitals. She clutched Yancey's arm. "Whose car is that?"

Yancey glanced at it indifferently. "Somebody drove Cim home, I suppose. Got enough dinner for company?"

Donna had gone to Oklahoma City to spend the weekend. It must be Cim.

"Cim!" Sabra called, as she entered the front door. "Cim!" But there was no answer. She went straight to the sitting room. Empty. But in the stiff little parlor, so seldom used, sat two massive, silent figures. With the Indian sense of ceremony and formality old Big Elk and his squaw had known the proper room to use for an occasion such as this.

"Why—Big Elk!"

"How!" replied Big Elk, and held up his palm in the gesture of greeting.

"Yancey!" cried Sabra suddenly, in a terrible voice. The two pairs of black Indian eyes stared at her. Sabra saw that their dress was elaborate; the formal dress reserved for great occasions. The woman wore a dark skirt and a bright cerise satin blouse, ample and shaped like a dressing sacque. Over her shoulders was the fine bright-hued blanket. Her hair was neatly braided and wound about her hatless head. She wore no ornaments. That was the prerogative of the male. Old Big Elk was a structure of splendor. His enormous bulk filled the chair. His great knees were wide apart. His blue trousers were slashed and beaded elaborately at the sides and on his feet were moccasins heavy with intricate bead-work. His huge upper body was covered with a shirt of brilliant green brocade worn outside the trousers, and his striped blanket hung regally from his shoulders. About his neck and on his broad breast hung chains, beads, necklaces. In the bright silk neckerchief knotted about his throat you saw the silver emblem of his former glory as chief of the tribe. There were other insignia of distinction made of beaten silver—the star, the crescent, the sun. On his head was a round high cap of brown beaver like a Cossack's. Up the back of this was stuck an eagle feather. His long locks, hanging about his shoulders, straight and stiff, were dyed a brilliant orange, like an old burlesque queen's, a startling, a fantastic background for the parchment face, lined and creased and crisscrossed with a thousand wrinkles. One hand rested on his knee. The other wielded languidly, back and forth, back and forth, an enormous semicircular fan made of eagle feathers. Side by side the two massive figures sat like things of bronze. Only their eyes moved, and that nightmarish eagle feather fan, back and forth, back and forth, regally.

Those dull black unsmiling eyes, that weaving fan, moved Sabra to nameless terror. "Yancey!" she cried again, through stiff lips. "Yancey!"

At the note of terror in her voice he was down the stairs and in the room with his quick light step. But at sight of old Big Elk and his wife his look of concern changed to one of relief. He smiled his utterly charming smile.

"How!"

"How!" croaked Big Elk.

Mrs. Big Elk nodded her greeting. She was a woman younger, perhaps, by thirty years than her aged husband; his third wife. She spoke English; had even attended an Indian Mission school in her girlhood. But through carelessness or indifference she used the broken, slovenly English of the unlettered Indian.

Now the two relapsed into impassive silence.

"What do they want? Ask them what they want."

Yancey spoke a few words in Osage. Big Elk replied with a monosyllable.

"What did he say? What is it?"

"I asked them to eat dinner with us. He says he cannot."

"I should hope not. Tell her to speak English. She speaks English."

Big Elk turned his great head, slowly, as though it moved on a mechanical pivot. He stared at his fat, round-faced wife. He uttered a brief command in his own tongue. The squaw smiled a little strange, embarrassed smile, like a schoolgirl— it was less a smile than a contortion of the face, so rare in her race as to be more frightening than a scowl.

"Big Elk and me come take you back to Wazhazhe."

"What for?" cried Sabra, sharply.

"Four o'clock big dinner, big dance. Your son want um come tell you. Want um know he marry Ruby this morning."

She was silent again, smiling her foolish fixed smile. Big Elk's fan went back and forth, back and forth.

"God A'mighty!" said Yancey Cravat. He looked at Sabra, came over to her quickly, but she waved him away.

"Don't. I'm not going to—it's all right." It was as though she shrank from his touch. She stood there, staring at the two barbaric figures staring so stonily back at her with their dead black Indian eyes. It was at times like this that the Marcy in her stood her in good stead. She came of iron stock, fit to stand the fire. Only beneath her fine dark eyes you now suddenly saw a smudge of purplish brown, as though a dirty thumb had rubbed there; and a sagging of all the muscles of her face, so that she looked wattled, lined, old.

"Don't look like that, honey. Come. Sit down."

Again the groping wave of her hand. "I'm all right, I tell you. Come. We must go there."

Yancey came forward. He shook hands formally with Big Elk, with the Indian woman. Sabra, seeing him, suddenly realized that he was not displeased. She knew that no formal politeness would have prevented him from voicing his anger if this monstrous announcement had shattered him as it had her, so that her very vitals seemed to be withering within her.

"Sugar, shake hands with them, won't you?"

"No. No." She wet her dry lips a little with her tongue, like one in a fever. She turned, woodenly, and walked to the door, ignoring the Indians. Across the hall, slowly, like an old woman, down the porch steps, toward the shabby little car next to the big rich one. As she went she heard Yancey's voice (was there an exultant note in it?) at the telephone.

"Jesse! Take this. Get it in. Ready! . . . Ex-Chief Big Elk, of the Osage Nation, and Mrs. Big Elk, living at Wazhazhe, announce the marriage of their daughter Ruby Big Elk to Cimarron Cravat, son of—don't interrupt me—I'm in a hurry—son of Mr. and Mrs. Yancey Cravat, of this city. The wedding was solemnized at the home of the bride's parents and was followed by an elaborate dinner made up of many Indian and American dishes, partaken of by the parents of the bride and the groom, many relatives and numerous friends of the young . . ."

Sabra climbed heavily into the car and sat staring at the broad back of the car ahead of her. Chief Big Elk and his wife came out presently, unreal, bizarre in the brilliant noonday Oklahoma sunshine, ushered by Yancey. He was being charming. They heaved their ponderous bulk into the big car. Yancey got in beside Sabra. She spoke to him once only.

"I think you are glad."

"This is Oklahoma. In a way it's what I wanted it to be when I came here twenty years ago. Cim's like your father, Lewis Venable. Weak stuff, but good stock. Ruby's pure Indian blood and a magnificent animal. It's hard on you now, my darling. But their children and their grand-children are going to be such stuff as Americans are made of. You'll see."

"I hope I shall die before that day."

The shabby little middle-class car followed the one whirling ahead of them over the red clay Oklahoma roads. Eating the dust of the big car just ahead.

She went through it and stood it, miraculously, until one grotesquerie proved too much for her strained nerves and broke them. But she went into the Indian house, and saw Cim sitting beside the Indian woman, and as she looked at his beautiful weak face she thought, I wish that I had never found him that day when he was lost on the prairie long ago. He came toward her, his head lowered with that familiar look, his fine eyes hidden by the lids.

"Look at me!" Sabra commanded, in the voice of Felice Venable. The boy raised his eyes. She looked at him, her face stony. Ruby Big Elk came toward her with that leisurely, insolent, scuffling step. The two women gazed at each other; rather, their looks clashed, like swords held high. They did not shake hands.

There were races, there were prizes, there was dancing. In the old Indian days the bucks had raced on foot for a prize that was a pony tethered at a distance and won by the fleetest to reach him, mount, and ride him back to the starting point. To-day the prize was a magnificent motor car that stood glittering in the open field half a mile distant. Sabra thought, I am dying, I am dying. And Donna. This squaw is her sister-in-law. Miss Dignum's on the Hudson.

Ruby's handsome head right had bought the young couple the house just across the road from Big Elk's—a one-story red brick bungalow, substantial, ugly. They showed Sabra and Yancey through it. It was furnished complete. Mongrel

Spanish furniture in the living room—red plush, fringe, brass nail heads as big as twenty-dollar gold pieces. An upright piano. An oak dining-room set. A fine bathroom with heavy rich bath towels neatly hung on the racks. A shining stained oak bedroom set with a rose-colored taffeta spread. Sabra felt a wave of nausea. Cim's face was smiling, radiant. Yancey was joking and laughing with the Indians. In the kitchen sat a white girl in a gingham dress and a kitchen apron. The girl's hair was so light a yellow as to appear almost white. Her unintelligent eyes were palest blue. Her skin was so fair as to be quite colorless. In the midst of the roomful of dark Indian faces the white face of the new Cravat hired girl seemed to swim in a hazy blob before Sabra's eyes. But she held on. She felt Ruby's scornful dark eyes on her. Sabra had a feeling as though she had been disemboweled and now was a hollow thing, an empty shell that moved and walked and talked.

Dinner. White servants and Negro servants to wait on them. A long table seating a score or more, and many such tables. Bowls and plates piled with food all down the length of it. Piles of crisp pork, roasted in the Indian fashion over hot embers sunk in a pit in the yard, and skewered with a sharp pointed stick. Bowls of dried corn. Great fat, black ripe olives. Tinned lobster. Chicken. Piles of dead ripe strawberries. Vast plateaus of angel-food cake covered with snow fields of icing.

Sabra went through the motions of eating. Sometimes she put a morsel into her mouth and actually swallowed it. There was a great clatter of knives and forks and dishes. Everything was eaten out of one plate. Platters and bowls were replenished. Sabra found herself seated beside Mrs. Big Elk. On her other side was Yancey. He was eating and laughing and talking. Mrs. Big Elk was being almost comically polite, solicitous. She pressed this tidbit, that dainty, on her stony guest.

Down the center of the table, at intervals, were huge bowls piled with a sort of pastry stuffed with forcemeat. It was like a great ravioli, and piles of it vanished beneath the onslaught of appreciative guests.

"For God's sake, pretend to eat something, Sabra," Yancey murmured, under his breath. "It's done now. They consider it an insult. Try to eat something."

She stirred the pastry and chopped meat that had been put on her plate.

"Good," said Mrs. Big Elk, beside her, and pointed at the mass with one dusky maculate finger.

Sabra lifted her fork to her lips and swallowed a bit of it. It was delicious—spicy, rich, appetizing. "Yes," she said, and thought, I am being wonderful. This is killing me. "Yes, it is very good. This meat—this stuffing—is it chopped or ground through a grinder?"

The huge Indian woman beside her turned her expressionless gaze on Sabra. Ponderously she shook her head from side to side in negation.

"Naw," she answered, politely. "Chawed."

The clatter of a fork dropped to the plate, a clash among the cups and saucers. Sabra Cravat had fainted.

Twenty-three

OSAGE was so sophisticated that it had again become simple. The society editor of the *Oklahoma Wigwam* used almost no adjectives. In the old days, you had read that "the house was beautifully decorated with an artistic arrangement of smilax, sent from Kansas City, pink and purple asters in profusion making a bower before which the young couple stood, while in the dining room the brilliance of golden glow, scarlet salvia, and autumn leaves gave a seasonal touch." But now the society column said, austerely, "The decorations were orchids and Pernet roses."

Osage, Oklahoma, was a city.

Where, scarcely two decades ago, prairie and sky had met the eye with here a buffalo wallow, there an Indian encampment, you now saw a twenty-story hotel: the Savoy-Bixby. The Italian head waiter bent from the waist and murmured in your ear his secret about the veal sauté with mushrooms or the spaghetti Caruso du jour. Sabra Cravat, Congresswoman from Oklahoma, lunching in the Louis XIV room with the members of the Women's State Republican Committee, would say, looking up at him with those intelligent dark eyes, "I'll leave it to you, Nick. Only quickly. We haven't much time." Niccolo Mazzarini would say yes, he understood. No one had much time in Osage, Oklahoma. A black jackanapes in a tight scarlet jacket with brass buttons and even tighter bright blue pants, an impudent round red cap cocked over one ear, strolled through the dining room bawling, "Mistah Thisandthat! Mistah Whoandwhat!" He carried messages on a silver salver. There were separate ice-water taps in every bedroom. Servidors. Ring once for the waiter. Twice for the chambermaid. A valet is at your service.

Twenty-five years earlier anybody who was anybody in Oklahoma had dilated on his or her Eastern connections. Iowa, if necessary, was East.

They had been a little ashamed of the Run. Bragged about the splendors of the homes from which they had come.

Now it was considered the height of chic to be able to say that your parents had come through in a covered wagon. Grandparents were still rather rare in Oklahoma. As for the Run of '89—it was Osage's *Mayflower*. At the huge dinner given in Sabra Cravat's honor when she was elected Congresswoman, and from which they tried to exclude Sol Levy over Sabra's vigorous (and triumphant) protest, the chairman of the Committee on Arrangements explained it all to Sol, patronizingly.

"You see, we're inviting only people who came to Oklahoma in the Run."

"Well, sure," said the former peddler, genially. "That's all right. I walked."

The Levy Mercantile Company's building now occupied an entire square block and was fifteen stories high. In the huge plate-glass windows on Pawhuska postured ladies waxen and coquettish, as on Fifth Avenue. You went to the Salon Moderne to buy Little French Dresses, and the saleswomen of this department wore black satin and a very nice little strand of imitation pearls, and their eyes were hard and shrewd and their phrases the latest. The Osage Indian women had learned about these Little French Dresses, and they often came in with their stately measured stride: soft and flaccid from easy living, rolls of fat about their hips and thighs. They tried on sequined dresses, satin dresses, chiffon. Sometimes even the younger Osage Indian girls still wore the brilliant striped blanket, in a kind of contemptuous defiance of the whites. And to these, as well as to the other women customers, the saleswomen said, "That's awfully good this year. . . . That's dreadfully smart on you, Mrs. Buffalo Hide. . . . I think that line isn't the thing for your figure, Mrs. Plenty Vest. . . . My dear, I want you to have that. It's perfect with your coloring."

The daughter of Mrs. Pat Leary (née Crook Nose) always caused quite a flutter when she came in, for accustomed though Osage was to money and the spending of it, the

Learys' lavishness was something spectacular. Hand-made silk underwear, the sheerest of cobweb French stockings, model hats, dresses—well, in the matter of gowns it was no good trying to influence Maude Leary or her mother. They frankly wanted beads, spangles, and paillettes on a foundation of crude color. The saleswomen were polite and acquiescent, but they cocked an eyebrow at one another. Squaw stuff. Now that little Cravat girl—Felice Cravat, Cimarron Cravat's daughter—was different. She insisted on plain, smart tailored things. Young though she was, she was Oklahoma State Woman Tennis Champion. She always said she looked a freak in fluffy things—like a boy dressed up in girl's clothes. She had long, lean, muscular arms and a surprising breadth of shoulder, was slim flanked and practically stomachless. She had a curious trick of holding her head down and looking up at you under her lashes and when she did that you forgot her boyishness, for her lashes were like fern fronds, and her eyes, in her dark face, an astounding ocean gray. She was a good sport, too. She didn't seem to mind the fact that her mother, when she accompanied her, wore the blanket and was hatless, just like any poor Kaw, instead of being one of the richest of the Osages. She was rather handsome for a squaw, in a big, insolent, slow-moving way. Felice Cravat, everyone agreed, was a chip of the old block, and by that they did not mean her father. They were thinking of Yancey Cravat—old Cimarron, her grandfather, who was now something of a legend in Osage and throughout Oklahoma. Young Cim and his Osage wife had had a second child—a boy—and they had called him Yancey, after the old boy. Young Yancey was a bewilderingly handsome mixture of a dozen types and forbears—Indian, Spanish, French, Southern, Southwest. With that long narrow face, the dolichocephalic head, people said he looked like the King of Spain—without that dreadful Hapsburg jaw. Others said he was the image of his grandmother, Sabra Cravat. Still others contended that he was his Indian mother over again—insolence and all. A third would come along and say, "You're crazy. He's old Yancey, born again. I guess you don't remember him. There, look, that's what I mean! The way he closes his eyes as if he were sleepy, and then when he does look at you straight you feel as if you'd been struck by lightning. They say he's so smart that the Osages believe he's one of their old gods come back to earth."

Mrs. Tracy Wyatt (she who had been Donna Cravat)

had tried to adopt one of her brother's children, being herself childless, but Cim and his wife Ruby Big Elk had never consented to this. She was a case, that Donna Cravat, Oklahoma was agreed about that. She could get away with things that any other woman would be shot for. When old Tracy Wyatt had divorced his wife to marry this girl local feeling had been very much against her. Everyone had turned to the abandoned middle-aged wife with attentions and sympathy, but she had met their warmth and friendliness with such vitriol that they fell back in terror and finally came to believe the stories of how she had deviled and nagged old Tracy all through their marriage. They actually came to feel that he had been justified in deserting her and taking to wife this young and fascinating girl. Certainly he seemed to take a new lease on life, lost five inches around the waist line, played polo, regained something of the high color and good spirits of his old dray-driving days, and made a great hit in London during the season when Donna was presented at court. Besides, there was no withstanding the Wyatt money. Even in a country blasé of millionaires Tracy Wyatt's fortune was something to marvel about. The name of Wyatt seemed to be everywhere. As you rode in trains you saw the shining round black flanks of oil cars, thousands of them, and painted on them in letters of white, "Wyatt Oils." Motoring through Oklahoma and the whole of the Southwest you passed miles of Wyatt oil tanks, whole silent cities of monoliths, like something grimly Egyptian, squatting eunuch-like on the prairies.

As for the Wyatt house—it wasn't a house at all, but a combination of the palace of Versailles and the Grand Central Station in New York. It occupied grounds about the size of the duchy of Luxembourg, and on the grounds, once barren plain, had been set great trees brought from England.

A mile of avenue, planted in elms, led up to the mansion, and each elm, bought, transported, and stuck in the ground, had cost fifteen hundred dollars. There were rare plants, farms, forests, lakes, tennis courts, golf links, polo fields, race tracks, airdromes, swimming pools. Whole paneled rooms had been brought from France. In the bathrooms were electric cabinets, and sunken tubs of rare marble, and shower baths glass enclosed. These bathrooms were the size of bedrooms, and the bedrooms the size of ballrooms, and the ballroom as big as an auditorium. There was an ice plant and cooling system that could chill the air of every room in the house, even on the hottest Oklahoma windy day. The kitchen range looked like a house in itself, and the kitchen looked like that of the Biltmore, only larger. When you entered the dining room you felt that here should be seated solemn diplomats in gold braid signing world treaties and having their portraits painted doing it. Sixty gardeners manned the grounds. The house servants would have peopled a village.

Sabra Cravat rarely came to visit her daughter's house, and when she did the very simplicity of her slim straight little figure in its dark blue georgette or black crêpe was startling in the midst of these marble columns and vast corridors and royal hangings. She did come occasionally, and on those occasions you found her in the great central apartment that was like a throne room, standing there before the portraits of her son's two children. Felice and Yancey Cravat. Failing to possess either of the children for her own, Donna had had them painted and hung there, one either side of the enormous fireplace. She had meant them to be a gift to her mother, but Sabra Cravat had refused to take them.

"Don't you like them, Sabra darling? They're the best things Segovia has ever done. Is it because they're modern? I think they look like the kids—don't you?"

"They're just wonderful."

"Well, then?"

"I'd have to build a house for them. How would they look in the sitting room of the house on Kihekah! No, let me come here and look at them now and then. That way they're always a fresh surprise to me."

Certainly they were rather surprising, those portraits. Rather, one of them was. Segovia had got little Felice well enough, but he had made the mistake of painting her in Spanish costume, and somehow her angular contours and boyish frame had not lent themselves to these gorgeous lace and satin trappings. The boy, Yancey, had refused to dress up for the occasion—had, indeed, been impatient of posing at all. Segovia had caught him quickly and brilliantly, with startling results. He wore a pair of loose, rather grimy white tennis pants, a white woolly sweater with a hole in the elbow, and was hatless. In his right hand—that slim, beautiful, speaking hand—he held a limp, half-smoked cigarette, its blue-gray smoke spiraling faintly, its dull red eye the only note of color in the picture. Yet the whole portrait was colorful, moving, alive. The boy's pose was so insolent, so lithe, so careless. The eyes followed you. He was a person.

241

"Looks like Ruby, don't you think?" Donna had said, when first she had shown it to her mother.

"No!" Sabra had replied, with enormous vigor. "Not at all. Your father."

"Well—maybe—a little."

"A little! You're crazy! Look at his eyes. His hands. Of course they're not as beautiful as your father's hands were—are . . ."

It had been five years since Sabra had heard news of her husband, Yancey Cravat. And now, for the first time, she felt that he was dead, though she had never admitted this. In spite of his years she had heard that Yancey had gone to France during the war. The American and the English armies had rejected him, so he had dyed his graying hair, lied about his age, thrown back his still magnificent shoulders, and somehow, by his eyes, his voice, his hands, or a combination of all these, had hypnotized them into taking him. An unofficial report had listed him among the missing after the carnage had ceased in the shambles that had been a wooded plateau called the Argonne.

"He isn't dead," Sabra had said, almost calmly. "When Yancey Cravat dies he'll be on the front page, and the world will know it."

Donna, in talking it over with her brother Cim, had been inclined to agree with this, though she did not put it thus to her mother. "Dad wouldn't let himself die in a list. He's too good an actor to be lost in a mob scene."

But a year had gone by.

The *Oklahoma Wigwam* now issued a morning as well as an afternoon edition and was known as the most powerful newspaper in the Southwest. Its presses thundered out tens of thousands of copies an hour, and hour on hour—five editions. Its linotype room was now a regiment of iron men, its staff boasted executive editor, editor in chief, managing editor, city editor, editor, and on down into the dozens of minor minions. When Sabra was in town she made a practice of driving down to the office at eleven every night, remaining there for an hour looking over the layout, reading the wet galley proof of the night's news lead, scanning the A.P. wires. Her entrance was in the nature of the passage of royalty, and when she came into the city room the staff all but saluted. True, she wasn't there very much, except in the summer, when Congress was not in session.

The sight of a woman on the floor of the Congressional House was still something of a novelty. Sentimental America had shrunk from the thought of women in active politics. Woman's place was in the Home, and American Womanhood was too exquisite a flower to be subjected to the harsh atmosphere of the Assembly floor and the committee room.

Sabra stumped the state and developed a surprising gift of oratory.

"If American politics are too dirty for women to take part in, there's something wrong with American politics. . . . We weren't too delicate and flowerlike to cross the plains and prairies and deserts in a covered wagon and to stand the hardships and heartbreaks of frontier life . . . history of France peeking through a bedroom keyhole . . . history of England a joust . . . but here in this land the women have been the hewers of wood and drawers of water . . . thousands of unnamed heroines with weather-beaten faces and mud-caked boots . . . alkali water . . . sun . . . dust . . . wind. . . . I am not belittling the brave pioneer men but the sunbonnet as well as the sombrero has helped to settle this glorious land of ours. . . ."

It had been so many years since she had heard this—it had sunk so deep into her consciousness—that perhaps she actually thought she had originated this speech. Certainly it was received with tremendous emotional response, copied throughout the Southwest, the Far West, the Mid-West states, and it won her the election and gained her fame that was nation wide.

Perhaps it was not altogether what Sabra Cravat said that counted in her favor. Her appearance must have had something to do with it. A slim, straight, dignified woman, yet touchingly feminine. Her voice not loud, but clear. Her white hair was shingled and beautifully waved and beneath this her soft dark eyes took on an added depth and brilliance. Her eyebrows had remained black and thick, still further enhancing her finest feature. Her dress was always dark, becoming, smart, and her silken ankles above the slim slippers with their cut-steel buckles were those of a young girl. The aristocratic Marcy feet and ankles.

Her speeches were not altogether romantic, by any means. She knew her state. Its politics were notoriously rotten. Governor after governor was impeached with musical comedy swiftness and regularity, and the impeachment proceedings stank to Washington. This governor was practically an outlaw and desperado; that governor, who resembled a traveling evangelist with his long locks and his sanctimonious face, flaunted his mistress, and all the office plums fell to her rapscallion kin. Sabra had statistics at her tongue's end. Millions of barrels of oil. Millions of tons of zinc. Third in mineral products. First in oil. Coal. Gypsum. Granite. Live stock.

In Washington she was quite a belle among the old boys in Congress and even the Senate. The opposition party tried to blackmail her with publicity about certain unproved items in the life of her dead (or missing) husband Yancey Cravat: a two-gun man, a desperado, a killer, a drunkard, a squaw man. Then they started on young Cim and his Osage Indian wife, but Sabra and Donna were too quick for them.

Donna Wyatt leased a handsome Washington house in Dupont Circle, staffed it, brought Tracy Wyatt's vast wealth and influence to bear, and planned a coup so brilliant that it routed the enemy forever. She brought her handsome, sleepy-eyed brother Cim and his wife Ruby Big Elk, and the youngsters Felice and Yancey to the house in Dupont Circle, and together she and Sabra gave a reception for them to which they invited a group so precious that it actually came.

Sabra and Donna, exquisitely dressed, stood in line at the head of the magnificent room, and between them stood Ruby Big Elk in her Indian dress of creamy white doeskin all embroidered in beads from shoulder to hem. She was an imposing figure, massive but not offensively fat as were many of the older Osage women, and her black abundant hair had taken on a mist of gray.

"My daughter-in-law, Mrs. Cimarron Cravat, of the Osage Indian tribe."

"My son's wife, Ruby Big Elk—Mrs. Cimarron Cravat."

"My sister-in-law, Mrs. Cimarron Cravat. A full-blood Osage Indian. . . . Yes, indeed. We think so, too."

And, "How do you do?" said Ruby, in her calm, insolent way.

For the benefit of those who had not quite been able to encompass the Indian woman in her native dress Ruby's next public appearance was made in a Paris gown of white. She became the rage, was considered picturesque, and left Washington in disgust, her work done. No one but her husband, whom she loved with a doglike devotion, could have induced her to go through this ceremony.

The opposition retired, vanquished.

Donna and Tracy Wyatt then hired a special train in which they took fifty Eastern potentates on a tour of Oklahoma. One vague and not very bright Washington matron, of great social prestige, impressed with what she saw, voiced her opinion to young Yancey Cravat, quite confused as to his identity and seeing only an attractive and very handsome young male seated beside her at a country club luncheon.

"I had no idea Oklahoma was like this. I thought it was all oil and dirty Indians."

"There is quite a lot of oil, but we're not all dirty."

"We?"

"I'm an Indian."

Osage, Oklahoma was now just as much like New York as Osage could manage to make it. They built twenty-story office buildings in a city that had hundreds of miles of prairie to spread in. Tracy Wyatt built the first skyscraper—the Wyatt building. It was pointed out and advertised all over the flat prairie state. Then Pat Leary, dancing an Irish jig of jealousy, built the Leary building, twenty-three stories high. But the sweet fruits of triumph soon turned to ashes in his mouth. The Wyatt building's foundations were not built to stand the added strain of five full stories. So he had built a five-story tower, slim and tapering, a taunting finger pointing to the sky. Again Tracy Wyatt owned the tallest building in Oklahoma.

On the roof of the Levy Mercantile Company's Building Sol had had built a penthouse after his own plans. It was the only one of its kind in all Oklahoma. That small part of Osage which did not make an annual pilgrimage to New York was slightly bewildered by Sol Levy's roof life. They fed one another with scraps of gossip got from servants, clerks, stenographers who claimed to have seen the place at one time or another. It was, these said, filled with the rarest of carpets, rugs, books, hangings. Super radio, super phonograph, super player piano. Music hungry. There he lived, alone, in luxury, of the town, yet no part of it. At sunset, in the early morning, late of a star-spangled night he might have been seen leaning over the parapet of his sky house, a lonely little figure, lean, ivory, aloof, like a gargoyle brooding over the ridiculous city sprawled below; over the oil rigs that encircled it like giant Martian guards holding it in their power; beyond, to where the sky, in a veil of gray chiffon that commerce had wrought, stooped to meet the debauched red prairie.

Money was now the only standard. If Pat Leary had sixty-two million dollars on Tuesday he was Oklahoma's leading citizen. If Tracy Wyatt had seventy-eight million dollars on

Wednesday then Tracy Wyatt was Oklahoma's leading citizen.

Osage had those fascinating little specialty shops and interior decorating shops on Pawhuska just like those you see on Madison Avenue, whose owners are the daughters of decayed Eastern aristocracy on the make. The head of the shop appeared only to special clients and then with a hat on. She wore the hat from morning until night, her badge of revolt against this position of service. "I am a lady," the hat said. "Make no mistake about that. Just because I am a shopkeeper don't think you can patronize me. I am not working. I am playing at work. This is my fad. At any moment I can walk out of here, just like any of you."

Feminine Osage's hat, by the way, was cut and fitted right on its head, just like Paris.

Sabra probably was the only woman of her own generation and social position in Osage who still wore on the third finger of her left hand the plain broad gold band of a long-past day. Synchronous with the permanent wave and the reducing diet the oil-rich Osage matrons of Sabra's age cast sentiment aside for fashion, quietly placed the clumsy gold band in a bureau drawer and appeared with a slim platinum circlet bearing, perhaps, the engraved anachronism, "M. G.-K. L. 1884." Certainly it was much more at ease among its square-cut emerald and oblong-diamond neighbors. These ladies explained (if at all) that the gold band had grown too tight for the finger, or too loose. Sabra looked down at the broad old-fashioned wedding ring on her own gemless finger. She had not once taken it off in over forty years. It was as much a part of her as the finger itself.

Osage began to rechristen streets, changing the fine native Indian names to commonplace American ones. Hetoappe Street became the Boston Road; very fashionable it was, too. Still, the very nicest people were building out a ways in the new section (formerly Okemah Hill) now River View. The river was the ruddy Canadian, the view the forest of oil rigs bristling on the opposite shore. The grounds sloped down to the river except on those occasions when the river rose in red anger and sloped down to the houses. The houses themselves were Italian palazzi or French châteaux or English manors; none, perhaps, quite so vast or inclusive as Tracy Wyatt's but all provided with such necessities as pipe organs, sunken baths, Greek temples, ancient tapestries, Venetian glass, billiard rooms, and butlers. Pat Leary, the smart little erstwhile section hand, had a melodramatic idea. Not content with peacocks, golf links, and swimming pools on his estate he now had placed an old and weathered covered wagon, a rusted and splintered wagon tongue, the bleached skull of a buffalo, an Indian tepee, and a battered lantern on a little island at the foot of the artificial lake below the heights on which his house stood. At night a search-light, red, green, or orange, played from the tower of the house upon the mute relics of frontier days.

"The covered wagon my folks crossed the prairies in," Pat Leary explained, with shy pride. Eastern visitors were much impressed. It was considered a great joke in Osage, intimately familiar with Pat's Oklahoma beginnings.

"Forgot something, ain't you Pat, in that outfit you got rigged up in the yard?" old Bixby asked.

"What's that?"

"Pickax and shovel," Bixby replied, laconically. "Keg of spikes and a hand car."

Old Sam Pack, who had made the Run on a mule, said that if Pat Leary's folks had come to Oklahoma in a covered wagon then his had made the trip in an airplane.

All the Oklahoma millionaire houses had libraries. Yards and yards of fine leather libraries, with gold tooling. Ike Hawkes's library had five sets of Dickens alone, handsomely bound in red, green, blue, brown, and black, and Ike all unaware of any of them.

Moving picture palaces, with white-gloved ushers, had all the big Broadway super-films. Gas filling stations on every corner. Hot dog, chili con carne, and hamburger stands on the most remote country road. The Arverne Grand Opera Company at the McKee Theater for a whole week every year, and the best of everything—*Traviata, Bohème, Carmen, Louise, The Barber of Seville*. The display of jewels during that week made the Diamond Horseshoe at the Metropolitan look like the Black Hole of Calcutta.

SMART DANCING PARTY

Social events of the week just closed were worthily concluded with the smart dancing party at which Mr. and Mrs. Clint Hooper entertained a small company at the Osage Club. The roof garden of the club . . .

SMALL DINNER

Mr. and Mrs. James Click honored two distinguished Eastern visitors on Wednesday at the small dinner at which they entertained in courtesy to Mr. and Mrs. C. Swearingen Church, of St. Paul, Minnesota. There were covers for eighty. . . . .

Mr. and Mrs. Buchanan Ketcham and Miss Patricia Ketcham left for New York last night, from which city they will sail for Europe, there to meet the J. C. McConnells on their yacht at Monaco. . . .

Le Cercle Français will meet Tuesday evening at the home of Mr. and Mrs. Everard Pack. . . .

The sunbonnets had triumphed.

Twenty-four

STILL, oil was oil, and Indians were Indians. There was no way in which either of those native forces could quite be molded to fit the New York pattern.

The Osages still whirled up and down the Oklahoma roads, and those roads, for hundreds of miles, were still unpaved red prairie dust. They crashed into ditches and draws and culverts as of old, walked back to town and, entering the automobile salesroom in which they had bought the original car, pointed with one dusky finger at a new and glittering model.

" 'Nother," they said, succinctly. And drove out with it.

It was common news that Charley Vest had smashed eight Cadillac cars in a year, but then Charley had a mysterious source through which he procured fire water. They bought airplanes now, but they were forbidden the use of local and neighboring flying fields after a series of fatal smashes. They seemed, for the most part (the full bloods, at least), to be totally lacking in engine sense,

They had electric refrigerators—sometimes in the parlor, very proud. They ate enormously and waxed fatter and fatter. The young Osages now wore made-to-order shirts with monograms embroidered on them the size of a saucer. The Osages had taken to spending their summers in Colorado Springs or Manitou. At first the white residents of those cities had refused to rent their fine houses, furnished, to the Indians for the season. But the vast sums offered them soon overcame their reluctance. The Indian problem was still a problem, for he was considered legitimate prey, and thousands of prairie buzzards fed on his richness.

Sabra Cravat had introduced a bill for the further protection of the Osages, and rather took away the breath of the House assembled by advocating abolition of the Indian Reservation system. Her speech, radical though it was, and sensational, was greeted with favor by some of the more liberal of the Congressmen. They even conceded that this idea of hers, to the effect that the Indian would never develop or express himself until he was as free as the Negro, might some day become a reality. These were the reformers—the long-hairs—fanatics.

Oklahoma was very proud of Sabra Cravat, editor, Congresswoman, pioneer. Osage said she embodied the finest spirit of the state and of the Southwest. When ten of Osage's most unctuous millionaires contributed fifty thousand dollars each for a five-hundred-thousand-dollar statue that should embody the Oklahoma Pioneer no one was surprised to hear that the sculptor, Masja Krbecek, wanted to interview Sabra Cravat.

Osage was not familiar with the sculpture of Krbecek, but it was impressed with the price of it. Half a million dollars for a statue!

"Certainly," said the committee, calmly. "He's the best there is. Half a million is nothing for his stuff. He wouldn't kick a pebble for less than a quarter of a million."

"Do you suppose he'll do her as a pioneer woman in a sunbonnet? Holding little Cim by the hand, huh? Or maybe in a covered wagon."

Sabra received Krbecek in a simple (draped) dress. He turned out to be a quiet, rather snuffy little Pole in eyeglasses, who looked more like a tailor—a "little" tailor—than a sculptor. His eye roamed about the living room of the house on Kihekah. The old wooden house had been covered with plaster in a deep warm shade much the color of the native clay; the gimcrack porch and the cupolas had been torn away and a great square veranda and a terrace built at the side, away from the street and screened by a thick hedge and an iron grille. It was now, in fact, much the house that Yancey had planned when Sabra first built it years ago. The old pieces of mahogany and glass and silver were back, triumphant again over the plush and brocade with which Sabra had furnished the house when new. The old, despised since pioneer days, was again the fashion in Osage. There was the DeGrasse silver; the cake dish with the carefree cupids, the mantelpiece figures of china, even the hand-woven coverlet that Mother Bridget had given her that day in Wichita so long ago. Its rich deep blue was un-faded.

"You are very comfortable here in Oklahoma," said Masja Krbecek. He pronounced it syllable by syllable, painfully. O-kla-ho-ma.

"It is a very simple home," Sabra replied, "compared to the other places you have seen hereabouts."

"It is the home of a good woman," said Krbecek, dryly.

Sabra was a trifle startled, but she said thank you, primly.

"You are a Congress member, you are editor of a great newspaper, you are well known through the country. You American women, you are really amazing."

Again Sabra thanked him.

"Tell me, will you, my dear lady," he went on, "some of the many interesting things about your life and that of your husband, this Yancey Cravat who so far preceded his time."

So Sabra told him. Somehow, as she talked, the years rolled back, curtain after curtain, into the past. The Run. Then they were crossing the prairie, there was the first glimpse of the mud wallow that was Osage, the church meeting in the tent, the Pegler murder, the outlaws, the early years of the paper, the Indians, oil. She talked very well in her clear, decisive voice. At his request she showed him the time-yellowed photographs of Yancey, of herself. Krbecek listened. At the end, "It is touching," he said. "It makes me weep." Then he kissed her hand and went away, taking one or two of the old photographs with him.

The statue of the Spirit of the Oklahoma Pioneer was unveiled a year later, with terrific ceremonies. It was an heroic figure of Yancey Cravat stepping forward with that light graceful stride in the high-heeled Texas star boots, the skirts of the Prince Albert billowing behind with the vigor of his movements, the sombrero atop the great menacing buffalo head, one beautiful hand resting lightly on the weapon in his two-gun holster. Behind him, one hand just touching his shoulder for support, stumbled the weary, blanketed figure of an Indian.

Twenty-five

SABRA CRAVAT, Congresswoman from Oklahoma, had started a campaign against the disgraceful condition of the new oil towns. With an imposing party of twenty made up of front-page oil men, Senators, Congressmen, and editors, she led the way to Bowlegs, newest and crudest of the new oil strikes.

Cities like Osage were suave enough in a surface way. But what could a state do when oil was forever surging up in unexpected places, bringing the days of the Run back again? At each newly discovered pool there followed the rush and scramble. Another Bret Hart town sprang up on the prairie; fields oozed slimy black; oil rigs clanked; false-front wooden shacks lined a one-street village. Dance halls. Brothels. Gunmen. Brawls. Heat. Flies. Dirt. Crime. The clank of machinery. The roar of traffic boiling over a road never meant for more than a plodding wagon. Nitro-glycerin cars bearing their deadly freight. Overalls, corduroys, blue prints, engines. The human scum of each new oil town was like the scum of the Run, but harder, crueler, more wolfish and degraded.

The imposing party, in high-powered motor cars, bumped over the terrible roads, creating a red dust barrage.

"It is all due to our rotten Oklahoma state politics," Sabra explained to the great Senator from Pennsylvania who sat at her right and the great editor from New York who sat at her left in the big luxurious car. "Our laws are laughed at. The Capitol is rotten with graft. Anything goes. Oklahoma is still a Territory in everything but title. This town of Bowlegs. It's a throw-back to the frontier days of forty years ago—and worse. It's like the old Cimarron. People who have lived in Osage all their lives don't know what goes on out here. They don't care. It's more oil, more millions. That's all. Any one of you men, well known as you are, could come out here, put on overalls, and be as lost as though you had vanished in the wilderness."

The Pennsylvania Senator laughed a plump laugh and with the elbow nearest Sabra made a little movement that would have amounted to a nudge—in anyone but a Senator from Pennsylvania. "What they need out here is a woman Governor—eh, Lippmann!" to the great editor.

Sabra said nothing.

On the drive out from Osage they stopped for lunch in an older oil town hotel dining room—a surprisingly good lunch, the Senators and editors were glad to find, with a tender steak, and little green onions, and near beer, and cheese, and coffee served in great thick cups, hot and strong and refreshing. The waitress was deft and friendly: a tall angular woman with something frank and engaging about the two circles of vermilion on the parchment of her withered cheeks.

"How are you, Nettie?" Sabra said to her.

"I'm grand, Mis' Cravat. How's all your folks?"

The Senator from Ohio winked at Sabra. "You're a politician, all right."

Arrived at Bowlegs, Sabra showed them everything, pitilessly. The dreadful town lay in the hot June sun, a scarred thing, flies buzzing over it, the oil drooling down its face, a slimy stream. A one-street wooden shanty town, like the towns of the old Territory days, but more sordid. A red-cheeked young Harvard engineer was their official guide: an engaging boy in bone-rimmed glasses and a very blue shirt that made his pink cheeks pinker. That is what I wanted my Cim to be, Sabra thought with a great wrench at her heart. I mustn't think of that now.

The drilling of the oil. The workmen's shanties. The trial of a dance-hall girl in the one-room pine shack that served as courtroom. The charge, nonpayment of rent. The little room, stifling, stinking, was already crowded. Men and women filled the doorway, lounged in the windows. The judge was a yellow-faced fellow with a cud of tobacco in his cheek, and a Sears-Roebuck catalogue and a single law book on a shelf as his library. It was a trial by jury. The jurors were nine in number, their faces a rogues' gallery. There had happened to be nine men loafing near by. It might have been less or more. Bowlegs did not consider these fine legal points. They wore overalls and shirts. The defendant was a tiny rat-faced girl in a soiled green dress that parodied the fashions, a pathetic green poke bonnet, down-at-heel shoes, and a great run in her stocking. Her friends were there—a dozen or more dance-hall girls in striped overalls and jockey caps or knee-length gingham dresses with sashes. Their ages ranged from sixteen to nineteen, perhaps. It was incredible that life, in those few years, could have etched that look on their faces.

The girls were charming, hospitable. They made way

for the imposing visitors. "Come on in," they said. "How-do!" —like friendly children. The mid-afternoon sun was pitiless on their sick eyes, their bad skin, their unhealthy hair. Clustered behind the rude bench on which the jury sat, the girls, from time to time, leaned a sociable elbow on a juryman's shoulder, occasionally enlivening the judicial proceedings by a spirited comment uttered in defense of their sister, and spoken in the near-by ear or aloud, for the benefit of the close-packed crowd.

"She never done no such thing!"

"He's a damn liar, an' I can prove it."

No one, least of all the tobacco-chewing judge, appeared to find these girlish informalities at all unusual in the legal conduct of the case.

In the corner of the little room was a kind of pen made of wooden slats, like a sizable chicken coop, and in it, on the floor, lay a man.

"What's he there for?" Sabra asked one of the girls. "What is that?"

"That's Bill. He's in jail. He shot a man last night, and he's up for carrying concealed weapons. It ain't allowed."

"I'm going to talk to him," said Sabra. And crossed the room, through the crowd. The jurors had just filed out. They repaired to a draw at the side of the road to make their finding. Two or three of the dance-hall girls, squatted on the floor, were talking to Bill through the bars. They asked Sabra her name, and she told them, and they gave her their own. Toots. Peewee. Bee.

The face of the boy on the floor was battered and blood-caked. There was a festering sore on his left hand, and the hand and arm were swollen and angry looking.

"You were carrying a concealed weapon?" Sabra asked, squatting there with the girls. A Senator or two and an editor were just behind her.

An injured look softened Bill's battered features. He pouted like a child. "No, ma'am. I run the dance hall, see? And I was standing in the middle of the floor, working, and I had the gun right in my hand. Anybody could see. I wasn't carrying no concealed weapon."

The jury filed back. Not guilty. The rat-faced girl's shyster lawyer said something in her ear. She spoke in a dreadful raucous voice, simpering.

"I sure thank you, gents."

The dance-hall girls cheered feebly.

Out of that fetid air into the late afternoon blaze. "The

dance halls open about nine," Sabra said. "We'll wait for that. In the meantime I'll show you their rooms. Their rooms——" she looked about for the fresh-cheeked Harvard boy. "Why, where——"

"There's some kind of excitement," said the New York editor. "People have been running and shouting. Over there in that field we visited awhile ago. Here comes our young friend now. Perhaps he'll tell us."

The Harvard boy's color was higher still. He was breathing fast. He had been running. His eyes shone behind the bone-rimmed spectacles.

"Well, folks, we'll never have a narrower squeak than that."

"What?"

"They put fifty quarts in the Gypsy pool but before she got down the oil came up——"

"Quarts of what?" interrupted an editorial voice.

"Oh—excuse me—quarts of nitro-glycerin."

"My God!"

"It's in a can, you know. A thing like a can. It never had a chance to explode down there. It just shot up with the gas and oil. If it had hit the ground everything for miles around would have been shot to hell and all of us killed. But he caught it. They say he just ran back like an outfielder and gauged it with his eye while it was up in the air, and ran to where it would fall, and caught it in his two arms, like a baby, right on his chest. It didn't explode. But he's dying. Chest all caved in. They've sent for the ambulance."

"Who? Who's he?"

"I don't know his real name. He's an old bum that's been around the field, doing odd jobs and drinking. They say he used to be quite a fellow in Oklahoma in his day. Picturesque pioneer or something. Some call him old Yance and I've heard others call him Sim or Simeon or——"

Sabra began to run across the road.

"Mrs. Cravat! You mustn't—where are you going?"

She ran on, across the oil-soaked field and the dirt, in her little buckled high-heeled slippers. She did not even know that she was running. The crowd was dense around some central object. They formed a wall—roustabouts, drillers, tool dressers, shooters, pumpers. They were gazing down at something on the ground.

"Let me by! Let me by!" They fell back before this white-faced woman with the white hair.

He lay on the ground, a queer, crumpled, broken figure.

She flung herself on the oil-soaked earth beside him and lifted the magnificent head gently, so that it lay cushioned by her arm. A little purplish bubble rose to his lips, and she wiped it away with her fine white handkerchief, and another rose to take its place.

"Yancey! Yancey!"

He opened his eyes—those ocean-gray eyes with the long curling lashes like a beautiful girl's. She had thought of them often and often, in an agony of pain. Glazed now, unseeing.

Then, dying, they cleared. His lips moved. He knew her. Even then, dying, he must speak in measured verse.

" 'Wife and mother—you stainless woman—hide me—hide me in your love!' "

She had never heard a line of it. She did not know that this was Peer Gynt, humbled before Solveig. The once magnetic eyes glazed, stared; were eyes no longer.

She closed them, gently. She forgave him everything. Quite simply, all unknowing, she murmured through her tears the very words of Solveig.

"Sleep, my boy, my dearest boy."

FAWCETT CREST BESTSELLERS

MESSAGE FROM MÁLAGA		
Helen MacInnes	P1716	$1.25
THE CONDOR PASSES		
Shirley Ann Grau	P1735	$1.25
GETTING HIGH IN GOVERNMENT CIRCLES		
Art Buchwald	M1739	95¢
VICE AVENGED: A MORAL TALE		
Lolah Burford	P1719	$1.25
THE SHADOW OF THE LYNX		
Victoria Holt	P1720	$1.25
CAPONE John Kobler	Q1704	$1.50
THE MOONLIGHTER Henry Kane	P1707	$1.25
ME AND THE ORGONE		
Orson Bean	M1709	95¢
THE DRIFTERS James A. Michener	X1697	$1.75
THE FIRES OF SPRING		
James A. Michener	P1701	$1.25
THE OTHER SIDE OF THE SUN		
Madeleine L'Engle	P1698	$1.25
PENMARRIC Susan Howatch	A1681	$1.65
THE OTHER Thomas Tryon	P1668	$1.25
G.P. William A. Block	M1669	95¢
UP THE SANDBOX!		
Anne Richardson Roiphe	M1656	95¢
MELBURY SQUARE Dorothy Eden	P1654	$1.25
THE WHEEL OF LOVE		
Joyce Carol Oates	P1655	$1.25
THEM Joyce Carol Oates	P1467	$1.25
EXPENSIVE PEOPLE		
Joyce Carol Oates	M1408	95¢
LOST ISLAND Phyllis A. Whitney	M1644	95¢
CARAVAN TO VACCARES		
Alistair MacLean	M1620	95¢
THE GODFATHER Mario Puzo	A1708	$1.65

FAWCETT WORLD LIBRARY

WHEREVER PAPERBACKS ARE SOLD